CELESTIAL SHIFTERS BOOK 3

THORNS OF NEPTUNE

TJALARA DRAPER

www.tjalaradraper.com

Edited by: Kirstin Andrews

Cover design by: Deranged Doctor Design

❀ Created with Vellum

To the lovely Treece Stubbs.
It's such an honour to call you friend!
Thanks so much for all your encouragement and support since the start of my author adventures. And thank you for being there when I want to have a whinge about my writing, and for giving me a good butt-kicking when I need it.

1
BLOOD OF THE DEFENSELESS

Imbeciles.

Matthias Branstone was surrounded by complete and utter imbeciles.

Crunch!

Once again, Axel, the trident-wielding hunter, shoved Kronan's head against the cliff wall with one meaty hand.

The pathetic Veniri cried out when his face slammed with bone-cracking force into the rock. Regardless of his biological advantages, the Veniri still felt pain just as much as any other shifter—or human, for that matter. Matthias couldn't help but admit to being entertained by Kronan's suffering, especially after the four-day trek through this hellish desert.

Shading his eyes with his hands, he blinked a few times to clear the sun's white afterimage before scanning the rocky wall once again.

Matthias wasn't one to ignore his instincts, especially after a lifetime of hunting shifters—the scourge of the damned earth. But nothing about this area tweaked his hunter's sixth sense. No markings, no openings, no signs of habitation. He'd been hunting all species of shifters practically his whole life. Hell, his first shifter kill back when he was only fourteen years old had been a Veniri. Even after forty years, the memory remained etched in his mind with crystal clarity. Surely after a lifetime of hunting shifters, he would just *know* when these scaly vermin were close.

But no matter how hard he glared at the wall of sand and rock, he didn't get even an inkling of any shifter presence, other than the whining Kronan.

"If this is a trick, slith, I'll shatter every crystal bone in your body," snarled Axel.

"It's not a trick! I swear!" Kronan continued to blither and beg as Axel barked threat after threat.

Matthias pinched the bridge of his nose. "Axel, enough."

The other hunter shoved Kronan one last time before taking a step back.

Kronan cowered and rubbed at his crushed cheek. The only reason his face hadn't been pulverized into mincemeat was his tough Veniri hide. Ironically, a Veniri hide could only be sliced open by their own crystal bones. Matthias's fingers twitched toward his Diamantium shard, one crafted into a Bowie knife holstered in his utility belt.

"Are you absolutely sure this is the place?" He put as much warning in his low tone as possible, his gaze steady on Kronan.

"Yes!" Kronan's head bounced up and down like a bobblehead in an earthquake. "I promise you. This is the place. I recognize my own hive when I see it."

"So?" Matthias raised an eyebrow. "Where is it?"

"We need to wait… We need to wait for the right time to enter." Kronan dropped his sheepish gaze to the ground.

"What is this?" Axel pointed an accusatory finger at the shifter but directed the question at Matthias. "Did we suddenly step into an Indiana Jones movie? Come on, Matthias. Four days we've been wandering around in the desert. Four blasted days! We left our vehicles behind a day and a half ago. We ran out of food last night. We're almost out of water. And it's so damn hot we may as well be walking on the sun! This desert is called the Boiling Void for a reason. It's because there's *nothing here*! Nothing but hot sun and sand. Freaking sand! I've got sand in my eyes, in my teeth, in my beard, and in crannies I didn't even know sand could enter.

"Face it, Matthias. We're lost. This slith has no idea where we are, and he's gonna say whatever he thinks you wanna hear just to save his own hide. In fact, I wouldn't be surprised if he's been leading us to our deaths this whole time. I say we cut our losses and kill him already so we don't have to drag his sorry ass back to the cars."

Axel huffed a few times once he'd finished his tirade.

Matthias blinked. It was the most he'd ever heard the gray-bearded hunter say at once. Before he could respond, the Veniri shifter dove to grasp Matthias's hiking boots.

"I'm not lying," Kronan cried.

Matthias sneered and kicked at him until the shifter scuffled back.

Kneeling, Kronan clasped his hands together and continued his begging. "Please, I promise, on my life, this is the place." Despite the desperate whine in Kronan's voice, his words were confident. "Any minute now. You'll see. I promise."

Matthias put his hands on his hips, making sure to reveal several more of the Diamantium blades hanging from his belt. "You have one minute, slith. After that, I'll let not just Axel have a piece of you, but all of them." He swept his hand toward the fifty other hunters scowling a few yards behind him.

Kronan glanced at the small army and audibly swallowed. Every single hunter had their resentful glares trained on him, their trademark hunter-black clothes grimy from the desert's sand. Sweat streams had engraved trails through the layers of dirt over their faces. Matthias's own clothes were so crusty that crystallized sweat had joined the sand in chafing every crevice of his body.

The journey into the Boiling Void had sorely tempted Matthias to add his own grumblings to those of his entourage; only his sheer determination to prove everyone wrong had silenced his complaints. After countless hours of Kronan leading them through the ravines of the Stony-Hearted Highlands, however, even Matthias's enthusiasm had barely reignited when the Veniri finally pointed to their ultimate destination: this nondescript cliff.

Matthias's fury began to simmer, but he'd worked too long and hard to lose face in front of all these expectant hunters, even if most of them were barely out of their teens. He'd long ago become fed up with handling new and inexperienced recruits, but after a few too many failed expeditions, his constant promises of riches and lifelong glory had worn thin with the older hunters from his own barracks. It didn't help that news of his failings had spread to the other legacy hunter families around the country.

He'd been nearly at the end of his tether by the time his men caught Kronan a little over a year ago. The groveling creature's loose tongue had spewed stories Matthias had never heard before—most interesting of which was his claim to be the Veniri queen's cousin. But when it became clear Queen Idalia didn't care whether Kronan lived or died, the shifter's self-preservation kicked into overdrive, and he spilled secret after secret after secret.

All the other hunters thought Matthias was stupid for allowing the slith to live, but his instincts had insisted Kronan was the key to finding their pot of gold at the end of the Diamantium rainbow.

Every hunter, young and old, dreamed of finding a Veniri hive, but to Matthias, the main prize was worth so much more. No hunter in history had ever encountered a Veniri queen in the flesh and lived to tell the tale. He was determined to be the first.

Kronan let out a strangled mewl.

Matthias's mustached lip curled in disgust at the sniveling creature. After today, never again would his father, his brothers, or any other hunter doubt him. They would all soon see that keeping the wretched Kronan alive had been worth it. And they'd understand that if he was right about this, he was sure to be right about the rest of his beliefs—one being that the Veniri queen possessed an item he would pry from her cold, dead hands if he had to.

And once he'd claimed his victory, *no one* would ever again dare say that his lifelong fascination with the so-called mythical winged shifters was a waste of time and resources.

"Are you sure this slith can be trusted, Uncle Matthias?"

He turned to Nika, who'd stepped up next to him.

Her nose screwed up in disdain. "I mean, seriously, how do you know this slith isn't leading us into a trap?"

Matthias laid a hand on his niece's shoulder. "No need to worry your pretty little head. Your uncle has this all under control."

Nika placed a hand on her hip, right where her Diamantium dagger was holstered. "Yeah, but what if he's lying? What if his plan is to lead us on a pointless journey into the desert only to have us all die out here from heat exhaustion and starvation?" She shot a sidelong glare at Kronan. "It's what I would do if I were a weakling slith like him."

Matthias regarded her through narrowed eyes. "How naive do you think I am, Nika?"

She opened her mouth to reply, but he cut her off.

"I am not stupid. I have spent my entire life around these creatures."

"Of course, Uncle, that's not what I—"

"Don't you think I would know if one of these beasts was trying to deceive me?"

His question hung in the air for a moment as Nika's brows drew together.

A cloud of doubt began to eclipse Matthias's eagerness. He knew that expression. He'd seen it before. Many times. On the face of his father, his brothers, his ex-wife, his current wife, the hunters back at the barracks, even those who'd followed him into the desert—*everyone*!

He rolled his shoulders and straightened his spine with a satisfying *crack-crack-crack*, allowing himself a few seconds to swallow his outrage before attempting a different angle. "My dear niece, for how many thousands of years have these shifters evaded us? No matter how many of them we hunt down, there's always more to replace them." He flung his arm out to the cliff wall, feigning an excitement he didn't quite feel after several days in the desert. "Our ancestors have tried and failed to find the source of the Veniri scourge. If this is it, then do you know what this means? It means that—"

"Today will be history in the making," said Nika. Her eyes held an edge of credulity, despite her furrowed brows.

"Exactly!" Matthias grabbed Nika's shoulders; her shoulder-length light brown curls bounced as he gave her a slight shake. "Can't you feel it, Nika? Today is going to be a monumental event, not just for us but for all the hunters and *all* shape-shifters."

Nika's large periwinkle eyes slowly blinked, and her face smoothed into an impassive expression as she regarded the rockface. "If you say so, Uncle Ty." She shrugged his hands off, then went to lean against the cliff wall by Axel.

Matthias curled his fingers into fists. He knew he was right.

"Look, Matthias. Up there!" the Veniri screeched.

Matthias's attention snapped to where Kronan pointed. A collection of awed exclamations rippled through the hunters as, at the very top of the cliff, about fifteen stories high, a spurt of water glittered in the sunlight.

No! thought Matthias. *That's not water.*

"What is that?" said Axel.

"Today is when Venus is at its inferior conjunction," explained Kronan.

"And... what the heck does that mean?" asked Nika.

"It means that Venus's orbit is passing between Earth and the sun," said Matthias.

Nika looked at him as if he'd grown a second head. "Okay... and what's that got to do with the water fountain?"

"That's not water," said Kronan. "In our culture, we don't do funerals for each individual Veniri. We hold a collective funeral every nineteen and a half months, during the inferior conjunction of Venus. The bones of our dead are stored in a sacred holding chamber. On the eve of the inferior conjunction, our holy men grind up the bones and set the dust free in a wind vortex that scatters it into the desert sky."

"No way," breathed Nika, raising her eyes to the dust cloud.

"You mean to say that you sliths store your bones—your *Diamantium*—in some kind of chamber, then grind it up to just... *throw it all away*?" Axel shook his head. "What a waste of profitable Diamantium."

"We don't think of it as 'throwing it all away,'" said Kronan. "It's a ritual every Veniri deems sacred."

Just as he finished speaking, the glittering dust began to rain down on them. A few of the hunters held out their hands to catch some of the majestic glitter. Matthias wasn't that foolish. He jumped under an overhanging rock.

"Don't let it touch you!" Nika shouted, running to join Matthias. But before she reached him, the screams erupted.

The Diamantium dust was like glass dust, except much, much worse.

The hunters scattered throughout the ravine, some running in the direction they'd come, others finding their own overhangs to hide under. Still others were dragged off kicking and screaming while they desperately tried to swipe away the tiny, razor-sharp shards shredding their skin. Smears of red appeared all over their exposed flesh.

"Don't wipe at the Diamantium dust!" Nika ordered. "Find some shelter!"

Those who had already rushed under rock formations rummaged in backpacks for canteens to splash what precious water they had left over their faces, necks, and arms. Kronan had scrambled to join Nika and Matthias, which was unfortunate for him.

Nika slammed Kronan up against the cliff wall, her Diamantium-studded knuckle-duster pressed against his throat. "So this *was* a trap!"

"No!" screeched Kronan. His eyes darted to Matthias. "I swear. Please! Tell her I wouldn't—"

His words ended on a gargle as Nika pressed the crystal tips of her knuckle-duster deeper into his neck. "Whatever water we had left is being wasted. Why did you bring us here, if not to lead us to our deaths?" A trail of teal blood dripped onto the collar of Kronan's dust-brown shirt.

"I'd say you have about three seconds to explain before Nika drains your jugular," said Matthias.

"The ceremony, *the ceremony*!" began Kronan, then started speaking at a hundred miles an hour. "Most of the Veniri will be paying their respects at the rites ceremony! I've brought you to a hidden entrance, one with the least resistance. Guards will be scarce due to the rites ceremony demanding their attendance."

"I don't see an entrance," growled Nika.

Kronan held up his hands and gargled something incoherent.

"Nika, give him some space," said Matthias.

Reluctantly, Nika released him, but she held her crystal-encrusted fist in plain view. Teal blood dripped from it onto the sand by her boot.

Kronan heaved in a shuddering breath, one hand clutching the new wound on his neck. With one last imploring look at Matthias, he held his other hand up, fingers undulating. After a moment, he grunted in frustration and hesitantly released his neck. Blood trickled freely from the cut as both hands danced in front of his face.

Nika shot a *what-is-he-doing-now* look at Matthias, who raised a finger to his lips, commanding her to remain quiet.

Kronan grunted again, face contorted in fierce concentration as he focused on the space between his palms. New trails of sweat gleamed down his brow and the sides of his face.

A bright teal light began to grow in the Veniri's hands.

Nika's jaw dropped. Even Matthias couldn't stop his eyes from widening in surprise.

The pea-sized light hovered several inches over Kronan's upturned palms. Matthias didn't know exactly what was happening, but the shifter seemed to be condensing the teal light into a tangible mass that rippled and swirled like a living glob of putty.

Veins bulged and throbbed in Kronan's temple. Within about a minute, the ball of light had grown to the size of a large apple. The Veniri prodded at the teal mass and then, with fumbling fingers, began molding it.

Matthias tried to guess what he was making—until Kronan growled in dissatisfaction, scrunched the sculpture back into a ball, and began again. Several minutes later, the shifter jumped into his third attempt. Nika huffed with impatience, and Matthias began tapping his foot.

Finally, Kronan managed to morph the tangible light into a jagged collection of teal spikes and extrusions. With one hand, he held the completed sculpture above his head while he summoned another globule of teal light over his other palm. This time the undulating globe flattened into a disc, paper thin and almost transparent, about three inches in diameter. It must have been easier to create, as he struggled less in achieving the task.

Kronan angled the disc until a beam of teal light streamed out onto the other sculpture's surface. The beam bounced off the various spikes before hitting the rock wall in several locations, like dots from a teal laser pointer. The dozen or so dots diffused into the rock face, then each bled out in a different formation. It took a moment for Matthias to understand what he was seeing.

"Those are words in the Veniri language, aren't they?" Nika asked.

No one answered her question. Matthias continued to stare at the inscription: nineteen symbols in a scattered pattern, each depicting a different word. He didn't know enough about the Veniri language to understand it. His expertise tended toward hunting shifters and priceless shifter artifacts—not shifter linguistics.

After a moment, each symbol began to fume with smoke before sinking about half an inch into the cliff face. A grinding crunch sounded from deep within the wall, like that of a giant mechanism being unlocked. The rumble grew louder and louder, reaching a crescendo as it approached the rocky surface surrounding the Veniri symbols. Then it instantly stopped, the sudden silence just as deafening as the quaking had been.

As Kronan took a step back, each of the reflected beams widened. The light caught shiny veins of what looked like mica, or some kind of crystal seam that hadn't been visible before the teal beams shone over it. Light shimmered up the veins in a cascading ripple, feeding teal up and around to form the jagged outline of a doorframe, tall and wide enough for a single man.

Matthias grinned from ear to ear, anticipating what came next with a shiver of exhilaration.

The illuminated outline cracked into a deep fissure, and with a ground-shaking rumble, the rock face pressed inward an inch, steam hissing from the seams. Kronan breathed a faint blue mist over the sculptures in his hands, and within seconds, they dissolved into tiny teal dust motes that floated off in the hot desert breeze.

The shifter placed his hands on the rock face. Before he could push, eagerness overtook Matthias, and he batted Kronan out of the way.

Axel took hold of the flummoxed Veniri, eyes wide with the amazement of a reformed believer. Holding Kronan firmly, he nodded for Matthias to do the honors.

The long-suffering hunter pressed both hands against the cliff. The sedimentary surface felt rough under Matthias's palms, and the heat of the sunbaked rock was almost unbearable.

He gritted his teeth and hesitated for a second, ignoring his searing flesh. The countless years and countless hunters Matthias had sacrificed all led up to this moment. Just as Nika had stated, he was about to make hunter history. Tears pricked his eyes as the thought overwhelmed him, only to have the desert heat instantly snatch the moisture from his eyes.

With a ragged breath, he pushed with all his might against the cliff. Hot grit rained down as the chunk of rock shifted inward several feet. The grinding of stone on stone reverberated through his hands and quaked in his ears.

The cliff wall they'd all been staring at proved to be about a foot thick, until a void appeared on his right. The farther Matthias pushed, the wider the entrance to the passage grew. By the time he could push no more, the passageway to his right was roughly three men wide, tunneling parallel to the rocky cliff.

A cool breeze softly howled out from an unknown source, whirling around him and winnowing the sand from his loose clothing.

"Heaven's above." A shiver fueled by both excitement and the sudden cold rushed down Matthias's spine. The hairs on the back of his neck stood on end, and he blinked several times as his eyes adjusted from searing desert light to pitch black.

Shock, horror, elation—he wasn't sure what caused the bubble of laughter to escape his throat. He cackled as he turned and patted Kronan on the head. "Well done, slith."

Laughter dying down, Matthias eyed Nika, expecting her to at least grovel in apology. Instead she stared into the gaping hole in the cliff face, suspicion etched deep in her features. Her crystal dagger was drawn in a white-knuckled fist, while her other hand flexed within the knuckle-duster.

He laid a hand on her shoulder and squeezed a little harder than necessary. "Never doubt me again, dear niece."

She did well not to flinch under his grip, but a fleeting expression of what had to be defiance crossed her face.

"Axel, call the men. We've got work to do."

Axel nodded and began barking out names. Responses rang out from various outcroppings in the ravine and echoed off the rocks and boulders. No one stepped into view, as the Diamantium dust was still raining down around them.

Impatient, Matthias growled at Axel, "Get the others to follow us when they stop being so petrified of a little Diamantium dust." He gave a pointed look at Kronan and inclined his head to the tunnel. "Lead the way, slith."

Darkness engulfed them. Both Matthias and Nika pulled out their Luxium-powered hunting flashlights, which cast magenta-tinged light over the wind-sculpted walls. The icy drafts of mineral-rich air tingled over Matthias's half-cooked skin.

Kronan led them through a passageway worthy of a tourist attraction. Glorious layers of reds, pinks, ochres, and browns—compacted into solid rock over hundreds, perhaps thousands, of years—made up the cavern's high walls. The remaining hunters soon shuffled in behind them, a few of their agonized whimpers echoing through the grand rocky tunnel.

"What's so special about this entrance, slith?" asked Nika. The light timbre of her voice bounced around the earthen walls.

"First of all, hardly anyone knows about this entrance," said Kronan. "And second..." Before he finished, he disappeared around a corner. When Matthias and Nika caught up, the sight before them stopped them in their tracks.

"Like I said, this way has the least resistance," finished Kronan.

"No kidding." Matthias screwed up his nose, suppressing the urge to pinch it in disgust.

The room spanned roughly fifteen by twenty feet and was filled with a mismatched assortment of baby cradles, all lined up side by side against the organically curved walls. Most of the cradles were occupied—by not just any babies but *Veniri* babies.

Matthias's lip curled. He estimated the room housed about twenty to thirty of the little vermin. Most were sleeping, while others cooed and kicked their little feet.

"Wow," Nika breathed. "I've never seen a Veniri baby before, especially not one that's in their shifted form. They're so—wait, are they… furry?"

"Yes, our young are born with fur and shed it in their adolescent years," Kronan explained.

Each baby had about an inch-long coat of aquamarine fur, with patches of white and dark blue. A faint impression of scales showed on the bare skin of their faces, throats, hands, and feet.

Matthias leaned over the nearest cot to peer at one of the pestilent spawn. The squirming thing burbled in its infantile language, revealing rounded crystal nubs beneath its top lip. He eyed the Diamantium, knowing just how lethal those nubs would become when they eventually grew into a set of triple fangs. And soft as the fur appeared, there was no way he was going to touch it to find out. He'd likely contract rabies or some other disease upon close contact with any of these screeching creatures.

Nika continued to look around in awe, but a moment later, her brow crumpled into a frown. "Hang on a sec. You mentioned there wouldn't be any guards because of the ceremony. Then who is supposed to look after all these babies?" Her voice hitched on the question, an emotion Matthias couldn't quite place.

"The human slaves." Kronan cast a sidelong glance at Matthias. "I assume you have no reservations about dealing with your own kind?"

From the corner of his eye, Matthias caught Nika's flinch. No doubt she expected him to reaffirm the hunter's code of "We don't kill our own." Over the centuries, his ancestors had protected the human race from all the heinous shape-shifters. It was the hunters' job to purge the earth of the abominations while the rest of the human species lived in their ignorant bliss.

Before Matthias bothered to respond, grit and gravel crunching underfoot announced Axel and the other hunters' delayed arrival. The stragglers spilled into the nursery, stunned gasps rippling through the group.

"Heaven's above, are those things in the cradles what I think they are?"

"As I live and breathe… Veniri *babies*."

"Matthias freaking found it this time…"

"Who would have thought Matthias would be the one to lead us to a hive?"

Crossing his arms, Matthias reveled in the collective disbelief. He was about to make a victorious proclamation when two women entered through an arched entrance at the other side of the nursery. Chains around their ankles clinked as they shuffled in. Mottled bruises covered their bare arms, metal cuffs encased their necks, and their gaunt features suggested malnourishment and neglect. There was no mistaking that these frail beings were, in fact, human.

At the sight of the half dozen baby bottles in the women's arms, Matthias recalled the Veniri shifters had a low female birth rate and had resorted to kidnapping human females to ensure the continuation of their species.

A sharp pang of horror stabbed his gut. Lyla-Rose, his daughter, had been kidnapped by the Veniri scum several years ago at the age of sixteen. In his mind, one of the slave women's faces morphed into the delicate features of his blue-eyed and fair-haired Lyla-Rose. Would this have been her fate? If she hadn't died, she'd have been brought here and locked into a metal neck cuff and forced to… *breed* with these foul reptilian fiends.

Matthias's disgust morphed into a boiling rage. Until this

moment, he'd never known how much of a mercy it was that his daughter had been murdered instead of made to endure this wraithlike existence.

In the seconds he spent pondering his daughter's demise, the slave women caught sight of him and his small army, and their sunken eyes grew wide.

A heartbeat later, four humanoid reptilian beings, scaled from the tops of their heads right down to their giant three-toed raptor feet, stalked in behind the women. Diamantium spikes jutted from their flesh—most prominently from their elbows, knees, and collarbones—and reflected rainbow flecks scatter all over the room. Initially unaware of the hunters, the creatures spoke to their slaves in the hissing and guttural drawl of their shifter language. From the way they groped the women, there was no need to guess what they intended to do during the rites ceremony with no one checking up on them.

The Veniri stopped their jeering and broke into a chuckle, only to cut themselves off mid-laugh when they finally spotted Matthias and the hunters.

The dumbfounded expression on the reptilian beasts' faces made Matthias smirk; it had taken the demons long enough to discover their sacred hive had been breached. From behind him came the melodic ringing of crystal weapons and blades being drawn from scabbards and holsters. In his periphery, Nika, Axel, and a number of other hunters gathered around him, bracing themselves for a melee.

Grasping the severity of the situation, one of the reptilian shifters sneered, putting his triple set of Veniri fangs on full display.

"Boss?" Axel asked.

"You know what to do," said Matthias.

The rising tension in the nursery shattered to pieces as

Axel and at least five other hunters raced past Matthias, eager to sate their bloodlust.

Crystal Veniri spikes and crystal hunter blades clashed with almost deafening ferocity, both sides swiping and slicing with expert precision. Three hunters managed to cut down the first Veniri. Another was impaled on Axel's trident.

Forgotten by the four shifters, the slave women had turned and fled. The clattering of dropped bottles and the splash of baby formula were drowned out by the vicious clangor and screams of the battle in the nursery.

"I'll deal with the women," said Nika, rushing after them.

Matthias frowned. He didn't think his niece had the gall to deal properly with the slaves. Regardless of their being human, they had been tainted and infected with shifter spawn. The only merciful thing to do would be to wipe them from existence along with their shifter captors.

The violent clamor grew louder, sparking the distressed shrills and screams of the infants around them. When the rest of the hunters looked to Matthias, it took only his glance at the shrieking spawn for them to understand the wordless order.

As the hunters spread out, he directed his attention to Kronan. The ever-spineless slith was practically hiding in the shadows near a nook by one of the cots.

Matthias raised an eyebrow. "Well? Lead the way, slith."

With a hesitant glance at the ongoing combat, Kronan gave a shaky nod and snaked his way toward the archway Nika and the slave women had disappeared through. Matthias followed, taking care not to be struck by a rogue Diamantium dagger or Veniri spike. The two remaining shifters had already sliced down three hunters, and continued to make Axel and his comrades fight hard for their victory.

Matthias stepped onto the rocky sections of floor that

hadn't yet been marred by the spatter of crimson or teal gore. The clang of weapons seemed to grow louder after they entered the narrow tunnel, but there was no sign of any more Veniri heading their way.

"Won't all this noise alert the guards?" Matthias asked.

Kronan shook his head. "The rites ceremony is held in one of the lower levels, many stories down."

"How long does the ceremony last?"

"For most of the day, until the last of the Diamantium dust is released into the vortex of wind." Leading the way into a twisting tunnel, he glanced over his shoulder to add, "The main living chambers of the hive are just through this walkway."

Matthias's stomach churned with eager anticipation.

The curses and shouts of the hunters, along with the ferocious chimes of clashing Diamantium blades, followed Matthias as he veered through the short passage. The tunnel spanned about twenty feet, with glowing teal orbs inside glass lanterns set at intervals along the walls. To Matthias, the orbs appeared similar to the tangible mass of light Kronan had sculpted his key out of earlier.

When they reached the final turn, Kronan hesitated.

"What?" Matthias asked.

The shifter darted him a nervous glance, then his shoulders sagged. "Nothing..."

When he didn't speak any further, Matthias said, "Don't tell me you've got a sudden dose of homesickness?"

"No, no. Of course not. Nothing like that, boss." Kronan shook his head in jerky movements, his expression a bit conflicted. "It's... strange to be back. I never thought I'd see this place again."

Matthias suppressed a groan of impatience. "From what I can gather, we haven't seen anything yet. All I see is the back of your head."

Without any further comment, Kronan shuffled forward. He'd hardly taken a step into the wide chamber beyond before Matthias grabbed his collar, yanking him back.

"One more thing, slith," Matthias hissed in Kronan's ear. "Don't even think about betraying me here, or I will make sure the rest of your life is nothing but severe agony. You will beg for death."

Not bothering to wait for a response, Matthias shoved past the shifter and stepped out onto a stone ledge. He stopped in his tracks to stare at the vastness of what lay before him.

A few moments later, the scuffle of boots and labored breaths announced Axel and the rest of the hunters had caught up. A glistening sheen of teal dripped from the prongs of the hunter's crystal trident as he gave Matthias a triumphant smile.

For a moment, all fell into an eerie silence as Matthias and the group of gore-painted humans took in their surroundings. If any of them had doubts before, no one could now deny they'd emerged into shifter territory.

The ten-foot-wide ledge they'd found themselves on was practically an infinite pathway, spiraling around the perimeter of an enormous chasm burrowing down, down, down into the depths of the earth. Matthias, along with all the others, peered over the edge of their stone perch. Not a single barrier obscured the sheer drop into the endless abyss below.

He and the hunters then craned their necks to gape at the void above. The circular walls of the massive chamber spanned about a hundred or so feet in diameter, hewn from the stone and earth.

"Wow. Now I understand why the sliths call it a hive," said Axel.

Though not hexagonal in shape, regularly spaced and

equally sized openings along the walls of the cavern called to mind a giant beehive. Judging by the collection of furniture and homely possessions in each opening, these were the main living chambers of the Veniri. A pale wash of teal light bathed the entire space, thanks to various globes scattered throughout the apartments. The spiraling path Matthias and his hunters stood on led down to each level, and a few wooden bridges crisscrossed over the dark expanse.

Matthias placed his hands on his hips and puffed out his chest. He would be going down in history as the first hunter to lead a group into a Veniri hive. Despite all the years of torment, the doubt, the hushed whispers and snide remarks, he had finally done it. Not his father, not his brothers, not even his own infamous son had achieved this.

It was *him*—Matthias Branstone. He alone had the determination and the gall to pull this expedition off.

A scuffle of boots caught Matthias's attention as Nika trekked up the spiral path to join them. He frowned at the sight of her. "Nice of you to finally join us. Did you encounter any issues?"

Nika shook her head. "The women have been dealt with."

"Oh, really?" He made a show of looking Nika up and down. "And not even a drop of crimson to show for it?"

Her expression was an iron mask. "I had four colors in my amulet. I'm quite efficient at what I do."

He eyed her for a moment before giving a wide grin. "Of course, dear niece. And yet, you can't have been all that *efficient* when your hunter amulet was destroyed. Come to think of it, I never did hear how that happened."

When Nika only scowled in response, he turned to Axel. "And those four sliths, they've also been 'dealt with'?"

Axel nodded, his bloodlust still evident in his grin. "Yup, along with all those brats."

"What?" The color drained from Nika's face as her head

whipped toward the tunnel they'd all come out of. "What do you mean 'those brats'? You don't mean… but… they were just—"

"Don't tell me that Nika 'The Iron Maiden' Branstone has started to develop a soft spot for these foul creatures." Matthias regarded her the way one would a maggot.

She glanced at him, then around at the other hunters, as if remembering the company she was in. "Of course not, Uncle."

"Good." He patted Nika on the head, and her scruffy curls bounced under his hand. "No need to worry your pretty little head over it. I'm sure you're aware that Axel and the rest of them are just as *efficient* at what they do."

All traces of emotion left Nika's face, but Matthias didn't miss the deadly glint in her eye.

"Think of it this way, Nika. Now that we've dealt with all the slith infants, we can now—"

Someone cleared their throat behind Matthias. "They haven't all been dealt with."

He snapped his attention to the one who'd interrupted him. "What did you say?"

Kronan cringed. "I, uh, said they haven't *all* been dealt with."

"Explain."

The slith pointed to several other openings, giving the locations of more nursery chambers farther down the spiral path.

With that many nurseries in this hive, and based on the number of cots Matthias saw in the previous nursery, his rough estimates almost had him snarling. No wonder the hunters never seemed to make any headway in decreasing the Veniri population. He almost didn't want to know how many human women were being held captive to contribute to the Veniri scourge.

"Fine, fine," said Matthias, cutting off Kronan's ramblings. "Clearly we've got a bit more work to do in eradicating this blight. Axel, take a few hunters with you and—"

"But you can't," blurted Nika.

Matthias slowly turned to his niece. "What do you mean I can't?" Despite the warning in his tone, Nika didn't cower as much as he would've liked.

"You can't," she repeated. "It's not right… I mean, they're all—"

"They're all *what?*" He took a step toward her. "Just *babies?*"

The set of her jaw and the fire in her eyes revealed the cracks in her previous nonchalance. "I was going to say *defenseless.*"

"And… the problem is?" He noted the slight twitch of her dagger hand, but a murmur from several of the hunters caused her to pause. She dropped her arm by her side.

"There's no problem, Uncle. I just didn't realize there was a vial in our amulets where we add the blood of the *defenseless.*"

Another murmur trickled through the hunters. The tone suggested Nika's comment had hit a nerve. No hunter appreciated their courage and skill being called into question, especially regarding their hunter amulets—the proof of their accomplishments and rank.

Matthias narrowed his eyes.

Nika matched him glare for glare. Her Shirley Temple curls, usually glossy swirls framing her doll-like features, now hung wild and drab from the four days in the harsh desert, adding to her fierce expression.

A few moments of silence passed before Matthias became keenly aware that every hunter had their eyes on him and Nika. He forced his glare into a placid expression and chose his next words carefully. "My dear girl, after a perilous trek through the desert, wouldn't you say that all these hunters have earned their right to cash in on their exorbitant payday? The payday that I graciously promised them?"

Rumbles of agreement echoed from a few of the hunters.

When Nika's glare didn't falter, he added, "Ah, I can see you still have a lot to learn. If a fortune's worth of Diamantium doesn't sway you, then what about your obligation as a hunter? Our duty is to rid this world of all that is heinous. A slith is still a slith, no matter the age. Do you understand, child?"

Nika held his gaze for a few heartbeats before she finally said, "Of course, Uncle. I completely understand now what my duty is."

"Good." Matthias grinned, his lips stretching wide. *Enough of these games.* He had work to do, but he'd be sure to deal with this impudence later.

He snapped his fingers, and on cue, Axel barked various orders. Nika's eyes widened in slight exasperation as several of the hunters peeled away from the group.

"For the record, you are right about one thing, dear niece," said Matthias. "This isn't the reason I've come." He patted a pocket on his chest pack, checking—not for the first time—on the five precious discs inside. Soon, very soon, another spangle would be added to his collection.

Tilting his head back, Matthias focused his gaze on the living quarters about fifty stories above, at the very top, where a highly engineered building hovered in the center of the circular chamber. If not for a network of wooden bridges connecting it to the sides of the hive, the structure would plummet into the deep heart of the bottomless pit.

"That is Queen Idalia's chambers," said Kronan, sidling up to Matthias.

"Yes, I gathered that." A tremor of excitement rushed through him as he pictured the grand prize inside.

Axel stepped up on Matthias's other side, scratching the gray whiskers on his chin. "Phase one of eradication is underway, boss." He indicated to army of hunters striding down the spiral pathway. "Although, I've got to ask, where do we find rest of the sliths?"

"I've already told you. Today almost everyone will be in the Vortex Chamber, paying their respects to the dead," said Kronan.

"Vortex Chamber? Everyone in one place, huh?" Axel stroked his bushy gray beard in thought. "I bet we can make quick work of it all with our Luxium shrapnel grenades."

"Fine. Whatever's necessary," said Matthias with a dismissive wave of his hand, eyes still fixed on the structure above.

Someone loudly cleared their throat behind him, and he turned to find about eight hunters who had stayed back from the group.

"Oi, what part of my orders didn't you understand?" Axel demanded.

No one answered. Instead, the majority of the remaining hunters turned their attention to a bulky man with a shaved head at the front of the group.

"Well?" Mathias asked. "What are you waiting for? A gilded invitation? Go! Your Diamantium awaits." He turned back to the royal chambers.

Crunching the gravel under his heavy boots, the bulky man stepped around Matthias and blocked his view.

Matthias calmly rolled his shoulders back and squared his stance, all while taking note of the glistening Diamantium sword the man held at his side. A drying trail of teal coated the deadly tip. "Got something to say, Brutus?"

The man regarded him with a glint of challenge in his eye. "With all due respect, Branstone, as much as a few Luxium grenades would make easy pickings for the Diamantium haul, a few of us have our sights set on a bigger prize."

"And what bigger prize would that be?"

As Brutus glanced up to the chambers at the top of the chasm, Matthias's heart skipped to a slightly quicker pace. He gritted his teeth and scanned the group of hunters, whose challenging gazes matched Brutus's.

"Have I not led you to the midst of a slith nest?" Voice rising, Matthias swept his hand in a wide arc, indicating the cavern around them. "This is not just a once-in-a-lifetime achievement. Since the dawn of hunters, who can claim they've infiltrated the Veniri in their own breeding ground?"

Brutus inclined his head. "True. But by the same token, who can claim they've seen, let alone captured, a female slith? Or better yet"—his gaze once again flicked to the top of the cavern before locking back onto Matthias—*"a slith queen."*

A muscle in Matthias's jaw twitched. "What is one female slith compared to the hoard of Diamantium for the taking? Diamantium is still Diamantium whether it comes from a female or not."

Brutus casually scratched the stubble on top of his head. "True again, if that's how you want to look at it. But a female slith—a *queen* slith—has the potential to rake in a monarch's worth of wealth for several years in, let's say... something like my own side business."

"Yes, yes..." Matthias's lip curled in a sneer. "I'm well aware of your shifter pleasure houses."

Brutus puffed out his chest. "What can I say? I excel at being a hunter *and* an entrepreneur. I know a good opportunity when I see one."

"Hmm... perhaps. But I, for one, am not so small minded as to presume that lust is the only potential to be found in this 'good opportunity.'"

Instead of being offended, Brutus gave him a big toothy grin. "I think you'll find that a few of the lads here would disagree."

The half dozen male hunters from Brutus's pack laughed, their grins greasy with lechery. One or two hurled a few bawdy comments about the slith queen, earning more chuckles from the group.

Matthias stepped past Brutus, cutting off the banter with a wave of his hand. "I will make myself thoroughly clear. Take whatever *other* female slith you find. Hell, take whatever female human slave you might find, for all I care. But as for the queen—"

"I say whoever finds the queen first can claim her," Brutus interrupted.

A few hunters voiced their agreement.

"Besides," he continued, "we're the ones doing all the hard work to earn our share of the loot. Other than a bit of desert sand, I've yet to see you getting your hands dirty, Branstone."

More mumbles rippled through the hunters.

Matthias glanced at Brutus over his shoulder. "You're right. Credit where credit's due. And payment where payment's due." He turned to give the man a wide grin. "But as for getting my hands dirty—"

With a lightning-fast jerk of his leg, Matthias kicked Brutus square in the torso. The pious expression on Brutus's face switched to fear. Arms flailing, the gore-covered hunter toppled over the edge of the spiral path. When his dying screams had faded into the abyss, the silence was as thick as syrup.

Axel came to stand by Matthias, his crystal trident aimed at the remaining seven hunters. Their expressions as they stared at their leader ranged from shock and anger to indifference.

Matthias made a show of dusting his hands off. "Anyone else have something to say?"

A few of the hunters shot nervous glances at Axel, then at

the dark void where Brutus had disappeared, but as a whole, they remained mute.

"Good. In that case, if anyone still needs me to make it perfectly clear… *the slith queen is mine*. All the rest is yours." He peered over his shoulder at the wide maw of the abyss. With a casual shrug, he added, "The way I see it, your share of the Diamantium just got bigger."

Axel took that as permission to order the group to either "get to work or join Brutus."

Heavy boots shuffled down the spiral path, following Kronan's directions to the Vortex Chamber.

After one more scan of the retreating backs, Matthias frowned. "Where's Nika?"

Axel scratched at his beard. "Maybe she rushed off to get her blades drenched at the ceremonial chamber."

"Perhaps…" Matthias said slowly, although after the way she'd spoken to him earlier, he had his doubts. After a few seconds of contemplation, he shook his head. "Forget my obstinate niece for now. I have my own prize to claim."

With Axel on his tail and Kronan scuffling ahead, they began their ascent to the suspended palace at the very top of the chasm.

2

CREATURES OF NIGHTMARES

FOUR DAYS EARLIER

"NO! STOP! LEAVE HER ALONE!"

Thane's desperate words roared dully in Violet's ears. Fighting to keep Solace in the safe cocoon of her arms, she tried in vain to console her baby daughter as they were yanked one way, then another by a variety of hands—webbed, clawed, covered in suction cups—some beyond anything she could describe. Ice-cold and slimy limbs dragged her closer to the cliff edge overlooking the ocean.

"No! Please no!" Violet dug her heels into the dirt. She craned her neck around to find Matthias Branstone standing in front of his army of hunters. "Please don't do this!" She didn't care how desperate she sounded. If there was a chance she could keep Solace safe, she'd take it. "Please help us. Don't you remember I was your daughter's best friend?"

Matthias's smug expression faltered for a second.

"Please!" Violet screamed. "Lyla wouldn't want you to do this."

But instead of the sympathy she'd hoped for, Matthias's face hardened. He folded his arms over his chest. "You know what is expected of you, Violet."

The last of her hope disintegrated. She had laughed, cried, and bled with Lyla-Rose Branstone, right up until the moment of Lyla's brutal murder. Did that not mean anything to Matthias?

Evidently not.

But what else could she expect from a man who had strapped an explosive collar around baby Solace's neck only moments before? Clearly Lyla hadn't gotten any of her compassion and human decency from her father.

Violet screamed in rage. She yanked back, trying to break free of her captors, but her efforts proved worthless. A tentacle whipped out and knocked her feet out from under her. Breath hitching, she braced for impact, but she didn't land on the hard ground. Instead, a surge of icy water slammed into her body—

And wrenched her and Solace over the edge of the cliff.

Violet's stomach flew into her throat. The briny air whipped her hair back and snatched away her screams as she plunged several stories into the crashing waves below. She managed to gulp in a desperate breath just before the freezing cold bit into her. Powerful swells buffeted her on all sides, forcing her to fight to keep both her and Solace's heads above water.

Moments later, with an almighty splash, something else hit the ocean a few feet away.

Thane's heaving gasps rang out over the surging waves, then quickly turned to grunts as he fought and thrashed against his own captors. It took four Nephezai shifters to keep him restrained and beyond reach of her.

"Violet, are you all right?" he called over the churning froth.

"Yeah." She managed the single word through swollen and split lips. Salt water stung the gashes over her face—a vicious reminder of Nika's merciless pummeling only moments before. Her brow, cheekbone, and jaw had been coated with a sticky layer of blood, which now washed away in the water.

That was twice now Violet had been graced with the fury of Nika Branstone's Diamantium-tipped knuckle-duster. If she ever saw Nika again, she wouldn't hesitate to smite that curly-haired hunter with her teal Magneii flames.

"What about Solace? Is she okay?"

Solace's piercing screams had begun long before Thane's question. The poor baby squirmed in Violet's arms. The cold, the water, and the army of Nephezai shifters were more than enough to cause a grown adult distress, let alone an infant.

Violet did her best to soothe her daughter, despite her own rising panic and shock.

When they'd been reunited only minutes ago after Solace's kidnapping, all Violet had wanted to do was take her child home and cuddle her. But instead, Nika and her uncle Matthias had handed Violet, Solace, and Thane over to Qozzlotl Nagahld, king of the Nephezai shifters.

She still didn't know why Qozzlotl would deem the three of them important enough to barter for. What did the Nephezai king want with them? *Oh hell...* Hopefully they weren't on the menu for some kind of Nephezai banquet. A shiver ran down her spine at the thought.

Solace's anxious screams almost shattered Violet's eardrums. They'd been bobbing in the water mere seconds, but in her mind, it had been a freezing and terrifying eternity.

She couldn't count the number of Nephezai shifters who had accompanied King Qozzlotl. Perhaps forty or fifty? The king and his ten or so personal guards had already dived under the crashing waves, and the rest of the thalassic shifters started to follow.

One of Violet's three captors—a female with flowing fins of radiant indigo and ruby red, like those of a Siamese fighter fish—snarled at her in a language she didn't understand. Violet flinched as the Nephezai held her webbed hand in front of Solace's face.

"Stop!" Violet cried. "What are you doing?"

The other two Nephezai held Violet firmly as a purple-tinged iridescent bubble formed in the fighter fish shifter's hand. It stretched like a thick membrane of bubble gum over Solace's entire head. A moment later, the same Nephezai formed a second bubble for Violet, then shoved them both beneath the surface of the ocean.

Violet gasped, heaving in lungful after lungful of air as the Nephezai shifters dragged her through the water. The bubbles remained over her and Solace's heads, and her three captors cut through the strong currents with little to no effort. Schools of numerous types of fish and the underwater scenery rushed by at a speed Violet couldn't imagine achieving on her own.

"Silence the screaming air breather!" the female Nephezai barked over Solace's slightly muffled cries.

Violet hugged Solace tighter and glanced at the shifter's rippling silken fins, whose indigo-and-ruby hues seemed somehow enhanced when fully submerged underwater. The graceful fins contrasted sharply with the numerous thorns—glimmering with mother-of-pearl—that embellished her shoulders and forearms.

One of Violet's male captors had the features of a stingray, while the other looked similar to a muddy-yellow octopus. When the octopus Nephezai caught Violet staring, he shot her a deadly glare at the same time a vibrant pattern of blue rings appeared all over his flesh. The magnificent mother-of-pearl thorns were the only feature all the Nephezai appeared to have in common—that and the neon-purple markings speckled over their bodies like psychedelic birthmarks.

She tore her gaze away from the octopus shifter's glare and squinted ahead. Within the school of Nephezai shifters, she could just make out the one with the giant eel tail from his waist down. From the waist up, he appeared more humanoid than many of the Nephezai, yet also more ferocious in appearance, his complexion gray like that of a giant shark. Weak rays of sunlight glinted off the crown of twisted mother-of-pearl spikes. Surrounded by his entourage, Qozzlotl Nagahld's power and sovereignty were unmistakable.

Only minutes ago, Violet had been ignorant of the aquatic shifter race's very existence. One minute, she and Thane were taking a drive in the early hours of the night with their friend Sagan; the next, he had betrayed them, handing them over to an ambush of bloodthirsty humans who hunted shifters for a living.

Matthias Branstone, the leader of the hunters—and Sagan's father—had met with Qozzlotl at the top of a cliff by the ocean and struck a bargain: Violet, Solace, and Thane in exchange for a *spangle*. One thing had become evident during the negotiations. Matthias was desperate for it. Even Violet didn't miss him constantly eyeing the transparent glass-like purple disc hanging around the Nephezai king's neck.

Violet knew next to nothing about the spangles—only that there were ten of them, one in each color of the different shifter species' blood. Sagan had told them his father had been searching a lifetime for them, but was aware he'd so far managed to acquire only the silver and pearlescent-white ones.

As for what the spangles actually did, no one seemed to know. Autumn had even utilized her hacking skills to try and find out more information, but nothing came up. Whatever Matthias's reasons for wanting them, though, Sagan was sure none of them wanted to find out.

Matthias had bargained hard for the king to hand over the spangle, but in the end, Qozzlotl was unwilling.

So now it was Violet's job to get it.

Her next breath shuddered as she looked down at the collar around Solace's neck. Terror, more icy cold than the waters surrounding her, sliced to her very core as she recalled Matthias's exact words after he returned her baby.

"Obtain that disc from the king. Once I have that disc in my hand, the collar will be removed, and your baby will live to see her next birthday."

Violet hugged her daughter tight. She'd only just got Solace back. How much longer would she have with her?

She choked back nauseating dread as Matthias's voice echoed in her mind:

"The countdown on the explosive is set for three weeks from today at midnight."

Three weeks.

Bile bit the back of Violet's throat. How the hell was she, as a prisoner, supposed to not only steal from the Nephezai king but also find a way back to the surface to trigger the satellite locator on Solace's collar? Assuming she was successful in this ridiculous heist, could Matthias even reach her in time to save her from the Nephezai horde that would likely be in pursuit? Who was to say Matthias wouldn't kill her and her baby himself after he got what he wanted? He'd probably allow Nika to finish what she'd started.

Under her breath, Violet cursed Matthias's and Nika's names with every phrase she knew.

Solace let out a cry again, clinging tight and snuggling into Violet's chest.

"Shhh, bubbah, shhh..." She tried to rock her daughter, but that proved difficult to do while being manhandled and dragged farther and farther into the depths of the ocean. She also didn't want to jostle the air bubble over Solace's head.

How strong were these bubbles? How long would they allow someone to breathe before the oxygen ran out?

On and on the panicked questions plagued Violet's mind. Worrying about their air supply was, in a way, preferable to worrying about the bomb strapped to Solace's neck.

Violet tried and failed to slow her panicked heaving. The bubble didn't mute the acrid scent of salt, fish, and seaweed. A fretful tear trickled down her face, joining the others pooling beneath her jaw at the base of the air bubble.

The powerful bodies of the Nephezai glided through the water with unending endurance, and icy turbulence rushed around Violet's non-streamlined body. She couldn't quite tell how much time had passed. Perhaps half an hour? An hour? Maybe more? However long it had been, they'd left the last of the sunlight long ago.

Down, down, down they went. As the water grew even more pitch black, the neon markings on the Nephezai began to glow, becoming beacons of royal-purple light.

The underwater scenery and sea life had changed with the loss of the sun. Delicate seaweeds and dancing anemones turned into sinister forests of spiny coral. Tropical fish that flitted around in darts of color were replaced by the eerie presence of glowing eyes and razor-sharp teeth.

Violet fleetingly wondered how her body could withstand the water pressure at these depths; she hadn't even needed to stabilize the pressure in her ears. Were her new Veniri and Magneii abilities to thank for that? Or did the strange purple bubble over her head do more than just allow her to breathe? Whatever the science behind it all, even Solace didn't seem to be struggling. Her cries had died down, although the poor thing still hiccupped with lingering sobs.

Ahead, the Nephezai king darted downward at a steeper angle. The rest of the Nephezai followed, a murmuration rolling down toward the seabed. There, without a word, the group began scooping up handfuls of what looked like sticky mud.

When the shifters began smearing the mud over their bodies, Violet shared a glance with Thane, but he looked just as perplexed as she felt. Only when she noticed her guards scanning the waters above did she realize the mud was being used to cover the glowing purple markings.

"What's going on?" Thane asked, but the lobster guard with a vise grip on one of his arms immediately shushed him. In fact, every shifter had become hypervigilant in assessing their surroundings.

Violet trembled with another shiver of horror. These shifters were by far the scariest creatures she'd encountered in the ocean so far. What on earth would make them want to hide?

She had no idea what kind of mud the Nephezai had coated themselves in—she wasn't sure she wanted to know—but it didn't easily wash off in the water. When every last inch of purple was smothered in goop, the king motioned for the troop to continue swimming.

This time, however, the shifters moved at a much slower pace, weaving through large rock formations and pausing periodically in giant clumps of seaweed. Those who had weapons held them at the ready. When the king gave a signal, they moved ahead, always pausing, hiding, searching.

Violet found herself also searching, heart in her throat every time she spotted a shadow or something brushed her ankle. But the shadows always turned out to be harmless boulders, and the tickles on her ankles were from the stirred-up seabed brushing around her feet.

They approached the entrance to a deep ravine. The sheer rock walls rose high above, making the path ahead especially dark and ominous. Violet wished with all her heart they weren't going to enter, but she had no idea how far up they would have to swim to avoid going through.

About twenty feet before the entrance of the ravine loomed the wreck of a massive cargo ship, nestled into the mud and murk. The Nephezai skirted around it, although Violet still didn't see any sign of what they were afraid of. Most scanned the waters behind and above them. No one seemed as perturbed by the ravine as she figured they should be.

The king came to a sudden stop and called out a warning. In a practiced flurry, the Nephezai darted out of formation and went to hide, some in the wreck, others among the nearby coral and rock mounds.

No one moved.

Violet and Thane were shoved into a rocky crevice right by the entrance to the ravine, large enough for their guards to also squish in. Violet would have hated being pressed up against the cold and slimy bodies of the Nephezai if her curiosity hadn't overwhelmed everything else. Unable to help herself, she peered through the cracks of their hiding place to get a good look at what was about to happen.

The rush and ripple of water became still, and the silence roared in her ears.

For several heart-pounding moments, nothing happened. Thankfully, Solace had become quiet, nestled in the crook of her mother's neck. Violet checked to make sure the air bubble wasn't squished against her baby's mouth or nose.

When she looked up again, little lights were bobbing around within the ominous ravine, meandering and dancing like graceful fireflies.

"What are they?" she breathed.

The speckles of lights blinked in and out, mesmerizing to watch.

"Ügovs," whispered the octopus shifter from just behind her.

"What are Ügovs?" Thane asked, in the same hushed tone.

"They're so pretty. I could watch them for hours," said Violet.

"And that would be your first mistake, air breather," said the fighter fish shifter, as if speaking to someone with the intelligence of a slug.

Violet frowned, then shook her head to break her hypnotic fixation on the little spectral lights. She scanned the area. The king and three Nephezai were the closest shifters to her own little crevice, hiding behind the big fins of the cargo ship's crumbling rudder. She wouldn't have thought it the safest place to hide, but there was something about the way the king and his companions were poised, taut like a bowstring. As if about to pounce—

"It's an ambush!" Violet whisper-shouted.

The fighter fish shifter hissed for her to be quiet.

Tension grew as all fixated on the phantasmal lights. Violet's pulse quickened when the half dozen or so lights doubled. Then tripled. What were they? A school of glowing fish?

The mesmerizing specks grew bigger as they moved closer to the entrance of the ravine, and their shapes became apparent.

Violet's breath caught in her throat. The lights weren't fish at all. They were eyes! Round, bulbous eyes made of a pale and sickly green glow. The eyes belonged to creatures she could only ever have imagined in her nightmares.

There were at least a dozen of them, all humanoid but disfigured—mashed-up mutations of fins, gills, claws, thorns, shells, and tentacles. Their attire consisted of scraps of metal, perhaps scavenged from shipwrecks, and were decorated with bleached bones from a myriad of underwater creatures.

Some held larger bones sharpened into long spears, with smaller spikes that edged the spearhead and upper shaft, resembling a cactus or the nose of a sawfish.

The leader of the creatures had not only a mouthful of jagged teeth but hundreds more in rows upon rows over his face and head. He scanned his surroundings as he approached the last few feet of the ravine.

Violet sucked in a breath and bit her lips hard to stop herself from making a sound. Every Nephezai in her immediate proximity became solid, causing not even a ripple in the water.

Moving forward, several of the Ügovs flicked lanky, slimy-looking tendrils about, giving Violet the impression of feelers on insects tasting and testing the environment around them. Her heart stuttered a few more beats as the creatures gradually, cautiously glided past her hiding place.

But before she could sigh with relief, the Nephezai king made a quick motion, and all hell broke loose.

Nephezai shifters swarmed out from all sides, surrounding the Ügovs. For a moment the creatures seemed startled, but they didn't hesitate to switch to attack mode. The fang-faced leader threw back his head and let out a high-pitched shriek that rippled through the water and drilled straight through Violet's eardrums. She and Thane groaned in pain, and Solace cried out. Thankfully, they no longer needed to worry about being overheard, not over the clangs, crashes, bellows, and screeches from the underwater battle.

The Nephezai fought with ferocious swipes of their claws. Tails whipped and hammered. Tentacles zapped, stung, and constricted. Mother-of-pearl thorns shot like darts through the water.

The Ügovs thrashed and shredded their enemies, tearing at the Nephezai with their overloaded mouths full of teeth and scores of crudely made weapons of scrap metal and bone.

Violet's stingray shifter guard gnashed his teeth and pummeled his fists together, shouting something in a language Violet didn't understand. The octopus guard made a sound of agreement, but the fighter fish shifter growled and planted a hand firmly on the stingray shifter's shoulder. "No, we have our orders. We stay and keep the air breathers alive." Her voice remained calm, controlled, but the tremor of her indigo-and-ruby fins gave away her adrenaline-fueled need to also join the battle.

The stingray shifter glared at Violet and Solace. When the octopus shifter turned his attention to them too, the vibrant blue rings flared where the sticky mud didn't quite mask his flesh.

Violet cowered, her back pressing against the rock wall. She tried her best to shield Solace with her body from the Nephezai guards' resentment.

A loud bang and bellow of rage claimed the guards' attention as a Nephezai battered one of the Ügovs with a rusted pipe torn from the nearby wreck.

On and on the Nephezai and Ügovs fought. A frenzy of bubbles, shipwreck shrapnel, and ocean floor debris in the water soon mixed with cracked claws, severed limbs, and blooms of bright purple shifter blood. The number of Ügovs had dwindled against the overwhelming number of Nephezai, but in the midst of the chaos, the fang-faced leader fought just as viciously and valiantly as the five Nephezai who had ganged up on him.

One Nephezai was cut down right before another stabbed the Ügov in the side. The Ügov roared but continued to claw and tear through his opponents. Just as Violet felt sure he'd be overcome at any moment, a screech rang through the dark ravine.

"Oh no," Violet breathed as many more sickly green lights headed straight for them. She held back a sob, the constriction in her chest growing beyond painful. Being captured by the Nephezai was one thing, but what would happen if the Nephezai lost this battle to the mutant Ügov creatures? Would they take prisoners of war or just feast on the remains?

A hand grabbed hold of Violet's. With a jolt, she went to shake it off, until she realized the fingers wrapped around hers weren't icy cold but warm.

She looked up at Thane, and he squeezed her hand tighter in reassurance. She should pull away, but instead she ended up squeezing back.

The gold flecks in his deep brown eyes flared with concern, anger, and possibly fear. Cuts and bruises marred his brow, cheeks, and jaw, courtesy of the hunters back at the clifftop. He tilted his head almost imperceptibly.

Violet gave a small nod, understanding his reassurance. Regardless of the fact that everything was certainly *not* okay, for a moment, all the seething fury and betrayal she harbored toward Thane was overshadowed by terror—and relief that she wasn't alone. She squeezed Thane's hand so hard the pain in her knuckles served as a reminder she wasn't dead yet.

Solace's cries had quieted to blubbering sobs. In a few more minutes, she might even fall asleep just from the exhaustion of crying. But with the circumstances they faced, what were the chances she'd be able to calm down completely anytime soon?

The new wave of Ügovs clashed with the remaining Nephezai, and this time one was vigilant enough to spot Violet's little group hiding in the crevice. The Ügov called out and earned the attention of five others, who followed a direct route to Violet's hidey-hole.

The guards rumbled with a mixture of alarm and excitement.

Thane drew Violet close as she waited for the melee to be unleashed around her.

The small group of Ügovs were five feet away when a new sound rang out through the water. This time, both the Nephezai and Ügovs froze. Weapons paused in mid-swing and jaws locked in mid-gnaw as all looked up toward the high-frequency *ping*.

A moment of silence followed. Then, just as another *ping* pulsed even louder, all the aquatic humanoids burst into a flurry. The Ügovs disappeared the way they'd come, dispersing into the black as if they never existed. King Qozzlotl barked out orders, and the Nephezai assembled and charged into the chasm behind the last of the Ügovs.

"Hurry," the fighter fish shifter ordered. "Get the air breathers out of here."

Thane and Violet were thrust out of the crevice and into the chasm. A bright white light was cast from above, and Violet looked up to the open ceiling of the ravine several stories beyond.

The light shone down into the cracks over their heads, momentarily blinding her. As the source passed over, she craned her neck to get a better look.

The contraption appeared to be some kind of submarine, about 150 feet long and 12 feet in diameter. The nose was made of a domed viewing window, with two bright spotlights on either side.

"What the heck is that thing?" she asked.

"Erathi," said the fighter fish shifter. "Erathi hunters."

"What? Erathi, as in *humans*? Down here at the bottom of the ocean?" Violet's eyebrows skyrocketed. Those human hunters were like pests. "But why would they be chasing us if they made a trade with your king?"

"These aren't the same hunters as on the cliff," said the octopus shifter. "These ones specifically hunt Nephezai and can be down in their submarines weeks to months at a time."

Violet shook her head in disbelief. She had so many more questions. How many hunters were out there? What on earth drove someone to be in a submarine for months at a time to hunt Nephezai? Squinting her eyes against the light, she could just make out the silhouettes of four people staring out from more domed windows along the craft's side. Thankfully, the people inside hadn't spotted them, as the submarine didn't veer off its course.

With a few more pings, the underwater vessel glided over the top of their chasm and out of sight.

The fighter fish shifter hissed a phrase, whether cursing or in relief, Violet couldn't tell.

The Nephezai didn't slow down, darting and weaving through the maze of underwater rock formations. Only just over half were left after the clash with the Ügovs, and a lot of the mud they'd covered themselves in had started coming off. The purple markings began to light up the chasm with their faint light, revealing the two sides of the rocky ravine had pinched together into a tight apex. Violet hoped the cavern ceiling would hide them in case the human hunters decided to circle back over.

Only when the group reached a dead end did the Nephezai come to a halt.

About five or six shifters moved forward to surround Qozzlotl. With the king taking the lead, the small group raised their arms and waved them above their heads in unison.

"Let's hope this doesn't take long." The stingray shifter glanced behind them, then all around the waters of their cavern.

"His Majesty has it under control," confirmed the fighter fish shifter, her eyes never leaving the king.

The octopus shifter also looked around nervously. "Do you think the Ügovs have sensed us?"

The fighter fish shot him a glare. "Do you doubt His Majesty's ability to lead us through the most untraceable route possible?"

Once again, blue rings flashed over the octopus shifter's flesh before his lips pinched into a tight line.

The corner of the fighter fish shifter's mouth curled into a sneer. "Scared of the Ügovs, Belitozzl? If I were you, I'd be more concerned about who you voice your skepticism of the king to."

The octopus and stingray shifters shared a surreptitious glance before returning their attention ahead.

Half a dozen Nephezai had positioned themselves in a semicircle in front of the rock face, with the king in the middle. Bursts of purple light blossomed to life in each shifter's palm, then intersected at a single point in front of the chasm wall. The tendrils of purple light rippled through the water, and within a few heartbeats, the beams collected into an undulating mass. It started out the size of an apple, then expanded to the size of a basketball, growing bigger and bigger with each passing second.

It took Violet a few moments before she recognized what the Nephezai were doing.

"They're light forging," she blurted.

"Looks like it," said Thane, a note of concern in his voice. "But what exactly are they light forging?"

"A gateway," said one of Thane's Nephezai guards.

"A gateway?" Violet frowned in thought. "Like a portal?"

The fighter fish guard shook her head. "No, you ignorant air breather. Portal-forging practices are extinct. Besides, portals are doorways into other dimensions and beyond the means of light forging. This is a gateway, a shortcut through the hundreds of miles of rock."

"A shortcut to where?" Thane asked.

"To Scylorethyz," said the stingray shifter.

"Or *home*, as we like to call it," said Violet's octopus guard.

"Or as the Erathi would say"—the fighter fish shifter turned her luminous purple eyes on Violet and Thane—"the Mariana Trench."

Violet's breath hitched.

The Mariana Trench? But… that was the deepest part of the ocean. The Mariana Trench was as deep as you could get on the face of planet Earth!

She felt the blood drain from her face as she stared, wide eyed, at the undulating light mass that continued to grow and expand.

The king swam over to the mass and, with two helpers, began sculpting. A minute or so later, Qozzlotl's gateway was complete. The light-forged structure, a circle twice as wide as the biggest Nephezai shifter, glowed ominously against the ravine's black-as-night waters.

Qozzlotl swam to the side of the gateway and gestured for the Nephezai to enter. One by one, the marine shifters disappeared through the circle's purple galaxy-like substance swirling in the center.

As Violet was dragged closer and closer, her breath quickened into shallow pants.

She couldn't—*wouldn't*—go through the gateway. She couldn't take her baby to the deepest part of the ocean. Not with an explosive device locked around Solace's neck!

"No, I can't." She turned tail and tried to swim away.

"Violet, don't—"

Thane's warning cut off as the guards surrounding him and Violet fought to keep them contained. Tentacles, fins, and other tendrils of who-knows-what latched on to her.

Once again, Solace shrieked with fear as Violet kicked and thrashed.

Then warm arms embraced her, much different from the cold Nephezai appendages. For a second she tried to fight the arms off, before Thane's calming voice spoke in her ear.

"I'm here, Violet. We'll do this together."

"No, you don't understand."

"I heard what Matthias said to you." He paused, allowing that to sink in. "I promise, no matter what it takes, we are getting that thing off Solace's neck and getting out of here."

By the time he'd finished his sentence, the Nephezai guards had rallied around them and moved them right up to the light-forged gateway.

Thane had only enough time to say "I've got you" before they were shoved through the vortex.

3

SUCK IT UP, IMHOTEP

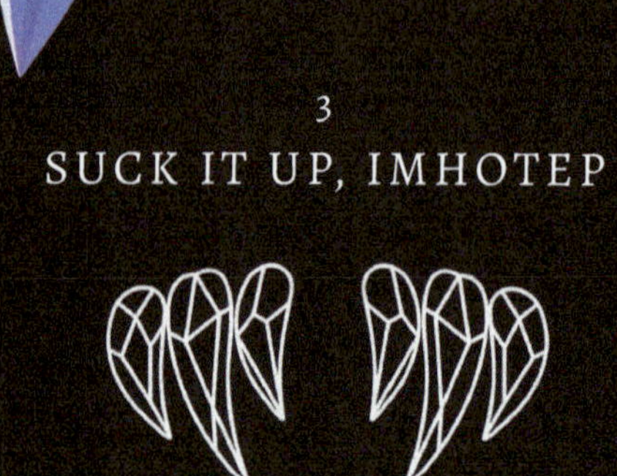

"WE HAVE A LIVE ONE HERE!" A VOICE SHOUTED.

Nathan ran.

He fumbled across the blackened beams and ash-covered rubble to the man calling out. En'gorr Droth, the crowned prince of the Jiovis shifters, sprinted alongside him, along with his three Jiovis guards. In a flurry, the group helped a few of the Maple Shire residents lift away a series of heavy beams. Dust and ash billowed around them, tainting each breath Nathan drew into his lungs.

"Careful!" warned Nathan as a cough and low groan came from beneath the rubble. He dug through large hunks of timber and tossed away chunks of concrete. The anxiety in his chest rose with each piece of charred debris they cleared away.

Please be her. Please. Please *be her...* The mantra of hope cycled over and over in his mind.

Finally, a face appeared among the debris. Black ash and dried blood coated the survivor's face.

A shriek rang through Nathan's ears when one of the other residents called out a name. "*Oscar*!"

The earth might as well have dropped out from under Nathan's feet.

It wasn't Violet.

Or even Thane.

Trying his best not to show his disappointment, Nathan made way for the men who carefully lifted the teenage boy from the ash. A mother ran over, crying tears of relief. A few other ladies huddled around the group of men as they carried the boy all the way to the infirmary tent.

Nathan dragged a bandaged hand over his bandaged head.

It was late afternoon on the second day since two explosions had torn through the peaceful off-grid community of Maple Shire.

Two days.

Two freaking days of digging through rubble to retrieve the dead and rescue the living. And yet there was still no sign of Violet or Thane.

Where are they?

Nathan clutched at the fabric of his shirt over his heart. The pounding in his ribs had reached an agonizing level. Sweat drenched his clothes and every bandage covering his body.

His breaths turned quick and shallow. Doubling over, he braced himself with hands on his knees. Was he having a heart attack? Was it possible for a Veniri shifter to even have a heart attack?

A heavy hand pressed down on his shoulder. "Sit, Nathan. Rest," came the deep rumble of En'gorr's commanding voice.

Nathan shook his head. "No time to rest. We still haven't found them."

"We will," said En'gorr.

"What makes you so sure?" Nathan peered up at the towering prince. "We've been digging for days." He pointed to the bulldozer clearing away the remnants of what used to be the home of Dr. Dawn Farrow and her family. The house where Violet had been staying. "We tore that place apart several times over. We pulled everyone out—Dawn, Lazareth, Gus, Autumn—everyone *except* Violet. There's been no sign of her, and heaven knows where Thane was during the blast. So I'll ask you again..." Nathan stabbed a finger into En'gorr's chest. "What makes you so sure we'll find them?"

"Nathan, calm down," said another voice. Tio, En'gorr's younger brother, clambered over the rubble to join them.

"I am calm!" barked Nathan, earning the startled attention of the other Maple Shire residents still close by.

The three guards drew closer to their princes but paused when En'gorr held up a hand. Neither he nor Tio needed the guards to protect them from Nathan's rising hysteria. In human form, the five Jiovis shifters were tall and broad—built for battle—yet the threat of their human forms paled in comparison to their "living metal" shifter forms. Even if neither prince was skilled in fighting, the Jiovis electrical ability would be more than enough to throw Nathan on his ass.

Despite Nathan's rage urging him to shove, kick, and scream at anyone who stood between him and finding Violet and Thane, a sliver of rationality reminded him that these shifters didn't deserve his abuse. None of this was their fault.

In fact, no shifter was at fault.

All blame rested on the human hunter Matthias Branstone. He and his pack of malevolent hunters had caused far more damage than Nathan could fathom.

With a shout of outrage, he kicked at the debris by his feet. He should have gone after Matthias and his hunters days ago. But instead, he'd been so busy searching for Violet and Thane in the wreckage that he'd missed his chance of exacting revenge.

"Nathan, listen," said Tio in a soothing tone. "It's probably time to consider why we haven't found Violet and Thane yet."

Nathan hung his head. "No..."

"We need to," pressed Tio. "The chance of finding Violet or Thane alive in the wreckage at this point is... well... What if they were in the midst of the explosions? What if instead of looking for bodies, we should be looking for—"

"Don't!" Nathan squeezed his eyes shut, but it did nothing to stop the gruesome images flashing in his mind. He couldn't take this anymore. He *needed* to prove Violet and Thane were still alive, and in one piece. He needed to get back to work.

Nathan whipped around.

Whoa... Big mistake. The world didn't stop spinning. Then it began to shift sideways.

"Nathan? Are you okay?" Tio's voice sounded as if it came from the bottom of a well.

The next thing Nathan knew, he was looking up at the clouds, with En'gorr's and Tio's ash-covered faces hovering over him.

* * *

"Here, drink this," said Lazareth Farrow, pressing a cup of warm soup into Nathan's hands. "It seems even the Veniri can suffer from physical exhaustion."

Nathan scoffed. "I'm not exhausted. I'm just a little—*whoa...*" Once again, the world started to spin when he stood up from his cot. En'gorr and two of his guards caught hold of him before he could face-plant at their feet.

"Careful," said Tio as En'gorr and his guards firmly sat Nathan back down.

"Give yourself a little time to rest," said Lazareth. "You've been working yourself ragged for the past couple of days."

"So has everyone else," countered Nathan. He gestured outside the window of Autumn's computer hut, at the many people traipsing past like worker bees. Along with those still in the midst of cleanup, many walked around with baskets handing out fresh-baked goods, homegrown fruits and vegetables, and flasks of ice-cold water.

"I'm not saying the others haven't been working hard," said Lazareth, "but everyone is also suffering. We're all trying the best we can to deal with our grief. Some people can't stop crying. Some people get angry. Some withdraw from everyone, while others try to overcompensate with humor. A few throw themselves into hard work to try and numb the pain of losing a loved one."

A fleeting anguish crossed Lazareth's features, and shame stamped out the rest of Nathan's frustration.

Lazareth had buried his wife, Dawn, mere hours after the explosions. And instead of throwing tantrums or provoking Jiovis shifters, he was still cooking large quantities of food to ensure none of the Maple Shire residents went hungry. When he wasn't cooking, he was checking up on and caring for everyone else, all with a reassuring demeanor.

"I'm sorry, Laz," said Nathan. "Regarding Dawn—"

"It's fine, Nathan. I already know how amazing Dawn is… was." For a moment, Lazareth closed his eyes tight, wringing his hands in front of him. "I should go check up on Gus and Autumn. They've been hammered at the infirmary tent and probably need a break by now." He gestured to Nathan's soup. "Finish that up, and perhaps give yourself the rest of the day off. Start fresh tomorrow."

Nathan shook his head. "I can't sit around here while the rest of you are working. I need to help."

"You'll be no help to us if you work yourself to the bone," Lazareth gently scolded. "You need food and rest— "

"No, I can't—I *need* to be doing something."

Lazareth finally nodded, his face grave with understanding. "Okay, in that case, just give yourself at least an hour to finish your soup, and have some water to rehydrate. I would recommend light duties for the rest of the day."

"What do you consider to be 'light duties'?" Nathan gruffed.

"Basically anything that doesn't include heavy lifting or overexerting yourself. Maybe take on one or two tasks away from the disaster site. Honey needs to be robbed from the beehives, goats need to be milked, lawns need to be mowed, there's a constant pile of linens from the infirmary that need to be washed—and that's only a few of the many community chores that are being neglected at the moment."

Nathan nodded, but his shoulders sagged. No matter what he did, it wouldn't be enough to quench his worry over what happened to Violet and Thane.

"I could always use an extra pair of hands in the kitchen," Lazareth added.

"Can I at least suggest Nathan has a shower first before handling food the rest of us are expected to eat?" said Tio.

Nathan raised an eyebrow.

"No offense," Tio rushed to say. "It's just that you might like to be reintroduced to this fancy thing called 'soap.'"

Nathan's temper flared. People's lives had been literally blown to pieces. Violet and Thane were missing. The full-to-bursting infirmary tent lacked supplies and resources, since the infirmary building had been destroyed. With all that weighing on his mind, the suggestion that he should be thinking about a shower—while the water house and pipes were still being repaired, on top of everything—felt utterly selfish.

This entire rant, and more, was on the tip of Nathan's tongue, until he saw the small smirk at the corner of Tio's mouth—and the undertone of insecurity beneath the expression. Then Nathan finally saw the dig for what it was.

He'd forgotten Tio was still in his midteens. The kid was struggling just as much as everyone else, but one of Tio's survival mechanisms was humor. Nathan had learned this when they'd both been locked up in Tempecrest with Thane and forced to fight Lycan shifters in the bloodthirsty human hunters' gladiator arena.

Thane was Tio's friend too, as was Violet. And Dawn had gone above and beyond in caring for Tio when he'd been mauled by a mutant leopard creature.

When Nathan didn't immediately respond, sadness began to eclipse the spark of humor in Tio's eyes.

Nathan made a point of looking the young shifter up and down before he said, "You're one to talk. You're so filthy you look like someone scraped you off the bottom of their shoe. Do you even have the word *hygiene* in your vocabulary?"

En'gorr and his three guards chuckled at Nathan's ribbing, although the laughter sounded a little forced.

Tio's white teeth flashed with a smirk. "Whatever, old man. No matter how many showers you take, we all know you can't wash away the stench of Veniri." He pinched his nose and mimed gagging, earning more animated laughs from his older brother.

"Good one, It'thio," said En'gorr, using Tio's full name and patting him on the back. He then added a comment in his own language to reconfirm the Jiovis's general opinion on the Veniri scent.

"Hey, I resent that," said Nathan, frowning in mock offense as Tio and the guards laughed harder.

Tio threw a few more lighthearted insults his way, and finally Nathan couldn't help adding his own small chuckle. It was more than worth being the butt end of the young shifter's jokes if it meant a fleeting reprieve from the overwhelming grief of the last few days.

He glanced over at Lazareth and earned a small reassuring smile. The joking may have been for Tio's benefit, but everyone in the room seemed to have a bit more sparkle in their eyes—even the most fearsome of En'gorr's guards.

"All right, all right," said Lazareth when the laughter died down, "I guess I'd better get back out there." He gestured to Nathan. "It looks like I should pick up some clean bandages while I'm at the infirmary tent."

Nathan looked down to find some of the bindings around his hands and arms had begun to unravel. He gave a slight wince at the filth ingrained in the once white bandages, then tried rewrapping the one around his left arm. "No, don't. Leave the clean bandages for the people who are *actually* hurt."

"It's not just the bandages on your arms that need to be re-dressed," said Lazareth. "The one around your head also needs to be redone."

"Yeah," confirmed Tio. "There are a few hints of your skin sparkling through some gaps in the bandage."

"Then I'd better find something else to cover my face instead of monopolizing valuable medical supplies," said Nathan.

"Nonsense," said Lazareth. "The clean bandages help sell the story that you were horrifically burned in the blasts."

"True," said Tio, "but Nathan's been helping out with the cleanup since the explosions. Won't people start to question how badly burned he really is?"

Lazareth shook his head. "Most people are sporting injuries and bandages, so Nathan's 'Invisible Man' appearance isn't much of an oddity. And everyone's a little too shell-shocked to take much notice of the details." He rummaged through some belongings on one of the tables. "Actually, let me check… I think I may have a spare bandage in the first aid kit, but… it looks like I've already used the last roll."

"I'm serious, Lazareth. Don't concern yourself over me."

Lazareth placed a hand on Nathan's shoulder. "I had hoped it would be obvious by now that I concern myself with everyone here." He made a point of looking at all the others in the room. "I may not be a shape-shifter myself, but we consider you all to be not only members of the Maple Shire community but also members of our family." He patted Nathan on the back. "You've been here during good times and now the worst of times. You've also helped protect us as best you can. You are now family."

Nathan dropped his gaze to the carpet, surprised at the rush of emotion Lazareth's words brought on. It had been a long, long time since anyone had made him feel like part of a family. The closest thing he'd had in recent years was Violet, who'd become his foster daughter.

Before Nathan could recoil back into harrowing worry over the whereabouts of Violet and Thane, Lazareth continued speaking.

"You need new bandages, Nathan. At least until we can figure out a better disguise for your… condition. I'll send some over after I check up on Gus and Autumn."

As Lazareth got ready to leave, En'gorr called on his guards. The prince spoke a phrase in the Jiovis tongue, to which all three responded with a nod. To Lazareth, he said, "My guards to help at infirmary. Autumn and cousin August may break their duties—"

"*Have a break* from their duties," corrected Tio.

En'gorr paused to cast a slight frown at his younger brother.

Since arriving in Maple Shire several weeks earlier, En'gorr had mainly spoken in the Jiovis language while Tio translated. But clearly being in Maple Shire was helping the prince gain confidence in speaking a language other than his native tongue.

En'gorr turned his attention back to Lazareth. "I to ensure Veniri staying hiding. Rest. Recover. As too, my brother, It'thio."

Tio scowled. "I hate it when you use my full name."

Judging by the glimmer in En'gorr's expression, Tio had reacted exactly as planned. Yet regardless of his brother's grumblings, En'gorr didn't seem likely to cast aside his princely formalities anytime soon, considering he also insisted on calling Gus by his full given name.

"Thank you," said Lazareth, addressing En'gorr and his three guards. "That would be a great help."

Lazareth and the guards left Nathan, Tio, and En'gorr alone in the computer hut, now turned into temporary sleeping quarters. Glancing over the hodgepodge of stretchers taking up most of the floor space, Nathan couldn't help but think of the absent beds.

Violet… Thane… Solace… Dawn… Sagan… Even if he left out Sagan's cousin Nika, the list of names was far too long.

A black cloud rumbled through Nathan's psyche. He no longer had enough fingers and toes to count off all that had gone wrong in the last few months—or rather, the last few days.

Despite the fact that the majority of Maple Shire's residents were human and ignorant of the world of shape-shifters, this place had been a haven for not just Nathan but also Thane,

Tio, En'gorr, and his guards. Lazareth's wife, Dawn, and her sister, Skye, had used this little community as a temporary shelter for shape-shifters who needed medical attention or a stable place to live as they searched for new homes, away from the lives they'd escaped from. It had also been the perfect place for Violet to birth her daughter, Solace, in peace and safety.

At least, it had been a place of safety, until tragedy started to find this tranquil little community a little too frequently.

No more than five minutes after Lazareth and the guards had left, Autumn entered the hacker hut, holding a bundle of bandages. Before she'd even taken a few steps inside, En'gorr strode over and engulfed her in a hug. Nathan glanced at Tio, who didn't seem nearly as surprised to witness En'gorr and Autumn's open affection.

Frowning, Nathan tried his best not to stare. He'd always considered himself observant to a degree, but since when had the hulking Jiovis and the dreadlocked young woman crossed over into the realm of PDA? He rubbed at his bandaged jaw. It now made a bit more sense why En'gorr had been working so hard on improving his language skills.

But what about Autumn? Wasn't it only a few days ago En'gorr had utterly freaked her out with the explanation of the Jiovis "love lock"? Autumn had seemed repulsed when he and Thane had tried to explain that En'gorr hadn't been trying to kill her the time he'd wrapped a hand around her delicate throat. Instead, as per the Jiovis culture, the prince had been claiming her as his soulmate.

Perhaps, considering recent circumstances, she'd had a change of heart. Nathan couldn't really blame her. On top of the explosions two days ago that killed her aunt and decimated her home, both her parents had died in a brutal Magneii attack not long before he'd arrived at Maple Shire. Finding some comfort from En'gorr could be the best thing for her.

When the two pulled apart, En'gorr placed his hands on Autumn's cheeks. The two murmured a few phrases Nathan couldn't quite make out, until En'gorr finally said, "Anything for you, Zhivotza."

Autumn's smile dimmed a little at the prince's use of the Jiovis word for "soulmate," but En'gorr either wasn't offended by her ambivalence or didn't notice. He took some of the rolls of bandages from her and strode over to Nathan.

"Hey, guys." Autumn gave Nathan and Tio an exhausted smile. "Uncle Laz said you needed some clean bandages. So, what's the damage?"

"No damage," Nathan confirmed.

"Lazareth thinks new bandages will help sell the concept that Nathan was burned by the blast," explained Tio.

Autumn eyed the filthy strips wrapped around Nathan's hands and arms. "Yeah, I suppose people will start to question how blasé we've become with hygiene and sterilization."

"I'm sure they'd be forgiving, considering the current circumstances," said Nathan. "I still think it's a waste to use perfectly good bandages on me."

"You're one of us, Nathan," said Autumn. "It's not a wasted resource if we're taking care of a member of the community."

"Yeah," said Tio. "So suck it up, Imhotep. You heard Lazareth. Until we come up with a better way to disguise your predicament, or find a… a cure, then bandages it is."

"Fine." Nathan gave a hesitant nod. "Then let's get this over with so I can get back to cleanup."

En'gorr made a disapproving *tsk* through his teeth, and Tio rolled his eyes. Regardless, no one decided to argue over Nathan's adamance to keep searching for Violet and Thane.

Autumn, En'gorr, and Tio assisted Nathan in unraveling the mass of wrappings. Even though he'd been dressing in bandages for only a few days, Nathan was surprised at how quickly he'd become used to them. Or perhaps he was just starting to notice how much apprehension rose with the removal of each layer.

Within a minute, a bundle of dirty bandages lay on the floor at Nathan's feet.

A few glimmers of light in the corner of his eye caught his attention, and he looked over at the full-length mirror Autumn had hung by the door. As expected, the sparkles of light came from his reflection. Nathan inspected himself, gritting his teeth when the intense fear in his chest froze him in place. No matter how many times he'd seen it, the sight of his skin condition—if that's what he could call it—still triggered crippling uncertainty, but also great curiosity. Never in his life had he seen or heard of anything that could describe his new image in the mirror.

He tilted his head from side to side. All his facial features were the same—his tawny eyes, the deep laughter lines framing his mouth, the salt-and-pepper stubble along his square jaw, and every new crease and wrinkle he'd gained in his forty-six years of life. All of it still looked like him, even with a few extra silver streaks in his dark hair. Yet the appearance of his skin had changed drastically. It now held a fractal appearance, like crystal in a sienna-beige skin tone. The facets flashed under the ceiling lights, and the sight was… what?

Fascinating? Mesmerizing? Eerie? Downright creepy?

Nathan still couldn't articulate what he thought about it.

"I don't get why you didn't tell me about this sooner." Tio folded his arms with a huff. "Not only were we freaking out when we found you unconscious in a rubble heap looking head-to-toe like… well, like this"—he gestured at Nathan's entirety—"but then we find out from Gus that this has been going on for a while. Since Tempecrest, for crying out loud. I thought that after you,

Thane, and I survived that hellhole together, we'd moved past this whole 'Veniri shifters don't trust Jiovis shifters' crap."

Nathan rubbed his temple. "That's not why I didn't say anything."

Eyes downcast, Tio grabbed a new roll of bandages and began to wrap Nathan's other hand.

"And you're right. After what we've been through, I do trust you." Before a year ago, Nathan never would have thought he'd say he trusted a Jiovis, or any other shifter species for that matter. "I didn't say anything because you're Jiovis. It was because... ugh, I don't know..." He shrugged his shoulders. "Maybe it was pride that kept me from saying anything... or fear."

At Nathan's raw admission, Tio looked up. His quirked eyebrow held a hint of surprise, as well as... Was that respect?

"So you said this crystallization began while you guys were locked up in gladiator prison on an island somewhere?" Autumn asked.

"Tempecrest Island." Nathan nodded, just barely suppressing a shudder at the awful memories. "It started as two tiny patches, but they'd grown to playing-card size by the time we reached Maple Shire. Sagan saw it one night when we were training with Violet. He was the one who forced me to tell Gus and Dawn."

A sharp pang stabbed his insides at the thought of Dawn.

Autumn's busy hands paused for half a second, and En'gorr, who had taken an almost sentinel-like position behind her, placed a hand on her back.

"I swear I'm going to hunt that Matthias Branstone down and kill him," Tio hissed through his teeth.

"Get in line," said Nathan.

"It's all my fault."

Nathan looked up in shock at Tio's choked words. "Of course this isn't your fault. Why would you say that?"

A shadow of profound grief washed over Tio's face. "If I hadn't run away from home, I never would've been captured by hunters and sent to Tempecrest. Then my brother wouldn't have had to go in search of me. Which means he wouldn't have had that run-in with Matthias that led him to Maple Shire. If it wasn't for me, they'd all still be here. Violet and Thane and… Dawn—"

"Stop!" Autumn clutched Tio's shoulder. "Don't you dare take this upon yourself. What happened to my aunty Dawn was definitely *not* your fault." She pointed to the scene out the window. "All that destruction, all those deaths—Matthias and *Matthias alone* is the one to blame. Well… and also all the hunters who helped him attack us."

Tio's tormented expression reminded Nathan once again that the Jiovis was only sixteen, something he kept forgetting. The young shifter already matched Nathan in height, his large frame bulky and strong.

"Now, you listen to me, kid," Nathan said in the most firm-but-gentle voice he could achieve. "I'm sure if Dawn could tell you herself, she would also say none of this is your fault. Do you hear me, It'thio Droth?"

Tio flinched at the use of his full name, but a spark in his eyes suggested the statement curbed at least some of his self-blame. "I hear you," he said with a slow nod, then with a ghost of a smirk, added, "Old man."

En'gorr moved silently to his brother's side and said a short phrase in the Jiovis language.

Tio gave a small smile. "Thanks, bro, I appreciate it."

En'gorr returned the smile and patted his younger brother on the back.

For a few moments of silence, the bandage wrapping continued.

"So, what is it again that caused this crystallization, or whatever, to grow over your skin?" Autumn asked.

Nathan shook his head. "I'm not one-hundred-percent sure. But after a bit of testing with Gus and Dawn, the only thing that seems close to logical is that it may have something to do with what the hunters called Aphrodite. It's a light cannon that casts condensed beams of artificial Venusian light."

"Oh, yeah, I remember you telling me that's what the hunters used when they tried to harvest your crystal bones and spikes. Then Sagan helped you escape, right?" said Tio.

Nathan nodded. "Gus came to the conclusion that the crystallization spreads further every time I haze into Veniri form."

"Sounds simple enough," said Tio. "Just don't haze."

Nathan chuckled without humor. "Easier said than done. I shifted more frequently than normal in the gladiator arena, and then again when we tried to rescue Violet's baby from Rivermyre."

Autumn hissed in a sharp breath. "I hate that I couldn't save baby Solace. And with what happened to Sagan, him being left behind at the god-awful place…" She didn't elaborate further, only screwed up her face and shook her head.

"And during the blasts, you ended up unconscious in Veniri form for at least ten hours." Tio pursed his lips. "It was kind of weird, you know."

"What was?" Nathan asked.

Tio hesitated. "The whole time you were unconscious, the crystallization slowly spread. Kinda looked like you had been frosted over with ice or something. It was so freaky."

A chill shuddered down Nathan's spine.

"And you're sure you've never seen this happen to another Veniri before?" Autumn asked him.

"Never."

"But what about the other Veniri the hunters used Aphrodite on? Surely one of them could confirm..." Autumn trailed off as Nathan once again shook his head.

"When Sagan helped me escape, he mentioned that no other Veniri had survived to see the aftereffects of Aphrodite."

Autumn frowned. "Why?"

"Because they were harvested."

"Yeah, you know," added Tio. "Harvested. As in, the Veniri are stripped of their Diamantium bones until they're nothing but a mound of meat and scales."

All color faded from Autumn's face.

Nathan's stomach flipped. "Gee, thanks so much for that gruesome image, Tio."

Autumn reached for a new roll of bandages. "Okay, so you survived Aphrodite, and—"

"It's not Aphrodite I survived. I survived by not being harvested."

A quick shudder racked Autumn's body.

"Yeah, yeah, details." Tio rolled his eyes. "As far as anyone knows, you're the only one who's lived, and you're now dealing with the consequences of being exposed to condensed artificial Venusian light. At least, that's what we're currently blaming for all this bling... right?" He gestured to the still-exposed facets of Nathan's skin. "So what now? Do you feel any different now that you're... well... covered from head to toe in what I assume is some kind of Diamantium crust?"

Nathan took a moment to consider Tio's question. "No. Believe it or not, I feel kinda the same. At least, I don't feel like I'm... dying." He gulped. "I mentioned to Gus and Dawn that this stuff feels different from Diamantium. For starters, it's not rigid." He poked at his skin, mesmerized by the way the microfacets still dimpled under his fingers, then bounced back, much like flesh. "To me it still feels like skin, except … it's more sensitive. It's as if I can register all the ridges of my fingerprints."

Nathan decided to leave it at that, still unable to articulate aloud what he'd been discovering. With the heightened sensitivity, he had no doubt he'd be able to tell each person apart just from a touch of their hand on his crystal skin.

Tio swiftly wound the last few lengths of bandage before rummaging through the pile of supplies for medical tape. Autumn began wrapping new bandages over Nathan's face and head while Tio taped down the loose ends.

"So, what other medical testing has my cousin got you doing?" Autumn asked.

"Nothing at the moment," said Nathan. "I think Gus has other things on his mind."

Tio sighed. "Right, poor guy. I can't imagine what it's like to find out you're a Pliokai shifter after thinking you're human your whole life. And then to find out your own mother isn't human either."

"And on top of that, he's got the impossible task of stepping into Aunty Dawn's role," added Autumn.

Another wave of grief engulfed Nathan at the thought of Dawn's passing. She was one of the most intelligent and selfless women he'd ever met, treating all people—humans and shifters alike—as equals. "I think Gus already knows it's impossible to replace his mother, but I don't think he fully believes the rest of us don't expect him to."

"No kidding. I don't envy being in his shoes." Tio applied a few more ripped-off sections of medical tape. "There you go. That should be about it."

"Great." Nathan rolled his arm around for a quick inspection. "Looks good. Thanks, kid." As he stood, he once again caught his reflection in the mirror. Autumn had allowed some gaps for his mouth, nose, and eyes, but he'd still have to put on a pair of sunglasses to completely hide his face. "I'm not sure I'm as optimistic about this 'Invisible Man' image as Lazareth is."

"I think you've got a few weeks, even months, to keep pulling this mummified look off," said Tio. "And after that, you could always claim you're a little insecure about your, uh… 'burn scars.' It shouldn't be too hard to sell. We all know how vain the Veniri are."

Nathan huffed. *Insecure? Vain?* If only scarring were the problem.

"Besides," Tio added, "I think the people of Maple Shire have a few more problems to worry about at the moment. Not many are going to be too concerned with why you're still covered in bandages."

Nathan heaved a sigh. "I suppose you're right. Anyhow, it might not be long before I'll have to…" What? Leave Maple Shire and find a new home?

Home. He jolted slightly at the thought. When had he started to consider Maple Shire his home?

His last home in Brookhaven had been burned to the ground by—surprise, surprise—Matthias Branstone and his pack of hunters. He'd loved that house: the first little piece of the outside world he'd claimed as his own after escaping the Veniri hive. And it had been Violet's home too when he started fostering her.

But that was before his world of shifters and Violet's world of ignorance erupted into chaos.

"I wonder how he's doing."

Nathan looked over at Tio. "Who?"

"Sagan."

"Oh." Nathan tried to rake his fingers through his graying hair, then remembered it was covered by bandages. "Yeah… me too."

He had every reason to detest the ex-hunter, yet in just

over a year, he'd developed a surprising level of respect for Sagan. The young man had done a lot to help him—and not just him, but Thane, Tio, Violet, and her daughter too.

"Do you think Sagan's… still alive?" Autumn asked.

Nathan couldn't bring himself to answer straightaway. The last time anyone had seen Sagan was during the failed attempt to rescue Violet's baby from Rivermyre, when he'd selflessly thrown himself into a throng of guards to give the others a chance to escape.

When no one responded, Autumn added, "As much as it's no longer a surprise how brutal Sagan's father and grandfather are, they wouldn't… hurt Sagan. Would they?"

Nathan knew that by *hurt* Autumn meant *kill*. "Sagan has a better chance than most to survive Matthias and Renard Branstone."

The taste of Renard's name on his tongue fueled his anger. The man led an underground facility that experimented on animals, humans, and shifters alike. To his mind, Renard the scientist and Matthias the hunter were equally despicable.

"I'm sure Sagan is fine," he added, not sure if he was trying to convince the others or himself.

"Maybe…" Tio's brow creased with uncertainty. "Just can't help feeling that we need to go back to that stinking underground lab and *try* to find him. At least get some kind of proof of life."

A pang of guilt sliced through Nathan's insides. If not for the explosions and the disappearance of Violet and Thane, he'd have gone to try and find Sagan already. "I can't say I disagree. Unfortunately, none of us are in any condition for another rescue attempt. We have to trust Sagan can look after himself. Best-case scenario, he's managed to find Solace and break her out, and he'll be showing up with her at any moment."

They all turned to the door as if hoping Nathan's statement was prophetic. The group remained somber when no one walked through.

Nathan reached for the pair of leather gloves Lazareth had lent him. "I need to get back to searching—"

The door to the computer hut swung open as Lazareth barged in. "Have any of you seen Gus?"

All four shook their heads.

"Hasn't he been with you at the infirmary tent?" Nathan asked.

"No." Lazareth cast Autumn a questioning look. "You told me Gus needed to duck out earlier. How long ago was that?"

Autumn glanced at her watch and frowned. "About forty-five minutes ago. Maybe an hour. Are you sure he hasn't come back?"

Lazareth shook his head. "No one has seen him. I'm starting to get a little worried."

"Hmm…" said Nathan after a moment's thought. "I think I know where he might be."

4

NO ESCAPING SCYLORETHYZ

PANDEMONIUM RECEIVED VIOLET, THANE, AND SOLACE ON the other side of the vortex.

Hundreds of Nephezai shifters crowded the gateway. They didn't wear the polished metals or pearl-like armor the guards did; in fact, the mob appeared to be made up of Nephezai civilians. Every single one greeted them with scowls, furious shouting, and vicious clicking and screeching sounds, like a whale song gone utterly wrong.

Violet's arms squeezed Solace closer, and Thane's tightened around both of them.

The throng began to fling seaweed, rocks, and coral. Violet and Thane's guards parried most of it, but they couldn't deflect the angry shouting.

"Filthy air breathers!"

"A thousand curses on the Erathi for banishing us!"

"Shred the air breathers to pieces!"

"Kill every last one of the Erathi!"

Nephezai guards huddled closer around Violet, Solace, and Thane as they tried to push through the hysterical shifters.

"What's wrong?" Violet asked. "Why are they so angry at us?"

"They think you're Erathi," said the fighter fish guard, her tone matching the anger of the crowd.

A few of the shifters tried to rush past the guards, lashing tentacles, fins, stingers, and claws. Before long, mother-of-pearl thorns joined the rock and coral projectiles.

The guards bellowed their fury. One or two peeled off to pummel the nearest offenders, but that didn't stop a rogue mother-of-pearl thorn shooting past Violet's ear. The thorn nicked and popped the bubble around her head. Ice-cold water gushed over her face, and salt burned her eyes, momentarily blinding her.

She tried to take a breath before her air disappeared but instead sucked in a mouthful of water. Panic kicked in. Her lungs were on fire. Logic fled, and instinct forced Violet to swim up, ignoring the fact that she was at the deepest part of the ocean.

Try to reach the surface!

Find air!

A booming *crack* resonated through the water, the rippling force ricocheting through Violet's body. Her chest spasmed with the effort to breathe. Just when she thought she couldn't last another second, a large hand covered her face.

Air! Oxygen-rich, life-giving air *whooshed* into Violet's nose, mouth, and lungs.

Her diaphragm kicked, and she started to cough up salt water, alternating between spluttering and greedily gasping in air. Thane kept her upright, holding her steady, while his other arm kept Solace in place in Violet's arms.

Violet opened her eyes to find her air bubble restored and the Nephezai king staring straight at her, his piercing purple eyes mere inches away. When the king seemed to deduce she wasn't going to die, he turned back to face a suddenly more subdued crowd.

Only then did Violet have the fleeting thought that the purple spangle had been in reach.

A group of guards rammed through the crowd's stragglers, forcing them to make way for Qozzlotl, just as another *crack* rattled right to the marrow of Violet's bones. The force of the sound flung the crowd even farther back. Violet realized the sound was coming from the king himself. He shouted orders in the Nephezai tongue, and the people responded with silence, residual anger still evident in their scowls and clenched fists.

Without another word, Qozzlotl swirled to face Violet, Thane, and Solace. As he waved his arms overhead in an arc, purple light collected in his webbed palms, then morphed into a bubble big enough to encase the three of them. The thick, opaque membrane cut off all vision and sound.

"What's going on?" Violet asked, the question eerily loud in the sudden quiet.

Thane finally released her, and coldness leeched over her skin where his arms had been. "Not a clue."

"I don't understand," she said. "That guard said they think we're Erathi. But why would that make them all so angry?"

Thane frowned, scanning the inner surface of their capsule. "Out of all the shifter species, the Nephezai hate the Erathi like no other. The hate is centuries upon centuries old."

"*Why*? Before today, I'd never even heard of the Nephezai. I didn't know these shifters—or the Ügovs or any other underwater humanoids—existed!"

"And the Erathi would prefer to keep it that way—keep the Nephezai existence a mystery. A species that most have long forgotten."

"But how did they all know we were here? They were waiting for us when we came through the gateway."

"No idea. Maybe news travels fast in these waters?"

Both Violet and Thane looked up when a shadow glided past their barely transparent bubble. Then another shadow swam past, and another. Once, something hammered against the membrane, but it was intercepted by a few more shifter silhouettes.

After a few heart-pounding seconds, all grew quiet. Solace began to wriggle in Violet's arms, her tiny brow crinkling. Surprisingly, she had been quiet the whole time they'd been in the bubble. Now she started to coo, almost as if asking what was going to happen next.

Violet squeezed her baby's tiny foot. Poor Solace. In just over ten weeks of life, she'd already endured much more than most beings did in a lifetime. The expression on her small, round face seemed wise beyond her infant existence. Was that because of what she'd already endured, or were Veniri children simply more aware than human children? Violet couldn't tell; she'd never had any experience with human babies to even compare.

Solace's worried look melted away as her focus shifted to the air bubble around Violet's head. Holding out a chubby hand, she began poking at the bubble with her tiny index finger.

Thane turned away from the shadows intermittently streaking past and watched her, as fascinated with Solace as the baby was with booping Violet's bubble. "Is she… all right?"

Violet nodded. "I think she's as well as can be expected, although I'm sure she'll be getting hungry soon. I have no idea when she last ate."

It struck Violet that this was the first time Thane had seen

Solace—at least, the first time he'd had the chance to focus on her after being thrown off a cliff, plunged into the sea, shoved through a light-forged gateway, and then assaulted by a throng of aquatic shifters. When Violet had fled Thane months ago—once she'd learned about his involvement in her best friend's death—he hadn't known she was pregnant. *She* hadn't known she was pregnant until she'd arrived in Maple Shire and Dr. Dawn had informed her during a bout of nausea.

She recognized the look on Thane's face. It was the same expression she herself used every time she looked at, or thought of, her daughter: he was completely smitten.

Solace turned her attention to Thane. She grinned at him, then reached out a hand.

Thane hesitated slightly, as if surprised Solace would acknowledge him. But he didn't keep her waiting long before holding his own hand out to her. She immediately grabbed one of his fingers and rocked his large hand from side to side, sending small ripples through their purple enclosure. After warbling a few things to him in her baby language, she began to bounce a little in Violet's arms.

"I think she likes you," said Violet.

"Really? Do you really think so?" Despite the scattered gashes, multiple bruises, and swelling around Thane's cheek and eye, he looked at Violet with a hope and longing she realized she could relate to.

"Yeah. Solace doesn't shy away from what she likes."

A small smile lifted Thane's whole demeanor, and his warm eyes seemed to glow, almost to the point she could see flecks of gold in his chocolate-brown irises. It reminded Violet of when they first met, when she was falling for him. When he was falling for Violet.

She had a feeling she should ask if he wanted to hold Solace. He was her baby's father, after all, and if she were in Thane's position, she would be desperate to hold her child.

But a glance at the crystal scorpion tattoo on his neck made her pause, a complex mix of emotions coursing through her. Instead, she turned her attention to the light-forged purple bubble around them. "What do you think they'll do to us?"

"I'm not sure." Thane didn't take his eyes off Solace, but his golden warmth faded, and worry turned his features rigid.

"Have you had much experience with these kinds of shifters?"

"No, I don't think anyone has in a long, long time. I was seriously surprised that Matthias, an Erathi hunter, was able to not only track down the Nephezai but also have a somewhat civil exchange that didn't end in bloodshed."

"But why? What did the Nephezai do? Some of the rioting Nephezai were yelling about the Erathi banishing them. Is that true?"

Thane had opened his mouth to reply when a loud *thunk* hit the outer side of the bubble. Violet jumped in surprise, lurching sideways into him. He softened her impact by wrapping his arms around her and Solace, and the trio glided through the water toward the edge of the sphere.

Just as they were about to bump into the purple membrane, the bubble burst. Its entire contents—Violet, Thane, Solace, and all the water—sploshed onto dry sand. Violet landed on her back, holding Solace out from her body to ensure she wasn't hurt. The water from their capsule seeped into the ground, the sand darkening around them.

A small *pop* went off in Violet's ears as the bubble around her head burst too. Half sitting up and trying to get her bearings, she found the three of them had been deposited into an enclosure in the middle of a vast underwater grotto. About ten feet above was a domed ceiling, and a bubble-like wall surrounded them on all sides. It felt like being in a giant snow globe, about sixteen feet in diameter, but with water on the outside instead of within.

Along the towering walls of the grotto, a vast array of other enormous bubbles covered the rocky cliff face. Violet realized with horror that this grotto was like a museum, a staggering menagerie of live specimens, all of which could be found on land. Animals, people, and creatures of all sorts peered out through their bubbles, staring intently at their new prison-mates.

To her dismay, she, Thane, and Solace were the centerpiece of the exhibition. Their enclosure was one of about eight to ten others, all on five-foot podiums, spaced out evenly along the grotto floor. And as far as she could tell, theirs was the only one currently occupied.

The Nephezai king and a half dozen guards surrounded their globe. The shifters' appearances rippled slightly as the bubble membrane swayed with the gentle ocean currents.

"Welcome to Scylorethyz," said the king, a triumphant gleam in his eye. "My Seh'Vuthi pair is a worthy addition to my collection." With a nod of approval at Solace, he added, "As is the Veniri princess."

Violet's flames ignited in her eyes. She hated the way this slimy eel shifter regarded her daughter.

Qozzlotl leaned a little closer to the barrier, his full attention on Violet. His unnerving grin revealed jagged rows of semitransparent needle fangs. "Yes. You, my little hybrid, are a fine specimen indeed."

Without another word, he turned and swam off, his eel-like tail snaking through the water as he disappeared down a corridor of rock and coral.

The guards followed their sovereign one by one until only the Siamese fighter fish shifter remained. Teal flames still burned from Violet's eyes, but the shifter held eye contact with a steady, thoughtful confidence. Violet didn't want to admit it, but the fighter fish shifter's gaze put her more on edge than the king's fang-filled smirk.

"Get comfortable, air breathers," said the Nephezai at last. "You will rot in here and be fed on by the bottom feeders like the disgraceful filth all Erathi are. There is no escaping Scylorethyz."

5
SPAGHETTI AND SELF-LOATHING

SAGAN'S FOOT BRUSHED AGAINST A PEBBLE. IT BOUNCED AND clacked over the rocky floor, creating echoes that joined the subtle singing from the other side of the underground lake—a gentle tune totally mismatched to the jagged, stygian environment. The cavern would be pitch black if not for the magenta-tinged light from the Luxium-core camp lights Sagan and his cousins had installed when they were children. Even after all these years, the Luxium energy cores still worked as efficiently as ever.

But efficient or not, Sagan couldn't help a slight sense of misgiving every time he focused on the lights. The fact that each Luxium core had been prized out of the smashed skull of a Magneii shifter should be reason enough for him to switch to basic LED. Once, he wouldn't have given the lights' origins a second thought, but that all changed when a close friend of his was bitten by a Magneii shifter and developed their lava qualities and fire abilities.

A deep stab of remorse sliced into Sagan's core, as it did every time he thought of Violet Chambers.

The delicate singing from across the lake switched its tune, bringing Sagan out of his current spiral of self-loathing. Setting his focus back on the task at hand, he stepped from one stepping stone to the next, through the shallows of the lake. When he reached the makeshift camp kitchen, he flicked the starter switch on his camp stove, whacked a pot over the burner, and filled it with tinned spaghetti.

The woman's voice continued to sing, this time a soft melody about a little boy who made friends with his echo in a well. The song sent chills down Sagan's spine, bringing with it the bittersweet memories of his childhood.

He looked over at the owner of the ethereal voice. Despite her disturbingly wraithlike appearance, some of his mother's features still rang true to the memories he had of her before she disappeared. She would always sing him to sleep as a child, assuring him the monsters he was being trained to fight and kill didn't actually live under his bed.

Even now, Odette Branstone's voice reminded him not only of warm hugs and confident encouragement but also strength and steadfast courage. All the other hunters Sagan had grown up with were quick to flaunt their so-called bravery, yet his mother was the only one he knew for a fact could glare Death straight in the face without flinching. She was the most courageous person he'd ever known.

And yet… could he still believe that of her?

Sagan squeezed his eyes shut. He couldn't reconcile his childhood memories with the frail woman before him. There was something… *wrong* about her singing now. It never quite matched the memory he had of her before she went missing, when he was only ten years old.

His shock still lingered from the moment he'd recognized his mother's song during the attempt to rescue Violet's daughter nine days ago. The haunting melody over the radio earpiece had called to Sagan like a siren's song. He'd fought hard through the labyrinth of Xabat Biogenetics to find her, leaving a trail of bodies in his wake, his soul-deep hope and grief driving him near the brink of insanity.

The astounding joy of seeing her again—*alive!*—was beyond words.

Yet his elation was instantly consumed by a toxic rage at the sight of his mother curled up in the corner of a metal cage. Her blonde hair was dull and scraggy, and the ragged brown gown with the Xabat Biogenetics logo hung off her like a billowing tent. Skin and bones didn't even come close to describing her condition.

Bile burned the back of his throat when he realized there was no hint of the fierce, strong, courageous woman she used to be. The rage that followed his heartbreak writhed through his entire being. But before he was able to break his mother free, an army of Xabat security spilled out from every direction. Beaten into submission and detained with electric shock cuffs, he had been dragged to the leader of the underground science facility, to Renard Branstone—his grandfather.

Sagan had always thought he couldn't detest anyone more than Matthias Branstone, his own father, but when he looked into the eyes of Renard, unparalleled hate eclipsed all else.

He'd spat in Renard's face. Juvenile as it was, he couldn't help but feel smug when his grandfather's triumphant grin dissolved into stricken disgust. But that small rebellious act was the last Sagan attempted, especially after Renard voiced an offer: his mother's freedom in exchange for the hybrid shifter Violet Chambers.

Immediately, he knew he should refuse.

When Sagan asked what Renard wanted with Violet, a malefic grin stretched across the man's face. His grandfather then proceeded to spout some sciencey mumbo jumbo, a lot of which Sagan didn't understand. Yet he still heard himself accepting Renard's offer. Shame burned his cheeks at the memory of practically begging his grandfather to promise he wouldn't hurt Violet.

In the end, his mother's freedom had trumped everything else. He'd sold his soul to the devil—or rather, he'd sold out his friends.

Sagan's shoulders drooped as he stirred the spaghetti in the pot. He could never deny that saving his mother was the right thing to do; he'd do it a thousand times over. But that didn't stop his insides from squirming with dread and self-hate. The transaction weighed heavier each day. A mere hour prior he'd been willing to die for Violet's cause, only to end up luring her and Thane to be captured by hunters.

Who does that to his friends?

Only a dirty rotten traitor like him.

Soon. Soon he would figure out how to make it up to Violet. Surely as a mother herself, she'd be able to understand his reasoning for what he'd done. Surely he could someday convince her to forgive him for his betrayal. And she'd forgive him... right?

An image of Violet, Thane, and baby Solace flashed in his mind, morphing into corpselike impressions of what his mother had been when he found her locked up in Xabat Biogenetics.

Stop it!

Sagan shook his head fiercely. He couldn't allow his mind to go there now. His mother needed him.

He turned off the camping stove, emptied the pot's contents into two stainless-steel bowls, then grabbed some spoons and recrossed the stepping stones. The singing stopped, leaving only the melodious *tink-tink-tink* of dripping water from the stalagmites into the lake.

"Here, Mom. Dinner's ready."

She didn't look at him. Didn't even register his existence.

Sagan tried his best to ignore the stab of hurt. Her indifference had been the same every time he'd tried to interact with her.

He held out one of the bowls. "I know, I know. We've had canned spaghetti for the last three nights. I promise I'll go shopping tomorrow."

He'd been promising that for days. The stockpile of supplies his cousin Nika had left from her stay previously was beginning to dwindle, yet he couldn't bring himself to leave the cave, with or without his mother. He wasn't quite sure how she'd handle herself without him, but he also had no idea how she'd react to a grocery trip after being locked up in an underground science lab for… who knows how long.

His mother turned her back to him. Sagan couldn't take his eyes away from the threadbare garment she refused to change out of. There was no point in tossing a blanket or a jacket over her. Despite the cavern's chill, she always threw the extra coverings off.

The bowls in Sagan's hands shook, the metal forks beginning to rattle. He barely registered the stainless-steel edges digging into his hands.

How did the scientists at Rivermyre have the gall to do this?

How could his grandfather have allowed this to happen?

Odette's simple brown dress exposed her shoulder blades and upper back, where the flesh was almost unrecognizable as human skin. Thick raised scars took up most of the real estate on either side of her spine, with birdlike pin feathers sticking out in scattered clumps throughout the scarring.

Sagan had a fair idea what his grandfather had been trying to achieve with his experiments on Odette. Small bonelike structures on either side of her spine looked like the beginnings of wings, but if wings had ever sprouted from his mother's back, they'd been hacked off, leaving only the disfigured stumps behind.

The heat of Sagan's rising fury could rival the flames of his camp stove.

Once, he'd thought the stories of the winged shifters were mythical, a fairy tale told to children at bedtime. Now he knew better, and he hated the lengths his grandfather and father would go to in order to claim the winged-shifter abilities for themselves. Sometimes he wished he could also hate the winged shifters and the heart-wrenching pain they represented, but despite the agony that sometimes threatened to crush his very soul, there was nothing about the winged shifters he could ever hate.

Squeezing his eyes shut, he forced himself to suppress all the rising memories he'd locked away in a very far and very sacred part of his mind. He didn't have the courage to revisit them.

Odette began singing again, the same song about the little boy and his echo.

"Come on, Mom, you've got to eat."

She ignored him, increasing the volume of her song to drown him out.

"Mom, please. For me?" He huffed out a breath. He wasn't sure he had it in him to fight this battle tonight. "You need to eat."

This time she covered her ears and pulled her legs up, curling into a ball on the cot.

Sagan's frustrations were reaching his threshold. For eight days, he'd waited as patiently as he could for her to acknowledge him, to actually *see* him when she looked at him. To recognize him as her son.

Did she remember him at all? Was she even aware she was free of that heinous lab?

Was there any chance the two of them could be a family again?

"Here, Mom." He moved the bowl of spaghetti into her periphery.

Odette screamed. Swatting at the bowl, she sent it and its contents flying. Spaghetti strands splattered over the floor and cavern wall, but most of the mess landed on Sagan's sleeping bag on the ground by his mother's cot.

He bit back his frustration, gritting his teeth so hard he risked grinding them to dust.

Still in a tight ball, Odette's body shuddered from head to foot. She peered at him through the lanky strands of her blonde hair, eyes wide, then covered her face with her hands and pressed herself farther against the wall.

For a confused moment, Sagan contemplated her actions. Then he almost dropped the remaining bowl of spaghetti when a thought struck him.

His mother was scared. No, she was terrified.

Of *him*?

How was that possible? He'd never done anything to make her question her safety around him. Right?

He glanced at the slimy clumps of spaghetti and goopy tomato sauce on his sleeping bag. What had he done to make her fearful of him? More importantly, what had those fiends at the lab under Rivermyre city done to her? They hadn't just broken her body; they'd obliterated her spirit.

Sagan heaved a deep sigh. He set the remaining bowl of spaghetti on the ground by his mother's bed.

"In case you get hungry," he said, and inclined his head toward the cave entrance. "I'm going to get some fresh air."

Knowing there was no use waiting for a reply, he trudged back over the lake's stepping stones and proceeded through the winding passages beyond. Darkness swallowed every glimmer of the Luxium lanterns behind him, but after many childhood adventures in the cave, he'd long ago learned each twist and turn by heart.

Within minutes, he stepped out into the fresh night air. The radiant light of the moon greeted him, filtering through the mighty trees around the cave's mouth. Even though his eyes were capable of seeing only the moon's silver beams, he still liked to imagine the other beams of light streaming down from the rest of the planets—teal for Venus, magenta for Mars, orange for Jupiter, absinthe green for Saturn, and so on.

Standing at the cave entrance, Sagan closed his eyes and tilted his head from side to side. With a *crack-crack,* the tension slightly loosened in his neck. He heaved in a long breath, taking in the subtle scents of pine, a variety of nearby wildflowers, decaying leaves and rotting wood, damp moss, and rich earth. A hint of water hung in the air, suggesting an imminent rain shower.

He took another moment or two to ground himself and remember the importance of what he was doing.

Terrible doesn't even come close to what Mom's been through, he reminded himself. He couldn't begin to imagine the horrors she'd endured in that hellish place. *I just need to be patient.*

Besides, what did he expect?

He snorted at his own naivete. For the past ten years, he'd been led to believe his mother had run off and abandoned her only son. At least, that was the story his father had fed him. He hadn't been convinced. There was no way his mother would have left him, especially with the likes of Matthias; she'd always disagreed with his father's harsh training and frosty treatment of his family.

But never—*never!*—in a million years would he have

guessed she'd been locked up and forced into his grandfather's sick science experiments.

After her kind of imprisonment, Sagan couldn't possibly expect them to just pick up where they'd left off. She'd been missing for over ten years of his life.

I just need to be patient, he told himself again. Odette needed time to heal. That was all. Then perhaps one day, everything would go back to normal.

But what if it never goes back to normal?

Fear mixed with grief trickled through Sagan's veins.

What if she never mended? What if his mother was damaged beyond repair and never remembered him?

What if he'd finally found his mother only to lose her in a different, more heartbreaking way?

The thought of that possibility made Sagan's world spin. His knees went weak, and he slumped down to the cold earth, digging his fingers into the dirt as a wave of nausea threatened to empty his stomach.

A gut-wrenching cry lodged in the back of his throat. There had to be a solution, something, *anything* he could do to help his mother, to bring her back to him.

A twig snapped.

Sagan whipped his head up. Still and quiet, he moved only his eyes, scanning the trees in the direction the sound had come from. Ever so slowly, he reached for his twin crystal daggers holstered on his utility belt.

Another subtle sound drifted from the forest.

He paused, unable to quite identify what he'd heard. Animal? Shifter?

...Human?

Another sound followed—was it a whimper?—and immediately after that, the soft hiss of someone shushing. He pinpointed the noise to a bushy area a few paces from the mouth of the cave.

Silent as the grave, daggers firmly gripped in his hands, he stood and took a few steps toward the little copse of bushes.

Just as he reached it, someone stepped out.

"Hello, Sagan."

His immediate shock fizzled, only to be replaced by volcanic fury. "What the hell are you doing here, Nika?"

6
THAT FATEFUL NIGHT

THE SHRILL CRY RATTLED VIOLET'S EARDRUMS.

"Shh, baby, *sssshhhh*." Wiping the sweat off her brow with a quick swipe of her forearm, Violet rocked and bounced, but nothing, *nothing*, made any difference. "Come on, Solace, *please* sleep."

Solace wailed for the hundredth—*thousandth!*—time. Violet couldn't really blame her. The last two days had been horrendous. At least, she guessed it had been about two days since their capture and arrival here. Night and day weren't exactly a thing thousands of miles under the ocean's surface.

She gritted her teeth. They were already two days into the three-week deadline Matthias had given her. Only nineteen days left before—

Stop! she mentally commanded herself. *Don't think about it. There's still time to figure out how to get the purple spangle from the king and get Solace out of here.*

Tears burned her eyes, but she refused to let them fall. Crying was useless, and besides, the last thing she needed was more salt water! Instead she tilted her head back, eyeing the domed canopy of their enclosure.

The bubble rippled with the gentle ocean currents, and it violently trembled whenever any of the more hateful Nephezai hammered their fists or slashed stingers and claws against it, but it never came close to breaking. From what she and Thane had observed, it would withstand any attempted break-ins—as well as any kind of breakout, although the severe risk of drowning prevented them from testing the latter theory.

Maybe because the king had made the bubble, only he had the power to destroy it, or even decide who and what had access in and out. A select few Nephezai guards had the ability to pass through items such as food and flasks of fresh water. One even had the job of removing the waste bucket.

Violet's cheeks heated with humiliation. The lack of privacy alone was enough to make her desperate to break free. Thankfully, they had been supplied with enough blankets that they could cover themselves from prying eyes. Still, what Violet wouldn't give for some soap, or even a fresh change of clothes. At least the guards furnished a steady flow of cloths she could use for Solace's diapers.

An eclectic assortment of furniture had also been provided—a queen-size bed, a bedside table, two sitting chairs, a coffee table, and a metal vase with a plastic bird-of-paradise arrangement. The theme of the decor could only be described as "scavenged from the surface," as it had no consistency in style or color scheme.

Thane had improvised the coffee table into a crib for Solace. He'd flipped it over and wrapped a blanket around the upturned legs, then used cushions from the chairs to line the bottom. Currently, Solace didn't want to go near it, preferring to scream from her mother's arms.

Violet huffed in exasperation, stomping back and forth through the sandy floor. She needed to figure a way out of this damned bubble. And yet, even if they could break out, neither she nor Thane could possibly escape without notice. For the past two days, an almost ceaseless crowd of Nephezai shifters had swarmed around their globe, coming to gawk at the king's new addition to his zoo. The bubble offered absolutely no escape from their impertinent eyes.

She continued to rock and shush Solace, trying her best to ignore the lingering Nephezai stragglers currently scowling at them with their hands clamped over their ears.

"Will somebody please shut that baby up!"

Violet didn't bother to look up and see whether a Nephezai spectator, one of the guards, or even one of the other captives had shouted at them. A few other voices soon added their own heckles from several bubbles along the grotto walls.

"Be quiet!" one called. "We're trying to get some sleep!"

Being at the bottom of the damn ocean, Violet had no idea what time of day it was, or even if she'd changed time zones after traveling through the light-forged doorway. But based on her circadian rhythm, it was well past her own bedtime. She'd already tried all the tricks in her repertoire to get Solace to settle: cuddles, songs, diaper changing… What did her baby need?

Solace writhed in Violet's arms, hazing back and forth from human form to Veniri. Soft teal fur and the beginnings of scales rippled in and out over her pudgy baby rolls. Glittering nubs that would one day be fangs protruded from beneath her top lip and disappeared in the next second. She would chew on her little fists with her human gums, then throw them out in a frustrated scream.

Maybe she was searching for food. Violet tried offering her the weird milk-like substance the Nephezai had provided —she was assured it was fed to the Nephezai infants—but despite normally chugging it down, Solace currently wanted nothing to do with the baby bottle.

But if she wasn't hungry, the gnawing on the fists could mean...

Oh no. Violet groaned. *Please,* please*, don't let it be that.*

Violet gently raised Solace's top lip and found a small dot of sparkle beginning to cut through the gum beside one of the prominent crystal nubs.

"Shut that thing up!"

Violet growled a curse as she glared up at the hecklers. Some of the other menagerie captives had started pounding their fists against their own bubble enclosures.

"Let me try, Violet."

Pretending she didn't hear that last voice, Violet continued to rock and pace. But still Solace screamed.

"Violet, you've been up for hours. Give her to me for a while. You need a break and some sleep."

"I can't sleep, Thane," Violet barked. She threw a hand up, gesturing to the other inmates. "No one can sleep, especially while Solace is *teething*."

Again she almost burst into tears. Talk about the worst timing ever. What she wouldn't do for some soothing teething gel. What she wouldn't do to be back at Maple Shire, surrounded by people who could help her. Surely Gus's mom, Dr. Dawn, would know exactly what to do.

"And don't you think I know I've been up for hours?" she added, swiping at the sweat along her temple. "In case you didn't know, you can't take a break from parenting. It's a twenty-four-hour, seven-days-a-week for the rest of your freaking life kind of gig."

"I'm well aware of that," said Thane after a pause. "But in the last two days, you've barely let Solace leave your arms. It's taking its toll on both of you. Please. Let me help."

Violet looked everywhere except at Thane. Shame burned her cheeks. She wasn't quite ready to hand Solace over to him—to share the responsibility of caring for her daughter.

She flinched. *Their* daughter. Not just hers.

"The thing is," Violet added in a quieter voice, "I've only just got Solace back. And I can't…" A lump grew in the back of her throat, choking off the rest of her words.

"You're not going to lose her again. I won't let that happen," said Thane. "I'm right here. And I'm not going anywhere."

Violet scoffed a laugh, minus the humor. "Is that supposed to make me feel better? Of course you can't go anywhere. *We're trapped here.*"

"You know what I mean, Violet."

Something in his tone made her stop pacing and look at him. Studying the determined expression on his face, she felt tempted to whip out her Veniri forked tongue to decipher his emotions.

Then she realized she did know what he meant. The moment Thane found out about Solace's existence, Violet had sensed Hell would freeze over before he would abandon his daughter.

Yet she was still hesitant. And why shouldn't she be?

Growing up in a chain of abusive foster homes had been rough, but none of that compared to when she was sixteen and both she and her best friend, Lyla-Rose Branstone, had been kidnapped. Nathan had rescued Violet, but tragically he'd arrived too late to save Lyla-Rose. At the time, Violet hadn't been able to recall much of what happened—except for a faceless man with a crystal scorpion tattoo on his neck, who'd haunted her dreams every night for the following three years.

Only after she'd met and fallen in love with Thane did the truth come out.

Thane had been one of the Veniri kidnappers.

Thane had been there when Lyla-Rose was brutally murdered.

Thane was the faceless man from Violet's nightmares.

When her memories had returned, it was like thousands of tiny glass shards pierced her mind and tore it apart. And the trigger?

The crystal scorpion tattoo on Thane's neck.

She wanted to continue hating him for what he'd done and for all his lies. But when the time had come to get Solace back, Thane had been willing to do whatever it took to bring her home safely.

Violet chewed on her lip as she continued to try and soothe her screaming daughter.

For the most part, she'd managed to be amicable toward Thane while being trapped in close proximity to him. But just because he'd helped rescue Solace didn't mean she was ready to drop her guard entirely. Especially when it came to *her* daughter.

Another shrill wail tore through her eardrums.

Indignation roiled through Violet's chest and throughout her extremities. This time, the rush of frustration came perilously close to tipping her over the edge.

For the love of all things merciful, when would this child *stop crying*!?

More rivulets of sweat cascaded down the sides of her face and dripped off her jaw; heat prickled down her back and under her arms. Add another thing to the mix of her never-ending concerns: she did not want to know how bad her odor was becoming. She needed a cool shower, to wash away not just the sweat but also the sand. There was freaking sand everywhere—in every crevice imaginable. She'd removed her shoes from her aching feet hours ago, but now the sand grated between her toes.

In exasperation, Violet collapsed on the edge of the bed, patting Solace on the back. Of all the damn places on this earth, why did Solace have to be teething here and now?

Whether Violet liked it or not, Thane was right. He was there.

She furiously blinked back hot tears before daring a glance at him.

He was sitting in the upholstered bucket chair, hands gripping both armrests, body rigid as if ready to jump up into action. As always, he waited patiently, allowing Violet to make the first move.

"Fine," she growled. "Come take her."

Thane didn't hesitate. He launched out of the chair and reached Violet in a second, arms outstretched for Solace.

"Careful," said Violet as he gently took the writhing baby. "Don't lay her on her back. She hates that."

"I know," said Thane. "I've been taking mental notes these last few days."

"Maybe you should try laying her over your shoulder," added Violet. "Be careful—"

"It's okay. I've got her."

Violet's knee rapidly bounced in place as Thane adjusted Solace in his arms. "Watch her head. Make sure you're supporting her head."

"Relax, Violet. This isn't the first time I've done this."

"It's not? What do you mean?"

Violet's questions were drowned out when Solace's fussing grew louder. Thane shifted the baby to support her against one forearm, and like Violet had, he checked Solace's top gum.

"Yikes. So that's what's causing you grief, huh?" He gently wedged his knuckle between her gums. "Here, try gnawing on that."

Solace chomped once or twice between wails. Within a minute, her cries died down.

"How's that, Little Fang? Feeling a bit better?" Thane said in a soothing tone.

Her droopy eyelids fought to stay open, but she soon succumbed to sleep, her body straddling Thane's arm and her cheek resting in the palm of his hand.

Violet frowned at Thane and her baby—her very quiet baby—through bleary eyes. "How did you do that?"

Not taking his eyes away from the now sleeping Solace, Thane gave a casual shrug. "When I was a kid, I used to help my mother out in the nursery. Back at the hive, she was a…"

"A breeder?" Violet finished when Thane didn't.

Sorrow clouded his face. "Yeah. How did you know?"

Violet shrugged. "I heard a little bit about them. Not much, but I once met a few ladies back at Maple Shire who had escaped from Veniri captivity." She paused briefly to wonder how the three mothers were faring. "Dawn and Skye told me about how human girls were being taken by the Veniri for breeding. At first I thought they were making up stories, but then when I remembered how Lyla and I were kidnapped… I suppose we were meant to end up being… Well, you were there."

The silence dragged on for several heartbeats. Thane held her gaze, even though she'd expected him to turn away.

"Would you tell me about it?" she finally asked, the question surprising even her. "About that night?"

Silence dragged out as Thane took care to adjust his knuckle for Solace's weary gnawing.

"I know nothing I say can bring you restitution. But for the loss of your friend, and the consequences you've faced since, I suppose…" His eyes panned around their enclosure, as if searching for the correct words. "The least I can do is tell you what you want to know." His chest expanded with a deep breath, and he settled back down in the bucket chair. "It's probably best to start with what you remember from that night. Then I can fill in the gaps for you."

"Okay." Violet dusted the sand off her feet before curling

her legs up on the bed. Might as well get comfortable before diving into such a deeply uncomfortable topic. Reaching for a pillow and hugging it tight, she swallowed the rising lump in her throat.

Was she really ready for this conversation?

"I remember Lyla-Rose and I walking down the street toward the skate park. I think we'd just been to the ice cream shop—or were we walking back to her place from the movies? Oh gosh, I'm a little hazy on the details.

"Anyway, out of the blue these guys appeared. I'm not sure how many, but I do remember a guy in a black hoodie. And the next thing I knew, Lyla and I were grabbed, shoved into the trunk of a car, driven to the middle of who-knows-where, and locked in some kind of shack. There were other girls there. Three, I think, and, oh… I'm ashamed to say I don't remember any of their names."

"Esther, Harriette, and Whinnie."

Violet looked up, eyebrows raised.

Thane gave her a sad smile. "I felt it was important to remember the names of the girls I helped kidnap for the Veniri. I remember all their names."

"Why's that?"

"I'm not sure." He looked off into the distance. "Perhaps it had something to do with my mother. She never spoke about her life before being taken, but I always wondered about her family. Did she have many friends? Any enemies? How many people noticed she went missing? Is there anyone out there who still misses her to this day?" He trailed off.

Violet brushed her hand over her pillow, smoothing out the wrinkles in the fabric. Thane had previously told her that his mother had passed away. The way he spoke about her then, and now, it wasn't hard for Violet to see how much he really loved her. "You miss her."

His nod was heavy, somber. "No matter how much time

has passed, I still love and miss my mother more than ever." The deep brown of his eyes shimmered slightly with a warm glow, then he shook his head as if waking from a trance. "I'm sorry, I interrupted. Go on."

Violet readjusted on the bed. "Where was I?"

"You and Lyla had just met the other girls."

"Right." She gave herself a few seconds to prepare before delving back into those dark memories. "We were locked up in that shack for days. It was awful. We didn't know how long you guys were going to keep us there, or even what you planned on doing with us. But I remember you were the one who would come into our room with food every now and then. I think one time, on a cold night, you brought us a blanket that the five of us all bundled up under."

"That's not exactly how I remember it."

Violet frowned. "Oh?"

"I gave the blanket to you. You'd given your jacket to Lyla, and I, uh... didn't want you to freeze. The other girls were deathly afraid of us... of me. They always scurried to the farthest corner of the room when the door opened. But you... you were brave. Still scared, but you were brave for the sake of the other girls. You looked after them. And when I checked on you later, you weren't under the blanket. It turns out the blanket wasn't big enough for all five, so you tucked the other girls under it. The others, understandably, were freaking out the whole time. Your friend was on the verge of hysteria. But you helped her through it. You protected her."

"I didn't protect her." Tears pricked Violet's eyes as memories of what happened to Lyla flickered in her mind like a strobing horror movie. "I failed her."

On that admission, she buried her face in the pillow. Silent, soul-quaking sobs shook her entire body as tears soaked the fabric beneath her face.

She wasn't sure how long she cried. At some point, Thane sat on the edge of the bed by her feet. He didn't touch her, only let her be aware of his presence—that he was there if she needed him. A part of Violet wanted to berate herself for allowing him to see her like this, so emotionally raw. Yet Thane had been there when Lyla was murdered. He, more than anyone, would understand what she was going through.

At last the tears dried up, and the sobs reduced to a sniffle. Violet raised her face and rested her chin on the pillow. "I'm ready," she said, her voice a little raspy.

Thane tilted his head to one side. "Ready for what?"

"To hear your side of what happened." Trying to regain some composure, she busied herself with wiping away a few escaped tears.

"Violet, it's been hard for you to bring this all back up. We don't have to—"

"You promised to fill in the gaps." She forced herself to meet his eye. "I need to know."

Thane's lips pressed together in a hard line. Finally, he gave a firm nod. "Okay. Where do you want me to start?"

"That guy in the hoodie, the Veniri. He was the one who…"

"The one who killed your friend."

Violet nodded. "Who was he?"

"He…" Thane cleared his throat. "He was my brother. Soren."

Violet's eyebrows shot up. "Brother?"

Thane kept quiet. He cuddled the still-sleeping Solace a little closer while keeping his focus on Violet.

"Wow. You two… the way you acted around each other, I never would have guessed."

"Yeah, let's just say I've never been close to any of my brothers."

"You have more? How many brothers do you have?"

"I'm the youngest of four. Soren was the second youngest. And other than me, he had the most to prove in the family."

"Oh." Violet bit her lip, then winced. It was still a little swollen from Nika's knuckle-duster. "But then… that would mean…" A thought struck her like a sledgehammer, and her mind suddenly became a racing jumble, making it hard to articulate her next words. "When he attacked Lyla, I tried to stop him. I fought him and then—" *…killed him.*

The memory had become so strong she could almost feel Lyla's dagger in her hand—the one she'd used to stab Thane's brother.

A whole new level of guilt washed over her. All this time, she'd hated Thane with the fury of a vat of boiling acid. She'd used him as the target for all her guilt, a scapegoat for all her heartache. And she'd felt justified, believing she was the only one who'd lost someone that fateful night.

Her head fell into her hands.

Heavens have mercy, I killed Thane's brother.

"You did what anyone would have done," Thane told her, an edge to his voice.

"How can you say that? This whole time I've been treating you like trash for what happened to Lyla. And it wasn't even you who hurt her. Now that I look back, in a way, you were trying to help us. But even though I lost Lyla, you lost a brother. Your brother was killed—*by me*!"

Self-loathing burned her chest with each breath. Every muscle in her shoulders, arms, and back constricted as her fingers dug into her scalp.

An arm wrapped around Violet's shoulders, and warmth flooded through her, thawing her enough that she couldn't stop her body from leaning into Thane's. His hand gently stroked her arm, enhancing the security she felt but definitely didn't deserve.

"Violet, you didn't kill my brother. Nathan did."

"What?" She snapped her head up, then gasped. Sorrow fled, only to be replaced by panic.

The world was awash in teal flames—her flames. She was entirely alight with her Magneii fire.

Yet Thane still sat hugging her with one arm, the other cradling Solace. Violet's teal inferno had engulfed both him and the infant.

"Whoa." Thane's half-startled, half-concerned expression began to turn confused.

"What's happening?" Violet asked.

Thane studied the still-sleeping Solace before looking back at Violet. He slowly shook his head. "I have no clue."

"Does it hurt?" Violet frowned down at her baby, searching for any sign of discomfort. But she looked just as peaceful as before, her little snores light and steady.

Thane shook his head again. "It doesn't hurt at all."

Becoming acutely aware of his arm still around her, Violet added, "Maybe it's because you're touching me?"

"Maybe… or maybe not. Remember when Nathan and I grabbed you back at Rivermyre when we were trying to rescue Solace? I definitely felt the blaze of your flames then. Veniri hide or not, it was *excruciating*." A slight shudder rocked his shoulders. "But now?" He unwrapped his arm from Violet and held up a hand, the teal flames dancing around his fingers. "I don't feel any pain at all. Instead it feels… pleasant. Almost like a cooling sensation. Like a menthol balm or something."

"Really? That's what it always feels like for me as well."

Thane continued to stare at the flames flickering over his hand. "No matter how many times I see your fire, I still can't get over the color."

"Oh yeah, I forgot. Magneii flames are meant to be magenta, right?"

Thane nodded. "Your hybrid abilities are certainly an anomaly."

The two fell into contemplative silence, transfixed by Violet's teal fire.

"Why didn't you tell me?" she finally asked. "About your brother."

A few heartbeats passed. In the silence, all the teal flames died out.

"In hindsight, I think I understand why you didn't tell me," she added when Thane didn't—or couldn't—answer. "But I'd like to hear your reasons."

"Fear," Thane finally said. His gaze stayed fixed on Solace's little hand, now clamped on to one of his fingers. "I couldn't face it—the fear of dealing with what happened that night. The fear of facing the monster I truly was." He caught Violet's eye. "The fear of losing you… It's almost as if all my life, all I've ever known is fear and loss. Whenever I found something valuable to me, no matter how tightly I held on to it, it was always snatched away. At the start it was my father and my brothers who took everything precious to me."

Thane swiveled on the bed to face her fully. "The first time I saw you, it was like… it was like I was…What am I trying to say?" He looked up, into the distance. "When I first saw you, it was like a shooting star had swooped in and smacked me straight between the eyes."

Violet half chuckled. "I'm not sure being showered with hot chai can be compared with a shooting star—"

"No, I'm not talking about the time you bumped into me at the coffee shop. I mean the *first* time I saw you."

"Oh, *that* first time."

"Yeah." Thane hesitated, as if plucking up the courage to continue. "The first time I saw you, you were a mere human."

Violet grimaced. *Mere* was an understatement. She'd felt

helpless all her life, even more so when she and Lyla were snatched.

"But even without your flames and crystal shards," continued Thane, "you still had a mean hook punch. I don't even know how many kicks to the shin my brother and I endured trying to get you and your friend into the back of the car, then into the shack. You fought us the whole time, Violet. You fought hard. And despite your own fears, you weren't fighting for yourself. You were fighting to protect your friend."

Another pang of shame hit Violet. *Fought and failed...*

"In my entire life, I've only ever seen that kind of selfless bravery from one other person," said Thane.

"Who?" asked Violet, wiping away a rogue tear.

"My mother. I could tell how far you were willing to go to protect Lyla—if need be, you would have died for her. The same way my mother died trying to protect me."

"What happened to her?" Violet immediately regretted the question. How rude was it to ask someone how they lost their mother? But thankfully, Thane didn't seem to take any offense.

His shoulders sagged. "The Veniri males don't always get to choose the human women they're paired with, not unless they're high up the Veniri hierarchy. So unfortunately for my mother, she was paired up with my father. The word *disgust* didn't even come close to what he thought when forced to breed with her."

"But she did give him four strong, healthy Veniri boys, right?"

Thane's nose crinkled. "Three strong boys, if you ask my father. By the time I came along, my brothers were his only reason to be proud, and they could do no wrong. I, on the other hand, could do no right."

"How come?"

Thane shrugged. "I've tried to make sense of it over the years, but the only thing I can think of is that there was a bigger gap between my next older brother and me. While my brothers were old enough to be out training with my father, I was left alone with Mother a lot. In the end, she had more influence over me than he did—and he hated it. He hated me for who I became under my mother's guidance.

"It didn't matter what I did, how much I tried, I could never earn his approval. There came a point where I stopped trying, especially when I realized I only cared what my mother thought of me. One day, my father figured out how much I no longer respected him. He exploded like never before. And my mother… even if she could have overpowered him, it never ends well for a human breeder if they try to stand up to a Veniri. There was never any hope for her resistance."

Violet tried to process Thane's story, but she quickly found herself in the familiar territory of "out of her depth." She'd never known her own mother. How could she find the right words to console someone who had lost theirs?

"What about your brothers?" she asked instead. "You said you didn't get along with them either."

"They were cut from the same cloth as my father. They hated me just as much as he did." He gave Violet a pointed look. "I know it's crazy—maybe even a little sociopathic—but if I'm being brutally honest, I didn't feel any kind of grief when Soren died that night."

Violet began to crumple in on herself from the overwhelming shame.

"Don't," he said, reaching out to take hold of her forearm. "I told you, you didn't kill Soren. And even if you had killed him, if you ask me, the world—the Veniri *and* human world —is much better off without the likes of Soren in it."

The gold in Thane's eyes burned brighter, and a flutter in Violet's stomach caught her off guard.

Just then, something grabbed her attention from the corner of her eye. A Nephezai shifter was hovering in the water just inches away from the wall of their globe.

Violet and Thane pulled apart and stood up. Strangely, this new shifter didn't ogle them like a patron at a museum, the way the other Nephezai did. He regarded them both with a cool, almost lazy expression; Violet wasn't sure if it brought her hope or doused her with more fear.

Thane pivoted to the side, using his body to shield Solace.

Violet's jaw clenched. How long had the shifter been there, watching and listening to their conversation?

The stare-down went on for a few more moments before the Nephezai raised his chin. "So you're my father's new pets that everyone's been talking about."

7
LIQUID GOLD

Nathan led Autumn, Tio, and En'gorr out of the computer hut. He paused after a few steps down the grassy path when he realized Lazareth wasn't following.

"Everything all right, Laz?" he asked.

Lazareth hadn't even stepped outside the hut. Several emotions crossed his face before he let out a long sigh. "Are you sure you know where my son is?"

"Not one-hundred-percent sure," Nathan admitted. "But if I were in his shoes, I know where I'd be."

Lazareth nodded but still didn't make a move to leave the hut.

"What's the problem?" Nathan asked.

"Since Dawn…" Lazareth grimaced. "Since Gus found out that his mother is a Pliokai shifter—that *he's* a Pliokai shifter—he hasn't spoken to me. He seems to rush out of every room I enter, and I can't help but feel he's avoiding me. In a way, I don't blame him. It's bad enough he found out we've been lying to him his whole life, then on top of that… the fact I'm not his biological father." His head bowed low, grief and shame etched in every line of his face.

"I'll talk to him," said Nathan.

"Would you?" Lazareth's demeanor lifted the tiniest bit. "Would you please try to explain that I never meant to hurt him. Every decision his mother and I made was always with his best interests in mind. At least, that's what we both believed… what his mother believed."

"It's okay," said Nathan. "I'll do my best to break the ice. But I think the rest of the explanation is best left to you."

Lazareth gave him a small smile. "Thank you, Nathan. I know he'll listen to you. He looks up to you."

As Lazareth made his way back to the infirmary, Nathan and the other three continued around the back of the hut, away from the hustle and bustle of the cleanup and toward the community's fruit orchard. A few of the vines and trees were bursting with fragrant flowers, and the consistent buzz of bees grew louder as Nathan passed a few of the hives.

They followed a small creek at the bottom of the orchard for a ways, then veered off into the woods. The hubbub of the working community gave way to the tranquil chirps and twitters of forest inhabitants, going along happily with their lives as if two bombs hadn't been detonated not even a mile away. The ashy air also gradually cleared, until every breath held rich, earthy aromas. With each step through the forest walkway, Nathan almost found himself forgetting Maple Shire currently lay in ruins.

But the spell broke when they reached a small graveyard in a clearing at the top of a hill. Only days ago the graveyard had been much smaller. Now a vast number of sites with freshly turned soil covered the grassy, flower-speckled mound. About three men on the west side busily dug graves with hand tools, while a few women sat together near the new tombstones, weaving floral wreaths while singing a solemn song.

A few rows closer to the east side, a lone figure knelt at another fresh mound of earth.

"Oh, poor Gus." Autumn's bottom lip drooped at the sight of her cousin. The group had halted a few meters away, a little out of earshot and out of Gus's sight.

"I haven't seen him much myself in the last few days," said Nathan in a low voice. "How do you think he's been coping, Autumn?"

She huffed a sigh. "I've tried talking to him, but he always changes the subject whenever I mention any of the Pliokai stuff. Of course, to add insult to injury, I was also in on the secret, so he's pissed at me as well. I'd happily be the target of his anger if it meant he'd stop avoiding Uncle Laz like the plague."

"So... should we go over to him?" Tio asked.

"Well, I should probably go to him," said Autumn. "But as I said, he's quite pissed that I knew about his heritage before he did. Besides, I haven't been able to bring myself to visit Aunty Dawn yet, especially because—" She shuffled from one foot to the other while twiddling a beaded dreadlock around her fingers. En'gorr wrapped his big arm around her shoulders.

Nathan could guess the source of her reluctance. Next to Dawn's grave were two others, added only a few months prior: Skye and Cruz Novak—Autumn's parents.

"I'll go," said Nathan. "Perhaps you three should go check on Lazareth and the others. We don't want the infirmary tent to be shorthanded for too long."

Without waiting to see if Autumn, En'gorr, and Tio heeded his suggestion, he walked on ahead.

Careful not to startle Gus, Nathan stepped up to Dawn's grave with as much grace as he could muster. The harmonious voices of the wreath makers filled the silence while Nathan took in the headstone. In accordance with Maple

Shire custom, a large tumbled stone from the creek had been engraved with Dawn's name, along with a heartfelt message from Lazareth and Gus.

In all the world we shall not find
A heart so wonderful and kind.
In our memories you'll always stay,
Loved and missed every day.
You're in our hearts forever,
Until we're once again together.

"There was no one like my mom."

Nathan almost didn't hear Gus's soft voice. He slowly crouched down on the grass next to him. "Agreed. I've never come across someone quite like your mother."

Gus's body sagged, and he fidgeted with something in his hand. Nathan mentally scolded himself when he recognized the item—and the way Gus could have interpreted his comment.

Laying a hand on Gus's shoulder, he said, "No one expects you to replace her, Gus. *No one.* And you shouldn't expect that of yourself either."

"Then what am I supposed to do with this?" Gus held up a cylinder, gold in color but not in material. A decorative, organic circuit-board-like pattern flickered and danced over the surface, illuminating more brightly where his fingers came in contact with it.

Before Dawn's death, Nathan had never seen a Glixus with his own eyes. He held out his hand, and after a slight hesitation, Gus allowed him to gently take the cylinder. The golden light didn't react as strongly to Nathan's gloved hands as it had for Gus. Maybe it preferred direct contact with skin. Or perhaps what remained of Dawn's essence came to life in recognition of her son.

A Glixus contained all the memories, knowledge, and thoughts of the Pliokai shifter it belonged to. Whereas members of other species could spend a lifetime perfecting their chosen skill only to lose it all at the expiration of their life, the Pliokai could store their wisdom, expertise, and inner thoughts and pass them on to other Pliokai.

This particular Glixus was Dawn's intellectual essence incarnate. Although sadly not sentient, the Glixus contained the deep etchings of Dawn's life—from memories of her childhood right up to the details of her medical training.

"Have you checked to see what's on it?"

Gus shook his head.

"I'm sure Autumn could help you. It seems like something she'd be capable of figuring out."

Gus turned his attention back to his mother's headstone. "She's already offered to help. More than once. But I… I'm scared about what I'll find."

Nathan raised an eyebrow. "These are your mother's memories. What is there to be afraid of?"

"I don't know." Gus shrugged a shoulder. "Maybe I'll find out just how great my mother was and realize I'll never be able to go on without her. She was a phenomenal doctor. And now, when the entire shire needs her most, the next best thing they have is *me*." He barked a dark laugh. "And here I am sulking in the dirt while everything else is in chaos."

"You're being way too hard on yourself."

"Yeah, well, that doesn't matter, does it? Not when a whole community needs a doctor. A *real* doctor. I know what Autumn and the others are thinking. I should just install my mother's memories, absorb what's left of her, and be all like '*Wah-bam!* I know kung fu!' and then swoop into the infirmary tent and save everyone with my brand-new surgery skills."

Nathan gave Gus's shoulder a squeeze. "For starters, I

don't think 'absorbing her' is exactly what happens, not that I'm an expert on Pliokai abilities. And second, I think there's one thing you're missing."

"Oh, yeah?" Gus swiped a forearm over his eyes. "What's that?"

Nathan held up the Glixus. "Your mom wasn't *just* a doctor. She was so much more. And I think a big part of what you'll find on here is how much she actually loved you, even though it may be hard to understand why she decided to keep things from you. Some of the answers you seek may be in here."

Gus didn't speak for a long moment. "You're right. I don't understand. And I do need answers. But I don't think I'm quite ready…" He glanced at the Glixus from the corner of his eye. "… for that, at least."

Nathan nodded. "Understandable. There's no rush. In the meantime, there is someone who may be able to shed a bit of light on some things."

"Yeah, I know." Deep shame washed over Gus's face. "I need to stop avoiding him. I just needed some time to adjust to the fact that he's… he's not Pliokai."

Nathan nodded, understanding what Gus meant. "Just because Lazareth isn't your biological father doesn't mean he doesn't love you like a father would a son. I've seen how he treats you, and trust me, Gus, to him, *you are his son*."

Gus released a heavy sigh. "Deep down I *do* know that. But I think I need some time for my heart-knowledge to catch up with my head-knowledge."

"Again, there's no rush," said Nathan.

The two fell into a contemplative silence.

"So, I'm Pliokai, huh?" Gus said in a monotone.

Nathan looked over at him, unsure how to respond. But before he could say anything, Gus continued speaking.

"Let me get this straight. You're Veniri, right? And Veniri have teal blood."

Nathan nodded with a frown. This wasn't news to Gus; he'd already seen many samples of Nathan's blood with all the testing they'd been doing.

"Tio, En'gorr, and their guards are all Jiovis," continued Gus. "And they all have bright orange blood."

Again, Nathan nodded.

"And then there's Violet. She's a hybrid, both Veniri and Magneii. The Magneii have magenta blood, which means Violet has the trippy kind of marbled teal-and-magenta blood."

"Uh, yeah." Nathan shifted on the grass, starting to get an idea where Gus was going with this.

Gus held up a hand a few inches from his own face. "You know, in my entire life, I don't have any memories of bleeding. Not a single scraped knee in a push bike accident. No unintentional nicks or cuts from a knife while helping out with dinner. No scabs to pick, no bloody noses. Nothing… Autumn fessed up that she played a big part in programming my mind to forget those memories, until a time my mother was ready for me to know."

Without warning, Gus brandished a scalpel with his other hand.

Nathan's eyes almost bugged out of his head. "Gus! What are you—"

In one fluid sweep of his blade, Gus cut a line in the pad of his index finger. Both he and Nathan watched in silence as a thick trail of golden blood oozed down his hand. Just like all shifter blood, it glowed with a distinct brilliance, a luminescence even in the sunlight.

Beautiful as the liquid gold was, it also triggered Nathan's memories of Dawn coughing up blood from internal injuries after the blasts. Of her gold-speckled hand removing the Glixus from her head right before she passed away.

Gus frowned. "Huh, no wonder I have no childhood memories of my own blood. You'd think I'd remember bleeding gold when everyone else around me bleeds red. Although I suppose this isn't an unusual sight for you, right, Nathan?"

"Actually, this is the second time I've seen Pliokai blood in person. Pliokai aren't exactly aggressive. At least, I've never met one who gave me a reason for bloodshed."

Instead of responding, Gus quietly observed the line of gold now trailing down to his wrist. Then he abruptly jumped to his feet and brushed the dirt from his pants. "We should get back."

Nathan stood up to find Gus staring at him. "What? Something wrong?"

Gus's eyes were still deep wells of sorrow, but they held an edge of amusement as he looked Nathan up and down. "How long do you think you'll be able to keep up the Tutankhamen cosplay?"

Nathan shrugged. "For now, it's better than the alternative."

"I suppose you're right. A walking life-sized Swarovski statue would be much harder to miss."

Nathan gave a small chuckle, then handed back Dawn's Glixus.

With Gus leading the way, the two wove back through the gravestones and down to the path alongside the babbling creek.

"Nathan?"

"Hm?"

"Can I ask you a favor?"

"Of course."

"Now that I'm... you know, a shifter, can you teach me

how to shape-shift, or—what was it you call it—*haze*? Can you teach me how to haze?"

Nathan rubbed the back of his neck. "I guess. I suppose hazing for a Pliokai could have the same principles as the other shifter species."

"Great." Gus's tone turned a bit more lively. "I know that technically I've been a shifter my whole life, but I still feel like it's been thrust upon me. It's probably how Violet felt when she went from being human one moment to a hybrid shifter the next after that Magneii chick bit her."

Right. Violet. Nathan frowned, panicked determination once again rising in his chest at the mention of her name.

Where in the world could she and Thane be?

8

DANCE MONKEY DANCE

VIOLET BLANCHED. DID THAT NEPHEZAI JUST SAY THE KING was his father?

"What is it about you three that has the citizens of Scylorethyz all whirled up?" The Nephezai narrowed his eyes as he appraised Violet and Thane through the rippling barrier of their enclosure. A half dozen guards floated in a protective formation behind him; Violet recognized the fighter fish shifter, the blue-ringed octopus shifter, and the stingray shifter among them.

Although the Nephezai prince had the same majestic and dominating presence as the king, his appearance held no similarity to Qozzlotl's eel-like qualities. Instead, this shifter was the humanoid embodiment of a sea nettle jellyfish. Long, thin tentacles mixed with coiled frills draped down his forearms, and a semitransparent bell adorned his hips, continually expanding and contracting in a steady rhythm. Beneath the bell, his body tapered into a twenty-foot-long jellyfish tentacle, embellished with even more frills and ribbonlike stingers, which twisted and undulated in the water behind him. The flounce and volume of the ruffles reminded Violet of the extravagant shirts worn by male aristocrats during the nineteenth century; however, she wasn't fooled into thinking this shifter's frills were any kind of fashion statement.

An organic pattern of variegated neon purple dappled the combination of off-white, gold, and reddish-gold hues that spanned the prince from head to tail tip. And as expected, a plethora of Nephezai thorns covered his shoulders and upper arms.

Tilting his head to the side, the prince slowly drifted along the circumference of the bubble dome. "My father journeys all the way to the surface with promises of nullifying our banishment, only to trade our treasury of ancient gold tomes for… what? A slith, a so-called hybrid, and"—he eyed Solace, still asleep in Thane's arms—"some kind of halfling?"

Thane gently placed Solace in the upside-down coffee table turned cot. He laid another blanket over the top, leaving a few inches open for airflow, before taking a position between Violet and the Nephezai.

Violet frowned, unsure how she felt about Thane taking a protective stance in front of her. Not to be underestimated, she stepped up beside him.

"What do you want?" Thane asked the prince.

With a raised eyebrow, the Nephezai glanced between Violet and Thane. "You don't look like a Seh'Vuthi pair to me."

Seh'Vuthi? Violet recalled King Qozzlotl using that same word to describe her and Thane when he was negotiating with Matthias. She tried her best to keep her expression impassive, thinking it best to conceal her ignorance.

The prince pointed to Violet. "Hybrid, I'm told you are both Veniri and Magneii. Is this true?"

She glanced at the Nephezai's vast number of mother-of-pearl thorns, then responded with a nod.

"Show me."

Usually, she ignored all the Nephezai's demands to put her shifter appearance and abilities on display, but the Nephezai prince's tone left no room for refusal. Violet pursed her lips. Would defying him help or hinder her chance of escape?

She went to take a step forward, but Thane threw his arm out in front of her. "Violet, you don't have to—"

"His Reverence gave an order, hybrid," barked the fighter fish shifter.

"Peace, Votloxo," the prince said, waving the guard off.

But a furious heat had already flared in Violet's core. "Screw this!" she hissed.

Slapping Thane's arm away, she stepped right up to the barrier and trained a deadly glare on the prince. "In the last two days, we've been ambushed by a group of human hunters, betrayed by a close friend, shot with paralytic darts, tossed into a box on the back of a pickup, bashed by a chick with small-dog syndrome, traded like cattle to a bunch of aquatic shifters—*who I never even knew existed before a few days ago*—and shoved through a purple gateway, taking us to the ass-end of the freaking ocean only to be dumped in this dome for all you freaks to gawk at."

"Uh, Violet..."

Ignoring Thane, as well as the prince's narrowing eyes, Violet continued her tirade. "You've tossed us into these atrocious conditions with nothing to eat except awful green crap. How can you guys possibly think any of this is suitable for us? We've had absolutely no privacy, while all you pervy creatures of the deep crowd around us like a peepshow. And *now* you want me to 'dance-monkey-dance' just because *you* say so?" She scoffed. "Why don't you go and impale yourself on your own thorns?"

The silence after Violet's little tantrum was almost deafening.

Every one of the guards glided closer to the prince, their scowls promising immense pain if he gave the word.

"Slith!" barked the fighter fish shifter at Thane. "You need to muzzle your female. How dare you allow her to disrespect Prince Exültov Nagahld, the sovereign prince of Scylorethyz and the Midnight Seas—son of Qozzlotl Nagahld, king of the Midnight Seas, heart of the bleeding ocean, and protector of the Scylorethyz realm."

Violet shot her deadliest glare at the fighter fish shifter. She opened her mouth to tell her exactly where she could shove her theoretical muzzle, but stopped when Thane gently rested a hand on her shoulder.

"Violet is fully capable of deciding for herself who she wishes to disrespect. But"—his tone turned low and deadly—"if *you* disrespect her again, the last thing you'll see is a Diamantium shard impaled in your eye socket."

The fighter fish shifter responded with a vicious tirade of threats, only some of which Violet understood. A few of the other guards also barked in the Nephezai language.

In the blink of an eye, a cluster of mother-of-pearl thorns shot through the bubble membrane, darted past Violet's periphery, and embedded in the timber headboard behind her and Thane.

"Silence!" roared the prince.

Violet turned and stared at the five thorns buried in the headboard. Her shock intensified when she and Thane spotted the torn fabric of his sleeve, where a thorn had just barely missed the flesh of his bicep.

Heart pounding, Violet snapped her head up and around, searching for any sign their bubble enclosure was compromised. Seconds passed, blood and panic roared in her ears, yet no flood of water came crashing down around them. A single tiny drop trailed down the inside of their dome, the only reminder that something had penetrated the membrane.

She looked over at her baby. Solace still slept peacefully in the upturned coffee table cot.

However, relief wasn't the emotion that engulfed her.

Rage fueled the hammering of her heart as she turned back to the marine shifters. She and Thane rushed at the iridescent barricade, teal flames ignited, Diamantium elbow shards unsheathed, both spewing their own tirade of violent curses.

"Enough!" roared Prince Exültov. A sonorous *crack* blasted straight into her and Thane's chests. Both flew back, bounced ungracefully on the bed, then toppled off the other side before ricocheting off the bubble barricade.

Violet groaned. She wasn't sure if those sonic booms were more painful while surrounded by water or not.

By the time she and Thane clambered back to their feet, Exültov had also flung the troop of guards back. He ordered them to remain and not come any closer. All obeyed, but the fury in their eyes showed their disdain for the command. Votloxo, the fighter fish shifter, directed her icy glare specifically at Violet.

Prince Exültov regarded Violet and Thane with an eerily calm facade. "My commander, Votloxo, is right to be concerned," he finally said, sparing a glance over his shoulder at the fighter fish shifter. "You, my little air breathers, are no longer in the realm of the Erathi. You are in my realm now, and I have every right to crush you like a crustacean if I see fit."

Violet rolled her shoulders back. If she got a chance, she'd be more than willing to do some crustacean crushing of her own.

"However," continued the prince, "if my father is willing

to make superficial bargains with air breathers, then I'm inclined to make some of my own."

"Not interested," said Thane.

"Not even to make your living arrangements more comfortable?"

As one, Thane and Violet glanced at their daughter, currently sleeping in an upside-down coffee table wrapped in blankets. Poor Solace must have been well past exhausted if the events of the last few minutes hadn't woken her up.

"What are the chances of getting a suitable bed for my daughter?" asked Violet. "And actual, edible food?"

"I can guarantee sustenance and sleeping arrangements that would be worthy of my own daughter," said Exültov, placing a hand on his chest.

"What's the catch?" Thane's tone held an edge of warning.

Exültov clasped his hands behind his back, drifting around the outside of their enclosure as he spoke. "Tomorrow night, my father is hosting a banquet. The esteemed members of the realm will be coming from far and wide for the occasion. I, of course, am expected to make an appearance, and in these late hours, I find myself in need of a companion, or a—what is the term you air breathers use?—a plus one?"

Thane gave the prince side-eye. "What exactly are you asking?"

Exültov paused his leisurely stroll around the bubble before turning back to face them. "In exchange for accompanying me to tomorrow night's banquet, I will arrange for better"—his eyes swept over the furniture in distaste—"amenities, for not only your halfling but all of you." With a pointed glance at Violet, he added, "Privacy considerations will also be taken into account."

Violet and Thane shared a glance.

"Well, we can't argue that your offer is more than generous." Thane clicked his tongue. "But I find myself in a bit of a predicament. I didn't think to pack any formal outfits before being dragged to the nethers of the ocean. And what are the chances of getting a hair appointment at the last minute, not to mention a mani-pedi?"

"Amusing," said the prince. "However, my invitation is intended for the hybrid."

"Her name is *Violet*, not hybrid. And she's not going anywhere with you, so you can forget it."

Exültov's smiled, but this time it lacked amusement. "Your chivalry is noted, Veniri. Yet I'm afraid the dress I've organized would only fit *Violet*."

"What?" Violet's eyebrows shot up. "A dress? For me?"

"Naturally. As much as having you by my side would already be a spectacle, I would prefer to avoid the kind of attention your current attire would bring."

Violet tried not to squirm as he looked her up and down. Her jeans, shirt, and dark green bomber jacket were tattered and still covered in dirt and blood stains that hadn't washed out during the ocean voyage.

"Trust me," Thane said to the prince. "No one will be paying attention to you if I'm the one in the dress."

This time an amused glimmer did reach Exültov's eyes. "As tempting as that image is, I am not swayed. It must be Violet."

"Over my dead body," said Thane, any veneer of humor gone from his voice.

"Either Violet goes or no one does." Exültov folded his arms, and the needle-tipped thorns along his shoulders sparkled with a more sinister edge. "And then there will be no extra provisions for the halfling."

"Fine. Enjoy the party by yourself," said Thane.

"Hold up," said Violet. "Don't I get a say about this?"

Thane winced slightly when he turned to her. "It would

be too dangerous," he said in a low voice. "I can't guarantee your safety. Not with these creatures who detest anything to do with the Erathi."

"But we still need better food and better provisions for Solace."

Thane's defiant resolve began to crumble. "These creatures have already proven unpredictable and volatile. What if… something were to happen to you?"

Violet glanced at Solace in contemplation, then at the five thorns still embedded in the headboard. "Whether in here or out there, they've proven they can get to us. And if the prince wanted to, he could just command my attendance. But he's given us a choice."

The furrows in Thane's brow deepened, but Violet could see him weighing her arguments.

"This could also—" She shot a sidelong glance at the prince, then lowered her voice to a whisper. "This could be our chance to get the spangle from the king. Or even find a way to escape."

"Exactly," said Thane. "Which is why I should go."

Violet frowned. "Why you? I'm just as capable."

"That's not what I meant. Of course I think you're capable —*more* than capable. But what if something happens? What if they don't even bring you back? I would never be able to live with myself if something happened to you—let alone Solace. The last thing I want is her growing up without a mother."

Slack-jawed, Violet couldn't figure out how to respond. She glanced at her baby. No matter what screwed-up situations they found themselves in, there was no doubt she'd make any sacrifice necessary if it meant Solace would be safe, even if it meant Thane would be the one left to raise her.

When she caught Thane's gaze again, flecks of golden glow had appeared in his brown irises. She did her best to suppress the familiar flutter of angry pixies reawakening in her belly.

"We can't let this opportunity slip by," she finally whispered, then turned to address the prince. "I'll do it. I'll go with you."

"Good. Expect my guards to retrieve you for the preparations tomorrow evening." Without another word, Prince Exültov swam off into the dark waters of the exit tunnel. His guards followed close behind, all except Votloxo, whose lip curled with a hiss at Violet before she turned to go after the others.

9

WHAT THE HELL, NIKA?

SAGAN LUNGED AT NIKA.

His cousin sprang back but not quickly enough—he grabbed her by the front of her black jacket. Almost instantly, she broke his hold with a swipe of her arm and sharp twist of her body, then aimed a kick at his diaphragm.

He sidestepped and deflected her kick with his forearm, sending her spinning. Using the momentum to continue to pivot, she drove her elbow back and cracked him in the cheekbone.

Pain lanced through his cheek; stars burst across his vision. But with years of training and muscle memory, he'd already seen his opening. He trapped Nika in a headlock with one arm under her chin and restrained the offending elbow with his other.

After growing up sparring with her, he expected her fury to peak at his attempt to render her helpless: foot stomping, violent thrashing, verbal abuse, attempted eye gouging. This time, however, a sharp pain bit into his abdomen.

"What the hell are you doing here?" he growled, cursing himself for overlooking her free hand.

"I'd back off if I were you, cuz, unless you want your insides to spill out," Nika warned.

Sagan glared into the night, heart booming in his ears. "Why so defensive, *cuz*? Are you here to spy on me and my mother? Isn't it enough that I helped you betray Violet and Thane? What's a little disemboweling to you, huh? Haven't you already caused enough damage?" His last sentence quaked with the fury he'd pent up over the last eight days—since he'd traded his friends for his mother.

He bared his teeth. "If I were you, I'd leave this place and run far away. Especially if you don't want to end up impaled on the end of *my* daggers." He twisted both his wrists, the crystal facets of his twin daggers reflecting the moonlight, their deadly blades inches from her face.

"Go on. Impale away, *cuz*." The venom in Nika's voice matched his own. "Do it."

Every fiber in Sagan's being wound tight; all he needed was a flinch from his cousin to spring into deadly action. He could slice just as quickly and efficiently as Nika would stab him before he could untangle himself from the headlock he had her in. With a bit more pressure on her neck, he could block the blood supply to her head and knock her unconscious. Or with a lightning-fast yank of his hand on her jaw, he could snap her neck… He was already on the road of total self-destruction.

Before he could make a decision, Nika hissed in frustration. She threw her dagger to the ground and, with a few practiced moves, stomped on Sagan's foot and wrangled herself out of his hold. She spun to face him but still kept both his daggers in sight. The moonlight glinted off her own crystal blade a few feet away on the ground.

Nika stared him down for several seconds. Never once did she break eye contact. Never once did she give him reason to react. "Damn it, Sagan. I didn't come here to fight you."

"Then why are you here?" He clenched his weapons so tight he risked crushing a handle.

Nika darted a glance at her dagger, then back at him, indecision now clear on her face.

Sagan's fury faltered. He'd never known his cousin to hesitate in a fight. Come to think of it, she would never put herself in a vulnerable position by tossing her weapon aside.

He lowered his blades but didn't return them to their holsters. "You've got some nerve showing up here."

Nika scoffed. "Drop the holier-than-thou act." Her tone dripped acid, burning straight to Sagan's soul. "For the record, I've left the hunters. I'm not going back—"

Sagan barked a mocking laugh. "Like I haven't heard that before."

"I'm serious."

"Nice try." He stabbed a finger in her face. "Last time, I almost believed you. I trusted you right up until you turned psycho freak on Violet and tried to kill her during training. But there's no chance I'll ever believe you, or trust you, after what you've done."

A heartbeat passed before Nika finally said, "Oh yeah? And what about you, huh? Do you want me to bring up all the monstrous things you've done in the past and shove them in your face too?"

Her words riled him, but an instant later, the threat of facing his sins had him deflated. With a few quick breaths, he made the conscious effort to holster his daggers. "How long had you known?"

Confusion replaced Nika's venomous glare. "Known what?"

"When you returned to the hunters, how long had you

known my mother was locked up and at the mercy of our grandfather's sick experiments?"

Nika opened her mouth, then clamped it shut. She finally had the audacity to look ashamed. "I only found out a few days before you and the others broke into the Xabat laboratory to rescue Violet's baby."

"You knew." Sagan's dizzying nausea returned. "You *knew* how long I'd been searching for my mother. Why didn't you tell me you knew where she was?"

Nika's mouth dropped open, then clamped shut. Sagan saw her mask returning, smooth and stoic as ever. He scoffed in disgust. A profound wave of exhaustion engulfed him, and he half stumbled back a step on the soft, leaf-littered ground.

"I didn't recognize her at first," Nika said. "She was so... different. But then I heard her singing, and I remembered that song she sang when we were kids, and I just knew. When I asked grandfather about her, he said she was a traitor, worse than a traitor to the Branstone legacy, and deserved a punishment worse than death—"

"Get lost, Nika." Sagan spat. It was all he could do not to clamp his hands over his ears to block out the heinous accusations. "You're a coward."

Only then did Nika's facade drop completely, and he realized how much the barb had stung her.

Forcing his rising guilt back down, and regardless of the risk, he turned his back to her. "You're not welcome here. Find yourself another hole to fester in."

He took a step back toward the cave entrance.

"Sagan, wait. Please." Her voice cracked. "I have nowhere else to go."

Sagan paused. He'd never heard her use that tone before. Pleading. *Begging*. Gone was the marble-hearted guise she always maintained: the Branstone Iron Maiden, tough on the outside but even more deadly on the inside.

The Nika before him was someone entirely different. Someone desperate. That tone reminded him too much of the internal agony he was facing himself.

But when his mother's face flashed in his mind, his compassion quickly faded. Nika was reckless, unpredictable, and he couldn't trust her. Not now that he finally had his mother back. He couldn't risk the chance that Nika would once again return her allegiance to the hunters, to the Branstone legacy—to their grandfather.

His shoulders sagged as his decision became steadfast. "I'm sorry, Nika." The words were like ash on his tongue. He had never turned his cousin away before. "But I can't—"

Another voice rang out in the night. "Nika?"

Sagan spun.

At first there was no sign of anyone else. Then leaves rustled in the nearby bushes, and a small figure emerged.

"Nika?" the tiny voice said again.

His cousin rushed over and stooped down. "Orson, why are you still awake?"

The little figure took another step into the moonlight. Sagan's jaw almost slammed into the ground at the sight of the small boy. By the way the child stumbled forward, Sagan could only imagine he'd learned to walk not long ago. He looked about two, maybe three years of age.

"Nika?" The child held his arms up; one hand clung to a stuffed toy Sagan couldn't quite make out in the near dark. Nika plucked him up from the ground, tucking him into the crook of her arm and half turning away from Sagan.

"What's going on?" Sagan asked. "What the hell, Nika? Whose kid is that?"

Her silence ignited a spark of fury in his chest. He reached out a hand, intending to swing her around to face him, but before he touched her, the little boy in Nika's arms hissed. A high rhythmic thumping noise followed.

Sagan's eyes grew wide as the mysterious child morphed into an all-too-familiar shape. In the dim light, the most distinct feature he could make out was the teal-tinged fur. A scattering of rainbow facets sparkled under the moonbeams, reflected from small crystal nubs hidden within the fur, signs of the larger, more lethal shards to come.

Sagan's instant fury dissolved into hollow shock. "Nika, *what have you done?*"

The thumping noise became more distinct, reminding Sagan of the deep, resonant war cries of the adult Veniri shifters he'd encountered. This toddler in Nika's arms was warning Sagan to stay back. The fierce expression on his chubby face would almost have been comical if Sagan could shake the seriousness of the situation.

Nika quietly shushed the boy, her hips beginning to sway as she gently rocked the child in her arms. She still hadn't faced Sagan, and it took him a moment to recognize her stance for what it was. She was shielding the boy from him.

"You need to tell me what's going on right now." Sagan hated how much his voice shook, whether from anger or panic, he couldn't tell.

"Will you let us in the cave?" Nika glanced at Sagan over her shoulder, the fear in her eyes as clear as a neon sign. He'd never seen his cousin show this kind of insecurity before, especially in regard to someone other than herself—and a shape-shifter at that.

Finally, he gave a slow nod. "Yeah, you'd better come inside."

Her whole body sagged in relief. Only then did the Veniri toddler's warning sound cease.

"Thank you." Nika's words were fragile enough to be snatched up by the night's subtle breeze.

Sagan stepped to the side, but instead of making her way

to the cave entrance, Nika inclined her head toward the bushes. "Can you help me with the others?"

His eyebrows shot up to his hairline. "Others?"

Nika pulled back a branch. Within the bushes was a small wicker basket, and inside the basket lay two much younger babies, both fast asleep.

10
WHAT IS SEH'VUTHI?

Violet growled as more sweat dripped from her brow, along her neck, and down her back. Not only had the anticipation of the upcoming banquet disrupted her sleep, but the heat was driving her to the brink of insanity. Rather than continue to toss and turn in the stifling bed, she'd finally opted for a spot on the sand, on the far side of the enclosure from Thane's chosen sleeping area on the ground. Pushing herself up against the cool bubble membrane helped to a degree, but her other side stayed as hot as ever.

Of all the shifter abilities she had at her disposal, why couldn't there be some kind of "frost" or even "cool breeze" power? The Veniri repertoire had absolutely nothing to do with temperature control, and as for the Magneii abilities—

Nope! Violet squeezed her eyes shut. Flames—teal, magenta, or otherwise—were the last thing she wanted to think about.

But by the time Thane and Solace awoke from the eternally long night, her mind had moved on to even more nauseating concerns. What kind of idiot agrees to accompany the prince of an underwater shifter species to a banquet hosted by the king who's holding her captive?

This idiot. Violet bit back another frustrated growl. The need to move, to do *something,* forced her to stand and begin pacing up and down the enclosure.

"Violet, stop," said Thane.

"Stop what?"

"Worrying is not going to help. Try to relax. You're going to carve a groove to the center of the earth with all that pacing."

"I've got to do something to try to get my mind off things." She waved her arms over her head like a crazy woman. "The banquet is *tonight,* and as far as I know, that stupid invitation from the prince was just to coax me into some kind of mind-twisted submission so they can chop me up and serve bits of me to their guests alongside some sea urchin strudel and clown fish frittata with kelp mayonnaise." Violet's voice had reached a higher octave than even she knew she was capable of.

A few heartbeats passed before Thane chuckled. "Clown fish frittata? Really?"

Violet sighed and slumped into the bucket chair. "I know, I'm overreacting. I just can't stand the thought that this might all be a waste of time and we'll be no closer to getting that *thing* off Solace's neck. What if I can't do this? What if I do or say something that makes the Nephezai decide to kill me after all? And then I'll have failed Solace again. What kind of mother allows her child to be kidnapped—twice!—and have a bomb strapped around her neck? She's not even three months old, and now she's going to… soon she'll…"

"*Stop.*" Thane took her firmly by the shoulders. "Listen to me. This is not your fault. *None* of this is your fault. You have done everything in your power to protect Solace—I know that for a fact. And as much as we'd like to, we can't change the past. Trust me, I'd be the first to go back if we could. What we can do is strive for a better future. We still have air in our lungs and life in our bones. Don't give up hope. We will find a way out of here. We *will* save Solace. Do you hear me?"

When she didn't answer straightaway, a crease appeared between Thane's eyebrows.

"What's wrong?"

"Nothing." She gave a slight shake of her head. "You just sound a lot like Nathan."

Thane chuckled. He dropped his hands from Violet's shoulders and rubbed the back of his neck. "Yeah, well, I've also gotten my fair share of scoldings from that old Veniri. Maybe some of his lectures are finally sinking in."

Solace began to stir with a few groggy coos. When she spied Violet and Thane, she waved her arms and legs, in a much better mood after a record-breaking sleep. Thane picked her up and started to entertain her with a thick gold-and-red tassel he'd ripped off one of the cushions.

Violet still found it hard to suppress her knee-jerk reaction to run over and snatch her daughter away from him, but the feeling wasn't as strong as it had been the last few days. After a few seconds of deliberation, she finally settled farther into the bucket chair, bringing her legs up and hugging her knees.

Thane continued to jiggle the tassel, and Solace responded with intermittent chatter. When she attempted to gnaw on it, he gently removed it from her mouth and looked around the enclosure.

"What are you looking for?" Violet asked.

"I'm just wondering if there's something better for her to chew on, to help her with her teething." He looked a bit defeated when he picked up his leather belt from the bundle of blankets on the floor. "So sorry, little one. This is the best I've got at the moment."

Solace didn't hold the same reservations as Thane. She gladly gnawed along the edge of the belt, her crystal fangs fading in and out as she chewed.

Thane smiled down at her. "Chew away, Little Fang. It's a bit better than a tassel to cut your teeth on."

"Is ten weeks old a little early for teething?" Violet inquired.

"For human babies, perhaps, but not for Veniri. One of the first things a Veniri baby learns is to control the hazing of their fangs. Shifter babies don't yet know they need to hide their shifter abilities. One day she'll develop the natural instincts and attributes to survive in this world."

Violet nodded, trying to imagine Solace as a grown shifter. Her fangs were still little nubs, not quite sharp enough to puncture the leather, though it wasn't for lack of trying.

For a moment, Violet felt herself relax, until Solace began to grizzle. "Oh no. I think she's hungry."

Just in time, two Nephezai guards approached the enclosure, one holding a tray containing a new flask of water, a new bottle of baby formula, and another bowl of the green goop that passed as food. The guard plucked the indigo baby bottle from the tray first and pressed it against the bubble. The membrane stretched like bubble gum, covering the Nephezai's arm in an iridescent film. When the bottle finally pierced through, the membrane remained sealed around the Nephezai's wrist, and when he pulled his hand out, it self-healed and bounced back into shape, leaving no trace of the puncture.

The Nephezai repeated the pattern for the other two items, placing everything on the bedside table. Then they turned and swam away.

"No extra food or better bedding yet," Violet observed.

"Doesn't look like it. Maybe our luxury upgrades won't be delivered until after you've fulfilled your end of the prince's bargain."

Violet gave a noncommittal *hmph* and picked up the bottle, dreading the battle ahead. Poor Solace seemed to be growing sick of the milky substance, resisting more and more each time. She took the writhing baby from Thane and wrangled her into one arm.

"I can try feeding her this time if you want," Thane offered.

Again, Violet's first impulse was to refuse. She was more than capable of looking after her own daughter. But as Solace's shrieks and kicking legs reached a new level, she couldn't help but entertain the idea. Besides, Thane had already shown at least a small level of competency by putting Solace to sleep the night before, and he'd helped with her teething.

Several moments passed while Violet deliberated. All the while, Solace became grouchier, her displeasure emphasized by her hazing between Veniri and human form.

"Okay," Violet said at last, and thrust the bottle at Thane.

Just like before, Thane was a natural. He spoke in calm, patient tones, assuring Solace that drinking the stuff in the bottle was the best thing for her and she'd feel much better with a full belly. Violet's jaw almost dropped when, thanks to Thane's gentle encouragement, the ten-week-old guzzled down the milky stuff as if it were some kind of magic elixir.

She could hardly believe it. Was Solace aware that Thane was her father? Was that why she was so comfortable with him?

This innocent child had no idea what kind of atrocities Thane had committed, but apparently that didn't matter.

Since being locked up in this underwater hellhole, Solace had found comfort in Thane's presence, and he in hers.

While Thane fed her, he spoke to the baby as if she could comprehend every word, chatting away as if to an old friend. He even chuckled once or twice when she did something he found amusing. How could this guy laugh at a time like this —in a place like this?

Dropping back down in the bucket seat, Violet looked on in amazement. After a few moments, she was astonished to discover within herself a genuine lack of resentment toward the budding relationship.

She'd never known what it was like to grow up with caring parents. She'd been determined for Solace to at least know the love of a mother, but *two* loving parents? It was more than she could've dreamed for her daughter.

"Want me to burp her?" Violet asked when Solace made it clear she'd had enough to eat.

Thane gave her a tentative glance. "Do you mind if I give it a go?"

"Um..." Again, she fought back the instinct to refuse. "Sure. I don't see why not."

Quicker than Violet could comprehend, Thane had Solace cleaned up, burped, and snuggled into a food coma over his shoulder.

"How did you do that?" she asked when Thane caught her look of disbelief.

He gave her a self-conscious smile. "It's nothing. When I helped my mother back at the nursery, I developed a knack for feeding fussy babies. If I'm honest, it was my way to avoid changing diapers. I always volunteered to feed the babies who drove everyone else nuts, and they were more than happy to dump that frustrating job onto me."

A smile played on Violet's lips as she imagined a young Thane dodging diaper duties.

After a moment, Thane's expression turned concerned, and he pressed a palm to the exposed skin on Solace's arms and legs.

"What's wrong?" Violet asked.

"I think she's a little cold."

"Cold?" Violet's eyebrows shot up. "How can she be cold? It's stinking hot in here."

Thane's frown deepened. "I have noticed you've been struggling to stay cool over the last few days."

"What? You mean you haven't been feeling the heat?"

"No. If anything, I've been next to freezing." He reached for the blanket on the bed and wrapped it around himself and Solace.

Violet shook her head. "How is that possible?"

"Uh…" Thane looked up through the bubble membrane, at thousands upon thousands of leagues of water. "I'd put it down to the fact that we're so far away from the sun. The water can't warm up down here."

That certainly made sense. Yet the idea of a blanket being anywhere near her was so repellent that more sweat prickled over her skin. She could barely stand to look at the two of them wrapped up snugly. "So what's the deal? Why am I so hot then?"

"I'm not sure. I've started wondering about that myself."

When neither of them could come up with a reasonable explanation, they fell into a contemplative silence—until another mystery struck Violet.

"Do you know what that word *Sevoovi*—or whatever it is—means?" she finally blurted. "The Nephezai keep calling us that. The king even said it to Matthias at the cliff. He said we were some kind of 'pair,' like we were a matched set or something."

Thane glanced at her from the corner of his eye but otherwise refused to look at her.

"You *do* know." She noted his taut expression; almost all color had drained from his face. "It means something bad, doesn't it?"

"Perhaps." Thane tilted his head from side to side. "Or it could be a good thing, depending on your perspective."

Violet bit the inside of her cheek. "Okay, so what does it mean?"

Thane stalled by gently laying Solace down in the makeshift crib. "The word is *Seh'Vuthi*. It's a common word in a lot of the shifter languages. And, well… it means…" His expression became pinched, almost as if he'd prefer to throw up instead of explain further.

"Just spit it out," Violet barked.

"The rough translation is 'soulmate.'"

Violet blinked several times. She must've misheard him. *Surely not...* "If that's a rough translation, then what's the non-rough translation?"

Thane's nose crinkled. "Are you sure you want to have this conversation? Now? Here, in this place?"

"Just tell me what it means, Thane." Violet swiped her forearm over her brow and cheeks. Had the temperature risen again?

"I don't know how to explain the correct meaning in your Erathi language, but… do you remember when Tio's brother arrived at Maple Shire? The word he called Autumn?"

Violet slowly nodded. Moments after showing up, En'gorr Droth had basically announced his undying love and commitment to her. "Yeah, I remember. But I also don't remember the actual word."

"He called her 'Zhivotza.' In the Jiovis tongue it means 'drug' or 'medicine.' But in the context En'gorr used it, it meant 'life source,' which is also a term of endearment for a Jiovis's… soulmate. *Zhivotza* is basically the Jiovis word for *Seh'Vuthi*."

Thane waited a few moments for that to sink in. Although his expression remained calm, his tense posture suggested he wanted to turn tail and flee.

"Okay." Violet dragged the word out a bit. "So, what would make the Nephezai think that about us?"

Thane shrugged. "Some shifter species are more tuned in to soulmate connections than others. That's how En'gorr knew straightaway that Autumn was his match. The Jiovis have a heightened sense of smell to distinguish their one true pair. I'm not sure what ability the Nephezai have when it comes to deciphering soulmates though."

"Hold up. Go back. When you say 'tuned in to soulmate connections,' do *you* think you and I are… that we're…"

Thane's eyes grew wide. He sliced his hand through the air. "Look, whatever these stupid Nephezai call us, it doesn't have to mean anything. Don't worry about it, Violet. You don't have to concern yourself with what they think—"

"Is that what you think though? Do you believe what they say we are?"

Thane slammed his mouth shut.

Violet's tongue tingled with the intense temptation to uncover whatever he was trying to hide from her, but she knew forcing the truth would only worsen the awkwardness. Almost as if he'd read her thoughts, relief smoothed out some of the concerned lines across Thane's brow.

"You didn't seem surprised when they called us that," Violet continued. "Why not?"

"I had a… suspicion," he said slowly.

"Care to clarify?"

Thane raked a hand through his vintage-gold hair. "There are a few signs that can suggest two people might be a Seh'Vuthi match." He held his palms up and added in a rush, "But you don't have to worry about being forced into any kind of commitment. The thing about the Seh'Vuthi soul-bind is that it's consensual. The bond is only fulfilled when both parties come to a complete acceptance of being matched, and I would never, *ever* expect you to commit to anything you're not interested in. I've already put you in a traumatic situation against your will once, and I've vowed to never do it again."

Violet chewed the inside of her lip. "Just to clarify, I have the choice to accept or deny this thing?"

"Absolutely."

"So... what will happen if I refuse it?"

Hurt flickered over Thane's face before his expression smoothed into a serene mask. "Nothing. You'll go on with your life, with no ramifications other than what you choose for yourself."

The relief Violet experienced was stronger than she'd expected. "Fair enough," she said slowly. "I think I understand. But you still haven't explained why you suspected this 'soulmate' thing. When did you first know?"

Thane's hard mask softened. "Do you remember that time I helped you with your college photography assignment?"

Violet's cheeks immediately flared with heat. She generally tried not to think of those moments they'd shared alone in her dorm room. But other than the intimacy, there was something else about that day she'd never been able to forget. "Are you referring to those golden specks of light that were floating around us?"

Thane nodded. "Apparently, that was the beginning of the Seh'Vuthi connection."

"Really?" At the time, they'd both been utterly confused by it, especially when they figured out the source of the floating lights was Thane himself. The luminous specks had appeared like small halos on his skin before drifting off to hover around the two of them. "Are you saying this whole time you knew we were soulmates... or whatever?"

"I didn't know at the time in your dorm room, no. I asked Nathan about it later, and he filled me in as to what had happened."

"So the lights are Seh'Vuthi?"

"It's one sign at least."

"What's another sign?"

Thane squinted one eye in a wince. "Are you sure you're comfortable talking about this?"

Violet considered for a moment, then nodded. "Yes."

"Okay." Thane huffed out a deep breath. "Another sign I've noticed is that I'm able to actually *feel* you looking at me."

"Oh." She'd forgotten about that. Not long after the floating lights appeared, Thane had claimed he could actually feel her gaze when she looked at him. At first she'd figured he was pranking her, but a small test proved his admission genuine. "Can you still feel it, even now?"

"Yeah, I think I can always feel you looking at me now. It became much more noticeable after I arrived at Maple Shire."

"Oh." Violet dropped her gaze, but curiosity caused her to keep glancing at him.

A ghost of a smile played at the corner of Thane's mouth.

"How come I don't feel it then?" Violet finally blurted. "If we're supposed to have this crazy, weird bond thingy, why don't I know when you're looking at me?"

Thane heaved in a deep breath, and Violet braced herself for whatever he clearly didn't want to say.

"I have a theory," he started. "I think—and again, there is absolutely no pressure on what you decide for yourself—but I think I've come to accept the possibility of… the Seh'Vuthi bond, between you and me. And perhaps my acceptance has led to the ability to feel your gaze."

Violet picked up the glass indigo bottle and turned it over and over in her hands.

Seh'Vuthi bond... you and me...

The weight of that admission was far more than she could process at the moment. Instead, she deflected slightly. "But why the ability to *feel* me looking at you?"

"I don't know." Thane scratched his chin. "Maybe it has something to do with trust. I mean, when it comes to people you don't feel safe with, the last thing you'd want is to actually feel them looking at you. At least, that's the best explanation I can come up with."

"Wow, that's a... pretty deep theory." After a pause, she added, "So you trust me?"

"Of course."

A breath caught in her throat. He hadn't even hesitated.

Violet once again gnawed on the inside of her lip, fighting the swell of shame. Thane trusted her—*her!*—the hypocrite with more trust issues than photos in a Kardashian's selfie stream. Sure, she had plenty of justification for her lack of faith in him. *She* hadn't been the one doing the kidnapping, or been the deceitful one hiding identities and tattoos.

Then why did she feel so guilty about not reciprocating his trust?

When she finally had the courage, she looked up and found Thane's gaze on her. The intensity in his eyes locked Violet in place. A golden glow radiated through the deep brown of his irises.

Leaning a little closer, she pointed. "Is that another sign of Seh'Vuthi?"

Thane frowned. "What do you mean?"

"The gold light in your eyes. I've noticed it a few times. Is that the Seh'Vuthi now?"

"I don't know what you're talking about. What gold light?" He rubbed his eyes.

"It's still there," she said when he looked back at her, "although it's starting to dim."

"You've seen this before?"

"Yep. A lot actually."

Thane's brows shot up in surprise. "How come you never told me?"

"I don't know." Violet shrugged. "I assumed you knew. The first time I noticed it was when those firefly lights appeared. Do you think it's linked?"

"I don't know."

Violet pulled her legs up to her chest and hugged her knees. "It's kinda cool, whatever it is."

Thane regarded her in contemplative silence.

Something flittered in her stomach. Unable to hold his intense gaze, her eyes fell to the crystal scorpion tattoo on his neck. For three years after Lyla died, that tattoo had plagued her nightmares. Just the sight of anyone's neck tattoo had been enough to trigger a panic attack. But now, she was pleasantly surprised that the image stirred almost no reaction.

"When we first met, you kept that tattoo hidden," she started, her tone deliberately light. "I'm assuming Nathan must've told you about my nightmares if you knew to hide it from me."

With a sheepish wince, Thane nodded.

"So how did it work? Nathan plays foster dad during the week, then catches up with you on the sly during the weekends? Is that how you stayed in contact?"

Thane laughed. "Something like that, but much less like the 'second wife' scenario you're making it out to be."

Violet couldn't help adding her own smile at the thought.

"But yeah," continued Thane, "Nathan was helping me out as well. He knew how hard it was to establish a new life after escaping the hive. With his detective job, he pulled some strings and set me up with documents and ID so I could get myself a job and a place to live. He checked up on me while you were at school, and watched my back in case anyone from the hive tried to track me down. The queen doesn't take too kindly to deserters."

"I haven't heard much about this Veniri queen, but it sounds like she's a piece of work."

"Most Veniri queens are. And apparently the Veniri empress is the worst—the queen of queens." Thane's mouth twisted into a scowl. "I've never heard of a compassionate or kind female leader of our species. They've all been vicious, stuck-up brats who deprecate every Veniri they encounter and stomp on all other females for the sake of plonking their entitled tushies on the throne."

Thane cleared his throat, his face stricken, as if he suddenly remembered who he was ranting to. "Of course, I don't mean to say that you're entitled or bratty. Especially now that you're a Veniri—I mean a hybrid. And even Solace. With her being a Veniri female, she's… I don't think she's…" He groaned and pinched the bridge of his nose, eyes scrunched tight. "I'm sorry. I shouldn't have said those things."

Violet shrugged. "It's cool. I didn't take any of it personally."

Thane's rigid features relaxed, and a small smile tugged at one corner of his mouth. "Still, as a Veniri myself, I shouldn't be saying anything so disrespectful about the Veniri royals."

"Why? What will happen?" Violet chuckled. "Does the Veniri queen have supersonic hearing or something? It's not like you're going to disappear into a puff of smoke for bad-mouthing her, right?"

"Nothing that bad. At least not for me, because Queen Idalia's not the one who I pledged my Divi—" He coughed a few times into the crook of his elbow, then cleared his throat.

Violet narrowed her eyes at his dramatic coverup.

She's not the one who I pledged my Divi—

What was Thane going to say? Div-eye… what? Divide? Device?

"Sorry," Thane finally said. "Uh, going back to your previous question about Nathan, he looked out for me almost as much as he looked out for you. And at times, I looked out for you when Nathan wasn't available."

Deciding to go along with Thane's far-from-subtle subject change, Violet asked, "So, bumping into you at the coffee shop that first day of college wasn't by accident?"

"That was definitely an accident. I didn't mean to interact with you at all." He rubbed the back of his neck. "At the time, I figured it was worth an extra pair of eyes scouting out your new surroundings. I only meant to be on lookout, to ensure you were safe."

"Oh." Violet took a moment to consider that revelation. "So to be clear, my whole time at college, Nathan had you following me around to keep an eye on me… for my safety?"

"Nathan didn't actually know I was keeping an eye on you," he admitted with a heavy sigh. "In fact, he explicitly warned me to stay away from you. But I knew Nathan couldn't be in two places at once with his detective job based in Brookhaven and you starting college in the city. So I took it upon myself to make sure you were safe at college." He grimaced. "Sheesh, that sounds way too creepy when I say it out loud."

Violet mentally catalogued her run-ins with Thane at college. "Other than the coffee shop and that night you followed me back to my dorm from the library, how many other times were you following me?"

"Well… there was the time you went to that UV party at that club in the city."

Her eyebrows shot up. "You went to that party too?"

"I waited outside in my car. I thought that perhaps, depending on the drunken state of you and your friends, I could come up with some excuse as to why I was there, then drive you all safely home. But I'm sure you recall that things turned out a lot different."

Details of that night flashed through Violet's head: super loud music, ultraviolet costumes, a huge guy with neon-green dragon body paint. Autumn disappeared, and they'd found her with the green-dragon guy's hand wrapped around her throat. They rescued her, then got chased into the street by one of the dragon guy's friends. He'd almost caught up to them when a car came out of nowhere—

Violet's jaw almost hit the ground. "Wait a second. Were you the one who hit that guy with the car?"

"Yeah." Thane's expression turned a little sheepish.

"Sheesh." She ran a hand down her face. "That night turned out pretty awful. I never would've guessed we'd see those guys a year later."

"Yeah. En'gorr's guard Va'atuu was the one I hit with my car. I'm lucky he didn't recognize me when they arrived at Maple Shire."

"Wow… So bizarre that the Jiovis way of proposing is to grab their potential soulmate by the throat. I thought he was trying to kill her. We all did."

Thane laughed. "I'll never forget the look on Autumn's face when she found out what that gesture really meant."

"Same. I've never seen her so stunned." Violet held her belly as they both chuckled. When their laughter died down, her eyes drifted to the crystal scorpion tattoo on Thane's neck. "I understand bumping into you at the coffee shop was a chance encounter, but what about your tattoo? Why hide it?"

"Uh… how exactly do you think that would've gone down? 'Hi, I'm Thane, but you might know me as one of your kidnappers. And just to prove it, ta-dah! Here's my tattoo, which has been giving you nightmares for the past three years.'"

Violet winced. "Point taken. But how long did you think you could've kept it from me?"

It took Thane a long time to answer. "If I had it my way, you would never have found out. I was terrified of you knowing who I was and hating me as much as you do now. But another reason—the main reason—was I knew how much you'd suffered, especially with the loss of your friend Lyla. I figured by hiding my identity, I was avoiding hurting you even further. Besides, I knew about the memory block Nathan put on you. I thought you would immediately recognize my tattoo, but I had no idea it was the key to unlocking your memories."

"Wait a second, go back. Memory block?" Violet almost launched out of her seat. "What do you mean Nathan put a memory block on me? And what do you mean your tattoo was the *key*?"

Thane blanched. His mouth repeatedly dropped open and then closed. "Uh… Nathan didn't tell you?" he said weakly.

"*No*. You mean to tell me the reason I couldn't remember anything about the kidnapping—about Lyla's murder—*was because of Nathan*?" Rage flaring, Violet saw red—or rather teal, as Magneii flames ignited from her eyes.

Thane held his hands up, as if attempting to calm a wild animal. "I really think you should talk to Nathan about this. It'd be better if he can explain it to you."

Spreading her arms wide, Violet gestured around their bubble. "I don't see Nathan anywhere, do you? And when do you think I'll see Nathan next? It's not like we're trapped at the bottom of the freaking ocean!" She stabbed a finger at Thane. "Tell me. *Now*."

"That's not my story to tell. I don't know the full details

anyway." He pursed his lips, locking away any further comment.

Violet's eyes widened in fury. The menthol sensation of her growing flames flickered over her brow. Nathan had taken her memories—blocked them. How would one even perform that kind of violation? A million questions flooded her mind, but Thane's hard expression didn't budge.

Fine. If Thane refused to give her answers, Violet would figure them out for herself.

She whipped out her Veniri tongue. The pink muscle gleamed under the overhead lights before disappearing back into her mouth.

An onslaught of flavors smashed through her senses. She distinguished as much as she could, then did her best to decipher what each flavor represented.

The pungent mix of salt and bleach registered first. Violet was relieved by the presence of bleach, which represented Thane speaking the truth, yet salt meant restraint. She almost scoffed. No need to guess what he was holding back. She nearly blasted him with more demands for information right then, but the presence of a few other flavors caused her to pause. Molasses revealed Thane's anxiousness, and burnt sugar his insecurity. Was he anxious about being trapped at the bottom of the ocean or because of the conversation he'd been having with her?

In contrast, the flavor of macadamia proved he was still hopeful. But about what? Escaping their captivity?

But the hint of lavender drew her attention, especially when it morphed into the aftertaste of sarsaparilla. It took Violet a moment to decipher what that meant. Lavender represented someone being comfortable—not comfortable like sitting on a cushion, but comfortable in the presence of a trusted person. Relaxed and free to be one's true self. And yet the opposite of that comfort was represented by sarsaparilla.

Only when Violet met Thane's glare did she understand the change in flavors.

As much as their conversation had no doubt been difficult for him, he'd still somehow felt comfortable talking to her. But by whipping out her tongue in a demand to know more, she'd pushed him back into the realm of insecure. Part of her felt a pang of regret. She was surprised by how much she disliked the idea of Thane being ill at ease around her.

An apology began to form on her lips, but the words died when she registered the family of menthol flavors—eucalyptus and peppermint. Violet's brows drew together. The presence of eucalyptus suggested Thane intended to keep secrets—whether Nathan's or his own. The undertone of peppermint tainted every other emotion, revealing whatever Thane felt, it was underlaid by a formidable state of terror.

Before Violet could open her mouth to speak, someone called for her.

"Hybrid!"

She turned to find the trio of Nephezai guards who'd dragged her and Solace through the depths of the ocean. Votloxo, the fighter fish Nephezai, along with the stingray shifter and the blue-ringed octopus shifter, swam right up to the bubble enclosure.

"Hybrid," Votloxo called again. "It's time to get ready for the banquet."

11
HIDDEN AMONG THE CHAOS

Nathan looked up into the velvet night sky. Other than the chilling breeze, the Maple Shire ambiance seemed much different from what he recalled prior to the bombings.

Usually at this hour, a scattering of Maple Shire residents would be gathered around a campfire, or taking a walk to the nearby creek, or venturing as far as the waterfalls to experience the ethereal glowworm caves. Yet for the last few nights, the shire had become eerily silent, with almost everyone going to bed early due to a mixture of grief and exhaustion.

He drew in a deep breath of crisp air, still tainted with ash and dust. Another day had passed, and still he'd found no sign of Violet and Thane among the rubble. It was time to try a new tactic. He was kicking himself for not doing this sooner, but the communal shock, anguish, and panic had left him disoriented.

Closing his eyes and suppressing his ever-growing worries, Nathan raised his face to the sky. He turned a few degrees counterclockwise, then opened his eyes to find the brilliant planet of Venus, shining brighter than all the other heavenly speckles within the inky blackness. It took only a few heartbeats for the vibrant morning star to hum its celestial song, privy to him alone. Like warm sunlight over his body, the Venusian beams washed over and through him, invigorating every fiber and cell within his being.

The melody grew louder, and for a moment, Nathan recoiled. The last time he'd hazed into his Veniri form, it had triggered the onset of his entire body being covered in a faceted exterior. At least, he hoped it was still limited to his exterior.

He glanced down at his bandaged arms and hands. What effect would hazing have on him now? Would it hurt him?

Kill him?

Nathan gulped, trying to release the tension in his throat. All the others had been asleep when he'd snuck out of the hacker hut and made his way to the remaining shambles of the Farrow family's home. If he chanced hazing, what state might they find him in tomorrow? What if he didn't do a full-body haze? Could he count on things not spiraling out of control?

Preparing himself, he sucked in a deep breath. No point worrying about hypotheticals. He needed to find out what happened to Violet and Thane.

Eyes drifting closed, he tuned back in to the sweet celestial melody of his connection with Venus. Before long, the familiar sensation of his Veniri inner eyelids glided over his eyes.

He hesitated.

When nothing concerning happened, he opened his outer lids. As far as he could tell, this partial haze had brought no cause for alarm. So far so good.

Nathan steadily traipsed through the debris of the Farrow's home. He came to a stop roughly where their guest room was, where Violet had been staying. As far as anyone knew, it was the last place she'd been—asleep in her bed, like the majority of Maple Shire—before two almighty explosions blasted all their lives into utter devastation.

Pausing, Nathan braced himself for the worst, then risked another small partial haze: he lashed out his forked Veniri tongue. Several inches of smooth pink muscle whipped out and back into his mouth within the blink of an eye. Immediately, he sensed a vast bouquet of flavors, and with the aid of his inner eyelids, the scene before him illuminated with a myriad of phosphorescent neon mists.

Again, Nathan didn't sense any harm to his person with the isolated haze of his Veniri tongue. But just to be sure, he figured he'd better get this scene assessed fast, with as few tongue whips as possible.

His eyes danced quickly over the phosphorescence, taking in as many details as possible while he assessed the different flavors. Each effervescent mist, or soul-trail, was imbued with the emotions, interests, and desires of a person —whether shifter or human—who'd passed through the area. A scattering of faded soul-trails belonged to various members of the shire who'd done their best to dig through the rubble in search of survivors.

The pungency of cinnamon almost overwhelmed him. Nathan wasn't at all surprised to pick up the scent of one's intention to murder—or in this case, the intention of a group of hunters to destroy the peaceful village of Maple Shire. The next strongest flavor was peppermint, which reflected the community's terror.

With another flick of his forked tongue, Nathan deciphered a few other scents: rhubarb for shock, sour apple for various other fears, and black licorice for deepest sorrow. So far, the emotional flavors revealed nothing he wouldn't expect from people enduring this devastation.

He began filtering out the trails of the rescue crew, as well as the overwhelming flavors of cinnamon and peppermint.

Instead, he zoned in on the trails of those who used to call this mound of rubble home.

Daring to call on his Venusian energy again, Nathan blew out a misty breath, but instead of the white cloud one might expect on a cold night, this was a soft teal. His energy-infused fog trickled over the remaining soul-trails. Clouds of light gathered in various places and condensed into figures of people, capturing the area's strongest emotions as snap-shots of the past.

The moment captured above the rubble appeared to be seconds after the explosion. Nathan recognized each trail: Autumn, Gus, Lazareth, Tio, the other Jiovis shifters, and even the late Dr. Dawn. Horror and panic infused every face and frozen action.

But of course, there was no soul-trail to represent Violet.

Nathan gritted his teeth, cursing—not for the first time—the night he'd decided to put a shield on Violet so no Veniri could track her. Of course, it was necessary to protect her from the Veniri queen who'd put a bounty on her head.

Frustrated, he lashed his tongue out again, and the mists pulsed with new vibrance. He scanned the debris, looking for something, *anything,* that might be a clue.

His pulse spiked when something caught his attention. He backtracked as the phosphorescent scene began to fade.

There!

Almost hidden among the chaos was another, familiar soul-trail—quite faint compared to the others, as if willing itself not to be found. A thought struck him, and his eyes grew wide.

It can't be. Sagan?

The hunter had an uncanny ability to blend into the background when he didn't want to be noticed. Nathan couldn't forget the time he'd found Violet and inserted the shield into the small of her back, only to later find out

Sagan had been mere feet away during the entire procedure.

He flicked his tongue out again. The soul-trail was difficult to decipher; he would have missed it entirely if his determination hadn't forced him to look for the tiniest of details. But every instinct he'd gained over his years as a detective told him this trail *certainly* belonged to Sagan.

But how?

His mind reeled. Had Sagan escaped Xabat? If so, where was he now?

With a little extra effort, Nathan isolated Sagan's trail and followed it out into the night. Past the house's gardens, past the communal areas. When Nathan reached the edge of the forest, he blew out another breath of teal fog, and a new scene of neon mist pulsed to life.

Nathan definitely knew that soul-trail scent. Thane!

But why had Sagan and Thane met up all the way out here? Did Thane have something to do with Sagan's escape?

He assessed the scene a little further. Thane's emotional cocktail was heavy with elderflower, representing suspicion, and the fizz of baking soda, confirming his distrust.

Nathan frowned. What had caused these strong reactions from Thane?

With another flick of his tongue, he registered the faintest hint of almonds and eucalyptus laced through Sagan's soul-trail. Once again, he breathed out a teal fog, which condensed into the frozen depictions of the two men. His frown deepened as he moved closer. Given the hovering positions of Sagan's and Thane's bodies, he could only assume they were sitting in some kind of vehicle. But Thane seemed to be sitting in the middle of the back seat.

Why was he sitting in the back?

Nathan's gaze fixed on a blank spot next to Sagan. Once

before, a few weeks ago, he'd registered a kind of "void" when tracking soul-trails.

Violet!

The pieces of the puzzle began to fall into place.

Violet was sitting in the passenger seat next to Sagan; he was sure of it. Sagan had somehow escaped Rivermyre and come back moments before the bombings to drive Violet and Thane… where?

His eyes narrowed on the frozen image of Sagan as he recalled the two flavors he'd scented on his trail. Why did Sagan's soul-trail reek of almonds for deceit? What secret did the flavor of eucalyptus represent?

More importantly, where the hell were they all now?

As Nathan's mind whirled with questions, another horror struck him. He'd been so focused on finding Violet and Thane he hadn't realized his entire forked tongue was no longer the slick pink muscle it used to be. Crystal facets now covered every inch of it, just as they did the rest of his body.

Dawn had warned him about the risk of his internal organs becoming crystallized as well. Was his tongue a sign she'd been correct?

And if Dawn was right about that, was she also right that the ongoing crystallization could prove fatal?

12

SILK AND TAFFETA FROOF

"Hybrid, are you deaf or just stupid?" Votloxo barked. The two other guards chuckled, then immediately stopped when she shot them a piercing glare.

Violet shared a look with Thane. Concern etched deep lines in his face.

"Hybrid! I said it's time to get ready for the banquet. His Reverence requests for you to look your absolute best." The Nephezai looked Violet up and down with a sneer. "And yet, I doubt there is enough time in the world for that to be a possibility."

"Hey!" Thane launched to his feet and jabbed a finger at Votloxo. "You better watch your mouth."

Blue rings flashed over the murky-yellow flesh of the octopus shifter. Both he and the stingray Nephezai glided closer to the bubble barrier, their fierce expressions a dire warning.

Votloxo elbowed both of them to move back. Her sneer deepened, revealing serrated teeth. "Or what, air breather? Your Veniri powers are useless down here. What can you possibly do to me?"

"Easy to say on that side of the barrier." Thane's glare dripped venom, yet his tone remained smooth as velvet. "Diamantium can still gut a fish."

The fighter fish shifter regarded Thane with a frosty gaze, her fins rippling around her with a lazy, nonchalant grace. Violet couldn't help casting a nervous glance at the vicious thorns over Votloxo's shoulders and arms, recalling the five that had easily sailed through the bubble membrane and barely missed Thane. She didn't know who'd fired them, but she wouldn't be surprised if it had been her.

"Votloxo," said the blue-ringed octopus shifter in a low tone. "You know what happened last time you tussled with one of the king's pets. Forget the Veniri. We're here for the hybrid."

After a heartbeat, Votloxo's eyes slid to Violet. "Let's go."

Thane took another step forward, but Violet held up a hand to stop him. "Will you look after Solace for me?"

"Of course." His tone suggested her question stung a little. Gently taking Violet by the shoulders, he half turned her away from the Nephezai. "I know I can't be there to protect you, and heaven knows you'll do as you damn well please, regardless of what I say. But—"

Votloxo began barking orders and threats again.

Anxiety rising, Violet made to leave, but Thane caught her in a hug. Startled, she went rigid. When was the last time she'd let Thane hold her like this?

Before she had a chance to react, he spoke softly in her ear. "Take these, just in case." He slipped something into the pocket of her bomber jacket.

When Thane released her, Violet shivered. The familiarity of his warmth, tenderness, and affections surged to the forefront of her memories. For the first time in a long time, a faint glimmer of… something she wasn't quite ready to name sparked in her chest.

A split second later, a tentacle cinched around her neck. Violet gasped, or she would have if her air hadn't been cut off. Her fingers clawed at the slimy bond, but the tentacle only gripped tighter, then yanked her back.

Thane lunged toward her, eyes wide in shock, as she crashed through the bubble barrier in a head-whirling, stomach-churning rush.

Icy water swirled around her body, rushing over her face and ears and cutting off Thane's booming shout. Her world turned into a blur of water swells and bubbles. She would have screamed if the tentacle around her throat had allowed it.

Mercifully, the tentacle released her seconds later. She heaved as a reflex, realizing too late she'd sucked in a lungful of water. Searing pain raced into her chest, and salt burned down her throat. Body thrashing, she expelled the water from her lungs, only to have a new gush of icy water replace it. Panic surged through her as black edged her already water-blurred vision.

A hand clasped over her face. Before Violet could struggle against the new attack, air gushed over her nose and mouth. At the same time, something wrapped around her middle and squeezed sharply several times. She choked up water, chest burning with each desperate breath of air. The tight coil continued to pump around her middle until ragged wheezes replaced her gagging.

Eyes stinging from salt water and tears brought on by her brutal fit of coughing, Violet blinked several times to clear her vision.

"Enough, Belitozzl," said the fighter fish.

The tentacle around Violet's waist quit pumping and loosened enough for Violet to heave in more air.

Votloxo's smug face drifted just outside the newly formed

air bubble over Violet's head. "When I tell you to do something, hybrid, do it."

Violet clenched her fists, wanting more than anything to punch the condescension off the fighter fish shifter's face. As if reading her mind, two more tentacles wrapped around Violet's wrists, holding her arms down by her sides.

The agony in her chest and throat deterred Violet from retorting verbally. Instead the teal fire in her eyes flared to life.

Votloxo's expression hardened, and her previous confidence seemed to diminish slightly, especially when her eyes dropped to Violet's hands.

Looking down, Violet gasped. Belitozzl, the blue-ringed octopus shifter, still held her arms firmly in place, but his tentacles flinched, coiling up and away from the teal fire coating her hands. The flames danced and swayed as if the water didn't affect them at all.

* * *

"Well, don't you look…" Prince Exültov's face puckered as he looked Violet up and down.

Blood rushed to her cheeks. She cringed, fighting hard not to fidget under the prince's scrutiny—not because she was concerned about pleasing him. Far from it. After what felt like hours and hours of Nephezai servants primping, frizzing, and zhuzhing, Violet looked as ghastly as she'd expected.

"I imagine if Björk and a wedding cake had a baby"—she gestured to her outfit—"this is what that baby's vomit would look like."

Exültov regarded Violet with a mixture of confusion and amusement. "I'm not familiar with the concept of procreating with baked confections, but is that your way of saying this isn't the latest—how do you say it?—*trend* in Erathi apparel?"

"Absolutely not." She pointed back to the dressing room where the wardrobe mistress and other servants had abused her with frilled silks and taffeta. "I tried to tell them that, but no one would listen to me."

Her embarrassment only deepened when she took note of Exültov's attire. He was naked by human standards, but his vast array of magnificent coiled tentacles and the ever-rippling jellyfish bell rendered clothing unnecessary. A few articles of jewelry had been added around his neck, wrists, and waist. The jewels and accent stones glittered as he moved but never came close to outshining the purple bioluminescent accents on his flesh or the foreboding tips of his mother-of-pearl thorns.

Exültov considered Violet's gown again with a more critical eye. "Hmm... What do you think, Jhutev?"

"The dress certainly makes a statement, Your Reverence," said a male voice.

Startled, Violet looked around. As far as she could see, Exültov, Votloxo, and herself were the only ones present in the small antechamber.

"If I'm not mistaken, Your Reverence," continued the disembodied voice, "a statement *is* what you're trying to achieve... yes?"

Violet zoned in on an area by Exültov, about two feet from his left, where the voice seemed to be coming from. Even with eyes squinted, she couldn't make out who or what was speaking.

The voice cleared his throat. "Perhaps, Reverence, you should explain who I am before the poor hybrid bursts an optic nerve."

A hint of amusement played on Exültov's lips. "That would be considerate."

He reached out a hand, and it connected with something solid at about waist height. At a flick of his fingers, a beam of black yet glowing light streamed up to the rocky antechamber ceiling. Within the beam, illuminated and visible only from the waist up, was a being much more tangible than what Violet could have imagined seconds before.

"What the?" Her eyebrows shot up to her hairline.

She'd never seen a being quite so fascinating. Nebulous colors and speckled starlight morphed and whirled over his midnight flesh like a hundred tiny galaxies. Whether a trick of the rippling waters or not, the edges of his body weren't quite defined, as if he might blink out of sight at any moment. Facial features like the mouth, nose, and ears also appeared blurred. His eyes, however, were strikingly bright. The irises looked like two radiant starbursts, or like the birth of a sun. A vibrant white light haloed each, and when the being's eyes shifted to a particular angle, a small beam of white light flashed out beyond his face.

An air bubble also encased his head. Despite being made from galaxy, he still couldn't breathe underwater.

He extended an empyrean hand to Violet, which she took. His fingers were like nothing else she'd ever touched. Maybe this was what it felt like to hold the night sky in your hands?

"It's an honor to be acquainted, Miss Violet the hybrid." The being drew closer, and for a second, Violet assumed he was about to plant a kiss on her hand. Instead, he briefly rested his forehead on her knuckles.

She tried not to cringe at "the hybrid" title. "Uh… thanks. Nice to meet you."

"I am Jhutev Iha, of the Arundhati lineage. I am at your service if His Reverence so wishes."

So many questions. Before she could choose which to ask

first, Votloxo interjected with a sharp warning directed at Jhutev.

"How many times must you be reminded, *Meruvo*. You are property of His Royal Reverence, and your lineage is no longer valid. Nor are you to—"

"Yes, yes," said the prince, swishing a dismissive hand. "Always with the formalities, Votloxo. There will be more than enough of that nonsense to deal with tonight." He pinched the bridge of his nose, then cast Jhutev a sidelong glance. Jhutev released Violet's hand and made an apologetic bow of his head to the prince.

The edge of steel in Votloxo's eyes suggested she wished to say more, but instead she opted to clamp her lips shut.

After a strained moment, the prince gestured to Violet's dress. "Regarding the matter at hand, I suppose there are quite a lot of… frills."

"'Quite a lot' is an understatement," said Violet. "I'm not sure there's any tulle or lace left on this planet." She swiped at the billowing fabric around her shoulders. Thankfully, the air bubble around her head kept the frills from entirely surrounding her face, but it was an effort to keep the froof from obstructing her line of sight. The voluminous fabrics puffed out into cascading tiers of dusty pinks, muddy purples, and muted navy all the way down Violet's body, and the circumference of pleated tulle at the bottom hem had to be large enough to border a small country. To top off the whole affair, Violet's hair had been teased and frizzed into an antigravity mass, with a massive pink-and-purple sequined bow attached to the side of her head.

She tugged on the collar, trying to get a reprieve from her climbing body temperature. Despite the icy water around her, heat still penetrated her core, and she wriggled at the prickles of hot discomfort trailing down her back. There was no point trying to wipe her dripping brow through the air bubble over her head. At least the wardrobe mistress hadn't deemed it suitable to put makeup on her.

"Hmm, who approved this outfit?" Exültov directed his question at Votloxo, who hovered a few feet behind Violet.

"I was assured by the wardrobe mistress this ensemble was acceptable," said Votloxo.

"Acceptable for a Lady Gaga music video perhaps." Violet waved her arms for emphasis, her hands and wrists barely clearing the layers upon layers of bunched-up fabric. "But it's unacceptable for functioning like a normal human being."

"But you're not a 'normal human being,' are you, hybrid?"

Violet shot a glare at the fighter fish shifter. Votloxo's face was practically begging to be punched.

"Enough, Votloxo," said Exültov. "You are excused."

"But, Your Reverence, I am to escort the hybrid to—"

"I am more than capable of escorting her myself." The steel in his eyes held no room for argument.

Votloxo dropped her gaze to the floor and bowed her head. "Of course, Your Reverence. I trust you'll enjoy your evening." With a swirl of her fins, she glided away into a side tunnel.

Violet almost sagged with relief to see Votloxo's tail fins disappear. That infuriating Nephezai had loitered like a plague the whole time Violet was being stripped down and dressed. Thankfully, the blue-ringed octopus and stingray Nephezai had been kicked out of the room, but Votloxo refused to leave, claiming it was her duty to ensure "the hybrid" wouldn't try to escape.

"Shall we get this blasted event over with?"

Violet looked up to find Exültov gesturing toward another arched tunnel on the other side of the antechamber. Dread caused her to pause. Exültov may have dismissed the guard, but she didn't for a second assume he wasn't a threat himself. She glanced at Jhutev, but nothing in his expression or posture gave anything away.

"Regrettably, there's no time to change," added the prince. "But the sooner we get this banquet over with, the sooner you can get rid of that dress. I'll even let you burn it if you like." He made a point of looking at her hands. No doubt he'd been filled in about her water-resistant Magneii flames.

Violet arched a brow. The thought of torturing the monstrous pink-and-navy fabric mound with her Magneii flames did give her a little satisfaction.

Returning her thoughts to the present, she went to slide her hand through the crook of the prince's proffered arm. But before making contact, alarm bells sounded in her mind, and she instinctively flinched back.

"What's wrong?" Exültov followed Violet's wary glance, and understanding smoothed his features. "There is no need for concern. My stingers will not harm you, unless you give me reason."

His warning rang loud and clear. For a split second she was glad to be wearing the ridiculous dress. It could be a barrier against the prince's stinging tendrils. She'd also discovered sections of the pleated material could be used as substitute pockets.

She subtly patted a small lump hidden in the floof at her waist, where she'd hidden the three Nephezai thorns Thane had slipped into her jacket pocket earlier. Somehow, she'd managed to keep them hidden from Votloxo and the wardrobe staff as they got her dressed. Thane must have saved the five thorns the guards shot through their bubble yesterday. He clearly thought they could be of some use, although Violet had no idea how. In the meantime, she'd been cautious not to prick herself with the three-inch mother-of-pearl barbs.

Not daring to arouse suspicion by hesitating longer, she

tentatively hooked her arm through the prince's. Exültov led her through the arched hallway, his firm hand pulling her along as her dress dragged heavily through the water. With the strain of the gown on her body, she'd never be able to navigate the underwater passageways by herself. Yet, like all the Nephezai, the prince glided along with no apparent struggle.

Jhutev flanked her, keeping up with the prince's swift pace. At the sight of her other companion, Violet's mind swirled with questions.

Votloxo had called him "Meruvo." Why was that term so familiar?

She racked her mind, trying to place where she'd heard it, when a flash of memories surfaced: her early days of becoming a shifter herself and receiving training from Nathan. He'd explained the different shifter races and touched on a few details of each, but he hadn't said much about the Meruvo shifters. She did recall, though, that they were associated with the planet Mercury.

Violet glanced at the ring of dark light illuminating Jhutev's upper half, confused about the emptiness beneath. Did he have legs? Or did the ring mark the end of his body? It also piqued her curiosity that Votloxo had referred to Jhutev as the prince's "property."

She slid another sidelong, empathetic look at the Meruvo. She couldn't help but notice he wasn't restrained; he swam freely by her side. What stopped him from just turning around and trying to escape from this underwater prison? Did he like it here? Was this place preferable to wherever he'd come from?

"I must extend my gratitude to you for accompanying me tonight," Exültov said, interrupting her thoughts.

Violet snorted. "What's stopping you from forcing me to go even if I refuse?"

The prince came to a stop, halting Violet along with him. A hint of surprise crossed his expression before his features smoothed into ironclad indifference.

For a moment Violet regretted her rash words. She may have been vocal about her dress, but she needed to remember she was in the presence of the prince of her captors.

Rein it in, Violet. She wouldn't be able to get herself, Thane, and Solace out of here if the prince decided to punish her for her disrespect.

"A valid question, air breather," he finally said. He released her arm, then gestured back the way they came. "By all means, if you do so wish, I will have Jhutev lead you back to the menagerie, and I will continue on to the banquet alone."

Violet blanched, her eyes darting between Jhutev, the prince, and the direction he pointed.

There was no mistaking what the prince's offer truly meant—return to the bubble enclosure with no extra bedding or food for Solace. Not to mention she'd lose her chance to learn more about her underwater prison and devise a plan of escape.

Her heart hammered in her chest; her fingers twiddled at her sides.

Just focus on getting out of here, she reminded herself. Solace wouldn't be living the rest of her days in a bubble enclosure just because Violet lacked the self-control to keep her mouth shut.

"My deepest apologies, Your Highness." She bowed low at the waist, hoping it was deemed humble enough. "It is truly an honor for you to consider one such as myself to accompany you to the banquet."

The prince regarded her with a contemplative expression. "A wise choice. And for the future, instead of 'Highness,' protocol is to address me as 'Your Reverence.' Or rather, ensure you address me as 'Your Reverence' in the presence of others, aside from Jhutev."

Violet nodded her understanding.

Exültov's mouth twitched into a smile at her silence. She couldn't tell whether he was unimpressed with her or pleased she'd fallen into some elaborate trap. Before she could decide whether she needed to be much more concerned, a high-pitched squeal rang out through the hallway.

Startled, Violet looked around, just as something *whooshed* past her out of nowhere. A split second later, another *whoosh* streamed past. The rush of swirling water would've caused Violet to tumble head over heels if Jhutev hadn't caught her and held her tight.

The squealing thankfully ceased, only to be replaced by an excited chattering Violet couldn't decipher. When she recomposed herself, she found two small creatures latched on to Exültov's waist. But instead of shoving them away, he leaned down with an affectionate glitter in his eyes.

"Children, children. Quiet down."

Children? Exültov has children?

Violet looked upon the trio with awe. Only when the two children stopped bobbing up and down could she see that the larger of the two was also a jellyfish shifter. She was the spitting image of her father, right down to the graceful tendrils of her frilled stingers. The smaller Nephezai boy had the unmistakable characteristics of a blue dragon nudibranch. His cheeky grin and infectious giggles indicated how much of a handful he likely was, yet his fins and mother-of-pearl thorns already promised intimidation and power when he got older. Violet guessed the jellyfish girl to be about eight or nine years old, whereas the younger brother couldn't be any older than three.

"You two should be in bed." Despite Exültov's firm tone, a smile tugged at the corner of his mouth.

"But, Papa, Zümgroz caught a sea sluggard, and I told him he has to let it go."

"No," wailed the little boy, eyes big as golf balls. "No slug-gah go!"

"Papa, tell him if he doesn't let it go, the sluggard will die!"

"Slug-gah no go! Slug-gah mine!"

"The sluggard doesn't belong to you, Zümgroz. You have to let it go," the girl interjected.

"Enough, children," Exültov said just as the two began to squabble. "Zümgroz, what are the rules with the pets you catch?"

The little shifter's lip drooped. "No pets in bed."

"And why do we have that rule?" asked Exültov.

"'Cause when I sleep, pets go squish."

Violet almost couldn't hold back her giggles when the little Nephezai made an adorable squelching sound.

"Yes," confirmed Exültov with a nod.

"But slug-gah fwend."

"That may be the case, but friends look after each other and make sure they don't go squish. Züm, you must let the sluggard go."

Zümgroz's head sagged. "Yah, Papa. I let go."

"And, Therizüs"—Exültov looked down at his daughter, cupping her chin—"as the oldest, you need to help your brother understand why things must be done instead of just demanding they be done."

"Yes, Papa." Her haughty expression crumpled with the rebuke, but a smile brightened her face when Exültov kissed the top of her head.

"Zümgroz! Therizüs! There you children are!" A leafy seadragon Nephezai bustled into the hallway, then glided to a stop. "Oh! Prince Exültov." She bowed her head over her little pot belly. "Your Reverence, I beseech your pardon. I had thought you'd be at the banquet by now. I regret to inform you the children slipped away from my supervision the second I turned my back. I can assure you they will be put to bed straightaway."

"Of course, Hildez," said Exültov, guiding the children toward her.

"But, Papa," whined the girl, "can't we stay up for just a few more minutes. Pleeeeeease."

"Yah, pweeeeeease, Papa," mimicked the boy.

"Now, now, little ones. It is already past your sleep time. Off to bed with you."

The two chorused a "Yes, Papa." Then with a final peck on the head each and a "Sleep well," Exültov sent the children off.

Without any further acknowledgment of the last few minutes, the prince continued to lead Violet and Jhutev down the hallways. At last, they reached a magnificent set of double doors, at least two stories high—an installation of living color made from a vast amount of coral and anemones of all sorts. A swarm of tiny fish frolicked from anemone to anemone, not at all perturbed by the three newcomers.

Two guards hovered on either side of the doors. Both bowed low to the prince before reaching for stone handles.

"Prepare yourself," Exültov said in a low voice only Violet and Jhutev could hear. "The pandemonium is about to begin."

13
WE FIGHT, WE STAB, WE KILL

SAGAN GROANED, DRAGGING BOTH HANDS DOWN HIS FACE. "Have you lost your freaking mind?" He'd lost count of how many times he'd said that to Nika.

Mercifully, his mother had already fallen asleep by the time he helped Nika bring the three Veniri children inside the cavern. He'd started to panic that Odette would recognize her. If she did, would she still consider Nika her favorite niece, or would she associate her with imprisonment at the Xabat facility? And who knew how his mother would handle the concept of shifter children. After all, Odette had once been a huntress herself.

Sagan looked over at the wicker basket, now sitting on a spare section of ground near the camp kitchen—on the opposite side of the cavern from his mother. He couldn't hide his utter disbelief. "Never in my life did I think I'd see the day that Nika Branstone would become the nurturing type—*for shifter babies*, of all things."

Ignoring his continual groaning, Nika fetched one of the spare sleeping bags and a stretcher bed and set them up next to the wicker basket. Sagan stood by while she settled the toddler, Orson, into the sleeping bag with his ragged green bear plushie. Every now and then, the child shot a look of curiosity in Sagan's direction, but with some hushed reassurance from Nika, the boy followed her suggestion to try and get some sleep. Once the toddler was fighting to keep his eyelids open, Nika dutifully checked the two—still sleeping—infants in the basket, then set a Luxium heater on the cavern floor nearby.

"What the hell, Nika," hissed Sagan after she tiptoed toward him. "Since when do you know how to look after a baby? No, forget that question—Where did you even get these babies? And in typical Nika style, you haven't just kidnapped one kid—*you've kidnapped three*!" He huffed a laugh. "Three teal-blooded, crystal-boned Veniri babies!"

"Will you keep it down? You're going to wake them," Nika growled through gritted teeth.

"Are you serious? You've got no idea how much responsibility it takes to raise a Veniri baby, let alone three!" Sagan's voice was reaching a hysterical pitch. "You need to take the babies back."

"No. I can't."

"Don't be stupid. Of course you can."

Nika held a finger to her lips, shooting him a glare that promised copious amounts of pain.

Sagan gaped at her. Who the hell did his cousin think she was? He went to grab the handles of the wicker basket.

Nika slapped his hand away. "You touch that basket and I'll rip out your intestines and dice them up into dog food."

He matched her venomous glare with his own. "Take them back to their parents. *Now*."

"I can't take them back because their parents are dead. They're all dead!"

Sagan froze.

Nika's words echoed around the cold cavern walls.

Before he could even begin to construct a response, a small wail called out from the wicker basket.

"Oh, no." Nika rushed over and gently raised one of the babies into her arms. The tiny infant kicked and fussed while she put him over her shoulder, rocking him like a pro. "Please, baby, shhh. Please go back to sleep. You're going to wake your brothers up."

Sagan looked on, resisting the urge to rub his eyes. Was he hallucinating. Who was this girl?

Despite Nika's efforts, the child continued to twist and writhe until his screaming reached a new decibel.

Out of nowhere, Odette appeared at Nika's side. On instinct, Sagan took a step forward, his body coiled to react at a moment's notice.

His mother peered down at the crying baby.

Then, to Sagan's bewilderment, his mother held her arms out. Nika took a step back and twisted away, shielding the baby with her body.

"Bubba?" His mother nodded at the crying infant. "Bubba, shhh?"

Nika glanced at Sagan, but he could only gawk in response. In eight days, this was the most animated and interactive his mother had been. After a few moments of hesitation, he shrugged.

Odette still held her arms out patiently.

After another nervous glance at Sagan, Nika passed the baby over. As if handling a delicate porcelain doll, Odette rolled the baby over and cradled his belly over her forearm. His head rested in the crook of her elbow, and his legs continued to kick the air. Using her free hand, she patted the baby on the back. With a gentle tone, she said, "Shh, bubba, shh," and a few other things Sagan couldn't quite comprehend. But it didn't seem to matter what his mother was saying, as the baby soon began to settle.

Nika shook her head. "Unbelievable."

Odette gave her a soft smile before setting her attention back on the baby.

Sagan couldn't help a pang of envy toward both Nika and the baby. For eight days, after he'd made a deal with the devil and freed her, fed her, and looked after her, his mother had hardly acknowledged his existence. And he was her own son!

Yet, as Sagan watched his mother calm the infant, his anger and resentment faded. Maybe this could be a step toward recovering from her trauma.

Just as the baby looked about to fall asleep, the little tot let rip an almighty burst of gas.

Sagan's and Nika's eyes bugged.

After a heartbeat, Nika cracked up with laughter, and Sagan couldn't resist a smile as well.

After that, the little baby's wails ceased. He closed his eyes and snuggled into Odette's arms. Less than a minute later, she gently laid him back in the wicker basket, then settled herself on the ground by the Luxium heater. She quietly hummed her little song, one hand stroking Orson's hair and the other patting the two in the basket.

Nika slowly made her way over to Sagan. "Well, who would've thought Aunty Odette had a liking for shifter babies?"

When Nika spoke, Odette waved her hands. She gestured at the three boys and hummed some unintelligible phrases. A few seconds of silence passed before Sagan realized she was waiting for a reply.

"Um..." Nika exchanged a confused glance with Sagan. "Sorry, Aunty Odette, what did you say?"

Sagan's mother repeated her gestures and hums, to which Nika responded with a grimace.

Bracing himself to intervene when Nika inevitably lost her patience, Sagan found himself frozen in shock when

Nika knelt down in front of Odette and calmly tried to comprehend what she was trying to communicate.

"Oh, I think I understand," Nika said after a few moments. "To be honest, I don't actually know what the boys' real names are. But I've been calling him"—she pointed to the older boy, who clasped the stuffed green bear tight even while he slept—"Orson. And as for the twins… well, I don't know for sure if they're twins, but I think they're pretty close in age, so I've just been thinking of them as twins. The one with the picture of an eagle on his shirt I've been calling Falco, and the one with the wolf picture I've called Raoul."

Odette tilted her head to the side as Nika spoke, as if trying hard to process the words. Then she pointed to Orson.

"That's Orson," Nika confirmed.

Odette slowly nodded as she contemplated the sleeping boy. She pointed to the green bear in his arms before holding her hands up like claws. Then, after pointing to Falco and the soaring eagle pattern on his shirt, she shaped her hands into flapping wings.

"Right," said Nika with an encouraging smile. "That's Falco."

Odette then pointed to Raoul, specifically the cute little baby wolf image on his shirt, before forming another sign.

"Sorry, Aunty Odette, I don't understand," said Nika, frowning.

"She's making the sign of a wolf," said Sagan. "It's a shadow puppet she taught me when I was young. It's a wolf's head, see?" He held up his own hands in the beam of one of the Luxium lanterns to demonstrate.

"Oh, I get it now." Nika looked back at Odette, eyes wide with clarity. "She's making up her own hand signs for the boys." She mimicked the signs back to Odette.

The smile on his mother's face was the most glorious thing Sagan had seen in the last eight days.

Nika stood up, leaving Odette to resume singing her ethereal song to the Veniri boys.

"Well, that was… interesting," Nika said once she was back by Sagan's side.

Sagan nodded, jaw slack with lingering wonder. He crossed his arms over his chest. "How did you do that?" He tried to keep his tone calm, despite the growing feeling of—what? Jealousy? Excitement? Bewilderment?

Nika arched an eyebrow. "How did I do what?"

He flung a hand at his mother. "*That*. How did you get her to talk to you? For the past eight days I've done everything to get her to talk to me, or even acknowledge my existence. But then you show up with three kidnapped Veniri, and she's busting out the hand signs and playing mother hen!"

"Sagan, *stop*," hissed Nika.

Only when she put her hand on his arm did he realize he'd raised his voice. Sucking in a deep, ragged breath, he counted back from ten—yet another technique he'd learned from his mother when his emotions were getting a bit too hot to handle.

Nika released her own heavy sigh. "Come on." She inclined her head to the "rumpus room" section of the cavern. "We should probably talk."

They crossed the stepping stones through the shallow water and settled into some camp chairs. Sagan slumped back, his arms and legs going limp as severe exhaustion overcame him. For several long moments the two just sat and watched Odette tend to the three boys, until at last she snuggled down on a spare blanket beside the wicker basket. The cavern became silent, bar the ambient dripping from the stalactites into the lake.

Despite the peace and quiet, Sagan's inner turmoil was deafening.

Nika reached for a dusty doll sitting among a pile of scattered toys and playing cards, all abandoned years ago after their last family camping trip.

Resting his elbow on the chair's armrest, Sagan grasped the black chain around his neck and absentmindedly rolled the metal links between his fingers. His attention wandered to Nika as she studied the doll with a nostalgic, almost sad expression on her face.

He raked a hand through his hair. "So, about the, uh… the Veniri babies. I think you need to—"

"I already told you I can't take them back. Their parents are all dead." Nika tossed the doll back into the pile of trinkets on the cavern floor.

Sagan opened his mouth to reply but stopped short when Nika swiped at glistening streaks on her cheeks. Was she… crying? Impossible. He'd never seen Nika cry, not ever. Even as a child, she'd refused to cry, no matter how brutal their hunter training had been.

He gaped at her as she choked out her next words. "We found it, Sagan. We finally found a Veniri hive."

A flurry of emotions swarmed through his core. A Veniri hive? But how? When?

No hunter in history had successfully located any of the hives where the Veniri shifters lived under the rule of each hive queen. Every young hunter dreamed of becoming the first to discover one.

And Nika had been there.

He pushed back a stab of envy as more questions flooded his mind. *Where is it located? What does a Veniri hive even look like? How many Veniri live there?*

Then a sudden fear gripped his insides.

If the hunters—if his father found the hive, the real question was, how many Veniri were left?

He glanced at the three sleeping babies.

"Fifty hunters, myself included, followed your father on

the expedition to the hive. All the while, Uncle Matthias promised us not only a king's ransom of Diamantium but also the eternal glory of being the first hunters who dared to do the impossible."

Nika paused for a few beats. Her periwinkle eyes glittered with fresh tears, and her head and shoulders sagged as she studied a small item in her hands. He recognized the knuckle-duster his father had given her one Christmas. It was Nika's favorite weapon, and as far as he could tell, she always had it with her.

"I'll be honest," said Nika, "the whole time I thought I was so stupid for letting Uncle Matthias convince me to join him."

Sagan scoffed. "I don't blame you. He's been obsessed for as long as I can remember. Finding a Veniri hive is like chasing gold at the end of a rainbow."

"But we did find a hive," said Nika, her tone laced with awe. "I never once believed Uncle Matthias would actually succeed in one of his ludicrous expeditions. I can't even begin to describe how I felt when we found it. But then what happened next…" Her face distorted with raw rage. "Never in my life have I been so ashamed to call myself a hunter."

"What happened?" Sagan gently prompted, although he already knew the answer.

"I've lost count of how many shifters I've hunted and killed. At first, when we arrived, I didn't think much of the slaughter to come. But we entered through one of the nurseries and… I couldn't do it, Sagan." Her words became thick with misery. "There was so much blood. Innocent teal blood *everywhere*. Some of the human breeder slaves tried to stop the hunters, but those women were skin and bone. Some had chains around their ankles. None of them stood a chance against the hunters.

"I'll never forget the screaming. The awful, awful

screaming will haunt my dreams until the day I die. They were just children. Harmless, defenseless *babies*." She gripped her knuckle-duster, her fingers turning white. "Call me a coward, but I turned and made for the exit. I wanted to run away from it all. I could have done it—finally left this blasted life and started afresh in a new town, or even a new country. But then I heard a noise in one of the too-quiet nursery rooms. I found them there, among all the carnage and... and death. Orson was huddled under one of the cribs, his little body trying to shield the younger two from me."

Sagan looked over at the sleeping children, imagining the serene and peaceful Orson trying to protect two babies at his tender age.

"I didn't think about the consequences," said Nika. "What I did next was either the best or the most stupid thing I've ever done in my life. I scooped the three children up and I fled. It was a tough trek back to find the cars, but thankfully no one had followed me by the time I drove off. At the first town I found, I bought some baby formula. A nice lady helped me pick out a few other items she said I'd need."

"And then you made it here," Sagan deduced.

Nika nodded. After a heartbeat, she said, "It turns out we were wrong."

Sagan furrowed his brow. "What do you mean?"

"All our lives we were taught that shifters are lesser than us. That they're nothing but animals—abominations that need to be eradicated. All my life I've believed that shifters were only worth hunting to be torn to pieces, so their profitable parts could be extracted and distributed throughout the hunter empire. But then I met Violet." Nika folded her legs up onto her chair and hugged her knees. Her light brown ringlets fell over her shoulders and face. "That night when I was sparring with Violet, I was so angry when you defended her."

"I had to," said Sagan, his words hard as steel. "You were going to kill her."

Nika barked a laugh. "With our upbringing, I suppose I just expected you to take my side over a shifter. And why wouldn't I? My treatment of shifters—my treatment of Violet—would have no consequences. None of us have ever been punished for all we've inflicted on the shifter races. All we've done is delude ourselves for generations, always convincing ourselves we do what we do in the name of honor, bravery—*for the good of humanity.* Never once have we faced the truth of what we really do. Murder, pillage, plunder..."

Nika's gaze remained locked on the knuckle-duster.

Sagan recalled that knuckle-duster making mincemeat out of Violet's face. The memory of her blood streaming down her neck and chest still jarred him. "We've all done terrible things, and who knows, maybe one day we will pay for what we've done. But what you did to Violet was unlike anything I've seen you do to any other shifter."

Nika regarded him with a steady gaze. "What is it with you and this Violet chick? Are you crushing on her or something?"

"No, it's not like that. If anything, I think of Violet like a younger sister, especially after she befriended Lyla-Rose. You remember what Lyla was like?"

Nika nodded, a cloud of grief engulfing her face. "She didn't have an evil bone in her body."

"Yeah, my sister was everything a hunter isn't," agreed Sagan, "which unfortunately made her the perfect target for bullies at her school. But then Violet came along and stood up for her. She even tried to protect her against those Veniri slavers who kidnapped both of them. She was there for Lyla when I couldn't be, and for that, I'll be forever grateful."

Pondering what he'd just said, Sagan internally sneered at himself. How could he say he thought of Violet as a sister when he was the reason hunters had loaded her and her family into Metallikite crates and taken them to his grandfather's bio-experimental facility? He wasn't there when Lyla needed him most, and now where was he when Violet needed him?

He looked over at his peacefully sleeping mother, trying hard to reaffirm the reasoning behind his decisions.

Nika huffed out a breath. "I didn't realize you thought of Violet like that—like she's family. I just figured she was some kind of distraction for you until you sorted out what to do after going rogue from our barracks. I suppose it makes sense why you reacted like you did when I sparred with her that night."

Sagan hung his head at the memory of what he'd done next. "I know I was angry about what you'd done to Violet, but I don't know what came over me to think that I… couldn't let it go unpunished."

Nika let out a halfhearted scoff. "So the best punishment you could think of was to destroy my hunter amulet?"

"No point crying over it in the end though, right?" He gave a pointed look at the black chain peeking above the neckline of Nika's shirt. "You got a replacement when you went back to the hunters. Besides, I doubt it will take you long to reclaim your lost shifter blood samples—if you haven't already."

Nika's nose scrunched in disgust. She cast a thoughtful look over at the sleeping children and muttered a soft "Screw that," then took hold of the black chain around her neck, pulled it over her head, and flung the necklace to the ground. The metal clattered along the stony floor until the medallion came to rest face up.

Sagan raised an eyebrow at the empty glass vials. "No colors?" He turned his inquiring gaze to Nika. "You were pissed when I destroyed your other amulet. I don't understand."

Nika fidgeted with the knuckle-duster, taking care to avoid cutting her hands on the embedded Diamantium shards. "Do you remember Elias Ragefire?"

"Yeah." Sagan slowly nodded. "Stellan's son. I remember Elias from when we were kids. His short fuse started a lot of fights. Didn't he try taking you on one day? You ended up giving him a black eye, or kicked him in the nuts or something."

Nika smirked, a tender fondness in her eyes. "I actually gave him a black eye *and* a bloody nose when he kicked me in the shin and thought he could get away with it."

Sagan chuckled. "Ah yes, I remember now. I'd never heard a ten-year-old screech like he did when he went crying to his mommy."

Nika snickered.

"Speaking of his mom, didn't she pass away a few years ago?"

"Yeah, about five or six years ago. It happened while she was… uh… on a hunting trip."

Nika's tone suggested she knew more to the story, but Sagan decided to drop it. Instead he asked, "So what's Elias Ragefire got to do with your change of attitude toward your amulet?"

"It's a bit of a long story, but… it started a few months after you disappeared. Elias, Stellan, and a bunch of other hunters from the Ragefire barracks showed up at ours to renegotiate peace and trade agreements."

Sagan groaned. "I'm so glad I wasn't there for that. My father would have forced me to sit through every one of those meetings. It's just a bunch of egotistical nonsense where all the barracks leaders try to flex their authority and prowess over everyone else."

"Isn't that the basic DNA of all hunters?" Nika asked.

Sagan huffed a laugh. "Yeah, I guess so. Still, those ridiculous meetings can drag on for weeks, or even months, before any agreements are made."

"Yeah, well, the Ragefire crew made themselves at home in our barracks for a few weeks. They even came along on a few of our hunting trips."

"I can just imagine how much your brothers hated sharing their hunting grounds with the likes of the Ragefires."

Nika rolled her eyes. "Yeah, Quill and Hestus weren't exactly impressed. But the Grimvast twins were way more threatened than my brothers."

"I bet. I've run into Elias a few times since we were kids. He's developed a bit of a rep when it comes to hijacking other hunters' prey."

"No kidding. I learned that the hard way," said Nika. "I was a dagger slice away from claiming a sample of Meruvo blood for my amulet when Elias freaking Ragefire crash-tackled me."

"A Meruvo, huh? That's a lucky find. I bet you were pissed. Did poor Elias get another black eye and bloody nose?"

"Something like that."

"What happened?"

"I may have made a scene in the cafeteria during the breakfast rush," said Nika with a shrug.

"Poor Elias." Sagan chuckled darkly. "I kinda wish I was there to see that. Was he smart enough to steer clear from you after that?"

"Nope. In fact, he did the opposite. He, um… asked me out for ice cream."

"He what?" Sagan's eyebrows shot up. "Whoa! Wait a second. You're telling me that you gave Elias Ragefire a butt-whooping in front of the whole Branstone barracks, then got asked out for ice cream? Only among hunters would something like that happen."

He half expected Nika to counter his jibe with an insult, or at least punch his arm. Instead, she focused on twisting a lock of curly hair around her finger.

"What happened, Nika?"

When she didn't respond, Sagan asked, "Did he hurt you?"

"No." Nika's reply was instant. "No, he never hurt me. He was… he and I…"

After a few heartbeats, Sagan said, "Don't tell me you like him."

She didn't answer.

"Oh" was all Sagan could think to say.

Nika's body tensed, grief flooding her blue eyes.

"So where is Elias now?"

She let the silence drag on for a moment. "He was planning to leave the hunters. His mother died not long after giving birth to his sister, and he'd taken over caring for Peony. It was his mother's wish for Peony not to be raised in a barracks." Nika took a moment to bite her trembling lip. "He asked me to join him. To run away with him and Peony. But when the time came for us to leave, your dad showed up after another of his expeditions, once again minus several hunters who'd gone with him. This time it was several missing hunters from the Ragefire crew.

"Elias's conscience got the better of him. Before we could leave, he said he needed to find out what was happening to the hunters. So he volunteered to go on Uncle Matthias's next expedition. But… Elias never came back." Tears streamed freely down Nika's cheeks. "I searched and searched. Just like I searched for you when you went missing."

A pang of guilt hit Sagan. It had never even crossed his

mind to let Nika know he was alive and how he was faring after he and Violet arrived in Maple Shire. He had no idea she cared that much.

"I couldn't find him, Sagan," Nika choked out through her tears. "My mother is gone. Lyla-Rose is gone. You were gone. Elias is gone. And even my—" She clutched at her belly as a sob racked through her hunched frame. "So much had been taken from me at the barracks. There was no longer any reason for me to stay. So I left. I came here, to this cave, to try and figure out what to do with myself. Then a couple days later, you showed up."

Sagan eyed Nika's discarded amulet. She'd chosen a guy over the hunters? And not just any guy but Elias Ragefire of all people—although the more Sagan thought about it, the more he suspected Elias might actually be the perfect guy for her.

A surge of sorrow twisted knots in his stomach. He could only imagine the heartache Nika was going through to find someone perfect for her, then lose him not long after.

"We've been trained our whole lives to be strong. Strong and unbreakable," continued Nika. "After leaving the hunters, I thought I was strong enough. But that night when I was sparring with Violet, I just… I couldn't hold the broken pieces together anymore.

"Violet has everything. She's a hybrid shifter with incredible abilities. She has Nathan, who's the best father figure I know, unlike my dad, who's never given a damn. She has Thane, who's always there to defend her, whether she wants him to or not. She has a daughter everyone just adores… Violet has everything, yet she doesn't even see it. She has the power, the family, love and support. She has everything I've ever wanted and dreamed." Nika's hands curled into tight fists. "And I hated her for it."

Sagan frowned, unsure how to deal with the mixture of

raging emotions her words spurred. "Your jealousy is no excuse for trying to kill her."

"I wasn't trying to kill her."

"Violet smelled cinnamon! When a Veniri smells cinnamon, it means someone has the intention to murder."

"Whether you believe me or not, I wasn't trying to kill Violet." Nika looked down at her hands and slowly uncurled her fingers. "I just wanted the pain to stop. The heartache, the anger, the hate—all of it. I wanted it to end. But the only way we hunters know how to deal with our problems is with these." She held up her hands. Her knuckle-duster hung from one of her fingers. "We fight. We punch. We hit. We stab. We kill. We're never taught to deal with our issues with peace or compassion, or even with love."

Nika's hands dropped into her lap, and her shoulders hunched. "I'll forever be ashamed of what I did to Violet. I was too ashamed to face her, or you, or any of the others after that. I had thought I'd turned my back on the hunters. But when you broke my amulet, it was like you'd destroyed the last piece of my identity. A hunter is all I've ever known how to be. After what I did, I knew I could never be anything other than a ruthless killer. So I went back. I went back to the barracks, and Grandpa practically welcomed me with open arms. For a while I could pretend I didn't care about anyone or anything back at Maple Shire, because all I'm good for is killing and destroying things.

"But then I started going hunting again, and every shifter had Violet's face. Or it had Thane's face, or Tio's, or Nathan's… Every shifter the others cut down and butchered was just another face added to my nightmares.

"I thought I would get over it. I thought maybe I needed to do more than just hunting, you know? So I went with Uncle Matthias on his grand expedition to find the Veniri hive. At first I was utterly amazed we'd actually found it—in fact, I was excited. But then the killing started..."

Nika sniffled, wiping her face with the sleeve of her jacket. "Do you wanna know the worst part? It's not like those stupid stories we've joked about. They don't live like animals. They're like us, like you and me. They have homes and families and children—heaven's above!—the *children*."

Bile seared the back of Sagan's throat.

"I'll never forget the look Orson gave me," said Nika. "He can barely talk, but he knew. He understood what was happening. I could see it in his eyes. He was terrified—of me. And yet he was willing to die to protect those two babies." She rubbed the tears from her raw red eyes. "I knew in that moment I could no longer be a hunter."

For several long moments, the two didn't speak; the melodic *tink-tink-tink* of dripping water filled the silence.

"So what's the plan now?" Sagan asked.

Nika shrugged. "I figured we could hunker down here for a few days, maybe weeks, until I can find a place to go where these guys will be safe from... well... safe from the likes of us."

Sagan snorted. "Yeah, like where?"

"I'm not sure yet."

A gentle humming broke through their conversation. His mother must have woken up.

"How is your mother, after... you know..?" Nika asked.

"She's fine..." Sagan sighed and shook his head. "Actually, I have no idea. She seems to be damaged on all fronts, physically, mentally, and who knows what else." He growled in frustration. "I don't know what they've done to her, so I have no idea how to help her or what she needs to heal."

Nausea joined his anger when he recalled his mother's mutilated back. He crushed his fingers into fists. "I swear on her life that I'm going to make them pay. Renard Branstone, everyone at that Xabat facility. They're going to suffer for what they did to her."

After a tense pause, Nika gave a firm nod. "This time, I won't stand in your way."

"Really? What about Quill and Hestus? You know they'll defend Grandpa."

An edge of sorrow brushed Nika's features before her expression hardened. "They've made their decisions, and now I'm making mine. Both you and I have trained all our lives to destroy. Maybe it's time we use our training to defend the innocent instead. And even if that means we go up against our own family, then... maybe it's time you and I start a new family legacy."

"Well, in that case, first things first. We need to go back to Maple Shire."

Nika's face turned a sickly gray. "No, Sagan. We can't go back there."

"Come on. You have to admit we need Dawn, especially her special Veniri baby formula. Not to mention she might be able to help my mother. Just swallow your pride for once."

"It's not that." Nika's face distorted with agony. "You haven't heard what's happened, have you?"

A tremor of fear washed over Sagan. "What happened?"

"Maple Shire was bombed by the hunters."

14
NO MORE BARBARIC THAN YOU

PANDEMONIUM INDEED.

Violet's jaw slackened at the riot of color and flurry of elegant creatures whirling and swirling beyond the giant doors.

The room was filled with Nephezai shifters: fins, claws, tails, fangs, and tentacles of all sorts. She figured it was the same crowd who came to ogle her each day, only now adorned in finery and glittering jewels. Just like in the world above, every guest seemed to be flaunting their wealth and status through extravagant possessions and exotic fashions. She even recognized the haughty upturned noses, the side-long glances and whispering in others' ears.

Violet rolled her eyes. She might as well be back at high school.

Exültov guided her into the room at a slow pace, with Jhutev still flanking her other side. The chattering and murmurs gradually grew quiet as the trio glided past.

Jhutev had said earlier that the prince wanted to make a statement, and it appeared he was successful. Eyes grew wide when they fell on the prince, wider when they landed on

Jhutev, and wider still when they reached Violet. Whispers swirled in their wake.

She leaned a little closer to Exültov. "I thought we were going to a banquet."

"We are."

"Oh." Violet glanced around, noting the lack of food. Did the Nephezai not use tables or chairs? "Is this the pre-party mingling before we're escorted to the dining room or something?"

"No. This is the room we will be dining in this evening." He tilted his nose up, and Violet's gaze also drifted upward.

Her eyes grew wide at the scene above the crowd. The cylindrical walls surrounding the grand ballroom spanned up, up, and up; she could only guess how many stories high. Just like the double doors they'd entered through, a forest of coral, anemones, and seaweed of all sorts covered every inch in an exploding spectrum of color and movement.

His arm still hooked with Violet's, the prince casually swam in a slow spiral through the gauntlet of Nephezai high society, up toward the tables above. The higher they ascended, the better Violet's view of their dining arrangements. Gold, silver, bronze, copper, and other precious metals had been crafted into an eclectic assortment of banquet tables and chairs—a level of grandeur she'd only ever seen in movies.

Violet counted about fifteen round tables that could seat about twelve to fifteen shifters each. Every one of the tables sat on a platform a few inches thick, held up by a plethora of purple-tinged bubbles ranging from bowling-ball to beach-ball size. The bubbles allowed the platforms to float and meander through the room.

As much as there didn't seem to be any rhyme or reason to the directions the tables floated, there did appear to be some kind of hierarchy. The lower tables never rose higher than those above them, and the number of tables within each tier decreased until there was only one above all, bigger than the rest.

Each table had a large cylindrical centerpiece. It took Violet a moment to understand what she was seeing, but when comprehension struck, her heart plummeted with dread. The centerpieces were, in fact, purple-tinged Nephezai bubbles, each of which contained a collection of living land creatures. Dogs, cats, chimpanzees, ferrets, owls, parrots, and even a swarm of butterflies had been plucked from the menagerie to be put on display here.

Four Nephezai huddled by one of the bubble displays, admiring a creature Violet couldn't quite see. Then one of them stabbed a clawed hand through the membrane to yank the creature out. She still couldn't quite decipher what poor animal was trapped in the Nephezai's hand, only that it had some kind of fur or soft downy feathers. But her gut twisted when the creature began to thrash, clearly unable to breathe.

Instead of appearing concerned, the huddled Nephezai just laughed.

"What are they doing?" Violet protested. "They're going to kill that poor animal."

"Keep moving," said Exültov, not looking in the direction she'd pointed.

"But that animal needs air."

Violet kicked her legs in an attempt to propel herself toward the table, but Exültov firmly clamped a hand over hers to pin her at his side. "Don't look at them."

But she couldn't help it. Horror squeezed her lungs more tightly with each table they passed.

Creature after creature was being plucked out of the air-filled enclosures. The Nephezai looked on with hysterical mirth, cackling and guffawing as each creature struggled desperately to find air.

"That's barbaric," Violet said in a soft voice.

"No more barbaric than what you land dwellers do to the marine creatures," said Exültov, his tone stiff.

"What do you mean? Land dwellers are not like this."

The prince spun, his tentacles swirling and snapping. His face halted inches from hers. "That is where you are wrong, hybrid."

Violet's fear spiked.

"How many of your kind have pilfered marine creatures from the ocean and looked on while that animal floundered in an environment where it couldn't breathe? And for what? Sport? Leisure? Food? How many of your kind show compassion when a fish thrashes and gasps at the end of a fishing line? And what about your pet stores, zoos, and circuses? We are not the only ones who have ensnared creatures and forced them into tanks, forever trapped for onlookers to ogle for the sake of entertainment. Do not presume to think your kind is superior to us. You are just as capable of despicable cruelty."

Violet's chest heaved with rising anger, a furious backlash on the tip of her tongue—except that his words rang horribly true. Shame burned her cheeks.

"Cruelty" was an understatement. She'd experienced human malevolence firsthand at the mercy of the foster system. And that didn't even take into account humanity's other damnable acts—human trafficking, child labor, war, and innumerable others—all over the globe.

And yet, among all those who performed evil, there still existed the likes of Autumn, Gus, and their parents; the residents of Maple Shire; and even Nathan.

They had taken her in, a nobody, broken and battered from the abuse and trauma of her world. They cared for her, gave her a home, and helped her heal and grow stronger than she ever thought possible. They nurtured her when she was vulnerable, and supported her during the birth of her child. And how many of them selflessly came to her aid to rescue Solace from her kidnappers?

"Not all of 'my kind' are as cruel as you say. There are many, many more who are caring and compassionate," she said, matching her passionate tone to his.

The prince's hooded gaze showed none of what was going through his mind. "Perhaps. I have heard stories of such air breathers but have yet to witness this 'care and compassion' myself."

"Maybe one day one of us will surprise you." It was the lamest comeback, but Violet couldn't think of anything better to say.

Only after the prince turned away did she hear him mumble something like "That's what I'm counting on."

Exültov's hold on her arm relaxed a little, and his pace slowed a fraction. He suddenly seemed different in the way he carried himself, although Violet couldn't pinpoint how.

"The same can be said of my people," he said after a long pause. "Not all the Nephezai are as 'barbaric' as you say."

Violet didn't have any suitable response, not when everything she'd experienced of the Nephezai so far seemed to prove otherwise. Although… she remembered the prince's children, still young, still vulnerable. Not yet tainted by the cruelties of the world.

They continued up, up, up, through each tier of tables. Some Nephezai regarded the prince with reverence as he passed; others remained oblivious due to their fixation on the animals within each centerpiece.

Violet's emotional cocktail of fury, fear, and pure helplessness started to make her nauseated. Once or twice the prince's grip on her arm tensed, then relaxed, only to tense again, making her wonder if he was equally distressed about the goings on around them.

Eventually, she cleared her throat. “We aren’t going to that table at the top, are we?”

Exültov huffed a noise, something between a laugh and a grunt of derision. “Where else do you expect a royal to be seated?”

Right, stupid question.

Exültov selected an elaborate copper chair fashioned, ironically, to look like abstract flames, then gestured for her to sit. Once she obliged, the prince and Jhutev sat on either side of her.

She took a moment to take in the splendor of the table settings. Each cup, plate, and piece of cutlery was on par with the extravagant furniture, made of a combination of precious metals and colored jewels. Just one of these items would probably set her up with a mortgage-free home, as well as pay for Solace’s college tuition in full.

Slightly distracted by the extravagant tableware, she noticed her anxiety had started to ebb—until her gaze drifted toward the seven-foot-wide domed bubble in the middle of the table.

“*No*.” Her hand flew to her mouth as Thane looked back at her, Solace clutched tight to his chest.

A vibrant array of tropical ferns, vines, and shrubs surrounded them, their foliage adorned with flowers of all types—hibiscus, bird-of-paradise, heliconia, orchids, and many more she couldn’t name. An impressive collection of animals darted in and out of the flora: parrots, toucans, chameleons, green tree pythons, a stunning array of butterflies, and even a small group of capuchin monkeys. Violet could have spent hours observing the living display, if not for the fact that Thane and Solace were also trapped inside.

She also wasn’t the only one who’d been forced to endure a ridiculous wardrobe change. Both Thane and Solace were dressed in exotic animal furs. Patches of zebra stripes, leopard spots, tiger stripes, shaggy lion's mane, and giraffe hide had been sewn together in a tacky ensemble akin to a Tarzan wannabe and his wild child. A large lion's head lay ungracefully over the flowers at the bottom of the tank. Thane must have been made to wear it on his head and then threw it off the moment he could.

Violet whipped an accusing glare at Exültov. "What's going on? Why are they in there?"

The Nephezai prince slowly turned to look at her, his expression an impenetrable mask.

The temptation to whip out her Veniri tongue became almost unbearable. Struggling to maintain control, she opened her mouth to demand answers, but a guffaw of collective laughter drowned out her words.

A group of Nephezai floated up to their table.

She cast a concerned glance at Thane, who gave a slight shake of his head. He didn't want her to draw attention to him, she guessed, and especially not to Solace. She responded with her own small nod before tearing her eyes away to observe the newcomers.

Instead of being hushed and reverent like the majority of the crowd had been, this group was loud and rowdy, as if already drunk. The five plonked themselves in the chairs on Jhutev's other side, lounging in their seats and continuing their chatter and guffaws. When a parrotfish shifter in the middle of the bunch spotted the prince, he threw out his hands and basically cheered. "Exültov!"

The other four immediately hushed and turned their attention to the prince.

Exültov inclined his head, his expression deadpan. An exchange followed in the Nephezai language.

The parrotfish shifter spoke in a booming and animated way, to which the prince responded with short, clipped phrases. Every now and then, a slight hardness would flicker in Exültov's eyes, especially when the parrotfish and his comrades let out more of their raucous laughter—the parrotfish shifter loudest of all. As the conversation continued, something in the parrotfish's tone struck Violet as slightly sinister.

"What's happening?" she asked Jhutev in a hushed voice.

"His Reverence is being reacquainted with some of his childhood… friends. Yigtheez, the parrotfish shifter in the middle, is currently visiting from a neighboring ocean. Yigtheez and His Reverence used to play a lot together as children, but due to their family dynamics, tension between them began to grow as they got older."

Violet's brows drew together. "Why?"

"Yigtheez's family holds a powerful social position in these oceans. It is no secret they wish to overthrow the Nagahld dynasty and rule in their place. Their ancestors have tried and failed many times in the last few centuries."

Violet was considering Jhutev's revelation when the five suddenly looked directly at her, making her heart rate spike. Yigtheez's comrades narrowed their eyes, as if they'd just discovered something putrid sitting at their table. One of the females, a mantis shrimp shifter, mumbled a phrase Violet didn't even want to understand.

The prince fired back a remark in an authoritative tone, and the mantis shrimp shifter dropped her head into a humble bow.

Yigtheez, however, held eye contact with Violet for several seconds, his gaze calculating. Then he finally shrugged his shoulders and said something that had all his comrades laughing again.

The group turned its attention back to the prince—all except one, a viperfish shifter seated next to Jhutev. He now had his gaze fixed on the Meruvo, bulbous eyes gleaming with what Violet could only describe as pure greed.

When the rest of the table guests launched back into raucous chatter among themselves, the viperfish shifter leaned closer to Jhutev and said something in a low voice.

The Meruvo stiffened.

When he made no further response, the viperfish shifter grinned, his razor-sharp teeth gleaming. He then picked up one of the knives from the table in an overly casual manner that made Violet wary. She glanced at the others, but no one else appeared to have noticed anything wrong. The prince had his steely gaze locked on Yigtheez and was paying them no attention.

Should she say something?

The viperfish murmured something else to Jhutev. His words held a coaxing edge, but the glint in his eyes suggested he was being far from civil. He angled the tip of the blade toward the Meruvo.

Jhutev slowly recoiled as the knife moved closer to his neck.

When Violet was sure the blade was about to slice through Jhutev's flesh, she slammed her fist on the table.

15
GLIXUS MERGING

The trills of the early birds grew denser and louder, especially when the rooster chimed in. After Nathan's night-time revelations, he'd been completely unable to drag himself back to bed and attempt to sleep. Worry, anxiety, and more unanswered questions had formed a colossal vortex in his core.

After realizing Thane and Sagan—and, he was certain, also Violet—had traveled in a vehicle, he'd gone back to borrow Lazareth's car to follow the road he suspected they'd taken. But then he came to the place the road split. Some tracks led to deeper parts of the forest, often used by hikers and campers. Another, more secluded road led to the ocean, where one could eventually find some lazy beachside towns. The most used roads headed inland toward bigger cities.

Nathan had driven down the more frequented tracks first, aiming for any logical direction Sagan might have gone. Perhaps back to Rivermyre? Or a nearby hunter hideout? Whenever his Veniri tracking instincts felt the trail had gone cold, he'd backtrack and try another road. Maybe Sagan had taken Violet and Thane to the closest town about a half hour down the highway. Maybe they'd needed fuel before making the two-hour journey back to the city.

On and on, Nathan's mind had swirled with different scenarios—guesses where they could have gone. And soon, he realized that was all he was doing: guessing. Somewhere along his nighttime travels, he'd gotten too caught up in his head. He'd forgotten to put his emotions aside, the way he used to when he was a detective.

When the fuel light had blinked on, he was forced to return right back to where Lazareth's car had been parked.

He got out and stood beside the car for a long time.

The details of what happened after were a little blurred. Somehow he'd managed to follow the weaving pathways back into the shire, even as his mind churned with all the possibilities, all the horrors, all the awful things that could have happened.

Violet, Thane, *and Sagan* were still missing.

He needed to try harder to find them. His skills in human form were useless compared to his Veniri tracking abilities, yet the memory of his crystallized tongue sent a shiver of fear down his spine. He'd been too freaked out to attempt any more Veniri tracking after that.

Nathan growled in frustration at his own cowardice. He should be doing everything he could to find them, damn the consequences…

Yet how much longer did he have left to search before the ongoing crystallization brought his demise—

Stop it!

Nathan thumped his forehead with the heel of his hand, determined not to let fear incapacitate him.

"Nathan?"

His body jolted at the unexpected hand on his shoulder. He turned to find Gus taking a step back, his eyes wide and hands up.

"Sorry, I didn't mean to startle you."

"Oh, no. You didn't. I was, uh…" Nathan looked around. It took a few beats for him to realize he was back at the graveyard, kneeling by Dawn's headstone.

"Are you okay, Nathan?"

He turned his attention back to Gus. Lines of concern creased the young man's face. It wasn't right. Gus was way too young for worry to mar his features.

"Uh… yeah, I'm okay." Nathan's words were flat. They both knew he certainly wasn't okay. Who was these days? He scrubbed at his face in a failed attempt to wipe away his exhaustion. The bandages around his head had long ago unraveled in the night; he hadn't bothered covering his crystallized flesh while everyone else in the shire was asleep. He was lucky it was Gus who found him.

"How long have you been out here?"

Nathan blinked. That was a good question. Come to think of it, he couldn't remember deciding to visit Dawn's grave, let alone the walk over.

"I couldn't sleep," he said in the end. After a slight hesitation, he decided to recount his discoveries, or at least his suspicions about what happened to Violet and Thane.

Gus whistled. "Sagan was here, huh? Did he escape from Xabat Biogenetics, or was he released?"

"No idea," said Nathan with a shake of his head.

"Well, either way, it's a relief that Violet and Thane weren't here during the blasts. We should get Autumn in on the search, use her hacking skills to track them down. In the meantime, you could try your Veniri abilities again, even if it's just to narrow down which direction they might've gone."

Nathan's shoulders slumped.

"What? What's wrong?"

He couldn't bring himself to meet Gus's gaze.

"Hang on a second." Gus's voice held an edge of worry.

"To find out what happened to Violet and Thane, did you have to haze into Veniri form?"

"No... not entirely," Nathan mumbled.

"What happened?"

Nathan recognized the "down to business" tone Gus had often used while helping his mother in the infirmary, a side of him he hadn't seen since the bombings. It was kind of nice to see hints of the old Gus returning.

With a bit more prompting, Nathan finally fessed up about the crystallized surface of his Veniri forked tongue.

"Oh no... does this mean the crystallization is now affecting the rest of your Veniri form? Your lungs... heart... brain?"

A shiver ricocheted down Nathan's spine at the question he himself hadn't been brave enough to voice. He shrugged. "It was the first time I'd hazed since the blasts."

"Hmm... I wonder what that means." Gus absentmindedly fidgeted with his turquoise wrist cuff. The faded fabric had frayed in spots, and a few strands of beads and charms clinked together with each flick of his fingers. Finally, he heaved a deep sigh. "I wish Mom was here. She would know how to go about testing your progressing stages of crystallization. She'd know how to get more answers."

Nathan looked over at the tombstone. "I'm sorry. I've monopolized your mom for a while now. You were probably hoping to spend some time with her, and I should..." He stood up. "I'll leave you with her."

"Actually," said Gus, before Nathan could take a step. "I came looking for you."

"Oh." He dug his hands into his pockets. "What's up?"

"I think... I might be ready to find out more about what Mom left me." Gus held up the golden Glixus.

A confusing mix of grief and curiosity surged through

Nathan as he looked upon Dawn's precious artifact. "Okay," he said carefully. "How do you want to go about it?"

Gus paused for a few moments. "I know I asked for your help in training me to be a Pliokai, and as much as I still think I'm going to need your help with the hazing side of things, I'm also wondering if… perhaps Mom—" His voice hitched, and he cleared his throat. "Mom might be the best person I can learn my heritage from."

Nathan nodded. "I can't think of anyone better to teach you."

"In that case, can you come with me back to the hacker hut, to talk it through with Autumn and… my dad?"

"Absolutely."

Gus rolled back his shoulders, as if releasing a heavy burden. For the first time in a long time, he cracked a smile. A small one, but it was a start.

Nathan clapped him on the back. "Let's go find your family then, plick."

"*Plick*?"

"Yeah, sorry, bad joke."

"I'm not sure I get it."

"It's the derogatory term hunters use for the Pliokai. They've come up with an insult for almost all the shifter species."

Gus quirked an eyebrow. "Yeah, but plick? It sounds a lot like—"

"I know," said Nathan, steering Gus through the graveyard. "Here's your first lesson in being a shifter: hunters are jerks."

* * *

"Wow, so you seriously think Violet and Thane are still

alive?" Autumn waved her arm in an arc. "And they're out there, somewhere, with Sagan?"

Once again, Nathan nodded in confirmation.

"And Sagan somehow escaped from Xabat?" Tio asked.

"I believe so."

"But how?" asked Autumn.

"Not a clue."

After a moment, Tio shrugged. "It is Sagan we're talking about. That hunter is pretty cunning."

Hope shone on Autumn's face. "If Violet and Thane were somewhere in Maple Shire during the explosions, we surely would have discovered some trace of them by now. So it makes sense they weren't here."

"That's still a worry though," added Lazareth. "They could be in some kind of trouble, especially if no one has heard from them."

"And what about Sagan?" asked Tio. "If he managed to get out of that underground lab and came back here, why only take Violet and Thane? Did they try again to rescue Solace? If so, why not tell any of us?"

Autumn wove through the stretcher beds to reach her computer desk. "If they returned to Xabat Biogenetics, then I'll be able to find some kind of proof from their security footage."

"And make sure you search the nearby towns' traffic cameras," said Gus. "Just in case they didn't go back there."

"Already on it," she answered, tapping away on her keyboard.

"Uh, before you get too far into it though, do you think we could have a chat?" Gus shot a nervous glance at Nathan, who gave him an encouraging nod. All eyes then fell on the illuminated golden cylinder Gus pulled from his pocket. "Can you help me with this, please?"

When Autumn hesitated, Tio jumped up. "I can start searching for the others while you help Gus."

She gave him a warm smile and relinquished her spot at the computer to go sit next to her cousin.

When En'gorr suggested he and his three guards give them some privacy, Gus shook his head. "I think you guys should stay. I'm guessing I've got a lot to learn, and the people in this room are the only ones I can trust with this stuff."

"If it pleases you, August," said En'gorr. He spoke to the three other Jiovis shifters in their mother tongue, and they all gave Gus a respectful nod.

Then Gus looked over at Lazareth, whose apprehensive expression melted into relief when his son waved him over.

Lazareth gave Gus a big bear hug and whispered something Nathan couldn't quite catch, but from the expression on both their faces when they pulled apart, all was okay between them. They sat down, side by side, on the edge of one of the stretcher beds.

Lazareth gestured to the Glixus. "Would you mind if I…"

Gus nodded with a knowing smile and handed the ornate cylinder to his dad, who handled it like delicate spun glass. The golden cybernetic pattern over the surface of the tube pulsed and glowed under Lazareth's touch.

"Wow." He held the Glixus up so everyone else could also see. "You know, this is one of those times I can verify that your mother was just as beautiful on the inside as she was on the outside."

"Agreed," said Autumn.

"Did you know… about Mom?" Gus worried his lip with his teeth as he glanced at Lazareth.

"That your mother was a Pliokai? I found out a little before we started dating."

Autumn sat down on Lazareth's other side. "How did you take it when she told you?"

Lazareth smiled. His tear-filled eyes remained on the Glixus, but his focus was on something far away. "I was smitten the moment I laid eyes on Dawn. She was the most beautiful, intelligent, brilliant person I'd ever met. Nothing she could have told me would have scared me away—not that she was pregnant with another man's child, not even something outrageous and crazy, like her being a shape-shifter associated with Pluto. I knew right from the start I wanted to be with her always."

He twirled the Glixus in his hand. Bright morning sunlight streaming through a gap in the curtains caught in the reflective golden details.

"I've seen Dawn's Glixus a few times before. She showed it to me when she first explained everything. Learning about her being a Pliokai just confirmed to me how magnificent your mother was. In the end, the only thing I struggled with was the idea that shifters were actually real. And understanding all the different types was a bit of a head spin."

"Yeah, no kidding," chuckled Gus.

Lazareth gave him a sideways hug. "Convincing your mom to marry me, and the added bonus of raising you, was the best thing that ever happened to me. And regardless of whatever questionable decisions you think your mother might have made, everything she did was to protect you."

A small divot appeared between Gus's eyebrows. "Yeah, that's what I'm finding the hardest to understand. Why all the secrecy? Why the need to protect me? How come you and Autumn knew but not me? Did Uncle Cruz and Aunty Skye know? Was Mom ever planning on telling me?"

"Yes, both Autumn's parents knew. And the reason for all the secrets was because your mother was in hiding… from her own kind."

Gus's eyebrows shot up, though Autumn didn't look half as surprised.

"You knew about this too?" Gus asked her.

"I suspected. No one told me anything outright, but there were a few hints along the way. In the end, I started doing my own research to try and find out what was going on."

"And what did you find?"

Autumn pursed her lips. "Not a whole lot. The Pliokai—all the shifters, for that matter—are pretty good at keeping their existence a secret, even from the deep dark corners of the web. But I did find out who she was hiding from."

"Who?" Gus, Tio, and Nathan said in unison.

With a slight grimace, Autumn glanced at Lazareth. Only when he gave her an approving nod did she continue. "Aunty Dawn was hiding from her own mother… and from your biological father, Gus."

"Why?" Gus asked after a few heartbeats of silence.

"That I don't know."

Everyone returned their attention to Lazareth.

He cleared his throat. "Well, one reason was that Dawn didn't want to be forced into the marriage her mother had arranged. She also didn't want to be forced into Pliokai politics, especially into the leadership role of Pre-Eminent, which her mother had been grooming her for since birth."

"Oh…" Gus frowned in confusion. "What's a… *Pre-Eminent?*"

"It's basically the leader of all Pliokai," said Lazareth. "The Pliokai value knowledge and skill over all else. The more knowledge and skill one attains, the more likely it is for a Pliokai to be elevated to the role of Pre-Eminent. And one way a Pliokai can fast-track their education is to inherit a Glixus from various others."

Lazareth looked down at the golden cylinder in his hands. "Around the time Dawn found out she was pregnant with you, Gus, she was horrified to discover her mother had orchestrated the murders of several Pliokai and obtained their skills and knowledge to give to Dawn."

"Whoa. So, basically, Dawn's mother was stealing other Pliokai's 'brains' and giving them to her daughter." Tio screwed up his nose. "Is it just me, or does that seem kinda gross?"

"It sounds awesome. Just imagine it." Autumn's eyes twinkled, her gaze far away as she pondered the possibilities. "How many great minds have there been throughout history? And how many of those minds have gone to waste, so to speak, the moment they've passed away? Einstein, Marie Curie, Galileo, Ada Lovelace... Imagine being able to download their minds into your own."

Tio's brow furrowed. "Who's Ada Lovelace?"

"Duh, she's only the first person ever to have published an algorithm intended for a computer. Only it took about a century for someone to appreciate her genius."

Tio nodded as if he understood, but his expression said otherwise.

"So Mom didn't like the idea of acquiring, uh... Glixuses? Glixiai... or whatever, from other dead Pliokai?" Gus asked.

"The plural is Glixees," said Lazareth. "And no. Dawn detested the idea of other Pliokai being murdered for her sake. In Pliokai culture, stolen knowledge is filthy knowledge. It is highly illegal to take one's Glixus either prematurely or without the owner's blessing. The punishment is not only death but also the destruction of the offending Pliokai's Glixus. The eradication of a Glixus is the most shameful thing that can happen to a Pliokai and their family legacy."

"Is that what happened to Aunty Dawn's mother? Did someone find out what she was doing?" Autumn asked.

"Yes and no." Lazareth readjusted on the stretcher bed.

"Dawn's mother and the man she had arranged to marry Dawn were coconspirators. The Pre-Eminent role can be held by a single Pliokai, but it's preferably held by a married couple who both share the title equally.

"When Dawn found out what her mother was doing, she went straight to her fiancé, only to discover he was in on the tangled web of murders. He had conned her—told her he loved her, then turned on her when she threatened his plans. Before Dawn could tell anyone in authority, her fiancé and mother were out for blood. They would have silenced her permanently rather than risk their own necks, so Dawn ran and went into hiding.

"Long story short, Skye found her. They were both seventeen when Skye's family basically adopted Dawn, which solidified her new identity and eventually allowed her to study medicine. What Dawn learned at medical school was a pittance compared to the wealth of knowledge she'd already acquired, thanks to her mother, but Dawn still insisted on starting afresh and acquiring her medical knowledge ethically. Unfortunately, after a while it became clear that all of the stolen Glixees were taking their toll on Dawn's mind."

"How do you mean?" Gus asked. "Was she becoming, like... possessed or something?"

"No, nothing like that. The Glixees don't take over one's mind or change someone's personality. They don't affect the basic essence of a Pliokai. They just enhance the intellectual parts of a Pliokai's mind. But Dawn was becoming overwhelmed. The over-influx of information nearly drove her insane."

Lazareth wrapped an arm around Autumn's shoulders and squeezed her tight. "However, at the tender age of five, our Autumn over here began showing how adept she was with computers and technology. It turns out this little munchkin had overheard and understood way more of our conversations than we anticipated. I'll never forget the day she brought out her new laptop, which was almost half the size she was at the time, and offered to help. 'You fix people. I fix your brain' is what you said to Dawn." He smiled warmly at Autumn. "It seemed almost too crazy to consider, but Dawn later told me there was something about your determination to help that led her to take the chance.

"I've got no idea how she did it, I still don't understand all that computer-techy stuff, but Autumn was able to offload all the extra mind clutter from Dawn's Glixus—which, by the way, no Pliokai has ever dared to do, due to the risk of diminishing their intellectual and social status."

Autumn smiled big and proud. "I remember those early days. I thought Aunty Dawn was like some kind of robot."

"Okay," said Gus. "I guess I can understand a few reasons why Mom did what she did. But I still don't understand how all of this led to me being... can I use the word *brainwashed*?"

Autumn's grin fell away.

Lazareth's expression grew grave. "When you were about five, Gus, Dawn's ex-fiancé somehow found out she had been pregnant with his son. He came searching, to kill Dawn and to take his son back. Up until then, we had only kept your Pliokai existence a secret from the rest of the shire. There didn't seem to be any reason to hide your Pliokai traits while you were at home with family. But fear drove Dawn to protect you as much as possible. She thought it best to raise you as human and for everyone else, even you, to treat you as one. So she made the tough decision to wipe your memory."

After a moment, Gus scoffed. "Yeah, okay. I can sort of get the *Eternal Sunshine of the Spotless Mind* treatment. But why did Autumn still get to remain all-knowing?"

"As unfair as it may seem, Autumn had become a key part in helping Dawn with her ongoing 'decluttering' issues," explained Lazareth.

"Trust me, Gus, I wanted to tell you so many times, but I thought it would be better if you heard it from your mom instead of me," said Autumn.

Gus's expression grew tense. "Yeah, well, it's a little too late to hear it from my mother now."

"Are you sure about that?" Autumn pointed to the Glixus still in Lazareth's hands.

Gus twisted his fabric cuff around and around his wrist; the sewn-on beads and trinkets jangled. "You're right, no point trying to delay this any longer." He expelled a deep sigh. "Autumn, would you please help me with this?"

She gave him a warm smile. "I thought you'd never ask, cuz."

Lazareth handed her the golden cylinder, then he, En'gorr, and the three Jiovis guards all moved back so Autumn and Gus could sit beside Tio at the computer. Nathan stayed leaning against the wall by the door.

"Now, I don't need to use my computer… not to start with, at least," began Autumn. "It's just a precaution, in case you have any problems trying to fuse Aunty Dawn's Glixus with yours."

Gus's nod was a little stiff. "'Fuse,' huh? Does it hurt?"

"I don't know. Maybe. I've never seen the Glixus-merging side of things. I only helped out with the decluttering for Aunty Dawn and the…" She pressed her lips together.

"The erasure of my memory," Gus finished.

After a beat, Autumn nodded, her expression deeply apologetic.

"It's okay. You did what you thought was right." Despite his words, Gus's tone still held an edge of resentment. "So, how do we do this?"

"Aunty Dawn explained the theory to me. This will be my first time doing the merging, but I'm pretty sure I'll be able to manage it." She held up a hand, hesitated for a moment, then rested her fingers against Gus's temple. A vibrant gold light glimmered under her fingertips, then a pulse of illumination radiated out beneath the surface of Gus's skin. The glowing pattern resembled the organic circuit board design that decorated Dawn's own Glixus.

"Whoa, cool," said Tio.

En'gorr and his guards watched in wide-eyed amazement. Nathan assumed his own expression looked much the same.

Autumn swiveled her fingers—once, twice, five times—until a section of Gus's temple spiraled open, revealing a circular opening about two inches in diameter. With a steady hand, she reached inside and pulled out a golden cylinder.

"What are you doing?" Tio exclaimed. "Are you pulling out his brain?"

"Relax," said Autumn. "Gus is fine. He can still function without a Glixus."

"Oh..." said Tio. "Does it hurt?"

Gus shook his head. "No. It's a little strange though. It's kinda like when you have an important thought you *need* to share with someone, but then it disappears suddenly, and no matter how hard you try, you can't remember what you were going to say."

The room fell quiet as all attention turned to Autumn, who held up both Gus's and Dawn's Glixees. The circuit board patterns flickered, glowing brighter where her hands came in contact with them. She fluttered her fingers over the length of both tubes at the same time, almost like a flutist playing a complicated tune on two separate instruments. Then came a subtle dual *ting*, followed by a sound Nathan could only describe as bio-mechanical whirring.

Autumn held her hands out in front of her, and for a second, both the Glixees sat on her flattened palms.

Gus and Tio gasped when the two cylinders rose several

inches in the air, making slow rotations above Autumn's hands.

A new kind of whirring commenced, this time in a steampunk-esque melody. Multiple sections of each cylinder spun or twisted, then removed themselves in midair, revealing layer after intricate golden layer within. Once the last layer parted, Nathan's breath caught in his throat.

Hidden at the center of each Glixus were several glowing tangles of a dense, writhing spiderweb-like substance. Though pea sized at first, once out of the confines of the Glixus, the tangles expanded to the size of small pumpkins, each a different color. Some were in colors Nathan couldn't even name. Dawn's Glixus contained about fifteen tangles, whereas Gus's had only three.

"These are what Dawn called *ethoseez*," explained Lazareth, speaking over the soft hum and crackle each tangle emitted. "Each is a different component of Dawn's mind, things like memories, knowledge banks, interests, passions, and other mental traits." He pointed to Gus's ethoseez. "You are still young, Gus. The number of ethoseez is dependent on how much you learn and experience over your lifetime. Of course, that number can be increased by fusing other Pliokai's Glixees with yours."

Autumn pointed to some grayed-out strands within Dawn's tangles. They outnumbered the glowing strands about two to one. "These are the ones I helped deactivate. As you can see, I couldn't erase them entirely. They've left a permanent scar. But Aunty Dawn said she was able to function much better regardless."

She gave a sad smile to Gus, then to Lazareth, who gestured for Autumn to proceed.

With her hands now free, she gently drew together two ethoseez—one of Gus's and one of Dawn's—and again fluttered her fingers over the tangles' surface.

"What are you doing now?" Gus asked.

"I'm programming the fusion process."

Tio cocked his head. "How are you doing that?"

"Easy." Autumn never took her eyes off the glowing tangles. "It's just like the basic concept of programming: you create a step-by-step list of commands for a computer. It turns out a Glixus essentially uses the same concept."

"Oh…" Gus's brow creased in concentration. "So, were Glixees inspired by computers or something?"

"I think it's the other way around. Computers were inspired by the fundamentals of a Glixus. At least, after working with both, that's my hunch."

"Hang on a second." Tio rolled his office chair a little closer to Autumn. "Go back to the part about programming. I don't get it. What programming language are you using?"

"What do you mean what programming language?" She gestured to the two ethoseez she was working on. "Can't you see the code?"

Everyone leaned in a little closer. Even Nathan squinted at the tangled masses.

"Nope," said Tio, finally shaking his head.

"Oh." Autumn continued fluttering her fingers along the ethoseez, almost as if they were computer keyboards. "Maybe because I've been working with Glixus programming since I was a kid, it's easier for me to read and decipher."

The moment Autumn spoke her last word, long, thin tendrils of Dawn's spiderweb-like tangles reached out for Gus's. In an instant, the tendrils latched on, and with a sight-searing flash of gold light, the clumps all merged within Gus's deconstructed Glixus. The three ethoseez hovering within had now become eighteen.

The tangled masses then snapped back to their previous pea size. Gus's Glixus interlocked back together with a melodic *ting-ting-tingle-tik-tang* before dropping back into Autumn's hand. Dawn's Glixus also interlocked back together, but with a hollow *ting-tang* sound. Its inner glow from before had also vanished.

"Dawn's cylinder looks like it's dead." The moment he said it, Tio shot a pained glance at Lazareth and Gus. "Sorry, I didn't mean it like that."

Neither acknowledged his comment.

"Is this normal?" Gus asked, pointing to Dawn's Glixus.

"Yes, very normal," said Lazareth. He gently took the dull cylinder from Autumn and hugged it to his chest. "This is now just a physical reminder of the amazing woman your mother was."

Autumn held up Gus's Glixus. "Are you ready?"

Gus studied the vibrant cylinder in Autumn's hand, then nodded. He tilted his head so she could glide it back into place through the circular opening at his temple.

"When I close the Glixus chamber, there's going to be a jolt with the influx of new ethoseez," Autumn warned. "It could be painful or slightly uncomfortable. Apparently it's different for each Pliokai."

Gus went rigid as Autumn twisted her fingers to make the chamber close. His eyes flickered shut, his head snapped back, and his hands flew up to clutch the sides of his head. The glowing pattern beneath his skin pulsed rapidly over his face and down his neck.

He gritted out a strangled cry, then sucked in a breath and became silent.

"Wow..." he said after several tense moments. "*Wow!* I can really see her memories. I can see everything—No! Not see. It's like I'm experiencing them myself, but... I can still tell they're not my memories."

"What do you see?" Lazareth asked.

"I can see..." Gus's closed eyes squeezed tighter. "Uh, it's a bit of a jumble, like my mind is being flooded with too many things at once. Except… there's one memory stronger than the others. I can see a vibrant memory of Mom writing a letter." His face slackened with sudden realization, then his lip began to tremble. "Oh… it's a letter to me. She's explaining everything, even the fact that she was going to burn the letter after she wrote it, but this memory would still tell me all I need to know. Mom knew there was a high chance she'd die before she was ready to tell me everything, but she assumed it would be because that ex-fiancé dude or her mother finally found her."

Gus rubbed his eyes, and Lazareth leaned over to hug his son.

"Mom's also added another memory giving me strict instructions to get Nathan to teach me to haze and control my Pliokai form."

Nathan gave a small smile. Even though he and Gus had already discussed the idea, the fact that it was one of Dawn's dying wishes made it even more of an honor. "Absolutely. We'll start whenever you're ready."

16
A RELATIVELY OBNOXIOUS EVENT

THE VIPERFISH SHIFTER JOLTED IN HIS SEAT.

Only when Violet locked fierce glares with him did she notice her world was awash in teal. His fleeting glance at her fist confirmed that flames also licked along her hands. Even in the water, her Magneii fire was starting to scorch the table.

"Is there a problem, Frizgitl?" Prince Exültov turned his attention to the viperfish shifter.

Even Yigtheez and his posse had become quiet, waiting for what would happen next.

Slowly, the viperfish shifter broke eye contact with Violet. A flash of silver caught her eye as, with quick sleight of hand, he removed the knife from Jhutev's neck and hid it out of sight. He gave the prince a humble shake of his head, uttering a phrase she guessed was some kind of apology, or some excuse for Violet's erratic behavior.

She wasn't sure if Exültov could have seen the viperfish shifter's knife from where he sat, but when the prince spoke next in precise syllables, his tone demanded the altercation go no further.

After a heartbeat, Frizgitl gave a single nod, but the final gaze he sent Violet and even Jhutev warned this was far from over. Without another word, he rose from his place and swam over to a seat at the other side of the group, farthest from Jhutev.

Only then did Violet extinguish her flames.

The prince didn't say anything more, to her or Jhutev. But he did regard the two with slight unease before fixing his attention elsewhere.

Violet heaved in a few breaths, regretting that she'd ever agreed to accompany the prince to this banquet. Things were already going terribly wrong, and they hadn't even brought out the food yet.

"Are you okay?" she asked Jhutev, leaning closer so only he could hear.

"Do not concern yourself about me, Miss Hybrid."

"Why can't I?"

A softness overcame Jhutev's celestial features, and he regarded Violet with a thoughtful gaze. Finally, he said, "I am fine. Thank you for asking, Miss Hybrid." He gave her a strained smile. "It has been quite a long time since someone showed concern for my well-being. I'd almost forgotten how to recognize sincerity."

"Perhaps you and I should stick together."

"I think I would appreciate that, Miss Hybrid."

"You don't need to call me that. Just call me Violet."

His smile grew a little wider. "Indeed I shall, Miss Violet."

"It's just Violet. You don't need to include the 'miss.'"

"That is kind of you, but my mother always insisted I show the utmost courtesy to everyone." Jhutev leaned a little closer and lowered his tone. "Especially to those whom I actually like."

Violet gave him a tight-lipped smile, trying hard not to

show too much hope over the budding friendship. Was it possible Jhutev could help her figure out a way to escape?

She flicked her eyes to the tank in the middle of the table. Thane's concerned expression bore into her; most likely the incident with the viperfish shifter had alarmed him. She gave a small nod, hoping to confirm she was all right.

The tension in Thane's shoulders relaxed but not by much. Still cuddling Solace close, he settled on a swing of twisted vines. A small cradle made of interwoven vines and leaves hung from one of the boughs higher up, but he glared at it as if it were made of stinging nettle. The four capuchin monkeys, on the other hand, had discovered the thrilling contraption, and Thane periodically had to duck if he didn't want to get slogged in the head.

Violet bit the inside of her lip, trying hard not to smile.

The jovial conversation from the group had reached a new decibel. Yigtheez, the parrotfish shifter, slapped at the table in an explosion of laughter. "Oh, Frizgitl, my friend. You are far too funny."

Violet leaned closer to Jhutev. "Can you explain something to me?"

"Of course, Miss Violet, I will try my best."

"I've noticed the Nephezai use a mixture of languages. Sometimes I can understand what's being said, and other times I'm assuming the Nephezai language is being spoken. Why mix things up? Surely it's not for my benefit."

"Not exactly, Miss Violet. The use of an air breather language is fashionable among the Nephezai. The Nephezai language is perhaps considered formal and perhaps a little… old fashioned. And as you've likely noticed, there are times it is a conscious choice to speak in Nephezai to ensure you don't understand what is being said."

"Yeah, I figured not many of these shifters would be keen

on me listening in on their conversations. But what about the prince's children? They weren't speaking in Nephezai."

Jhutev nodded. "The young prince and princess prefer to communicate in your air breather language. And His Reverence encourages it."

"He does? Why?"

"He..." Jhutev cast a fleeting glance the prince's way. "He wishes to prepare his children for whatever they may encounter in their future."

Violet frowned. That seemed a little cryptic. "One more thing," she added. "I forgot to ask, what is this banquet in celebration of?"

"In my opinion, there isn't any reason to celebrate."

She looked up, startled that the prince had been the one to answer.

Exültov reached for a glass flask that held a shimmering navy liquid. A bizarre kind of metal valve wedged in the narrow neck seemed to keep seawater from leaking in and the navy blue from leaking out. He raised the flask to his lips and drank straight from the odd-looking valve.

"For millennia, we Nephezai have been stuck in our ways... always in need of celebrating our so-called superiority." The prince plonked the flask back down onto the table. "Even while banished to the bottom of the ocean, we still continue to convince ourselves we are above all the other shifter species. Yet it was that kind of thinking that got us into this banishment mess in the first place."

"Careful, Reverence," Jhutev said in a hushed voice. "There may be keen ears close by. You don't know who will repeat what you say to your father."

Exültov snorted. "Let them repeat what they like."

A hand slapped down on his shoulder. Violet glanced up to find it belonged to the parrotfish shifter.

"Ah, Exültov, dear friend, I fear we've had a rocky start to this event. You must excuse my new friend Frizgitl and his fascination with your Meruvo. I've only just recently explained to him the benefits of keeping such a pet. My new friend Frizgitl has a lot to learn, since I took him into my household, along with the very few from his village who survived a hunter attack. You, of course, know what these Nephezai who live on the outskirts of the city are like. So naive and unrefined, barely better than Ügovs."

"*You* live on the outskirts of the city, Yigtheez." Exültov gave a tight-lipped smile. "You can't fool me into thinking you see yourself as naive or unrefined, regardless of how benevolent your so-called charity appears to those lesser than you. You've always thought so highly of yourself your head may as well be in the clouds."

"Better one's head in the clouds than in the sand like your father, wouldn't you say, dear friend?"

For a long moment, Exültov leveled a contemplative expression at Yigtheez, without offering a response. There seemed to be something in the parrotfish shifter's bold statement the prince didn't care to dispute. Instead, he reached for the flask of shimmering navy liquid and took a long swig.

Yigtheez smirked, then peered down at Violet with open interest. "Tell me, dear prince, what has brought you out of your hidey-hole? Surely it's more than just honoring us with your presence this evening?"

"Yes, it has been a while since we'd been graced with an appearance from our charming Reverence," cooed the mantis shrimp shifter. She flounced her hips from side to side as she glided through the water to sit in the spare seat next to Exültov. "This seat isn't taken, is it?"

"Of course that seat isn't taken, dear Giztherrel," said Yigtheez. "It's not as though she who used to sit at his right hand is able to claim her place anymore."

Jhutev gave a small jolt.

Exültov's grip on the glass flask tightened, his knuckles going white. "You dare speak ill of my wife?"

"Me? Speak ill of the late Princess Nepthyz? Never, dear prince." Yigtheez placed a hand on his chest. "It hurts you'd think I would ever do so. I'm merely stating facts for the benefit of our friend Giztherrel. Perhaps I am mistaken?" He covered his mouth with one hand, eyes wide in mock innocence. "Is the seat not available? Has it been claimed without my knowledge?"

"Careful, Yigtheez." Exültov's soft voice sent shudders down Violet's spine. "Loosen your tongue too much and you may lose it altogether."

"I mean no offense, Your Reverence." The parrotfish shifter bent at the waist and swung his arms out in a dramatic bow. The exaggerated movements disturbed the water enough that Violet bobbed from side to side on her chair. "However," he added with a pout, "I do believe it's a shame we can no longer banter like we used to as children."

"Some of us had to grow up. Childish behaviors needed to be set aside for the good of the realm."

"Ah, yes… 'the good of the realm.'" Yigtheez leaned over Violet to retrieve the flask of navy-blue liquid directly in front of her. "It has been a while since I've been back here, in the glorious realm of Scylorethyz. Business endeavors have kept me away for longer than I'd intended. I'd almost forgotten how *humbly* everyone stoops to ensure all is done 'for the good of the realm.'"

"While you're here, what exactly are your intentions, Yigtheez?" Exültov said, narrowing his eyes.

"Tonight, I intend to strike formalities from my mind and embrace all the frivolities I've missed. Hysterically, gluttonously, and lecherously." Yigtheez gave the prince a sly grin, then took a swig from the flask he'd pinched from Violet.

Exültov responded with a taut smile. "By all means,

Yigtheez. Just ensure your viperfish friend doesn't forget the Meruvo belongs to me."

Yigtheez chuckled and patted Exültov on the shoulder. "Don't worry, my dear prince. I've never forgotten the lesson of what happens when someone plays with your toys." He subtly emphasized the word *toys* by turning to look at Violet with confident curiosity. Then he said a phrase in the Nephezai tongue, and both he and the mantis shrimp shifter returned to their seats on the other side of the table.

Several long moments later, the tension in Violet's neck and shoulders remained. She had a feeling this dinner would provide no opportunity for her to relax her guard.

More marine shifters swam up to the topmost table, each new arrival more glamorous than the next; soon, almost all the seats were taken. The chatter among the underwater shifters was difficult for Violet to follow, although every so often one would look in her direction and hiss a few familiar words and phrases she'd overheard over the past few days. She was beginning to believe some of the familiar phrases meant something particularly nasty.

A hush fell over the group, and after a few seconds, everyone in the entire room had gone silent. All faces turned upward. Violet tilted her head back too to see what had captured everyone's attention.

Violet's table, although at the topmost tier, was not at the very top of the cylindrical dining room. The circular walls spanned much, much higher. King Qozzlotl descended through the water, followed by an entourage of decorated guards.

Perhaps in other circumstances, she would have been awed by the exuberant jewels and adornments the king wore, but her focus immediately fused on the purple spangle hanging dead center at his chest, surrounded by at least a dozen other golden chains and bejeweled necklaces.

When the giant eel shifter reached the table, everyone else remained silent until he took his place one seat away from Exültov. The seat on his right remained unoccupied, just like the one to the right of the prince.

The two unoccupied seats stuck out glaringly at a table full of guests. Violet couldn't decide if she admired the homage to loved ones or if the constant reminder of their absence was just more salt to the deep wound of grief.

The four guards who had followed the king down lined up a few feet away from him, all at attention, staring directly ahead.

Qozzlotl reached for a glass flask served to him by a dolphin shifter cupbearer, and the shimmering navy liquid sloshed inside as he raised it above his head. He called out a phrase in the Nephezai tongue, which boomed around the room. Everyone else raised their own flask and repeated the phrase, then all took a drink.

Violet couldn't join in the ritual even if she wanted to, as Yigtheez had already taken her own flask of whatever everyone was drinking.

Qozzlotl then raised his arm. With a single hand gesture, a number of openings appeared in the coral-encrusted walls. A flurry of servants swarmed out to the tables, serving platter after platter of food, each one more astounding than the last. Every dish could be considered a work of art—a vibrant mix of colors, shapes, and textures. Despite the cuisine's obscure and unfamiliar nature, it all looked much more delectable than the green goop served to captive creatures in the menagerie.

Violet looked around at what everyone else had been served, and it became apparent no one was eating yet. Instead, all watched and waited while a few servants selected food and laid out platters for the king. The moment the servants darted away, the king gave a nod of his head, and the rest of the Nephezai began eating. A subtle murmur of conversation resumed, accompanied by the tinkling of cutlery.

Violet shot a quick glance at Thane and Solace, and shame immediately drowned out the grumble of her belly. How could she possibly eat any of this wholly appetizing food in front of Thane when all he'd had since their capture was that weird goopy green stuff?

"Do you not find anything to your liking?" Exültov asked.

"Oh, on the contrary, I, uh..." She couldn't stop herself from glancing over at Thane again. "I don't know what to try first from this wonderful selection."

She went to give Exültov an apologetic smile, only to make eye contact with the king. For a split second, Qozzlotl's eyes widened in surprise, as if he'd just then registered who she was. When he turned his attention to the tank in the center of the table, understanding crossed his features, and he glared daggers at Exültov.

The king uttered a phrase to his son, voice mild but words clipped. There was no mistaking his fury.

But the Nephezai prince didn't appear at all intimidated. "I assumed when you practically begged me to choose anyone to accompany me this evening, I had the privilege of doing just that."

"And of all the eligible *Nephezai*, you decided my new pet was the most suitable choice? For the next event, are we to expect another from my collection to accompany you? The baboon? The water buffalo? Or perhaps the skunk? And do you also intend to dress them up in such ghastly attire?"

Violet gritted her teeth. The temptation to fire back her own insults almost slipped past her control. But a single thought of Solace brought her back to her senses—and the real reason she'd agreed to be Exültov's companion.

There had to be some way for her to snatch the purple spangle from the king's neck.

While the heated discussion between Exültov and his father continued, Violet just sat, trying her best to appear casual while she looked around—hoping, wishing for some kind of inspiration to resolve her predicament. But absolutely nothing stood out to her.

Disappointment alternated with frustration. The purple spangle was a mere few feet away, but so were several hundred deadly mother-of-pearl thorns. Even if she did get close enough to swipe her prize, there was no way she'd get away with it, not with four guards and a table full of witnesses.

She may have developed the skill of lock-picking during her fostering years, but sadly she never thought to master thieving.

More waiters brought more platters of food, and the chatter became more animated with every delicacy consumed. To an extent, she was relieved she couldn't understand the likely odious conversations; she couldn't afford being goaded into losing her temper. The underwater shifters had given her no reason to regard them with high esteem. Her opinion only got worse with each passing day of her captivity.

Something about the prince's demeanor, however, suggested he might be different from all the rest. She didn't know yet if that could be a benefit to her or not.

"Are you not hungry, Miss Violet?" Jhutev inquired.

Breaking out of her thoughts, Violet gave him a tight smile. As if on cue, her tummy growled; hungry was an understatement. "I'm not exactly familiar with this cuisine." She leaned toward him and said in a hushed tone, "I suppose it would be too offensive to ask about the possibility of a double cheeseburger, or some kind of deep-fried chicken?

What about some doughnuts? Glazed ones, not the cinnamon kind."

The orbiting stars within his night-sky flesh appeared to glimmer brighter with Jhutev's amused smile. He leaned a little closer and, matching her tone, said, "I am not familiar with anything you've mentioned, and I would recommend you don't make any special requests. However, I do suggest you try some of these."

With a pair of small, delicate silver tongs, Jhutev picked up a few finger-length clusters of vibrant green beads that reminded Violet of caviar.

"What is it?" she asked.

"It's a type of seaweed. I'm not sure what you'd call it in your language, but I've heard one Erathi captive call it 'umibudo,' if that is of any help."

Violet shook her head. "Sorry, it doesn't sound familiar to me."

A delicate voice rang out, speaking a phrase in the Nephezai language. When Violet looked up, she found all eyes at the table were on her.

"We have the finest chefs in all of Scylorethyz and the Midnight Seas. Is none of this worthy of the hybrid's standards?" the mantis shrimp shifter said, voice saccharine sweet.

Neither the prince nor the king interjected, but Violet thought it best not to risk offending Qozzlotl if it could be helped. Not really knowing the best way to respond, she gave a small smile and picked up one of the clusters of tiny green globes. When she went to put it in her mouth, she remembered she still had an air bubble over her head.

Warmth flooded her cheeks, though she wasn't entirely sure if it was from embarrassment or anger at the soft sniggers coming from around the table.

Before Violet could voice the obvious, Jhutev reached out

and pinched her air bubble near where it sealed over her neck. Gently, he pulled the bubble outward, stretching it wide enough to engulf her plate and a few of the nearby platters. He then helped her draw one of her arms inside the bubble as well.

"Wow," said Violet, her mind racing with thoughts and questions over what Jhutev had just done. Still hyperaware of her ever-attentive audience, however, she pushed her musings away and skewered one of the tiny grapelike clusters with her copper fork.

Making a quick prayer that this stuff wasn't poisonous or ghastly to taste, she bit into it. As expected, the tiny bubbles burst in her mouth, just like caviar, releasing a fresh briny flavor with each bite. The mildly salty "taste of the sea" also held a hint of acidity and an undertone of sweetness. Surprised by how much she enjoyed this bizarre underwater food, she immediately took another bite.

Her reaction was clearly not as dramatic as most of the Nephezai had hoped, and they soon lost interest in gawking at her.

The mantis shrimp shifter regarded her with a sly sneer.

Violet let out a huff. So it was going to be like that, was it? Whether she ate the Nephezai food or not, there was no pleasing these shifters. On land or at the bottom of the sea, mean girls were all the same breed of despicable.

She leaned in to speak with Jhutev. "How is it that you could do that with the air bubble? Why didn't it burst?"

"A Nephezai bubble is not the same as what the Erathi are used to on the surface," he answered. "They are much stronger, although you've perhaps already discovered that about your enclosure in the menagerie."

"Hmm..." Violet pondered that for a moment. "How are the bubbles made? Is it just a Nephezai ability, or is light forging involved?"

Jhutev opened his mouth to answer, only to have another voice speak first.

"Why do you ask?"

Violet inwardly cringed as she recognized the regal voice of the king.

"No reason," she rushed to say, forcing herself to turn and acknowledge Qozzlotl. "Before a few days ago, I didn't know the Nephezai existed, and I suppose I'm a little curious."

A fork clattered to a plate, and this time all eyes glared at her.

"What's wrong?" Violet looked between Jhutev and Exültov. "What did I say?"

"Nothing but the obvious," said Exültov, his tone as dry and palatable as ash. "Our punishment is not limited to banishment. We've also been forgotten and erased from all air breathers' minds."

This time when Violet looked at the king, fear creeped down her spine at the rage in his eyes. *Yikes…* Talk about causing the biggest offense without even trying.

Before anyone could react further, a low *boom* sounded from somewhere outside the dining chamber.

All conversation abruptly stopped when an aftershock sent ripples through the water. Plates and cutlery clattered. Hands, tentacles, and claws clutched at chair arms, the edge of the table, or each other.

"What's going on?" Violet whispered to Jhutev.

"It's the Erathi hunters" came the Meruvo's shaky reply.

Fear leached into Violet's core. Hunters? Here? But how?

She then recalled the strange submarine that had disrupted the battle between the Nephezai and the mutant Ügov creatures. When another faint *boom* rattled the dining hall, the gathered Nephezai, in their glamour and glitz, looked just as petrified as they had that day.

Violet caught Thane's taut, angry expression. He had

dealt with more than his fair share of human hunters—she couldn't imagine the horror he'd endured in the gladiator prison. Was it selfish of her to be relieved to have him here, as an ally in protecting Solace?

Not even half a minute had passed when there came a louder *boom-boom-boom,* followed by startled cries from servants and distinguished shifters alike. Some of the Nephezai rose from their chairs.

Violet's own terror spiked.

The king also rose from his chair, arms wide as he spoke over the impending panic. His voice was calm, authoritative, as he motioned for his guests to remain seated. Gradually, everyone returned to their places, though tension and fear still percolated through the seawater.

Another *boom* sounded, though this one was much farther away. Even so, it sent a small tremor through the dining room.

"Who are the hunters shooting at?" Violet asked.

"Perhaps some Nephezai who were out beyond the city stronghold," said Jhutev. His eyes darted around, as if searching for any indication that another boom was about to go off. "The hunters have never been successful in finding the exact location of Scylorethyz, yet I swear their attacks are getting closer and closer with each passing year."

The king instructed the servants to continue bringing out dishes and refilling flasks, but Violet's appetite had dissolved with the first boom. Not wanting to waste this opportunity, though, she swiped a few of the items off her plate and hid them within the mountainous ruffles and frills of her dress. Just because she'd lost her appetite didn't mean Thane wouldn't be starving. And even if he wasn't, they still needed to plan for their escape. Stocking up on food didn't seem like a terrible idea.

There came a lull in the Nephezai's subdued conversations, and Violet looked up to find about a dozen guards had entered the dining chamber from one of the servants' entrances in the coral wall. They swam directly to the king. The leader leaned in and whispered a few short phrases, and Qozzlotl replied with a stern nod.

When the king rose, the entire room directed its full attention to him. He made a short speech and then, without any obvious warning, turned and swam to the top of the chamber, where he'd entered at the beginning of the event. The dozen guards trailed closely behind him.

A pang of disappointment and despair filled Violet. Any chance of retrieving the purple spangle had passed.

The moment Qozzlotl disappeared from sight, Exültov rose from his seat and made his excuses for retiring for the evening, despite the disapproving expressions on several of the guests' faces. Ignoring the raucous exclamations from Yigtheez and his comrades, he gestured to both Violet and Jhutev.

"Time to leave, Miss Violet," Jhutev explained.

Exültov once again held his arm out for her to take. Before he could lead her away, she cast a furtive glance at Thane and her child.

"No need for concern," Exültov said in a low voice. "I will ensure the Veniri and halfling are returned to the menagerie as soon as possible."

Violet gave a small nod of her head, fighting the urge to demand they be released instantly. Who knew which moronic Nephezai would attempt to yank them from the tank for the purpose of cruel entertainment?

Just when she thought her list of problems had reached capacity, Yigtheez caught her attention. A chill clasped her heart. She swore she could feel the parrotfish shifter's unwelcome gaze boring into her back as the Nephezai prince swept her past him.

Only when Exültov had led her back out of the dining chamber and through the hallways did she breathe a small sigh of relief.

"I must commend you, Violet, for enduring a relatively obnoxious event. I'd like to say it's not always like that, but sadly, that was tame compared to the usual undertakings of a formal gathering." Exültov pursed his lips, then forced a small smile. "In any case, your presence has been appreciated. I wish to extend an invitation for you to join me for breakfast. You will be retrieved in the morning for the wardrobe mistress to dress you for the occasion."

Before Violet could muster a response, the prince turned his attention to Jhutev.

"Please escort Violet back to the menagerie. For my own peace of mind, I must go check on my children."

Jhutev had only enough time to reply with "Of course, Your Reverence" before the prince hurried away.

17
CAVE OF CHAOS

"*What!*" Sagan launched himself up, sending his camper chair flying behind him. "What do you mean Maple Shire was bombed?"

The blood drained from Nika's face, leaving her ashen.

A flurry of emotions swarmed through Sagan's core. How? When? He was there less than two weeks ago.

He clutched his head, his fingers digging into his scalp. A sudden fear gripped his insides. How many were wounded or, heavens forbid, killed?

Heavens, no.

"How is everyone? Nathan? Gus? Autumn? Dawn? Lazareth? Tio...?" He rambled off name after name, faster and faster.

"I don't know," Nika said over the top of him. "I wasn't there when it happened. Grandpa may have been happy I returned to the hunters, but the rest of them still didn't trust me. I wasn't privy to a lot of plans and details. I had no idea what was in store for Maple Shire until it was too late."

"*Explain,*" Sagan demanded through gritted teeth.

Nika held up her hands, as if trying to placate a vicious

beast. "All I know is it happened in the middle of the night when everyone was sleeping. The bombs were set off in the community buildings. Chances are no one was in those buildings at that time of night, and everyone might be safe and—"

"You can't know that for sure!" Sagan almost shouted. "When we were there, how many times were we up at all hours of the night, training at the pavilion, planning for Solace's rescue, and everything else we did?"

Only when Nika leaned back in her chair did Sagan realize he'd been advancing on her. But her nervous glances weren't directed at him. Her eyes kept darting to the sleeping children still huddled by his mother.

For a split second, Sagan registered a whimpering sound, but his panic and rage couldn't process what that meant.

Images of blasted buildings, broken bodies littered throughout the wreckage, entered his mind. Every face on the bodies belonged to one of the names he'd listed moments ago.

He'd tried so hard, and yet he'd failed. He'd failed Violet and her daughter. He'd failed his sister, Lyla-Rose. He'd failed his mother. And now he'd failed everyone at Maple Shire.

He glared at Nika. "How could you let this happen?" His roar echoed around the rocky chamber as his rant went on and on; in the end he didn't even know if his shouts were coherent. The white noise of his mental overload sent a shrill squeal through his skull.

Crack!

Nika's fist slammed into Sagan's cheekbone.

His head snapped to the side, making his body and world spin. He crashed down to the stony cavern floor, and momentum sent him rolling into the shallows of the lake. Ice-cold water jolted through him and sliced his rage and fury to shreds. For the second he was fully submerged, it even muted the cacophony in his head.

He sat up, breaking through the surface of the shallow water. Ragged wheezes replaced his nonsensical shouting, but the high-pitched scream, once again, tore through his skull.

Sagan stood, water sloshing all around him. The cold air in the cavern sent a chill right to the marrow of his bones. Mere seconds had passed since Nika knocked him into the water, but it took a few more for him to understand the chaos happening before him.

Nika was bolting over the stepping stones, shouting at the top of her lungs, "Stop!"

A triptych wail from the three Veniri children shuddered through the cavern. But their cries were drowned out by the clashing, banging, and shattering of the camp kitchen and surrounding furniture being destroyed by Odette.

Sagan's eyes grew wide with shock, trying to make sense of it all. It struck him that the shrill screeching was coming from his mother. It was spine chilling—unlike any noise he'd ever heard, unlike any noise a human could possibly make.

Nika's shouts became desperate as she snatched the hysterical Orson out of harm's way. But before she could retrieve the wicker basket, Sagan's mother latched on to one of the handles.

"No!" roared Sagan.

He darted through the water toward his mother.

Startled, Odette released the basket's handle as if she'd been zapped by electricity. She scrambled away from the two screaming babies and stared at her hands in horror.

By the time Sagan reached her, Odette's feet were cut up from the broken glass and twisted metal of the smashed items littering the floor. Red blood smeared a trail in her wake.

"Mom, it's okay." Sagan reached for her, but she recoiled.

Odette huddled in a small, dark recess of the cave and hugged herself tight, hands tucked deep in her armpits. Her shrill, otherworldly scream had died down to a sob that clawed at Sagan's broken heart. She looked at him through the strands of hair hanging over her face, the soft magenta light of the Luxium lamps catching the glint of her eyes.

Sagan recognized the sorrow in her face. It was the sorrow of one who realized the enormity of their actions and hated themselves for it.

"Mom, please. Tell me what to do. Tell me how to help you." The painful lump in his throat almost strangled his plea.

Odette responded with an anguished whimper. Then a sharpness entered her eyes.

Sagan's breath hitched. He had only a second to react.

His mother lunged.

For a split second she was airborne, her arms outstretched toward him. Just before impact, he whipped out an atomizer and spritzed the contents into Odette's face.

Her whole body fell limp in his arms. He dropped the atomizer, and the little metal canister clattered and rolled along the rocky ground.

"Shh, it's okay, Mom," he said, cradling her close.

Odette's eyes found his.

Sagan's heart skipped a beat when he saw the clarity in her eyes. A single tear rolled down her cheek, a silent message of thanks and relief.

He nodded, trying to show he understood.

Then his mother closed her eyes.

He had no idea how much time passed as he held her, but by the time he turned back to Nika, she'd managed to calm the hysterical children down. Orson and one of the babies were on the verge of going back to sleep, but she still rocked the third baby back and forth, gently shushing his soft whimpers.

Sagan picked up his mother and carried her to one of the camp stretchers, then laid her down with the care of someone handling fine porcelain. As he pulled a blanket over Odette's frail body, Nika appeared next to him.

"Is she…?"

"She's sleeping," confirmed Sagan.

Nika reached down and picked up the atomizer Sagan had dropped. "Myst?"

He nodded.

Nika winced. "Can't say I'm a fan of this tranquillizer stuff, but in this case, good call, cuz."

"How are the boys?"

"They're still a little shook up but as good as can be expected." She inclined her head to the sleeping children, the older boy with his arms wrapped around his green bear again. "I think exhaustion got the better of them in the end. They should be fine after a decent sleep. But as to how they'll react to Aunty Odette in the morning, I can't say for sure."

Sagan pressed his mouth into a hard line. He sagged to the ground by the head of Odette's bed. "I'm not sure how Mom will react in the morning either."

Nika hmmed in a tone that suggested she didn't want to find out. "So what now?"

After a long pause, Sagan said, "I need to find out what happened to her. I need to know what I'm dealing with—what *she's* dealing with. I need to go back to Rivermyre, to the Xabat facility, and find answers." He glanced over at the sleeping children. "But before I go back to that hellhole, these boys and my mother need to go to a safe place."

Silence dragged on for a few uncomfortable seconds.

He stumbled over to one of the camp chairs and sank down into it before his head started to spin. His cheek throbbed where Nika had punched him. It was just as well. He wasn't sure how much damage he would have caused with his meltdown if she hadn't been there to knock him out of it.

He looked up at her and attempted an apologetic smile, and she gave him a small nod of acknowledgment. The interaction took him right back to when they were kids—to the times Nika looked out for him in her own brutal way.

"We still need to go back to Maple Shire, don't we?"

Sagan nodded. "We'll leave in the morning."

18
STAR-BLADE

Thane and Solace were brought back to the menagerie only minutes after Jhutev returned Violet.

The moment the guards shoved him through the bubble membrane, Thane yanked Violet in for a hug. "I'm so glad you're all right."

"Me all right? What about you and Solace?"

"We're fine." Thane loosened his arms just enough to glance down at the baby. "She was a little distressed while the hunters' submarine was making itself known, but the monkeys soon distracted her. That is, until that parrotfish shifter and his friends started plucking them out of the tank." The corners of his mouth turned down in disgust. "That viperfish shifter was the worst. He'd drowned all the birds and the chameleon and was moving on to the butterflies by the time those guards came to bring us back here."

Violet's stomach heaved.

"Wow," said Thane, looking past her. "Looks like Exültov followed through with his end of the bargain."

She joined him in admiring the new silver-plated crib for

Solace. In fact, the entire enclosure had been redecorated, in a way Violet could best describe as "no expense spared."

Covering most of the sand on the ground was a large circular rug, with a detailed design of purple grapes, vines, bees, and colorful flowers. Violet had kicked off the wet silk slippers she'd been given by the wardrobe mistress and luxuriated in the glorious feeling of carpet under her feet.

A larger bed had also been provided, furnished with more pillows than Violet could count and a selection of elaborately embroidered blankets. A canopy surrounded the bed, with curtains made of transparent white gauze. It didn't offer too much privacy while sleeping, but it was better than what they'd had to deal with before.

Following the theme of privacy, a tent-like structure now enclosed the new bathroom amenities, which now included a shower. Beside it, a wardrobe contained a selection of clothes for both Violet and Thane. All the clothes were much more glamorous than what Violet would ever choose to wear —no jeans or T-shirts in sight. Thankfully, though, most were much less gaudy than the absolute joke of a dress she'd been forced to wear for the banquet.

The moment Violet discovered the new clothes, she somehow bundled herself and the mountain of tulle into the amenities tent to change into a simpler V-neck dress with an intricate rosebud pattern. She thought about setting the mound of dusky-pink-and-navy fabric alight with her Magneii flames but it was still a sopping wet pile of frills. Plus, filling the bubble enclosure with smoke would be less than ideal.

Solace had been gifted a whole new nursery suite, complete with a highchair and day rocker, all plated in silver to match the crib. Within the crib was a set of iris-pink blankets, more cushions, and even a fluffy bunny. A mobile of colored glass animals hung from an arched canopy of mint-green curtains.

Solace fussed a little more, a sign she probably needed sleep. Thane passed her to Violet.

Hugging her daughter tight, Violet eyed the new crib but didn't move any closer to it. As beautiful and practical as the new accessories were, she couldn't stand the idea of releasing her baby. Not just yet. Not after the event they'd all endured. Instead, she settled down among the cushions in the new silver-plated rocking chair to change Solace out of her dripping animal skins and into a dry, white frilly romper. It was the closest she could find that had any kind of resemblance to baby pajamas.

Like Violet had earlier, Thane made a beeline for the new wardrobe. After a few seconds of riffling, he crinkled his nose.

Violet gave a soft snigger. "There aren't any casual clothes. I've already checked."

"Figures." He shook his head with an eye roll. "Although I had hoped to find something better than this king-of-the-jungle atrocity."

"And here I was thinking there could be nothing worse than that stupid froofy thing they put me in."

Thane laughed when he looked over at the waist-high mound of silken flounce. "Part of me thinks I'd prefer that over the animal skins. But then, you did look like some kind of cotton-candy cream puff."

Violet responded with a halfhearted groan. "Don't remind me."

"I suppose, considering what we've had to put up with the last few days, having to wear crappy clothes is the least of my worries." After a half-second hesitation, he yanked some items off their hangers and disappeared into the amenities tent.

He emerged with a buttoned-down black shirt and stone-gray vest ensemble. All he needed was a black tuxedo jacket and he'd be fit for a ball—except for the waist down. He'd selected what looked like midnight-blue silk pajama pants.

His lips pursed in an unimpressed line as he tossed his drenched animal skin costume on top of the ruffled heap of Violet's dress. "How's the little one?" he asked.

"Fast asleep," said Violet, still cuddling Solace and gently rocking in her chair.

He crouched down in front of Violet and tilted his head to look at her. "And how about you? Are you all right?"

She nodded. "Yeah. A little shaken by the whole thing, but I'm fine."

Thane let out a heavy sigh. "There is no way that is happening again. I'm not letting you out of my sight."

"No, Thane. You can't do that."

"Well, I can damn well try. These shifters are crazy!" He gestured to the tunnel that led out of the menagerie. "That banquet was a joke. It was nothing but a vulgar display for the Nephezai to showcase just how vulnerable we are down here. As land dwellers and *air breathers,* we have no chance of taking them on or defending ourselves if we need to. Not here. Definitely not at the bottom of the damned ocean."

"Shhh. You're going to wake Solace," Violet whispered when her baby began to stir.

Thane softly groaned in frustration and slumped into a new black velvet wingback chair studded with crystal buttons.

Violet patted Solace on her back until the little girl settled once more. "I hear you though. Our situation seems hopeless. But we can't give up. Especially not with that freaking collar still strapped around Solace's neck."

"I know. I know." Thane leaned forward to brace his

elbows on his knees, and his head fell into his hands. "I just don't know what to do."

Violet gnawed on her lip. "I need to try and get the purple spangle from the king."

"No. It's too dangerous."

"I have to, Thane."

"No." He gave a sharp shake of his head.

"What choice do we have? Because as far as I'm concerned, allowing Matthias's freaking bomb to detonate is *not an option*." Now it was Violet raising her voice.

Startled, Solace flinched, her eyes fluttering open before slowly closing again. Maybe it was time to make use of the crib. Placing her baby inside, Violet drew the canopy curtains closed.

Thane waited a few seconds to ensure Solace was still sleeping, then said, "So, what is your plan to get the spangle?"

Violet tried not to wince. "I'm still working on it."

He raised an eyebrow.

"Okay, okay. So I'm not exactly a jewel thief kind of gal. I'll start with breakfast tomorrow and see what happens."

Thane frowned. "Hang on a second, what do you mean by 'breakfast tomorrow'?"

"Oh… well, Exültov said I'm also to accompany him to breakfast tomorrow. Before you say anything," she rushed on, just as Thane opened his mouth to respond, "I know it's dangerous. But this is the best opportunity we have to try and get the spangle and find a way out of here."

Thane made a disapproving noise deep in his chest. "I don't like that you're the one taking all the risks. It should be me. Why is the prince fixated on you anyway? What's his endgame?"

"I've got no idea."

"Did he mention anything while he was with you? Any

hints as to his motives for having you paraded around like one of his playthings?"

Violet grimaced, not sure she liked what Thane seemed to be insinuating. "No, he didn't mention anything."

"Hmm..." Thane rubbed his jaw. "Do you still have those thorns?"

She jutted her chin toward the pink-and-navy mountain of frills. "Yeah, they're tucked away in some folds in the dress still."

"Good. From now on, I suggest you carry them with you at all times. And if possible, you should keep this with you as well."

He held up his hand. On his palm was a switchblade.

Violet almost launched out of her chair to snatch it from him. "That's my switchblade. Where did you find it?"

"I came across it when Nika and the hunters ambushed us." He pulled out two more knives, one teal and the other magenta. "I also kept these."

"Oh, wow. Are those the light-forged throwing daggers I made?"

"Yep, the very ones that sailed into the car door before I got in."

Violet's cheeks grew hot. "I'd forgotten about that. You know I wasn't aiming for you. I didn't know you were there."

Thane shrugged. "I know."

"And you've kept them this whole time?"

"You said I could." His expression turned a little concerned. "Should I not have?"

"No, it's not that. It's more to do with, well..." She eyed the two small blades. "It was my first time light forging any kind of weapon, and the result was a little crude."

"Not at all," said Thane. "I told you before, you're very good at light forging. And I still think these are really good. You're being too hard on yourself."

Violet pursed her lips. "Perhaps, but maybe with a little practice I can create some better things."

"I'd be interested to see what you come up with." He held the three weapons out to her.

"You can keep the throwing daggers," said Violet as she reached for the switchblade. She latched on to the weapon, admiring the beauty and craftsmanship of the piece. "How did you hold on to this through all the chaos that's happened?"

Thane chuckled. "Yeah, sorry. I would have given it to you earlier, but with all that's been going on, I just flat-out forgot. But after those last few hours at the banquet, with that jelly-fish prince dragging you around like live bait, I remembered where I'd hidden it. Besides, I figured it was sentimental, something you didn't want to lose."

"Sentimental?" Violet palmed the switchblade, its familiar presence fitting nicely in her hand. "I suppose it is. Nathan gave it to me not long after he started fostering me and teaching me self-defense. Although I considered throwing it away when I found out he… um…" She gave Thane a side-long glance.

"When you found out he never told you he knew me, and that he also knew what I'd…" He cleared his throat. "…what I'd done to you."

"Yeah. I suppose he thought he was protecting me," she said with a scoff.

"He protected both of us. Me from the toxic mire of my past, and you from, well… from the likes of me."

"Yeah, and look how well that all turned out. He wasn't there to protect me when I found out who you really were." Violet ran her thumb over the pearly-white handle of her weapon until she found the button. "Nor did he protect you from me stabbing you." She gave the button a gentle press, and the blade shucked out with a *shnik*.

When she'd first been given the knife, Violet had assumed the stunning emerald-green-and-magenta blade—shot through with lines of blood red—had been painted with some kind of enamel. But since being immersed in the world of shape-shifters, she'd started to suspect the blade wasn't made out of metal at all.

"If you ask me," said Thane, "you didn't need Nathan to protect you. Especially not when you've got a weapon like *that*."

Violet couldn't suppress her sinister grin. "You know, you're the only person I've stabbed with this thing."

"That's probably just as well. I'd only heard stories before, but I now know for sure that being stabbed by a star-blade hurts like a freaking mother."

"Star-blade?" One of Violet's memories resurfaced at the name. "That's right, I remember you telling me about it. What's the reason behind its name again?"

"Uh…" Thane raked a hand through his hair. "I'm not entirely sure, but I think one reason is because of the scar it leaves behind."

Her eyes fell to his chest at the area she recalled stabbing him.

The tension grew dense as Thane watched her, silent and motionless. Mere heartbeats passed, but to Violet, it may as well have been several long minutes.

"Can I see the scar?" she finally asked.

Thane nodded. He'd mentioned before he wouldn't hide anything from her again, and clearly he still meant it. After undoing the top three buttons of his shirt, he pulled the collar aside.

A sharp breath hissed through Violet's teeth at the sight of the cruel scar. "Did I seriously cause that?"

"Yeah." Thane's nose crinkled, his admission reluctant.

Violet continued to gape. Several knotted lines of

bubbled flesh coursed out from the center of the bluish-black scar over Thane's heart; they looked as if they'd been caused by a severe acid burn. The effect did, in fact, have the appearance of an irregular star.

"Why does it look like that? It happened about a year ago, yet it still looks pretty nasty." Her hand reached out toward the angry scar, but just before her fingers could brush over it, she recoiled, clutching her fist to her chest. "Does it still hurt?"

Thane shrugged one shoulder and shook his head. "No. Not anymore."

Only when his breath ruffled a lock of her hair did she notice how close she'd come to him. Her cheeks grew warm as she took a step back, reestablishing a suitable gap.

"It looks like it really hurt." She winced at how lame that sounded.

"'Really hurt' is an understatement." Thane's eyes grew wide, and he rushed to say, "But don't worry, I definitely deserved what I got."

Violet made a noncommittal noise, trying to mentally uphold the justification for her actions. Considering the circumstances, most would probably affirm she was well within her right to defend herself. Still, a wave of remorse washed over her when she recalled Thane's soul-wrenching roars of agony, and judging by the scar, her switchblade had caused far more damage than she'd intended.

She looked down at the offending weapon, then glided her thumb along the gemstones running along one side of the handle. There were ten in total. Each corresponded to a shifter species, and when a shifter was close by, the stone for that species would glow.

Currently, three were alight: teal for Veniri—no surprise there, with Thane, Solace, and herself only a few feet away; magenta for Magneii, due to the other half of Violet's hybrid nature; and bright purple for the Nephezai. At the moment, she couldn't see any Nephezai around the outskirts of their enclosure, but perhaps a few guards lurked in the shadows.

"That other shifter I was sitting with at the banquet…" Violet began as a thought struck her.

"The one that creepy viperfish shifter took a bit too much interest in?"

"Yes, that was Jhutev. He said he's a Meruvo."

Thane nodded. "He definitely looked like one to me."

"What color is a Meruvo shifter's blood?"

"Black."

Violet couldn't help grimacing as she tried to picture it. "Black? Like horror-movie, monster-blood black?"

Thane huffed a laugh. "No, not like that. I haven't seen it personally, but I hear the blood of a Meruvo is the most mesmerizing of all the shifter races. Just like how all the other shifters' blood has a radiant quality to it, Meruvo blood also glows."

"But how is it possible for *black blood* to glow?"

"Like I said, I haven't seen it myself. I've only heard from others that their blood gives off some kind of paradoxical luminescence. It's even distinguishable in the dead of night."

"Wow…" Violet took a moment to consider the new information.

Solace began to stir, and Thane hurried over to gently pat her on the back. She grizzled a little more, to which he responded by humming a soft tune.

Violet settled down in the rocking chair and watched as Thane calmed the baby down within minutes. Even after a short time of being trapped in this underwater prison, he'd proven time and time again how much he cared for Solace. Perhaps even as much as Violet did.

"Thane?" she said, a slight tremor in her voice.

"Yeah?"

"I… um… just wanted to say thank you for looking after Solace while I was unable to—during the banquet, I mean. And don't take this the wrong way, but… I'm glad you're here."

Thane looked up, brows slightly raised in surprise.

"What I'm trying to say is," Violet blurted, "it's clear Solace, well… she likes you. And of almost everyone I know, I can't think of someone better to be trapped down here with us."

Thane studied her for several long seconds as she tried not to squirm. "You really mean that?"

Violet nodded. She nearly let out a sigh of relief when he didn't whip out his Veniri forked tongue to confirm her emotional state—but then her whole body tensed. Specks of gold had begun to illuminate Thane's brown eyes.

The impulse to flee flooded through her, especially now that she knew exactly what the glowing gold meant.

Seh'Vuthi.

The word still felt foreign to her—still alien. The idea of soulmates and love-at-first-sight stuff was a whole lot of fairy-tale bullcrap. There was no such thing as "the one," especially not for her.

Was there?

She gnawed on the inside of her cheek as she considered it. Maybe, just maybe, she would be open to the idea. After all, she had fallen for him… once.

Her gaze fell to the crystal scorpion tattoo on his neck, and her uncertainty reemerged. Far too much had happened between her and Thane. Surely they could never mend all that had been shattered.

Before she could even begin to make up her mind, several small flecks of golden light started to float in the air around them.

When Thane caught sight of the tiny lights, he slammed

his eyes shut. "Sorry…" He grunted and rubbed his eyes. "I didn't mean to make things weird. I wasn't aware that was happening."

"It's okay." Violet was a little taken aback by how truly okay it was.

Thane shot her a squinted glance.

"Really," she confirmed. "It's okay."

Regardless, Thane refused to look at her again. "It's getting pretty late. We should probably, uh… sleep."

Without another word, he gathered a pillow and blanket from the bed, then settled into a place on the floor at the base of Solace's crib.

"Good night," he said, rolling onto his side, his back facing Violet.

"Good night," Violet said in a hushed voice. She looked up to find a few remaining glimmers of the Seh'Vuthi lights floating about a foot in front of her face. Three lights floated toward her, and then, one by one, they blinked out.

19
HAZING PLIOKAI

"NOT A BAD NIGHT FOR SOME SHIFTER TRAINING," LAZARETH said.

"Agreed." Nathan craned his head back to get a good view of the skyscape. A few fluffy clouds blocked out some of the stars, while others trailed across the bottom half of the moon. Laying a hand on Lazareth's shoulder, he added, "Are you ready for this?"

"Shouldn't you be asking Gus that? I'm not the shifter in training here."

"No, but you're his father. And this can't be the easiest thing for you to adjust to either."

"I've had plenty of time to adjust since Dawn filled me in all those years ago. I just wish there had been a better way for Gus to find out." He cast a look over his shoulder at Gus and the gang carrying some bench seats over to their chosen field, away from the sleeping Maple Shire residents. "I hope he still thinks of me as his father."

"Of course he does. You've been there for him. Yeah, it may be a bit of a challenge to accept all this new information, but Gus is a smart young man—who you helped raise. And I'm sure it won't take him long to comprehend just how much you mean to him."

"Thank you, Nathan." Lazareth gave a shaky smile and clutched at the chest pocket of his shirt, where the golden edge of Dawn's Glixus peeked out. "I just want to make her proud."

"You have," Nathan assured him. "All of you have."

A dull *thunk-thunk* sounded from a short distance away as Tio and En'gorr dropped a heavy wooden bench seat on the ground.

"Good luck," Lazareth said to Nathan before heading over to the newcomers. Gus had already peeled away from the group, and the two met in the middle. Nathan couldn't quite make out the short exchange between them, but it ended with Gus nodding his head and Lazareth drawing him in for a big hug.

"So, where do we start?" Gus asked, bounding over to Nathan. "What's the first step in hazing?"

"Um, well..." Nathan scratched at his bandaged jaw. "I suppose we could begin where we did with Violet. Start by closing your eyes."

"Okay." Gus's eyes snapped shut.

A corner of Nathan's mouth rose into an amused half smile. Unlike Gus and his instant compliance, Violet had resisted even the simplest of instructions during her first hazing lesson.

He suppressed a familiar pang at the memory. Right now Gus needed him. He'd figure out what to do about finding Violet, Thane, and Sagan later.

"Try to drown everything out and focus on the shifter side of you."

A crease appeared between Gus's eyebrows. "Uh... how

exactly am I supposed to do that? How do I know if I'm focusing on the shifter side or not?"

"There's a kind of 'inner melody' that's also a link to your allied planet."

Gus's frown deepened. "But the Pliokai are connected with Pluto—the *farthest* planet from us. How am I supposed to find a link with a planet that can't even be seen with the naked eye?"

"This is where you need to exercise a little faith. Trust that it's there, even if you can't see it. Try and see it with your heart, or with your soul… if that makes any sense at all."

Gus's face tensed with concentration, and a few beads of sweat formed across his brow.

"Anything?" Nathan asked after about half a minute.

Gus shook his head.

"Try angling your face up to the sky and moving around a bit. When I'm focused, even with my eyes closed, I can find the general direction that Venus is located."

A few more seconds passed before Gus's eyes flew open. "Still nothing," he growled, then glanced over at the group seated behind him. "Hey, Autumn, did Mom happen to mention anything about what to do when it comes to hazing?"

Autumn shook her head. "Are there any hints in her memories?"

"Oh, right…" Gus smacked a hand to his forehead. "Hang on a sec, I'll see what I can find."

He closed his eyes again, and the movement beneath his lids seemed to go at double time. "Sheesh, there's just so much information she has here. I think I'm going to have to categorize a few of these memories for my own sanity. The timeline of things also seems a little jumbled and—*Yikes*!" He violently whipped his head from side to side. "Ugh! I did not need to see that."

"What was it?" Autumn called out at the same time Tio said, "What did you see?"

Gus's face screwed up. "Ugh! Not another one." His palm pounded at the side of his head. "Seriously, how do you turn this thing off? Oh… it's okay. It's gone now."

By now, everyone had abandoned the wooden bench seat and crowded around Gus, each face etched with concern.

"Son, is everything all right?" Lazareth asked.

Gus quickly nodded, but his lips still pressed together in distaste.

"Dude, what just happened?" Tio asked.

A violent shiver racked Gus's body even as he replied with "Nothing."

"Gus." Autumn placed her hands on her hips. "What happened? If there is anything wrong with your Glixus, or if there was a problem with the transfer of Aunty Dawn's ethoseez, I need to know."

"No, no, it's nothing like that," Gus blurted. "As far as I can tell, there's no problem at all. In fact, it's all coming in loud and clear. Ugh, maybe even a little too clear."

"Then what's the problem?" Tio asked.

"It was nothing. I just didn't think… I didn't realize I was going to come across the likes of…" Crossing his arms and digging his fists deep into his armpits, he cleared his throat a number of times. "…Mom and Dad's 'home videos.'"

Silence followed for several long seconds.

As one, Autumn and Tio erupted with laughter.

Nathan bit the inside of his cheek, trying his best not to react, but the pure horror in Gus's expression almost sent him over the edge. Even the stern guards cracked a grin when En'gorr explained the situation in the Jiovis language.

Tio was now thumping Lazareth on the back, his loud laughter ringing out into the night. Lazareth calmly stood with his arms folded; the expression on his face could only be described as "someone trying to seem apologetic while having absolutely no regrets."

"Sorry you had to see that, son" was all he said in the end.

"Yeah, okay…" Gus shuddered and swiped his hands through the air. "I don't think I want to go rifling through Mom's memories again. That was enough to scar me for life. Any other suggestions?"

He had to wait for the residual laughter to die down before anyone offered serious attempts.

Nathan glanced over at Autumn and Lazareth. "Just out of curiosity, has Gus ever hazed before?"

"A few times when he was a baby," said Lazareth.

"There was one time I remember when we were kids." Autumn's face screwed up as she tried to recall the details. "We were about five… or six? Anyway, we were having a sleepover, and Gus shifted into his Pliokai form. It was only for about a second, but he freaked right out. Aunty Dawn asked me to help with the memory wipe after that."

"How did you do the memory wipe?" Nathan asked.

Gus followed up with his own question. "Can it be reversed? Maybe that's what's inhibiting my awareness of this weird… inner song… thingy." He cast a sidelong glance at Nathan. "No offense."

"I can give it a try," said Autumn. "But I'll have to tap into your Glixus again."

Gus nodded his permission, and all fell silent as Autumn pressed her fingers to the side of his face. It still utterly amazed Nathan to witness the Glixus being extracted from Gus's temple, as well as to see the intense magnificence of the glowing golden cylinder.

Instead of opening the cylinder like Nathan expected, Autumn tapped away at the surface in the same way she would a computer keyboard. The glowing pattern pulsed brighter with each press of her fingers.

"I think... I... *got it*!" Autumn grinned just as the entire cylinder pulsed a bright rusty red before fading back to its original gold. "Try this."

The Glixus chamber spiraled shut once Autumn replaced it, and a final pulse of the circuit board pattern glowed over Gus's temple and across his face.

"Whoa..." he said after a heartbeat. "Yeah... I can feel something a little different now." He nodded his head several times. "I think I can hear that song thing you were talking about."

"Great." Nathan shot Autumn a smile of thanks. "Now, Gus, try focusing on that melody. Maybe look up at the sky again and see if you can pinpoint—"

"There!" Gus stabbed a finger over Nathan's shoulder. "Pluto is over there. Wow, this is so... *weird*. I can feel where Pluto is. *Freaking Pluto*."

Nathan chuckled.

"What's next? What's next?"

Nathan placed his hands on the shoulders of the now jittering Gus. "Just brace yourself for this next bit. Hazing can be a little bit... uncomfortable."

"Or downright painful," called out Tio, which earned him an elbow in the ribs from Autumn. "Ow! What was that for?"

Ignoring the hissed argument between Tio and Autumn, Nathan began to explain the next step. But before he'd even finished speaking, Gus's features began to change.

His flesh shifted color to a very pale grayish green, and deep seam lines appeared along his brow, down one cheek, across his jaw, and back up the other cheek, giving the impression of a mask made up of panels. A few other smaller "panels" materialized over his neck and the rest of his exposed skin. Even Gus's ears elongated and split into panel-like structures. A golden glow shone out from each of the seams, as well as from distinct markings over his face that looked like a cross between Viking warpaint and cybernetic face tattoos.

Gus's eyes, too, held an almost mechanical glow, but instead of golden, they were a deep peridot green. His hair had also changed from thin strands to transparent cords, or perhaps wire cables, where dots of light pulsed from his skull to the tips of the twenty-or-so-inch lengths. His "cable hair" was a mixture of glowing gold, peridot gray like his skin, and bright peridot green like his eyes.

By the time Gus had finished hazing, the best way Nathan could think to describe him was "cyborg elf."

Gus held his hand up in front of his face, his gemstone-green eyes wide. Glowing seams marked each knuckle and fold, giving the appearance of robot hands, though more biological than artificial.

"How do you feel?" Nathan asked as Gus flexed and rotated other parts of his body.

"I feel good—whoa!" His hand flew up to his throat. "My voice sounds different."

"That's normal," said Nathan. Of the few Pliokai he'd met, all had a tri-tone inflection to their voices, almost as if there was a half-second delay to one of the bass tones in their register.

Gus tested out his new voice, reciting random song lyrics and movie quotes before landing on a plethora of Jim Carrey impersonations that had Autumn and Tio clutching their sides in laughter.

When he'd finished his repertoire, he grinned at Nathan. "What's next?"

"Well…" Nathan scratched the top of his head. "Once the hazing has been figured out, we usually get into fighting techniques. But the Pliokai are generally a peaceful race that relies on their intelligence rather than combat."

"Fighting techniques, huh?" Gus tapped his chin. Without warning, he took off into the forest at the edge of the field. Within half a minute, he returned with a nearly straight stick almost as tall as himself.

He started by holding the stick out to his side. Then, slowly, he spun it parallel to his body. As the spinning got faster, he flicked the stick over to his other hand.

Gus spun the stick faster and faster until it became nothing but a blur. Once he grew comfortable with the momentum, and with tossing the stick from one hand to the other, he threw it behind his head and caught it with his other hand behind his back.

Nathan's jaw almost dropped. Everyone else continued to watch in stunned silence.

Finally, Gus threw the stick high in the air, caught it expertly, and stabbed it into the grass. For several long seconds, he looked over at his audience, his eyes just as wide with surprise as everyone else's.

"Turns out Mom learned bōjutsu," he explained with a shrug.

"You got all that from your mother's memories?" Nathan asked.

"Yeah. When you said 'fighting techniques,' it triggered a memory, or I suppose some kind of neurological and physical response. It was almost like I could actually 'feel' Mom's muscle memory."

"Damn, Gus," said Autumn. "Remind me not to try and piss you off anymore."

"Did your mom learn any other sweet skills?" Tio asked. "Anything like Krav Maga? Parkour? Hold up, what about dance fighting?"

Autumn jabbed her elbow in his ribs again. “Seriously, Tio? He’s not a jukebox.”

“How about a duel?” Lazareth called out before Autumn and Tio could begin bickering again.

Gus raised an eyebrow. “You want to duel me? In bōjutsu? What makes you think you’ve got what it takes?”

“Oh, I’ve got what it takes.” Lazareth flashed a wicked grin. “I’m the one who taught your mother.”

20
IMPOSSIBLE DEMAND

THE NEXT MORNING, AS PROMISED, JHUTEV AND A FEW OF THE guards came to escort Violet to the breakfast banquet. To her chagrin, the guards included Votloxo, along with her two right-hand men, the blue-ringed octopus shifter and the stingray shifter. In time she'd learned the stingray shifter's name was Pwevül and the octopus shiver was Belitozzl.

Votloxo gave Violet a chilling glare, which she returned with equal intensity.

Though she tried not to let it show, her nerves spiked right before Belitozzl's tentacle snatched her from the bubble enclosure. Knowing what was coming this time, she grabbed the chance to take a deep breath. It was a good thing too, as Votloxo seemed to take longer than usual putting the bubble over her head.

Violet fought to remain calm while she waited for air, hating how much Votloxo enjoyed this power over her. How satisfying it would be to sock the fighter fish shifter in the jaw… but there was too much at stake to entertain small rivalries.

Relief flooded her when the bubble finally formed and sweet, life-giving air filled her lungs.

She expected to be escorted out of the menagerie, but to her alarm, Thane and Solace were taken by the guards as well. Pwevül gave her a wicked grin in passing, enjoying Violet's horror as he and Belitozzl took them down a separate passageway almost immediately.

Violet's slew of concerned questions landed on deaf ears. Even Jhutev gave her only hushed murmurs, refusing to offer any explanation. Eventually, despite her rising fears, she was shoved into the wardrobe chamber and thrust into the frenzy of preparation.

"Don't fuss, girl," the sea turtle wardrobe mistress tutted, annoyed by Violet's obvious distress. "We don't have time for your nonsense. The prince will be expecting you soon, and we can't have him dealing with you like this."

Snapping and clicking her turtle beak, she quickly had her assistants strip Violet down to nothing.

Violet gritted her teeth and crossed her arms over herself. Her nude body didn't freeze in the cold ocean water; it never did. In fact, the lack of clothing brought a tiny bit of relief in her struggle to stay cool. But she was always much more relieved to be covered up, no matter how hideous the outfit.

About half an hour into the dressing process, a faint *boom* brought everyone to a halt. Violet sucked in a breath, recalling the booming they'd all heard during dinner. A few seconds passed, and then a shudder rippled through the water.

Everyone looked up and around, waiting. A second *boom* followed, and a third, along with a few small cries of terror.

Votloxo barked at the panicked wardrobe mistress and the servants, who did their best to ignore a fourth and much closer *boom* as they continued dressing Violet.

"What's happening?" Violet asked Prince Exültov the

moment Jhutev and Votloxo escorted her into the antechamber.

The prince's mouth pinched into a grim line at Violet's question, but before he could answer, another faint *boom* sounded. This one, thankfully, felt much farther away than the last.

Violet was about to demand answers once again when, with a cry and a squeal, Exültov's children rushed into the room. The exhausted leafy seadragon nanny appeared a few moments later.

"It's all right, Hildez," said Exültov when she tried to hustle the children away. "I think I would prefer them to be by my side." He turned his attention to Violet, Jhutev, and Votloxo. "Come. We have breakfast to attend."

Votloxo flanked Exültov and his children, while Violet and Jhutev trailed along behind. Jhutev was kind enough to take Violet's arm, helping her swim through the passageways.

Before long, they arrived at a very different dining room from the last one Violet had been taken to. This chamber was elongated rather than towering. It was set out like typical dining halls on land, but less elaborately decorated than the banquet hall from last night. The tables floated on bubbled platforms along either side of a thoroughfare, and at the head of a grand U-shaped table at the end, the Nephezai king was already seated.

There were also fewer Nephezai present. Jhutev quietly explained to Violet that those who had attended the previous evening's feast were likely still sleeping off their raucous celebrations.

The chitter-chatter of the dining hall patrons grew quiet as Exültov's little procession traveled through the center of the room. All eyes turned to them, and those that landed on Violet narrowed with disgust. Jhutev patted her hand on his arm, and only then did she realize how tightly she'd been gripping him. The beady, bulbous, and slitted eyes still unnerved her, no matter how many times she'd been dragged into the presence of these creatures.

"It's okay, Miss Violet. This will be over soon," said Jhutev in a whisper.

About halfway through the room, Violet spotted more cylindrical tanks, much like last night's centerpieces, except this time, the tanks stood at regular intervals between the tables. Each was once again filled with land animals and plants.

About half a dozen tanks surrounded the royal table at the end of the room. Violet's heart sank with fitful worry—though not surprise—when she found Thane and Solace. It startled her to see other kinds of shape-shifters as well. One male shifter was unmistakably a Magneii in his shifted form. His skin was blackened like cooling lava, with fissures revealing the magenta inferno within. Based on his wide-eyed, freaked-out expression and banging fists on the purple-tinged membrane of the tank, he seemed to be a new addition to the king's collection.

The Magneii man yelled after the prince when he passed. When Exültov ignored him, the captured shifter became alight with fury. Magenta flames crackled over his charred, molten flesh, licking across his hands and eyes.

Violet stared in awe at the magenta blaze. She'd become so used to her own teal flames that the Magneii's magenta struck her as odd, even though she herself was the actual oddity.

But her interest fizzled when she drew closer to Thane and Solace's tank. Violet couldn't figure out if their attire was supposed to be Roman centurion–themed or Viking warrior. Her confusion must have been evident when she glided past, because Thane gave a slight shake of his head with a "don't ask" expression on his face. She would have grinned in response, if not for the distress eating at her gut.

Jhutev held firmly to her arm, perhaps sensing her need to stop and ensure Thane and her daughter were all right. Before she had a chance to cause a scene, he seated her at the table, with Thane and Solace's tank at her back.

Loud, discordant laughter drew her attention to the seats directly across from her, at the other arm of the U, occupied by none other than Yigtheez and his posse—the viperfish shifter and the mantis shrimp shifter included. Violet had hoped this bunch were among those still sleeping off the previous event. As her gaze wandered over the raucous group, she made the mistake of catching the obnoxious parrotfish shifter's eye.

The sly grin Yigtheez gave her caused chills of revulsion. Much as it galled her, she held his repugnant gaze for a heartbeat longer, fighting the urge to turn away or give him any reason to think she was easy prey. As he watched her, he drew a long swig from a flask of the same navy-blue liquid they'd served at dinner. Violet was starting to think she wouldn't recognize Yigtheez without a flask in his hand.

With as much nonchalance as she could muster, she tore her attention away from the parrotfish shifter, only to find the king staring at her with cool calculation. Casually spinning an enormous gold ring around one finger, he looked between her and Exültov.

For a split second, Violet glanced at the purple spangle hanging from his neck. Her subtle relief at the sight of it fled the moment she caught the king's eye again. A small, knowing smile crossed his mouth.

Fear gripped Violet's heart.

Did he know she was after the spangle? Was it possible he'd overheard what Matthias Branstone had said to her? She hadn't even considered that possibility until now.

This time she did look away in timidity, hoping against hope Qozzlotl was none the wiser about her plans.

The section of the table where King Qozzlotl sat contained five places, with him in the centermost position. The unoccupied chair to his left, which Violet suspected once belonged to the queen, was just as elaborately decorated as his own. The other seat on the king's far left also remained unoccupied.

Votloxo had ushered Exültov to the seats on the king's right hand. The prince had placed his daughter, Therizüs, between himself and the king, and his son, Zümgroz, in the seat adjacent to Violet. When the prince's children were settled, Votloxo peeled off to join the other half dozen guards stationed behind the king.

Violet looked down at the young child next to her. She hadn't been this close to the little shifter before, and his blue dragon nudibranch features were even more stunning up close. His silvery-gray and vibrant blue face looked up at her with both caution and curiosity.

Just as she was starting to wonder if she needed to offer him a smile or some kind of reassurance, he held a hand up in front of her face. Startled, Violet couldn't quite suppress a wince at the fetid brown-and-toxic-yellow lump seeping slime between his little fingers.

"Slug-gah go squish," he said.

Violet let out a small snort, remembering the conversation about his little pet from the previous evening. Even Jhutev, on her other side, gave a soft chuckle.

"Oh dear," was all she could say, trying to suppress her grin.

"Zümgroz," came Exültov's quiet voice. "What have you got there?"

Zümgroz turned his deadpan expression to his father. "Slug-gah go squish," he said again.

"Oh, Zümgroz." Exültov released an exasperated sigh when he caught sight of the mangled goop in his son's hand. "What did I say about letting the sluggard go *before* going to bed?"

"Slug-gah go squish," was Zümgroz's response. "Slug-gah yuck."

Before anyone could react, the princeling dropped the poor creature onto the table and shook the remaining goop off his hand, splattering yellow slime and sluggard entrails onto the surrounding plates and cutlery. Some of the goop even slapped onto the outer surface of Violet's bubble.

"Zümgroz, *don't—*" Exültov grabbed his son's wrist just as he was about to wipe his slimy hand on the gold chiffon vest he'd been dressed in.

Violet shared an amused look with Jhutev as servants hurried over to clean up the mess. The leafy seadragon nanny also appeared, taking on the job of cleaning the sluggard remains from the little prince's hand and clothes.

"His Reverence's children don't always have the honor of dining with the rest of us and thus don't get the opportunity to practice their etiquette and table manners," Jhutev said to Violet.

"It's fine." She used some excess frills of her iceberg-colored gown to wipe away the slime on her bubble. "No harm done. Except to the poor sluggard."

Jhutev bit his lips together to stifle a chuckle.

Shortly after the food started to arrive, there came another faint *boom*. Everyone froze, waiting for the tremors to subside.

"I understand why the prince wants his children close," Violet said in a quiet voice only the Meruvo shifter could hear. She turned her head just enough to spy the edge of Thane and Solace's tank behind her. "In case the worst was to happen."

"Precisely, Miss Violet."

"Is it usually like this?"

"This hasn't been unusual, until about three or four months ago," Jhutev answered. "The hunters are persistent. In recent days, though, it does seem to be becoming much more frequent."

"Is anything being done about it? Can't the Nephezai fight back, or maybe leave? Find a new place the hunters won't find them?"

"And where do you suggest we go?"

Violet's cheeks flushed when the king himself answered her. She hadn't thought her conversation was loud enough for Qozzlotl to hear.

When she didn't answer straightaway, the king continued to speak. "Not only have we been banished from above, but we are forced into further hiding from those who wish to eradicate our species." Another faint boom and a subtle quake followed, as if to emphasize his point. "The Erathi banished the Nephezai to the bottom of the ocean all those centuries ago and sent Erathi guards after us, to ensure we never again set foot on dry earth. But over the years the Erathi guards grew restless, and soon their work of securing the banished Nephezai turned into hunting them for sport, and eventually for profit. The Erathi submarines have hunted us through every sea and every ocean, forcing us deeper and deeper into hiding."

"But my great-great-grandfather found this place where we would be safe, right, Grandfather?" said the sea nettle jellyfish princess. "Great-Great-Grandfather built the city of Scylorethyz for us to be safe, didn't he?"

"That's right, Therizüs," said Qozzlotl with a smile, stroking his granddaughter's long hair. "The city of Scylorethyz, and the need for the light-forged gateways to enter, has ensured this is a safe haven for all the Nephezai."

A disagreeable scoff echoed through the water.

Along with the others at the table, Violet turned to find Yigtheez lounging in his chair and shaking his head, as if someone had told a terrible joke.

Qozzlotl leaned a forearm on the table as he turned his full attention to the parrotfish shifter, who took a lazy swig of the navy-blue liquid from his flask.

"Care to explain what is so humorous?" Qozzlotl asked.

"Oh, nothing," said Yigtheez, waving an idle hand. "Just something you said caught my amusement."

The group of Nephezai surrounding Yigtheez gave subtle sniggers behind their hands and exchanged knowing glances with each other.

"By all means, I can appreciate a humorous remark as much as anyone," said Qozzlotl. He gave the group a calm smile, but a prickle of warning up the back of Violet's neck suggested the king was far from jovial. "I'm interested to know specifically what I said that evoked your amusement."

Yigtheez set his glassy eyes on the king.

Violet could practically hear everyone within listening distance mentally shout for him not to answer. But as the perfect amount of arrogance and intoxication would have it, he dove straight into the king's trap with enthusiasm, as if he were doing a victory dance.

"I found particular amusement in… hold up, what was it you said?" He paused to hiccup. "Ah, yes… you said this lovely, very pretty little city you've made for yourselves here is a 'safe haven for all the Nephezai.'" He threw his head back and chortled. "*All* Nephezai."

By now, even the parrotfish shifter's friends had begun to understand he was plunging into dangerous territory. Grins and smirks started to morph into looks of concern.

Violet half expected the king to demand Yigtheez stop talking, but when Votloxo and the other guards drew closer, rage evident in their venomous scowls and white-knuckled fists, Qozzlotl held up a hand for them to halt.

Oblivious to the discomfort all around him, Yigtheez pointed to Exültov. "If this place is so safe, then explain to me why his wife, Princess Nepthyz, was killed by hunters?"

The mantis shrimp shifter gently shushed him, but apparently Yigtheez was just getting started. Next, he jabbed a finger at the king.

"And what about you, hmm? What about your wife? I'm a little fuzzy on the details, but remind me again how Queen Sozzüxl died all those years ago?"

"Yigtheez, that's enough," hissed the mantis shrimp shifter.

Yigtheez shrugged off his friend's plea and swept his arm in a wide arc. "For such a marvelous city where supposedly *all* Nephezai are safe, you would think they could extend support to *all* Nephezai, such as my father, who sent for help when the Erathi hunters discovered our homes. But what was the reply we received from the king himself? Oh, yes. I remember. The king who claims to be the protector of the Midnight Seas refused to extend *protection* to those who 'unwisely put themselves in danger by living beyond the fortress of Scylorethyz.'"

"I told your father to come and live in the city, along with the rest of the petulant residents of your quaint little village," said Qozzlotl.

"My father was your best friend!" Yigtheez yelled.

"And still he refused to listen to his king. He refused to listen to reason." Qozzlotl rose from his chair. "Time and again he was warned of the dangers of living beyond the capital."

Yigtheez hooted a laugh. "What is it they call you? 'King Qozzlotl Nagahld, the heart of the bleeding ocean,' isn't that right? 'Bleeding ocean' is fitting for all the Nephezai blood that has been spilled under your rule."

"How dare you." The king slammed a fist against the table. "I've brought you into my care, *into my own home,* and you repay me with insults and disrespect. Your father would be ashamed of you."

"No, he wouldn't," spat the parrotfish. "My father died surrounded by the screams of his wife, his daughters, and his other sons—by the death of my entire family. I'd wager my own life he was ashamed to ever call you friend." The finger Yigtheez pointed at the king may as well have been a dagger as Votloxo and her comrades swooped in and took hold of him.

"If it weren't for your father, I would have you executed for your insolence," said Qozzlotl as the guards escorted a struggling Yigtheez from the dining hall.

"You call yourself the sovereign ruler of the Midnight Seas and all the Nephezai!" the parrotfish shifter screamed. "You claim to protect your precious city of Scylorethyz from the Erathi hunters, and yet you can't protect your own queen, or even your son's wife. The Nephezai are dying out, and there will be no one left to blame except yourself, oh Sovereign Highness, King Qozz—"

The slam of the dining hall door cut off the rest of Yigtheez's raging.

For several long moments, no one moved or said anything. Even the servants remained still.

Qozzlotl stared at the closed door Yigtheez had been booted out of. Then with a shake of his head, as if remembering where he was, he barked an order in the Nephezai tongue. The servants began to once again bustle about. Conversation started up again, quiet at first, then soon back to regular volume.

Thankfully, breakfast ended a short time later. Most everyone seemed to have lost their appetite.

The king disappeared first, and then Exültov claimed he needed to get his children ready for their tutors. Jhutev was left to escort Violet back to the menagerie.

Yet her excursions at Exültov's side were far from over. In the days that followed, it became routine for Jhutev and a handful of Nephezai guards to collect Violet, send her to the wardrobe mistress to be zhuzhed, and then present her to the prince to accompany him at regular gatherings and appearances.

To Thane's rising frustration, they still had no clue regarding the prince's endgame. Even more exasperating to Violet, she still hadn't figured out how to steal the spangle from the king. She was always under the watchful eye of the prince, or his guards, or all the other Nephezai aristocrats and servants. And if not them, Jhutev always hovered only a few feet away.

"Blast Matthias Branstone and his impossible demand to get that blasted spangle from the blasted king!" Violet raged in the menagerie a few days after the Yigtheez incident, after being subjected to the utterly boring Nephezai equivalent of a Shakespearean play. "How the hell am I supposed to get the spangle from the king if I can't get anywhere near him?"

"Violet, shh." Thane pointedly glanced up at the nearby captives within their own bubble enclosures.

Violet gritted her teeth and forced herself to take a few seconds, suppressing the string of curses she wanted to scream. Instead, her rising emotions manifested in teal flames igniting over her hands. The fire also blazed from her eyes, along with a bitter stream of tears.

Only when Solace crawled over and raised her hands to be picked up did Violet quench her fury. In mere days, her baby had been racing through more milestones. Her little

Veniri daughter had learned to crawl in roughly a two-day period.

With Solace snuggled safely in her arms, Violet blinked away her tears and sank into the rocking chair.

"We will figure this out," Thane said, taking the seat across from her.

"How can you be so sure? It's been *days*, and we're still no closer to getting the collar off Solace's neck." A tear fell down Violet's face before she could stop it. She dashed it away and hugged her daughter a little tighter.

Thane rubbed his jaw, brow furrowed in contemplation. "Maybe you need to mix things up a little."

"How? I'm escorted directly from here to the wardrobe mistress, who's always waiting for me with another hideous frock. And then I'm led to whatever awful event I'm expected to attend. Then straight back here."

"That's what I mean. I think you need to try and stray a little. Break up the routine. Don't do anything so unexpected you'll raise suspicion. Try taking an interest in… I don't know, maybe the Nephezai culture. See if you can play to their egos and 'explore' a little, under the guise of being interested in their history and whatnot."

"Do you think that would actually work?" Violet chewed on the inside of her cheek. She'd have to stop that habit soon before she chewed all the tender flesh away.

"What else have you got to lose?" When they both turned their attention to Solace, Thane added, "Don't answer that."

Only a couple of hours passed before Violet was called upon to accompany the prince to yet another exhibition, this time of a new glass sculpture garden made by the Nephezai's master artisans.

When Jhutev and the guards escorted her through the menagerie's exit tunnel, she glanced over her shoulder at her daughter tucked snugly in Thane's arms. The ever-growing anxiety over the repugnant collar around Solace's neck made her throat constrict. If something happened while she was away at another frivolous Nephezai gathering, she'd never forgive herself.

After the tedious exhibition, Violet accompanied the prince to dinner in the grand dining room. As expected, the Nephezai guests were all dressed as extravagantly as at the last glitzy event.

Violet's own flamboyant gown once again matched the outrageous attire, but this time the wardrobe mistress had, thankfully, selected something made of light chiffon in sunset orange. Beaded strips of fabric in yellow, orange, and golden hues trailed in the water behind her. For once the simple task of breathing wasn't hindered by frills, faux-leather straps, and boned corsets—not to mention the outfit felt light and relatively cool.

She'd practically been begging the wardrobe mistress for something that wouldn't make her so flustered and hot. Previously, when she'd been forced to wear a charcoal-black ruched velvet ensemble, she'd almost passed out from heat exhaustion. Only after this incident, and by the prince's command, did the wardrobe mistress finally begin to consider more comfortable outfits.

Violet always made a point of not caring what the other Nephezai thought of how she looked, especially when she herself thought all of her outfits looked atrocious. But there seemed to be a shift in the way the Nephezai were regarding her this evening. When Prince Exültov guided her up through the tiered tables, the Nephezai women in particular sent her the usual prickly glares, and yet, Violet thought she sensed another collective emotion. Surely that wasn't… jealousy?

Was it?

As for the men, most didn't even try to hide the fact that

they ogled her, looking her up and down with hooded eyes and bemused smiles as she and the prince passed by. The new way they all ogled her was as if she was… covetable?

Surely not. She had to be misunderstanding things… right?

What had changed? Mildly distracted when she took her seat, she racked her brain, trying to understand the situation. As far as she could tell, she hadn't started behaving any differently since her first appearance with the prince. Even Exültov didn't seem to be acting any different.

Violet twiddled with the beaded lengths of her orange-and-sunset-yellow dress as she contemplated. And then her hand froze.

Her heart began to pound, hammering away in her chest as a disturbing thought crept into her mind. Was she imagining things, or was the inspiration for her dress taken directly from Prince Exültov's own sea nettle jellyfish appearance?

Thane had been adamant the prince had a specific reason for parading Violet around the way he did. Now a question arose in her mind—one she wasn't sure she wanted to know the answer to.

Was Exültov's intention to claim her as his new bride?

21

DO I LOOK LIKE THE JOKING TYPE?

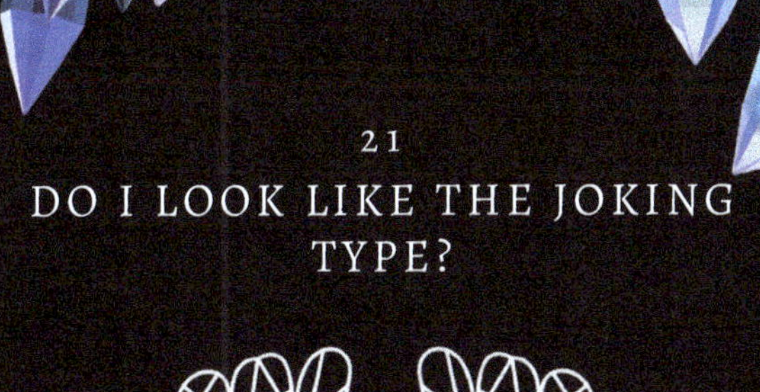

THE DOOR TO THE HACKER HUT FLEW OPEN, AND TIO BARGED in. "Nathan, you're not going to believe this."

Nathan's head fell into his hands. "What now?"

"Nika is back." Tio dashed out the door without even waiting for a response.

Nathan rushed after him, straight to the outskirts of Maple Shire. He almost bumped into Tio's back when the young Jiovis shifter came to a sudden stop on one of the side roads.

Sure enough, there in the middle of the road stood Nika, roadblocked by the ever-vigilant Jiovis guards. Farther up the road was a banged-up mud-colored sedan, most likely the vehicle Nika arrived in. Why she'd gotten out and walked a good fifty or so yards from it, though, didn't make a whole lot of sense to him. Then again, he didn't understand much about this woman, and he didn't care to.

The huntress's periwinkle-blue eyes didn't look quite so murderous as the last time Nathan had seen her, although she wasn't a bubbling ball of sunshine either. Hands on hips, she gave disdainful side-eye to the pewter twins flanking her. Urg'vhul had his arms crossed, keeping his steely gaze on her, while Tior'vul blocked her from going any farther.

Nathan would have expected Nika to try to knock them on their asses by now. Being raised by hunters usually came with the side effect of prejudice and a hefty dose of slice-and-dice. They tended to have a "kill now, ask questions later" policy when it came to all shifters. Nevertheless, that wasn't the reason the pewter twins regarded her as a criminal.

Nika had practically pummeled Violet's face into mincemeat. When Sagan and Thane had stopped her, she'd taken off, conveniently disappearing a few hours before the bombings.

Nathan balled his hands into fists, the bandages pulling taut over his knuckles.

When she spotted him, she looked him up and down with an expression of confused amusement.

"Evening, Nathan," Tior'vul said, while Urg'vhul just nodded in greeting.

At the mention of Nathan's name, Nika's smug expression fell.

He opened his mouth to tell the twins to turn the huntress around and send her back to whichever hovel she'd emerged from. But then he spied the desperation in her face and bit his tongue. Damn his curiosity.

When he drew closer, he gestured for Tior'vul and Urg'vhul to give Nika some space, but they blatantly ignored him. Clearly one had to be a Jiovis royal to have any kind of sway with the pewter twins.

Nika kept steady eye contact with him—that is, as best she could while Nathan glared at her from behind the wrap-around sunglasses hiding the gaps in his bandages. He came to a halt a few feet from her and, after a moment's pause, took the glasses off. Her ironclad resolve glitched for a heartbeat, and her gaze dropped to the ground.

Interesting. He'd started to think the ruthless huntress was incapable of remorse or humility. What had happened to crack that prickly exterior?

Nika's mask of indifference returned as she looked Nathan up and down. "What's with the Halloween costume?"

"You've got some nerve showing up here." He made a show of observing her hands. "No bling for the knuckles today?"

Nika folded her arms, then immediately dropped them to her sides in a huff. She fidgeted a little more, flicking her fingers and shuffling her feet, before finally blurting, "I'm here to see Dawn."

Nathan whipped out his forked tongue.

Nika's top lip curled. She leaned back an iota but remained resolute, calmly allowing him to sense her emotions.

Nathan's tongue sparkled in the sunlight. He ground his teeth in frustration. He could have kicked himself. How could he have forgotten how serious his crystallization condition was getting? Yet the need to test Nika's intentions was instinctual, an ingrained habit to guarantee he wasn't welcoming danger into their midst.

Much as it wasn't a secret from the Jiovis twins, he wasn't sure if his tongue whip had been quick enough for Nika not to notice anything unusual. The last thing he needed was for her to discover any further weaknesses she could exploit.

Suppressing the worry threatening to cripple him, he tuned in to deciphering the information his Veniri senses had picked up.

Among the plethora of scents, he didn't pick up any hint of cinnamon. That at least was a relief. However, murder wouldn't be the only way Nika could cause harm to the shire.

The scent of baking soda for distrust didn't surprise him, nor did black cherry for resentment. The flavor wasn't fresh and sweet, but rich and matured like fine wine. Whatever the reason, she'd been harboring the scent of black cherry for a very long time.

Another, more tart flavor complemented the black cherry: the crisp flavor of lilly pilly berry, showcasing how tense Nika was. But he hadn't needed the scent to tell him that. Her rigid posture, the forward dominant foot, the hand on her hip next to her holstered Diamantium dagger—all indicated how ready she was to spring into action.

A sticky, pungent flavor of molasses represented Nika's anxiety, but it had a macadamia aftertaste for her hopefulness. What could Nika possibly be anxious about? Surely she wasn't that desperate to return to the shire. Weren't there other people in the world she could torment?

He could detect her drive and motivation in the subtle burn of chilies sizzling through all the other flavors—not mild and easily dissuaded like a jalapeño, and yet not as brutal as a ghost pepper. More in the mid to high heat range of red cayenne. Whatever her reason to seek Dawn, how much would Nika's chili heat fade when she found out what had happened to the doctor?

One emotion almost bypassed Nathan's attention; he almost wasn't convinced of its presence.

Persimmon. It was suppressed under all the other flavors, barely perceptible, as if Nika had tried to hide it completely. She was ashamed.

In the seconds after Nathan examined her soul scents, Nika held up both hands in surrender. That was certainly out of character.

He crossed his arms. Was she sincerely humbling herself, or had she figured out how to play poor-little-pretty-girl right before diving in to slice a few jugulars? Branstones never displayed any kind of weakness. They certainly refused to show submission to anyone else.

"I know I'm not exactly welcome here," she began.

Nathan cut in with an "Understatement."

Nika sighed heavily. "Look, I may have been a little out of line while sparring with Violet that night—"

"If you think your attempt on Violet's life was a little out of line, then I'm the freaking Queen of England. And what about the heinous crime your uncle and his minions committed against a community of innocents—of *humans*? I thought you hunters considered yourselves honorable in keeping humans safe from all us oogedy-boogedy shape-shifters."

A plethora of emotions crossed her face. "I can promise you this, I knew nothing about those plans. Nor did I have anything to do with it."

"You're joking, aren't you?" Nathan sneered.

Nika placed a hand on her hip, her resting "just about to stab you" face locked in place. "Do I look like the joking type?"

Nathan gripped his sunglasses, and the plastic creaked under the pressure. "You would have me believe that you, Nika Branstone, niece of Matthias Branstone, didn't have anything to do with him and his cronies showing up in the middle of the night to blast this community to rubble?"

Nika gave a small shake of her head. "When I returned to the hunters, they were all skeptical of me. No one would tell me anything and—wait." She looked Nathan up and down. "Your bandages, is that why you're—"

"I'm fine. I can't say the same for the rest of the Maple Shire residents." His sunglasses cracked into two pieces in his fist.

He studied her face for a long while, watching as all the

harshness gave way to what he could only imagine was deep remorse.

"I didn't know," Nika finally said in a quiet voice. "I swear I didn't know."

Nathan huffed out a breath. "Regardless of what you did or didn't know, the damage is done. The residents here have suffered enough. And after what they've been through, and what you put Violet through, I'm sorry, Nika, but it's best you leave."

He gestured to the pewter twins. "Tior'vul, Urg'vhul, if you wouldn't mind, please make sure Nika makes it safely out of here."

"You can't be serious." Nika scoffed, glaring up at the two hulking Jiovis guards. "If either of you touch me, I'll gut you, make ugly jewelry out of your metal flesh, and sell it at a makers' market."

Nathan turned to walk away, ignoring the scuffle of gravel behind him.

"Wait," Nika called after him. "Seriously, you can't throw me out—*what did I just say about touching me?*—Nathan, wait. I need to see Dawn. I'm not leaving here until I see Dawn."

"*She's dead.*" Nathan spun on his heel. A small breeze picked up the dust he'd ground underfoot, swirling it in the air between them before the particles eddied away.

"What?" Nika said, eyes wide with shock. "No, it can't be true. You're just saying that to get rid of me."

Nathan shook his head. "Remember those bombs I mentioned earlier? Turns out one of them obliterated the Farrow household while Dawn was asleep in her room. I'd dig up her body to prove it, but unlike you, I respect the members of this community, no matter which side of the grave they're on."

"But..." Nika's mouth worked, soundless.

"Just go, Nika."

"Wait," she called out again. "I don't have anywhere else to go."

"Not my problem. Get her out of here, guys."

"No." Nika sidestepped out of the twins' reach, weaving and ducking past their attempts to grab her, as fast as he'd seen Sagan sometimes move.

Nathan took a step back as she approached him. "I don't have time to deal with your drama, Nika. Not now, not ever—"

"I'm sorry!"

Jaw slack, he gaped at her. Surely his ears deceived him. "What did you just say?"

Nika's mouth twisted into a grimace. "I said… I'm sorry."

Struck dumb by astonishment, Nathan glanced up at the pewter twins. Tior'vul looked just as shocked as Nathan felt, but Urg'vhul only frowned at Nika, his expression dubious.

"Not sure I've ever heard a hunter apologize for anything," said Nathan. "Just to clarify, what exactly is it you're sorry for?"

Nika's shoulders sagged. "I don't need to list it all, do I?"

"I get that the likes of you aren't well practiced in the respectable art of apologizing, but you could at least make an effort, especially considering that lives have been lost—"

"But I didn't have anything to do with that. I told you, no one would tell me anything, other than the plan to dupe Sagan into luring Violet and Thane out to—"

Nathan dropped the broken sunglasses. The plastic pieces crunched under his boots as he darted forward and grabbed Nika's shoulders. "What do you know about Violet and Thane? What do you mean *lured out*? Where are they?" He practically shook the huntress with each question.

Before she could answer anything, a high-pitched squeal resounded through Nathan's ears. Something small, not much taller than his knees, rushed over from heaven-knows-where.

"No! No hurt Nika!" Small hands shoved at Nathan's shins.

He looked down to find the angriest little face glaring daggers up at him.

When the little boy shoved him again, Nathan released Nika and took a step back, not because the boy had the power to move him but because of pure shock. The little boy had hazed into the teal shades and furry features of a Veniri toddler.

"No hurt Nika," the tiny Veniri growled again. He held up the not-yet-sharp crystal nubs on his elbows and bared his crystal fangs.

Nathan might have laughed at how adorable the young Veniri looked if he weren't still reeling from the entire situation.

Right when he thought he'd seen it all, the wail of a baby caught his attention. Standing on the side of the dirt road was a female waif holding two infants in her arms. One howled while the other stuck out its bottom lip, on the verge of crying too.

A cool breeze swirled around the waif and the babies. Tendrils of the woman's dull brown hair whipped over her face and shoulders, and the hem of her thin gray dress fluttered around her knees. She looked like an illustration from a storybook, a fae creature who'd wandered out from deep within the woods—whether a pixie who granted wishes or a harbinger of death and destruction, Nathan couldn't decide.

The waif paid no mind to the crying babies in her arms, her unnerving attention locked directly on Nathan.

Nika gestured to the woman. "Uh, Nathan. This is Odette Branstone. Sagan's mom."

He had a thousand questions. But none could be articulated before the little Veniri boy kicked him in the shins.

22 ONE SINGLE WISH

"Come along, Miss Violet," Jhutev said in a quiet voice. "Time to return you to the menagerie."

"Okay, thank you," she said with a tight smile.

They swam in silence through the opulent hallways. Violet tried to start up some small talk to fill the awkward lull, but as she turned to Jhutev, she caught sight of Yigtheez and the viperfish shifter trailing a few paces behind them. They both grinned at her, showing their sharp transparent teeth. Thankfully, after a few moments, they took the tunnel to the right, while Jhutev escorted her to the left.

"You must excuse the arguments between the king and Prince Exültov this evening," said Jhutev, as if he hadn't caught sight of their two shadows. "His Reverence and his father are becoming less and less discreet about their differences of opinion."

"Can't say I blame them," said Violet, recalling the hushed conversation between Exültov and his father. Most of it she hadn't been able to understand, but the vicious scowls and clipped phrases hadn't indicated a pleasant conversation. "What else can you expect from people who are forced to live at the bottom of the damned ocean and don't have the freedom to escape those around them?"

When she saw the expression on Jhutev's celestial face, she immediately wished she'd kept her mouth shut. "I'm sorry, Jhutev. I didn't mean—"

"Of course you meant it, Miss Violet." Jhutev's attention remained on the path ahead. "If one has the luxury to express the truth of their heart, one must do so."

Violet's brows drew together as she considered his words. As the seconds dragged on, she began to fidget with the beaded trim of her sunset-colored gown, her face hot with embarrassment. Had she offended the one person in this Nephezai kingdom she deemed worthy of her respect?

The longer the silence endured, the more her mind raced to think of something to change the subject. But just as she opened her mouth to blurt out the tamest thing that came to mind, Jhutev spoke.

"I was born into captivity, Miss Violet. My mother was the king's prized Meruvo at the time, and when she bore me, the king gave me to his son, to be His Reverence's personal Meruvo."

Violet's face screwed up in a mixture of disgust and horror. "That's awful."

"Perhaps it is awful, Miss Violet, but I have heard that it is not so unusual for my kind to be sold into captivity, whether on land or in the depths of the ocean."

"But that's even worse. Selling pregnant women, shifter or not, is utterly barbaric."

"I cannot disagree. However, no one, not even my mother, knew she was with child at the time King Qozzlotl claimed her. It was a great surprise for everyone."

"Oh." Violet wanted to inquire further but didn't know how. Anything she might ask would be touching on some super painful issues.

Jhutev raised his chin to look upward. She followed his gaze to a number of gaps in the ceiling, like glassless windows, naturally carved from years and years of water currents. Each one granted a view into the vast midnight ocean above.

"Like you, my kind is not meant for life in the water," said Jhutev. "But I have never once seen the world beyond the depths of the seas. Sunlight, clouds, rain, towering trees and skyscrapers, birds that soar on the winds of a blue sky. All of it is foreign, yet it's all so vibrant in my imaginings.

"I have never truly understood the term *freedom*. I've only ever been at the mercy of another's whims. Where I sleep, what I wear, what I eat, whom I speak to or even look at, all is decided for me. From the moment I was born, it has been ingrained in me never to nurture a thought or desire of my own, let alone consider fulfilling a destiny granted only to myself."

"And yet, you do have dreams and desires of your own, don't you?" Violet asked, trying to keep her tone as light as possible.

Jhutev squeezed his eyes shut, obscuring their brilliant light for a number of heartbeats. "Your perception is remarkable, Miss Violet."

She wrapped the beaded fringe tighter around her fingers, trying and failing to comprehend the life Jhutev must have led. There was no way for her to guess the Meruvo's age, but she had a feeling he'd been trapped at the bottom of the ocean far longer than she dared to contemplate.

"How did the king capture your mother?" She almost immediately regretted her question; Jhutev's face couldn't possibly bear any more sadness.

"The king has a few hunters he is willing to risk trading with for items and information from the surface. One such hunter captured my mother when she was quite young and traded her to the Nephezai king. As you can imagine, King Qozzlotl was elated to add her to his 'living collection.'"

"So was your poor mother forced to live in one of the enclosures in the menagerie?"

"No, Miss Violet. Being a Meruvo, she was never allowed to leave the king's side."

Violet balked. "Why? That seems a little... extreme?" All of a sudden, she felt bad about how much she'd complained about the prince dragging her out of the menagerie to all these ridiculous parties and events. How much worse would it be to *never* leave the prince's side?

"Do you know much about my kind?" Jhutev asked.

"About the Meruvo shifters?" Violet screwed her nose up in a wince. "A little. Only what Thane explained to me."

"And what did the young Veniri say?"

"Well... he said that you have black blood that glows, even in the dark. He also said you're somewhat ethereal and unlike any of the other shifters."

Jhutev nodded. "The young Veniri is quite right in that regard. Did he inform you of anything else?"

"No. But I figure, like all the other shifters, the Meruvo have some kind of special powers."

"What makes you say that?"

"Well..." Violet unwound the beaded tendril from her finger as she gathered her thoughts. "For one, all the shifter races seem to have some kind of 'superpower' compared to mere humans. And also, you said your mother was captured by a hunter. I have a friend who used to be a hunter, and as far as I'm aware, they're only interested in shifters who attract a hefty profit, whether from what they can harvest from the shifter"—a slight shudder of disgust trembled down Violet's spine at the thought—"or from whatever special ability the shifter may have."

"Quite right, Miss Violet. Of all I've endured in my lifetime, I can at least say I've been fortunate enough to never encounter a hunter myself."

"So what abilities do the Meruvo have?" Violet inquired. "Laser powers? Telekinesis? Mind control?"

Jhutev chuckled. "Nothing quite so aggressive. Oddly enough, I have heard some Nephezai fairy tales where a Meruvo has the ability to read minds. I cannot say whether it is true or not, as the only other Meruvo I've encountered is my mother. However, I will say she was quite intuitive when it came to what others were feeling and thinking."

"So, no mind control then." Violet confirmed with a grin.

Jhutev shook his head. "No, at least not for me. But we do yield a much more powerful ability."

Violet's eyes widened. "Oh yeah? What's that?"

He paused for a few moments before answering. "We have the power to grant a single wish."

Violet cracked up laughing. "A wish? What, like 'blue-skinned guy who lives in a lamp' kind of wish?"

"Blue skin?" Jhutev's brow furrowed. "I've not heard of another shifter race with blue skin who grants wishes. Is this a new kind of hybrid I'm unaware of?"

"No, nothing like that." Her laughter died down when Jhutev's confused expression deepened. "Uh… never mind. But hold on a second, are you serious? About the Meruvo granting wishes?"

Jhutev nodded. "Yes, quite."

Violet's jaw dropped and her eyes narrowed, searching for any sign he might be joking. "A Meruvo can grant wishes? Really? How is that even… possible?"

"Not 'wishes.'" Jhutev held up a finger. "Just one. One single wish."

Violet blinked rapidly, trying to comprehend all this new information. Three wishes would no doubt be awesome, but even a single wish… just imagine the possibilities!

"Ah… I am all too familiar with that gleam in your eyes, Miss Violet. I have seen that same avid expression on many faces over my lifetime."

Embarrassment at being so transparent heated Violet's cheeks, but it swiftly turned into shame when she recognized the deep disappointment etched in Jhutev's features. The way the viperfish shifter oogled Jhutev the other night made a lot more sense.

"I'm sorry. I didn't mean—"

"Again, Miss Violet, indeed you meant it. I may be naive to life above the surface, but I am not naive to the fact that all beings are tempted by the power I possess."

Violet let out a self-conscious chuckle. "Can you blame me for dreaming? What I wouldn't give to free my daughter from this underwater prison."

Jhutev came to a sudden halt.

"What? What's wrong?" She glanced around, only to find Jhutev's utmost attention locked on her.

"Miss Violet, do you mean to suggest that if you had the opportunity for a wish to be granted, you would make it on behalf of a being other than yourself?"

"If it meant my daughter was safe and sound, back on land where she belongs, then absolutely." She gave a firm nod to emphasize her point.

"No riches, no extra power, no heightened self-esteem? You would forfeit a world of possibilities for yourself to ensure the betterment of another?"

"For my daughter, I would forfeit a thousand wishes. I would even forfeit my life if I knew it would guarantee her a safe and happy life *not at the bottom of the ocean.*"

A spark of light glistened in the corner of Jhutev's eye. Before she could decipher his expression, he once again tilted his head back to look up at the inky-black ocean through the gaps in the ceiling.

"Did I say something wrong?" Violet asked after a few seconds of silence.

"I do not believe your heartfelt concerns over your own child are wrong, Miss Violet. But I will admit, I have never in my lifetime heard anyone declare someone other than themselves worthy to benefit from a Meruvo's sacrifice."

"Would your mother not do the same for you?" She ignored the stab to her own heart at the question; after all, her own mother had abandoned her at the hospital when she was only a few hours old.

"On the contrary. My mother only ever hoped the best for me. And if she had thought a single wish would ensure a better fate for me, I'm sure she would have used hers."

"I don't understand. If your mother had the power, why didn't she wish for your freedom?"

"Because I begged her not to. I did not have the courage to live without her."

"Without her? What do you mean by that?"

"The power of a wish comes from the very essence of a Meruvo."

Violet frowned. "Oh… so when you said 'sacrifice' earlier…?"

"Yes, I meant that in the literal sense. The power of a Meruvo's wish is fueled by their soul. For my mother to have granted my freedom, she would have forfeited her life, and I could not bear to live a life of freedom without her."

"But your mother… where is she now?"

"She has long since passed."

"But… you said… What about her wish?"

"There was no chance for her to make her wish." Jhutev shook his head, his starlit eyes dull with grief. "Another Nephezai village located in a ravine on the outskirts of Scylorethyz was attacked by hunters. My mother was visiting there with the king at the time, and sadly, she was among those caught in the torpedo blasts. She and several others were never found. I can only hope her passing was swift and she didn't suffer."

Tears pricked Violet's eyes at the absolute heartbreak in his expression. "Do you regret your mother not making her wish?"

Jhutev gave her a long look. "Not for a second. She lived well into her old age and was present for a large portion of my existence. I suppose, in a way, she did grant me the wish to not live a life without her."

What a horrible tragedy. Even when she considered the similarities to her own situation with Solace, at least she had Thane for support. Jhutev and his mother had only had each other. And now his mother was gone.

"And what about your wish?" Violet asked. "Do you have any plans for it?"

"There are many times I believe I would wish for this power to be removed from me, to put an end to it all. The torture, the mind games, the persistent pressure to relinquish my power, and for what? Greed? Lust? Selfish glory?"

Violet gave a small gasp. "Torture? You've been tortured because of your wish?"

Jhutev's grunt of laughter held an edge of darkness. "My mother once told me of how resilient our kind is, or perhaps how stubborn we are."

"But why?" Violet shook her head in disbelief. "Why put up with the torture?"

"Are you asking if I've been tempted to just wish for something silly to end the pain and agony? I'd be lying if I said I'd never considered it. But a Meruvo wish is not so easily granted. I myself have to want—have to *need* the wish to come true with every fiber of my being. A harsh hand, stinging words, or even gentle caresses are not enough to manipulate my kind. Our wishes are granted on the authority of our own creation. In an ironic way, the wish, and therefore our demise, is the one thing we have absolute control over."

Jhutev paused for a few moments, then gave Violet a wicked smile. "If there's one thing I've also learned through all my grief and pain, it's that never releasing my power is the greatest revenge I can commit. Especially against the Nephezai king."

23
URBAN JUNGLE TO ACTUAL JUNGLE

Sagan stepped out of the car, his face twisting in distaste as he scanned the urban terrain of Rivermyre for any signs of life. Eyes narrowed, he peered into the deepest shadows. Just because this place had been dubbed "The City of Silence" didn't mean there wasn't anything lurking in the gloom, watching and waiting.

A prickle ran along the back of his neck, and he palmed his twin crystal daggers, tuned in to even the smallest flicker of danger.

His phone buzzed. Scanning the message, he got the gist of Nika's update on how things had gone with her arrival at Maple Shire: *You're still a coward and a douche for not coming with me. But you were right, the people here are way too kind to refuse helping three young children and your mother. Although I suspect they were more concerned about them being in my care in the first place...*

She continued with a few more details on how his mother and the boys were settling in. It felt like a million-ton weight off his shoulders, knowing they were all in a safe place.

Sagan couldn't stop himself from wincing when he

recalled the argument he and Nika had had before leaving the cave. When she figured out he wasn't coming with her to Maple Shire, *outraged* was an understatement. She'd ranted and raved, calling him all kinds of names—*coward, wuss,* and *weakling* being some of the tamest.

He hadn't budged in his decision though. He'd insisted he needed to return to Xabat Biogenetics as soon as possible to find out what had happened to his mother. Nika had still been stewing when they went their separate ways—she in her sedan toward Maple Shire and he in his Defender toward Rivermyre, the city he hated most in the world.

The wind whistled and howled through the metal carcasses of half-built skyscrapers. Sagan began to wonder if he should have gone with Nika after all. Maybe he could have recruited someone from Maple Shire to come with him.

He snorted out a breath. Since when did he need someone to hold his hand for a mission? Besides, it was too late to be having regrets.

Get over it, you're here now. Just focus on the task at hand.

He walked along the middle of the road, and the soft thud of his lightweight boots echoed up and around the abandoned buildings. The light of the moon shone brighter as the cloud cover dispersed; its silver beams reflected over the few remaining windows in the skeletal skyscrapers. Most of the glass had shattered, decorating the sidewalk with scattered fragments that sparkled like jewels in the night. Weeds, wildflowers, clumps of grass, and tangled scrubs had also taken up residence within the cracks and crevices of the concrete.

Several shop front signs remained, all rusted and discolored: cafés, dress shops, jewelry stores, and a collection of other boutiques on the ground floor of each building. Once expected to be a grand utopia, Rivermyre was now a cemetery of unfinished towers and condos from a developer who went bust.

Sweat trickled down Sagan's spine as he walked. He'd long ago mastered any fear of the shifters he'd been raised to hunt, but the mutant creatures that roamed these deserted streets gave him a new kind of heebie-jeebies. Only his desperation to help his mother could have convinced him to return to this backend of hell.

A cold zephyr whistled down the two-lane road, bringing with it the foul aroma of decay. Sagan made the mistake of taking a deep breath at the same time, and he half gagged on the stench of death in his lungs.

There was no mistaking the scent of rotting meat. It wouldn't surprise him if the stink came from the dead Godzilla worm that had attacked him and his friends during one of his recent visits to this ghost city.

His stomach heaved. If the stench was this bad, then he had to be getting close.

He turned down another street, and the fetid atmosphere hit him like a brick wall. Involuntarily, his legs locked up, refusing to take him any closer to the huge mound of dead Godzilla worm about twenty yards down the road.

But if he recalled correctly, the entrance he and his friends had used to get inside Xabat Biogenetics was just a few feet beyond the worm's corpse.

Before he attempted another break-in, there was something else he wanted to seek out first.

Covering his nose and mouth with his black jacket, Sagan forced himself to take a step down the putrid street. To distract himself from the smell, he did his best to focus on the night the Godzilla worm was killed—specifically, the few moments after the worm was killed, and by whom.

Something gently swung in the breeze over by one of the buildings. Was that what he was looking for? He moved closer to the structure's metal-and-concrete base, to where a cable hung down the side of the construction. To someone who didn't know what they were looking at, it might have seemed like just a leftover length of cable, but a loop at the bottom told Sagan otherwise. He spotted one or two more dangling down buildings farther down the adjacent streets.

If memory served him correctly, he'd found the cable he wanted.

He took one last look around before deciding it was safe enough to holster his twin daggers. Grabbing hold of the cable, he put his foot into the loop at the end, then gave a sharp tug with both hands.

His stomach dropped as the cable yanked him up, up, up, several stories high. The breeze zipped past him as he left the fetid rank of the street below. The higher he went, the farther Rivermyre appeared to stretch out below him. The ghost city looked like an inkblot in the landscape, especially compared to the bright, sparkling lights of the city on the other side of the river.

Sagan's knuckles turned white as he gripped the cable tighter. How high did this thing go? Was he going to the very top? He couldn't tell how many stories he'd soared past already.

He glanced up, trying to make out where this ride ended. Directly above was a cantilevered concrete slab with a hole in the middle, through which the cable passed. Sagan braced himself for whatever awaited on the other side of the hole—hopefully not the crushing of his skull.

The rush of wind came to a sudden stop as he shot through.

His stomach lurched when he jerked to a halt several inches above the slab, the ground a nauseating drop below. Stepping out onto the ledge, he didn't let go of the cable until he had both feet firmly planted on the concrete.

Palms sweaty and knees weak, he wiped his hands on his

jeans, pulled out a flashlight from his utility belt, and scanned his surroundings.

The flashlight's bright magenta beam illuminated the interior of the abandoned building. Surprisingly, some panels of floor-to-ceiling glass remained intact, blocking out the rushing wind and allowing a glorious view of the urban cityscape.

The space he'd found himself in appeared to be some sort of hallway. An array of non-distinct doors lined the wall opposite from where he'd just sailed through the floor. Perhaps this had been the beginnings of residential apartments. A pile of dusty rubble and fallen concrete columns blocked the majority of the doorways on his left, but to the right, a clear path led to a door at the far end of the hall.

Carefully, Sagan made his way over and tested the handle. Surprise flickered through him when it turned easily. Perhaps the person who lived here figured a locked door unnecessary, considering the only way in was a reverse bungee cable.

When he pressed softly against the door, it swung silently open. Keeping his flashlight behind him, he peered into the dark room beyond and waited for a few breathless moments. Nothing happened.

He pushed the door a little wider. The moment he took a step inside, the lights turned on.

His arm flew to his face to block out the harsh brightness. Heart booming in his ears, he expected someone to jump out and attack.

But, again, nothing happened. Eyes still squinted, he looked around and noticed a little sensor on the wall by the door. Thin wires trailed from the sensor to the LED lights in the ceiling.

When his eyes further adjusted, his jaw almost dropped in amazement.

The spacious area appeared to be the beginnings of a penthouse, with all the internal structures—like the walls, hallways, kitchen, and dining areas—still intact. Sagan caught glimpses of designer tiles, marble surfaces, gold and crystal fittings, and other finishes that screamed luxury living, albeit they looked a little ragged from neglect.

Yet it wasn't the glam factor that took his breath away; it was the numerous plants that filled every available inch of wall space, from the small hallway he'd just entered to the living areas beyond. He felt as if he'd stepped out of an urban construction jungle directly into an actual jungle.

Smaller plants in individual pots were stacked on floor-to-ceiling shelves, while larger plants had been placed along the floor. No two looked the same, with leaves of all shapes and sizes, in every hue of green imaginable. Sagan didn't recognize many of them, if any.

The farther he walked into the apartment, the more vivid and diverse the plant specimens became. Some looked as if they came straight out of a sci-fi or horror movie. Many had flowers or fruits of some kind, a lot of them otherworldly, and he couldn't even begin to guess if they were edible or deadly.

Sagan slowly traipsed through the lush greenery, careful not to touch anything. Large windows lined the inner edge of a spacious balcony, with a recess for a pool on one side. Most of the tiled area surrounding the pool had been commandeered by a number of solar panels, and a collection of wires from the panels, as well as pipes from the pool, trailed inside through a gap in a broken window.

As if on cue, the moment Sagan spotted the water pipes along the ceiling, a mechanical thrum sounded, and a fine mist of water spritzed down.

He hustled away from the automatic watering system to the edge of a lounge room. Amazement held him in place as some of the more alien plants immediately responded to the added humidity.

One plant had bulbous pods that opened, fanning brilliant ultramarine petals with rows upon rows of glistening silver spikes; it gently waved its bloomed face toward the ceiling, as if trying to catch as much mist as possible. Another had long sunset-red tendrils that whipped out in various directions, snapping at the air. Still others responded with subtle color changes, and a few even seemed to hum a faint happy tune.

He made his way over to a dark corner of the room, where some other plants floated in water tanks. Sagan didn't know much about plants in general, and even less about underwater ones, but these were the most beautiful he'd ever seen. Many glowed with their own bioluminescence, lighting up the water with pops of neon. A small filtration system circulated bubbles through the tank, and the plants gently waved to and fro with the currents.

Sagan found no sign of anyone being home, but the kitchen had a small collection of canned food and supplies for simple meals. He peeked his head into one room and spied a futon mattress with a jumble of blankets piled on top. A few stacks of neatly folded clothes sat in the corner, and some trinkets that looked like cat toys lay scattered across the floor.

As much as this odd little abode had struck Sagan's curiosity, he now feared he'd crossed over into "snooping like a creeper" territory.

A message alert buzzed on his phone. Nika.

Hey Cuz,

Did you find that ninja-star chick yet? No sign of another freakout from Aunty Odette. I've been keeping the Myst on hand... but may end up using it on a Jiovis or two.

How are things on your end?

Don't get killed.

Nika

Sagan marveled at the message. His cousin wasn't one to send him multiple messages in one night—or many messages at all, for that matter. Perhaps Nika had changed in more ways than he'd expected. Could it be she wanted to reassure him that his mother was in safe hands? Whatever the reason, he found himself grateful for the update.

He quickly sent back a reply, briefing Nika on his current circumstances. After hitting Send, he noted the time. He didn't like the idea of looking at plants all night while waiting to see if someone showed up or not.

Was it best to hang around?

Just as he decided to make his way to the exit, a quiet scuffle in the outer hallway caught his attention.

Swapping his flashlight for one of his crystal daggers, he followed the noise. A few little chirps or titters joined the scuffling, followed by a faint cry of pain—which startled him into moving more swiftly.

As he approached the hole in the concrete, it took him a second to process the scene in front of him. The cable flailed as if it had just been released, and a young woman was hanging on to the edge of the slab for dear life. Her fingers, slick with crimson smears of blood, clawed for purchase at the concrete as she slipped farther and farther down the hole.

Sagan immediately holstered his dagger and raced over. He helped her climb up onto the slab, pulling her safely away from the treacherous edge. Then, as gently as possible, he turned her over. With a soft groan of anguish, the woman sagged in his arms.

She wore a midnight-blue-to-black ombre leather jacket, decorated with a Japanese flag button badge and another of a cartoon cherry blossom. Both badges were now speckled with blood. More blood streaked her cheeks and caught in clumps of her long, purple-tipped raven hair.

Her glassy eyes, deep brown like smoky quartz, glanced around before landing on Sagan's.

"Hello, Umbra," he said.

A small dimple appeared in her cheek as her lips curled up in a knowing smile. "I know you. You're that hunter who tried to steal my star-blade. Sagan, right?"

He nodded. "Have you been out hunting Godzilla worms again?"

Umbra forced a confident grin, but before she could respond, her features twisted with agony. She curled in on herself, hands shaking, and clutched at a gash in her side.

All the relief Sagan had felt upon finding her switched to distress when he saw the amount of blood seeping from the wound in her torso.

Umbra's head rolled clumsily to the side, her eyes fluttered shut, and her body went limp.

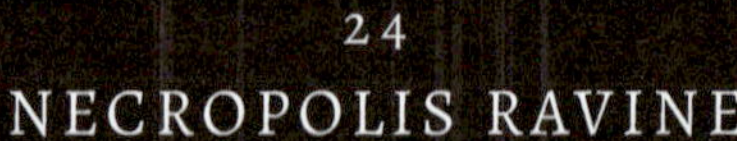

24
NECROPOLIS RAVINE

After yet another dinner banquet, Violet had to restrain herself from swimming as fast as possible back to the menagerie. Before, she would have done anything to get away from the bubble enclosure, but following her little epiphany about the prince possibly grooming her for marriage, the menagerie now seemed like a suitable hideaway.

It didn't help her anxiety that Jhutev seemed to be lagging farther and farther behind in the passageway, leaving her and Exültov to glide through the water side by side, alone. After all the previous events she'd attended with him, the prince had been quick to take his leave and entrust her to Jhutev's care, yet this time, he'd insisted on escorting her back to the menagerie himself.

She hated that Thane's conspiracy theories were starting to get to her. Suspicion set her whole body on edge when the prince's shoulder bumped hers as they rounded a corner. Even that gentle impact sent her off course.

"Whoa there." Exültov caught her arm before she could

spin too far away. He brought her close to his side, helping steady her as the currents settled. "Are you all right?"

Violet nodded. "Fine. No problem."

"Good." He released her, then placed a hand on her back to continue guiding her through the water.

She became hyperconscious of the three mother-of-pearl thorns hidden in her dress.

Unlike the majority of the Nephezai, Exültov had never given her reason to believe she might have to defend herself against him. But if it ever came to that, she hoped the self-defense techniques Nathan had taught her would translate against a Nephezai shifter.

Keep it together, Vi, she warned herself. Adding more worries to her ever-growing list was not what she needed.

She tugged on the tendrils of her dress. This time the wardrobe mistress hadn't been so blatant in matching Violet's gown to the prince's features, but the strands of pastel freshwater pearls and crystal bead ensemble still reminded her of a jellyfish.

Despite her attempts to suppress it, apprehension grew with each moment the prince's hand remained on her lower back. Her fear spiked when she realized he'd guided her into an unfamiliar passageway.

"Uh, not to be obnoxious or anything, but isn't the menagerie back that way?" She jerked her thumb over her shoulder.

"Quite right, Violet," said Exültov, not deviating from his course. "I had thought we would take a different way back. Change up the monotony a bit."

"Oh, okay." Violet forced a smile.

The tips of her fingers started to tingle from the beaded tendrils wrapped tightly around her hand. Just as she was sure the beads would cut into her flesh, there came a subtle pop, and a few came loose in her fist. Unsure what to do with the little collection of lentil-sized crystals and pearls, she let them go one by one, dropping them like Hansel and Gretel's breadcrumbs. She was moving too quickly to see them gently fall through the water and settle on the ground, but chances were they'd only be carried off by the currents anyway.

"Here we are," said Exültov.

They'd arrived at a pair of golden doors twice Violet's height. Only when the prince came to a halt did Jhutev rush forward, open one of the doors, and patiently wait for Violet and the prince to swim through. She couldn't help but look around in awe at what she could only describe as some type of underwater courtyard.

"Wow, it's beautiful," she breathed. "What is this place?"

They were at the base of a deep trench about three football fields wide. The rocky walls rose several stories high, disappearing into the midnight water above, and all along the ground stretched a whole host of Nephezai statues. Each one gave off an inviting purple glow—the same color as the luminescent markings on the living shifters—eliminating any need for lights or lanterns.

The statues were mounted on pedestals, ranging from a few inches to several feet high. Most contained just one statue, while others could accommodate two or more. Violet spied one with what appeared to be a family of two parents and their six narwhal-like children. Elaborate pathways made of polished stones—agate, jasper, tiger eye, petrified wood, fluorite, and obsidian—wove between the statues' plinths.

"Is this some kind of artists' sculpting chamber?" Violet asked. "Do the Nephezai specialize in making statues or something?"

"This is our Necropolis Ravine," said Exültov. When Violet raised a questioning eyebrow, he added, "It's the memorial grounds for our dead."

"Oh," said Violet in a quiet voice, taking in the scene with much more reverence than before. "There are... so many."

There seemed to be no end to the Necropolis Ravine. The collection of monumental statues went on forever, vanishing into the dark waters.

"How many are there?" she asked.

"I cannot say. We have long ago lost count."

Violet followed Exültov as he floated along one of the wider stone pathways.

"While it's true our necropolis was established when my great-grandfather founded the city of Scylorethyz," he continued, "the number of monuments you see here is far more than the number of those who have passed during the existence of our city.

"Due to the tides and currents, the ocean floor is ever changing, so it is not ideal to bury our dead. Instead, the bodies of our loved ones are escorted into the outer city waters, then drifted farther out to break down and be reclaimed by the ocean. Their memory is embodied in these effigies."

"Wow," said Violet. "That's quite a heartwarming concept. For land dwellers, statues are usually reserved for historical figures who did something remarkable or admirable. If someone were to make a statue of themselves, we would think them extremely conceited."

Exültov gave a low chuckle. "With that in mind, it sounds like this is definitely suited to the general disposition of the Nephezai." He flashed her a small smile. "You're probably already aware that we're a very proud race."

"I did pick up a hint or two," Violet replied with her own smile.

For a few moments, neither of them said anything.

"You know, it has been a very long time since I have been able to talk to someone with such simplicity," said Exültov.

Violet quickly dropped her gaze to the stone path. Part of her wanted to empathize—she certainly understood loneliness and grief—but the direction the conversation was taking made her wary. Instead, all she said was "That's a shame."

They continued to float along the stone path, passing a group of servants who were diligently clearing away all traces of silt, barnacles, and algae from the statues. The servants paused to bow low when the prince glided past them. A few gave Violet curious looks, and one narrowed his squid-like eyes at her with cold derision.

But before Violet could give the glaring Nephezai any thought, Exültov turned, leading her and Jhutev, who lagged a few meters behind, onto a pathway that ascended toward one of the ravine walls. She gave a small gasp when she spotted all the statues positioned in alcoves along the rock face.

"Wow, there are so many more," she exclaimed.

"You'll find that the effigies in the wall alcoves belong to the Nephezai royals." Exültov made a beeline for one statue in particular. "This one over here… is my wife, Nepthyz."

"She's very beautiful," said Violet.

"Yes. More than this effigy will ever show." He floated up to be at eye level with the statue, a sad smile on his face.

Violet would have been able to figure out who the Nephezai woman was even if Exültov hadn't explained it. She had the same distinct blue dragon nudibranch features as her young son, and there was no mistaking the regal glint carved into her expression. Her pure gold plinth rose about five feet high, engraved with inscriptions Violet couldn't read, and the entire alcove surrounding her was adorned with a decorative mosaic of tiny sparkling jewels. The mosaic depicted snapshots from Nepthyz's life—meeting Exültov, their wedding day, her coronation, the addition of their two children—all glinting in the glowing purple light from the statue itself.

"If you don't mind my asking," Violet said, "what happened to her?"

When the prince didn't answer straightaway, she began winding strands of her beaded dress around her hands again, wondering if the question was out of line. An apology had started to form on her tongue when the prince spoke.

"It was much like any other day. She hated the fact that we lived here in this city. 'Trapped,' she called it. Even when we were children, we would sneak out beyond the fortress walls and go exploring. But as we got older, my royal obligations forced me to grow out of my childish escapades.

"Not long after our marriage, I lectured her on her adventurous habits. But she promptly explained she no longer left the Scylorethyz boundaries for her own selfish desires, but to help those beyond it: those who were cut out, banished, or simply willing to remain with the loved ones who were not fortunate enough to live within the city. My father would have had her severely punished if he ever found out what she was up to. She had started to devise different strategies to smuggle food, clothing, energized heating rocks for warmth, toys and entertainment for the children—if the Nephezai outcasts said they needed something, she'd figure out a way to bring it to them."

"It sounds like she cared about the Nephezai people a lot," said Violet.

"She did. She cared far more than anyone would ever imagine. If there was a need, she wanted to fill it. When not diligently pursuing her philanthropy, she was the most dedicated mother I've ever had the privilege of witnessing."

Violet nodded as the prince continued to reminisce; however, her attention was divided between Exültov's lighthearted stories and the sweat prickling down her back. She still hadn't acclimated to the intense heat she'd experienced since being dragged to the bottom of the ocean. She tugged at some of the frills of her dress, wrapping them tight around her hands.

"Then came the day I would forever curse," continued Exültov. "About two years ago, when Therizüs was six and Zümgroz one, my dear wife was beyond the Scylorethyz boundaries when a hunter submarine chanced upon the village she was visiting." An anguished shudder strangled his next few words. "By the time the devastating news reached me, the little village had been decimated. No one was left alive."

Violet didn't know what to say. She could never bring herself to use the phrases "Sorry for your loss" or "My condolences," not after she'd heard them far too many times when her best friend Lyla-Rose had been killed.

"I'm sure your children miss her dearly," she said in the end.

"Sadly, Zümgroz didn't have enough time with her to form many memories, but Therizüs speaks of her often." He smiled and gave an amused shake of his head. "That girl becomes more and more like her mother with every passing moment. I'm sure I'll be batting the overconfident suitors away with a harpoon."

Violet laughed at the thought.

"It's regrettable that they have to grow up without a mother." Exültov's smile morphed into a frown. "My father has been pressuring me to marry again, his new angle being that any mother is better than no mother for my children. I'm always reminded of the list of suitors he deems appropriate."

He scoffed and shook his head. "I won't marry for the sake of political negotiations to further my father's power over this kingdom. My children deserve more than that.

They deserve a new mother who would love them as her own, someone who would teach them the kindness and compassion Nepthyz always strove for. And I have long ago come to the conclusion that there is no Nephezai in these godforsaken waters worthy of being entrusted with the title of 'mother' to my children. No Nephezai can give them the freedom their mother deeply desired."

The more Exültov spoke, the more Violet fidgeted with the frills and beads from her dress. Her heart pumped faster as the prince's compassionate speech edged far too close to territory she did not want to enter.

Without warning, Exültov turned to face her. The speed of his movement caused the waters to swirl around them. "Violet, I need to ask you a very serious question."

Violet's eyes grew wide. *Oh no.* Surely he wasn't about to—

"I wish to ask you to—"

"I can't marry you," she blurted.

Exültov gaped at her.

"I'm so sorry," Violet rushed to add. "It's not that I don't like you. I... I do. And I think your children are great, wonderful even. But I can't. I have my own daughter, and she needs me. Not only that, she needs sunlight and air and... grass and trees. But aside from that, your wife sounds like she was the most amazing woman, and there is no way I could—I mean, I'm seriously struggling with recently becoming a mother. But me as a *wife*?" Oh gosh, she was totally rambling and really needed to shut up, but her mouth had other ideas. "I'm sure that many women would kill to be in my position right now. I mean, who doesn't dream of being proposed to by a prince? But in all honesty, I'm not cut out for royalty. I'm the worst choice. The Nephezai already hate me—"

"Violet, I don't want to marry you."

Violet paused mid-sentence, allowing her brain to catch up with what Exültov had just said. "Wait—what?"

"I said I don't want to marry you."

"Oh." Violet's mouth opened and closed like a guppy. Her confusion turned to embarrassment when the prince's features pinched with mild aversion.

"Whyever would you think I'd want to marry you?"

More heat flooded into her cheeks. Blaming Thane for her blunder would, without a doubt, be childish, but she'd definitely kick his ass when she got back to the menagerie.

"Because you've had me dragged from the menagerie multiple times a day to be primped and zhuzhed in every absurd outfit imaginable, so I can be paraded around by your side at an endless number of social events. Everyone has noticed you've been paying particular attention to me, while poor Solace and Thane have been subjected to those awful display chambers in the dining halls." She held up the beaded strands of her dress, her words getting faster and more frenzied by the moment. "Your wardrobe mistress is even dressing me up to match your appearance. And now there's all this talk of how awful it would be for your children to grow up without a mother, and how you believe no Nephezai could take her place, and that you had a very important question to ask me. And it all led me to believe you were, you know, going to… propose."

Violet sucked in a deep breath.

For a moment the prince stared at her.

Then he threw his head back and laughed.

Violet glanced at Jhutev. He was still a few feet away but had clearly heard the whole exchange, as he was doing a terrible job of hiding his own mirth.

"Okay… so I must have made a mistake." She scrubbed a patch of algae on the gemstone pathway with her bare foot.

"Believe me, Violet, I have no interest in marrying you," said Exültov when his laughter had died down.

She frowned. "I still don't understand. Why all the special treatment, and silly dresses, and formal escorts?"

"To be candid, I got the idea from an argument with my father. When our disagreement over me finding a new wife became heated, I stated I'd rather flounce around with one of his pets from the menagerie than have him force me to marry a Nephezai of his choosing."

"Oh." Violet pursed her lips.

Exültov's expression turned apologetic. "I'll admit, it was rather infantile of me to follow through on my remark. I initially intended that first event to be the one and only with you as my companion, but your presence brought a pleasant change to the monotony. Plus, it helped deter all those annoying Nephezai women from throwing themselves in my path."

"Okay, well..." Violet let out a small sigh of relief as the tension in her neck and shoulders released. "But, wait a second, you said you had a very important question to ask."

All traces of Exültov's humor dissolved, leaving a stoic mask. "I wish for my children to live in the freedom my wife always dreamed for them." With a slight pause, Exültov tilted his head back and looked up into the inky-black ocean. "The Nephezai have been banished for thousands of years. The world above has long forgotten us, progressing in more ways than we can imagine down here. But my father refuses to change, believing that when the Nephezai return to the surface, we will reclaim our rightful place of dominion over the Erathi and all the other shifters."

He looked down at Violet, his face taut with a mixture of emotions. "The Nephezai are still paying for the sins of my ancestors. And as long as we refuse to embrace the other shifter species and treat them as equals, we will forever remain in this prison of our own making."

"So, what is it you need from me?" Violet said after a few heartbeats. "I don't have the power to change your father's mind, if that's what you're thinking."

"No. I already know he is immovable. I've already tried." His eyes clouded with resentment. "You must know that I have never agreed with my father's entrapment of the creatures in his menagerie."

"Then why can't you set us all free?" Violet asked.

"Even if I did, there are still the hunters and their submarines to contend with. And, sadly, I do not possess the power to light forge gateways like my father can. But I believe there is another way for you and your family to leave this place. In return, this is all I ask..." He took hold of Violet's shoulders. "When you, Thane, and your child escape from here, please take my children with you."

"What?" Violet's jaw dropped. "You can't be serious."

"Yes, Violet, I am."

"No, I can't do that. I can't take your children away from you." She violently shook her head, trying to shut out the remembered anguish of her own child being taken from her. "No, I won't take someone else's children away from them."

"Please." His grip on her shoulders grew strong, desperate. "I need you to take them."

Violet's resolve began to falter at the pleading in his eyes. "But... they were born here, underwater. They're aquatic creatures. They have gills and tentacles. Can they even survive—"

"They are shape-shifters, just like you. It's true, they have never had the opportunity to experience their human forms, to breathe air and walk on land. But they will learn. Their human forms will survive on land. You need to teach them how to *live* on land."

"But why me? Why do you want *me* to take them?"

"Because you were once Erathi, and now you are a Veniri and Magneii hybrid. You are also a mother, with a strong and willing partner to help guide and raise your child."

Violet wanted to correct Exültov's use of the word *partner* for Thane, but she bit her tongue as he continued.

"You already have an understanding of the Erathi culture, and you are now learning to embrace the Veniri and Magneii way of life. We, the Nephezai, need to learn the lessons you are learning. Please take my children. Teach them how to adapt on land. Teach them to be compassionate and understanding toward mankind and shifter-kind alike. I believe if they have the opportunity to be immersed in the land dwellers' way of life, it will prepare them to one day return to the Nephezai and lead them out from their banishment."

Violet's mind whizzed with the enormity and complexity of Exültov's request. "I still don't understand. Why can't you escape with them and teach them yourself?"

"I want nothing more than to escape with my children and turn my back on this life. But my people still need me. One of the many things I learned from my wife is that even after many centuries, not all the Nephezai have dwindled into self-absorbed, resentful creatures.

"Just like all the Nephezai here, she was born in the depths of banishment. Yet she still found enough compassion in her heart to become a beacon of light and hope—even risking her life to spread it to others. She was determined to serve not just the Nephezai in Scylorethyz but the entire Nephezai species. What better way can I ensure her light never dims than to continue her work?

"Severe changes need to be made, but I will no longer subject my children to the punishment for my ancestors' sins. I will grant my wife's wish to give our children a life of freedom, even if it means I must ask someone else to raise them in my stead. I will do it, to honor them and their future, and to honor my wife and her dream.

"Adjacent to all that, I must remain here in earnest for the day I take over from my father. All while pursuing my best to be a bridge between ocean and land. I need to prepare my people for the day my children return from the surface and lead all the Nephezai in a new regime of freedom and allegiance with the land dwellers."

Violet remained silent for a long moment, until she could muster the courage to speak. "Let's say that hypothetically—and I'm not saying I am agreeing to this—but *hypothetically,* if I do as you ask and you help us all to escape from here, then how? How do we leave? What is the earliest we can escape?"

Her heart rate quickened, and her pulse hammered in her ears in anticipation of his answer.

"If I were to say I may have figured out a way, you would have to put your complete trust in me. Is that something you're able to do?"

More strands of beads snapped in Violet's clenched hands.

How can someone ever completely trust another?

And yet, the only person she'd ever fully trusted was Lyla-Rose. Her dear friend had never lied to her, never betrayed her, and always helped Violet keep her own secrets. Lyla-Rose was always there for her.

Could Violet trust the prince with the safety of her daughter? She'd only just started trusting Thane with Solace.

Then again, Exültov was taking a big risk himself. How desperate would a father have to be to trust his own children with a near stranger?

"The truth, Violet."

After a few seconds, a tingle formed under her tongue. Before she could restrain it, her forked tongue whipped out and snapped against the air bubble around her head.

Exültov's brows rose, his countenance slightly stunned.

Violet's own shock overcame her for a heartbeat, but not because her tongue had lashed out. Her surprise came from the bouquet of flavors exploding through her senses. Even with the filter of an air bubble and a foot of water between her and the prince, she could still taste his emotions as clearly as she could anyone's on land.

Exültov's expression morphed into a guarded mask, but he couldn't quite hide his fascination. "I've heard about the Veniri ability of sampling and deciphering emotions. I'm curious, what have you learned from me?"

"Uh…" Violet tugged on her dress; a bead of sweat rolled down her temple.

"What emotions did you taste?" Exültov prompted.

She had picked up a variety of flavors, but which ones to admit to? She riffled through her mental list of the emotions corresponding to each flavor. "Well, I scented vanilla for one, and ironically the flavor of seaweed."

"And what do they mean?"

"Vanilla represents your inspiration and passion to do something, and the seaweed confirms your determination to see it through."

A rush of relief washed over Exültov's face. "That was all?" When Violet hesitated, he prodded, "Go on, what other flavors have you sensed?"

She explained the presence of ginger for his curiosity, macadamia for his hopefulness, molasses for his anxiety. She also noted that black licorice tainted each flavor, making known his deep sorrow.

"Hmm" was Exültov's only response.

"There are a few other minor flavors, not strong enough for me to pay too much attention to, but one is the acrid tang of bleach, which confirms you're telling me the truth. So because of that, my answer is yes. I believe I can trust you."

"Good." Exültov turned his attention back to the effigy of his wife. "Regarding the plan of escape, as I said before, I do not possess the skill to light forge gateways. My father is the only living Nephezai who possesses that skill, to ensure no other can enter without permission… or escape. Anyone who is caught practicing light forging is executed.

"I, myself, have had a few lessons from my father, to prepare me for the time I will be king. But I am ashamed to say I do not have the gift. As a result, I fear the Nephezai realm will truly be trapped here in Scylorethyz come the day I take the throne."

Violet nodded, understanding just how dire Exültov's circumstances were.

"I wish there were a better solution. Sadly, escape from here would not include a shortcut through the underwater mountain ranges. The alternative route involves many other dangers, larger predators, and the chance of getting lost, not to mention the risk of running into hunters, all before reaching the safety of the surface."

A few of Violet's loose beads fell from her hands. "Great. You're not really giving me much confidence in this idea."

"As much as I'm willing to help you and your family escape, I cannot guarantee there will be no casualties. If I were to send you all out beyond the city borders alone, there would be no hope for you. But with a guide, and extra protection, there is a much higher chance you can reach the surface safely. Of course, you'll need someone who is well acquainted with the dangers and passageways to get you out and up to the surface."

"A guide?" Violet looked up, through the ceiling of dark water. "Why not swim straight up?"

"Because my ancestors established the city of Scylorethyz in the heart of an extinct underwater volcano. The opening of the volcano has eroded and caved in over time. Swim up, and you will eventually reach the ceiling of the largest cavern. Open water is at least a three-day journey away."

"Three days?" Violet's knees might have gotten weak if she were standing on land. In the water, her body became slack. "Three days." She took a few more moments to let that concept sink in.

"As I said, you will need a guide, and I will provide you with the best guide and the best protection I can offer."

Violet heaved in a deep breath. "Okay, so who's this guide you have in mind? And please don't tell me you're going to send Votloxo and her two besties."

"No, none of the Nephezai can be sent. There'd be too great a risk of someone noticing their absence and notifying my father." Exültov hesitated. "This may be the part of the plan where your trust in me would be tested most."

Violet's rising hopes plummeted. "Why? What's the problem? Who would you send?" She looked over at Jhutev.

"Jhutev is also unable to go with you. My father may be enraged to find you have escaped, but he would immediately send out his own hunting parties to bring back the Meruvo."

Jhutev's shoulders sagged. She hated to see the hopeless expression on his face.

Exültov turned and looked somewhere over Violet's shoulder. Following his line of sight, she saw that the group of servants who'd been cleaning the statues and pathways were now leaving the Necropolis Ravine. Their work shift must have ended.

When the doors shut behind them, Exültov swam a few meters above the statue of his wife and called out a phrase that seemed foreign even to the Nephezai language.

"What's going on?" Violet asked. Her eyes darted to the area where Exültov had set his fierce gaze.

No one answered.

Prince Exültov swam a bit farther up, his sea nettle tentacles gracefully trailing through the seawater.

Violet chewed on her lip. Unease fluttered in her belly when she caught sight of an oblong shadow a few hundred yards behind the prince. Still facing the other way, he hadn't seen it yet.

She squinted. Was that another Nephezai heading toward him?

Her fear spiked as the ominous shape grew larger—large enough for Violet to make out some distinguishing features.

Shark!

Terror practically punched her in the gut. Her legs kicked out involuntarily, and her wrists fluttered as she tried to propel herself back. But the frills and tulle of her dress allowed no smooth or rapid getaway.

It took her a second to register the prince still hadn't noticed the threat.

"Look out!" Violet screeched with alarm. Without a second thought, she changed trajectory and swam toward the prince. "Exültov, look out!"

He turned to her but still didn't see the monstrosity heading straight for him.

Violet wished she had strong fins or some kind of epic swimming superpower—any of the Nephezai abilities would be helpful right now! Her panic screamed at her to turn back, to save herself from the shark, but the massive shadow was almost upon Exültov. Sharp teeth glistened in the purple light.

Instinct screamed at her to flee, but she couldn't just leave the prince to his demise, especially not when the images of his two young children came to mind. Nephezai or not, those children couldn't lose both their parents. But she was still too far away to help...

A bright teal light ignited in Violet's periphery, and the

flames over her hands flashed in and out of her sight as she swam. Maybe the shark would be afraid of fire—or perhaps it'd be attracted to it.

Oh gosh, hopefully it wasn't the latter.

Before she could let her worries consume her further, something caught her from behind, dragging her back.

"Wait, Miss Violet."

"Let me go, Jhutev. That monster is heading right for the prince!" She tried to wriggle out of the Meruvo's grasp.

The prince had made no sign of retreating from the incoming shark. What was wrong with him? Another few feet and those teeth would be in chomping distance.

"Exültov, what are you doing? You have to get away!"

"Peace, Miss Violet," Jhutev said in a calm voice. "His Reverence is not in danger."

Even though Violet heard his words, they did nothing to tame her terror.

Her next warning cry choked off as the shark brushed straight past Exültov, then darted back to face him. No alarm or fear crossed the prince's features. Instead, he smiled. Then he laughed as the shark nuzzled its nose into his belly.

Exültov patted the shark's head. "Hello, old girl. It's been a while."

Violet gaped.

"His Reverence and Ebele first met when she was a pup. She comes to visit him along with the others."

"Oh," was all Violet could manage to say as Exültov started to give the shark belly rubs.

"Would you like to meet her?" Jhutev asked.

"What? Me? Meet a giant shark?" She waved a dismissive hand. "No, no, I'm fine. It's probably best if I don't interrupt."

Before Violet had even finished speaking, she looked up to find herself face-to-face with the shark. Heart in her throat, she kept deathly still—or at least as still as she could in the water's currents—as the creature made a tight circle around her and Jhutev.

Casually gliding over to join them, Exültov observed the situation with a bemused expression. "It appears Ebele is curious to know who you are."

"Do you mean curious in a 'wonder how I taste' kind of way, or...?"

Jhutev gave Violet a subtle smile. "There is no need for concern, Miss Violet."

"Really? Are you sure?" Sweat prickled on her brow and trailed down her temples.

"Quite sure," said Exültov. "She's already eaten."

Violet didn't reply as the shark nuzzled her belly, just as she'd done to Exültov.

"At least I think she's eaten."

Violet's eyes snapped to Exültov, only to find him smirking at her. She gave him her deadliest glare, which only made him grin wider. The tips of his transparent teeth glinted in the subtle light.

Despite her terror, Violet found herself surprised at how gentle the shark was when nudging her stomach.

"She wants you to rub her head," said Exültov.

"Oh..." Violet bit down on her lip as she considered how fatal the next three seconds would be, whether she refused to pat the shark or not. A tingle under her tongue caught her by surprise. Would her Veniri forked tongue even work on a shark?

Without another thought, she whipped her tongue out.

Of the flavors that engulfed her senses, cinnamon wasn't among them, nor any other flavor resembling some kind of murderous intent.

"What do you sense?" Exültov's intense gaze sparkled with interest.

"Uh... I don't sense I'll be fish food, at least not yet." Even though Violet still didn't like the idea of patting the shark, it gave her no choice as it nuzzled under her arm.

Exültov and Jhutev looked on with grins on their faces.

Each time the shark swam out and then darted back toward Violet, it caused her breath to hitch. She just couldn't get used to the idea of petting a shark. But, thankfully, all limbs were still in place, and all pints of blood remained in her veins.

"Uh… is someone going to do something about this creature? Can someone please help?"

Exültov laughed again. It had a nice melody to it, especially when Jhutev joined in. She'd never heard either of them laugh this much before, even amid all the other jovial Nephezai at every event they'd attended.

"Come here, Ebele." The prince beckoned her back as one would a puppy.

"Good grief…" Violet placed a hand on her heart, willing it to slow down. Only then did she notice her flames had gone out.

Jhutev must have noticed her confused expression. "Your flames extinguished when Ebele came close to you."

"But how? Why? When I'm under threat, my flames usually don't go out unless I intend them to."

Were her flames broken? Holding a hand up, she willed her flames to ignite, and teal fire licked over her hand and wrist. Everything seemed to be working fine.

"Perhaps you knew instinctively Ebele was not going to hurt you, so you switched off the flame before you could hurt her," Jhutev said with a shrug.

"Huh… maybe." Violet frowned. Her desperation to flee had waned a little since watching Exültov pat and cuddle the shark. "Hang on a second. You said 'She comes to visit the prince with the others.' What others? Are more sharks coming?"

"Not sharks, Miss Violet."

As if on cue, more dark shapes swam toward them through the inky-black waters. This time, Exültov and the shark swam over to join Violet and Jhutev.

"Don't fear, Violet. They've just come to talk," said Exültov in a soothing tone.

"Talk? To us?" Violet didn't know how much more shock she could handle as eight creatures made of horror and nightmares swam into their vicinity.

25
DO YOU HAVE A SUBMARINE?

NATHAN FIDGETED WITH A LOOSE BANDAGE AROUND HIS WRIST as he scanned all the people crammed into the hack-shack.

Autumn, En'gorr and his three guards, Tio, and himself patiently listened as Nika filled in the group on what had happened since she'd disappeared from Maple Shire. Everyone periodically glanced over at Sagan's mother, who sat on the carpet in the corner of the room, dutifully watching the three Veniri children. A big part of Nathan wanted to remain dubious about Nika's reasons for returning, but the three children and the wraithlike woman certainly piqued his curiosity.

Once Nika had finished talking, everyone remained silent.

Seconds dragged out.

Nika may be petite, but it was no secret that she could still pack a punch. Turns out she could also pack a massive punch to the gut even without her fists.

They now had a lead on Violet, Thane and Solace… however, they were trapped at the bottom of the freaking ocean.

Nathan's shoulders hunched, his head sagged, stopping only when his chin touched his chest.

Also, apparently Nika had nothing to do with the Maple Shire bombings. Yet, in what world was that the good news, especially in comparison to the fact that Sagan was the one who lured Violet and Thane out to their new watery prison.

Sagan Branstone.

Under his breath, Nathan cursed his name. He had trusted that hunter. Hell, Sagan had even been the one to rescue Nathan from a hunter barracks, saving him from having his crystal bones harvested.

He'd fought side by side with Sagan, on more than one occasion.

Sagan had even stood up for Violet when Nika went psycho-freak on her.

And it was all for what? So Sagan could toss Violet and Thane into a watery grave the first chance he got. How did that make any kind of sense?

If he ever saw Sagan again…

The muscles in Nathan's neck ached from the constant clenching of his jaw. His hands squeezed into fists. The bandages over his fingers and hands constricted to the point of being painful.

Just as Nathan had thought Nika couldn't report any more bad news, she then recounted the events of how she'd come by three Veniri children.

After lifetimes upon lifetimes of the Veniri shifters keeping their hives hidden from human hunters, a hive had now been breached and desecrated. And not just any hive, Nathan's own hive. And out of all the iniquitous creatures who could commit such a heinous act, it was of course Matthias Branstone's doing.

Nathan's head began to spin. Was the air in the hut becoming a bit too dense to breathe?

He jumped up and opened the window that faced the forest behind the hut. Gripping the windowsill, he drew in a lungful of the fresh air.

"Nathan? You alright?"

Nathan waved off Tio's concern. "Yeah, just give me a moment. I think the bandages are a bit tight. Just need some air. Hard to breathe."

After a moment, his head cleared a little, but he still felt a bit shaky in the knees. Turning back to face the group, he sat on the windowsill, hands on either side, anchoring him in place.

"What the heck is a Nephezai?" Autumn finally blurted. Her long, bead-adorned dreadlocks swung around her shoulders as she looked around the room for answers.

Nika opened her mouth to respond, but Tio beat her to the punch.

"They're water shifters. Their shifter energies are allied with Neptune. Think mermaids, but more amphibious and much more freaky looking. They're the kind of water monsters you definitely do *not* want to come across while you're out in the open seas, especially if you're a human."

"Why?" Autumn asked.

"Because the humans and the Nephezai have been enemies basically since the dawn of time," said Tio. "The Nephezai enslaved the humans. Then, hundreds of years ago, the humans overpowered the Nephezai."

"Humans banished the Nephezai to the deepest depths of the oceans," added Nathan.

Tio nodded. "Yeah, and because of that, the Nephezai hate the humans even more. They're like the real-life selkie and siren mythologies all rolled into one species. They love luring humans into a watery grave."

"Only stupid-brave Nephezai dare breach banishment and swim to ocean top," said En'gorr.

"So… that's it then? Violet, Thane, and Solace are dead? Dragged under the ocean and drowned to death?" Autumn's voice hitched on the last few words, her eyes rapidly blinking.

"No, I don't believe they're dead," said Nika.

"How do you know for sure?" Tio asked.

"Because the Nephezai king showed way too much interest in Violet and Thane just to immediately kill them."

"What exactly did the Nephezai king want with them?" Nathan asked.

Nika's knee bounced up and down. "I have no idea."

"So, you think they're still alive, even now?" Autumn asked, eyes wide with hope.

"If the Nephezai continue to believe Violet, Thane, and Solace are more valuable alive than dead, we can only hope."

"What are the chances of finding that out?" asked Tio.

"And what are the chances of rescuing them?" Autumn added.

"Unless you're all planning on growing gills and raking the entire seabed, then chances of a rescue are almost impossible," said Nika. She glanced around at everyone's shocked expressions with cool nonchalance. "What's the problem? Were you expecting someone to say that all we needed to do was wave a magic wand, add a sprinkle of unicorn dust and the blessing of a mushroom troll, and everything would be all better?"

Autumn rolled her eyes.

"Sheesh, do you have to be such a jerk about it?" Tio asked.

Nika placed a hand on her hip. "If you've got a plan on how to rescue two land shifters and a baby from the bottom of the freaking ocean, I, for one, would love to hear it."

Tio's pious expression faltered, then hardened into a frown. "So let me get this straight, Nika. You're willing to rescue three Veniri babies from your sadistic uncle, but when it comes to Violet, Thane, and their *baby*, you're more than happy to leave them for dead. Is that what you're saying?"

"Of course not." Nika crossed her arms. "What I'm saying is, I don't have a submarine parked out on the driveway. Do *you* have a submarine?"

The bickering started to escalate, with Autumn and En'gorr interjecting their own arguments.

Nathan pinched the bridge of his nose. "*Enough*."

The squabbling died down at Nathan's command. All eyes turned to him, but his attention shifted to Nika. "What did the Nephezai trade for Violet and Thane?"

"Uh… Uncle Matthias wanted the Nephezai king's spangle."

"Spangle?" Tio's brows drew together. "Do you mean one of those disc thingies that looks like a glass coaster? Like the orange one Autumn stole from En'gorr?"

"Yeah, but the king had a purple one. He had it strung around his neck like an amulet."

"So, now that your uncle has the Nephezai's purple spangle, what does he plan to—"

"Uncle Matthias didn't get the purple spangle," said Nika, cutting Tio off.

"What do you mean he didn't get it?" said Tio.

"Yeah, Matthias Branstone doesn't strike me as the type to leave empty-handed," added Autumn.

"In the end, the king decided to hold on to his spangle and gave Uncle Matthias a bunch of golden tomes instead. But before Violet was taken away, he forced the mission to retrieve the spangle onto her," said Nika.

"Forced how?" Nathan asked.

Nika grimaced, her downcast eyes filled with more shame than Nathan had ever expected to see from her. "My uncle strapped a collar around Solace's neck—a collar with a timed explosive that can be deactivated with a remote control. Except the collar can only receive a signal above the ocean's surface."

The shock that engulfed the room felt tangible enough to slice a blade through. Several jaws dropped. A few expressions simmered with fury.

"So," started Autumn, "when you say the collar is timed..."

"Uncle Matthias has given Violet three weeks to find a way to get the spangle. Otherwise... well, I'm sure you get the idea."

Again the room fell silent.

"Do you still have the orange spangle?" Nika asked Autumn.

She shook her head. Her face and shoulders sagged in defeat. "No, your uncle took it from us just after the explosions went off."

"What is purpose of spangles? In our family, orange one just heirloom, trinket passed to Jiovis prince for throne," said En'gorr. "Why Matthias need?"

"No idea." Nika scrubbed at her eyes with the heels of her hands.

Mind racing, Nathan tried to make sense of the jumbled mess in his head, searching for any kind of solution. Violet, Thane, and Solace needed to be saved, and things needed to be set right with Maple Shire—all while thwarting Matthias's mission, whatever that was.

The group continued to discuss and analyze everything, yet no one could come up with a plausible plan. Eventually, the discussion moved on to Sagan's mother. Nika filled everyone in on the details, describing the escalating concerns.

"Not only does it turn out I need help with the Veniri children, but I figured Aunty Odette could also benefit from, uh… Dr. Dawn's help." Nika's shoulders slumped. "But now that she's gone…"

Nathan's stomach dropped. It still seemed unfathomable that someone as ingenious, kind, and humble as Dawn Farrow was no longer alive. He looked around the group, at the heartfelt grief evident in every teary eye, every drooping head. Autumn wrapped her arms around herself and softly sniffled, and En'gorr responded by drawing her into his side.

"And Gus?" Nika asked.

"He's fine," said Autumn, her voice sharp. "At least, physically he's fine. But as you can imagine, losing his mother has been beyond devastating."

Nika shot a glance at the three orphaned Veniri boys, perhaps understanding a little too well what she meant.

"Uncle Lazareth is okay too," Autumn went on to add. "He's dealing with his grief the best he can by keeping busy."

Nika looked over at Nathan. "And what about you? Looks like you earned some decent injuries."

Nathan grunted.

"Those bandages aren't a result of the bombs. They're just a front to hide the real problem," said Tio.

Nika groaned. "Good grief. I don't think I can handle any more bad news or epic surprises."

26
ZASF

Violet's heart stuttered as the eight nightmare creatures paused a few yards before them. She'd seen these creatures before, way back on the day she, Solace, and Thane had been dragged to their underwater prison and their group had a skirmish with the… what did Votloxo call them?

Ügovs?

Exültov approached the leader. They both bowed low, then clasped forearms and clapped each other on the shoulders, over areas where jagged bone armor and mother-of-pearl thorns weren't present.

Violet blinked in astonishment. It was the warmest meeting she'd seen the Nephezai prince have with anyone.

"Violet, I would like to introduce you to Zasf, one of the Ügov clan leaders." Exültov gestured to the newcomer with a smile, as one would when introducing an old friend.

She remembered seeing this particular Ügov before. Transparent fangs spilled out of his mouth, and rows upon rows of jagged teeth covered his face and head. This Zasf had slain a fair number of Nephezai in the skirmish by the shipwreck.

"Hi," Violet said, trying her best not to sound high on helium, especially when the leader of the Ügovs turned his bulbous eyes on her. Their sickly green color illuminated with an eerie glow. In fact, all the Ügovs had the same glowing green eyes.

Zasf swam closer to Violet and, as he'd done with Exültov, bowed low to her. His Ügov companions followed, also bowing at the waist. "It is an honor to meet you, Hybrid Violet. We have learned many things about you."

"Uh, great. Nice to meet you too." She couldn't help shooting Exültov a questioning look.

The expression on his face turned apologetic, but before he could explain, Zasf continued.

"Do not be concerned with what this jellyfish may have said on your behalf, Hybrid Violet. Be assured, all that was spoken of you was in high regard."

The Ügov leader's accent contrasted greatly with the Nephezai's, consisting of various throaty drawls, added clicks and chirrups, and what seemed to be odd emphases on a few select words. Zasf also didn't speak of Exültov in the formal fashion one usually used for a prince. As obvious as Exültov's sea nettle jellyfish features were, she never thought anyone would be brave enough to address him as "this jellyfish."

"Yes, please forgive my lack of forewarning, Violet," Exültov added. "I would have mentioned things sooner if I had thought it was safe to do so. Plus I needed to ensure you were someone I could trust with an interaction such as this."

"Our alliance with the prince is prohibited. The rest of the Nephezai would aggressively oppose his sympathizing with myself and my ilk," added Zasf. "All who attempt to acquaint themselves with us are deemed traitors."

"Is that because of what happened between the Nephezai

and the Ügovs the day we were brought down from the surface?" Violet asked.

Exültov's features hardened. "That particular clash was an unfortunate event, one I was ashamed to be informed of after it happened." He turned to Zasf. "I know I've already expressed my deepest condolences—"

Zasf held up a hand. "Do not trouble yourself with something out of your control, Friend Exültov. You have already done more than enough to ensure medical supplies reached those in need. We are also grateful for the small tokens of comfort granted to those who lost loved ones."

Exültov placed a fist over his heart. "I only wish to continue the hard work my dear Nepthyz started in striving for reconciliation with the Ügov kingdom."

Both he and Zasf looked upon the illuminated purple statue of Exültov's wife.

"It was a sorrowful day when we lost her," said Zasf. "We owe her more than we can ever repay. And you too, Friend Exültov."

The prince bowed his head. "I'm humbled by your gratitude. But there is much more work to be done."

Zasf nodded in understanding. "So, I am to assume you have come to a decision about the relocation of the young prince and princess?"

"Yes, I have decided." Exültov rolled his shoulders back, as if adjusting a heavy burden. "I will accept your offer to take them to a safe location on the surface. However, I need you to also take three others—Violet and her family."

Zasf absently patted the shark while contemplating Exültov's request. "Adding three more would bring further challenges, but it would not be impossible. I could add another warrior or two." He gave the prince a pointed look. "And with the additional protection, we could add an extra—"

"No." Exültov shook his head. "We've already discussed

this. I cannot leave. I am needed here, for the sake of the Nephezai and the Ügovs. Once I have achieved peace among our people, then I will be reconciled with my children and bring them to a home they deserve."

"Understood. I am willing to proceed with your blessing then," said Zasf. "And what about you, Hybrid Violet? I have seen the discomfort in your eyes since our arrival. We, the Ügovs, are aware of our startling appearances. It has long been an issue when interacting with those not like us. Regardless, we will endeavor to get you and your family to the surface. Will you endeavor to trust us and obey our instruction?"

"I think so."

"The journey out from Scylorethyz is too perilous for uncertainty," said Zasf.

Violet chewed her lip. She'd promised in all her silent prayers that she'd do anything to get Solace to the surface—to get her daughter home safe. And though she'd known Exültov only a short time, if he trusted these creatures with his own children, surely she could as well. "Yes, I am willing to trust you. I will do all you ask."

"Good, then it's settled," said Exültov.

"We leave tomorrow night," said Zasf, "after the king and his entourage have departed for their intended week-long journey."

"If all goes well," Exültov told her, "you will have a week to get to safety before my father comes back and discovers you're missing."

They'd finally be getting out of here *tomorrow night*. Violet forced a smile, although her gut started to sink with an awful realization.

She now had less than twenty-four hours to snatch the purple spangle from the king. How on earth was she going to achieve that?

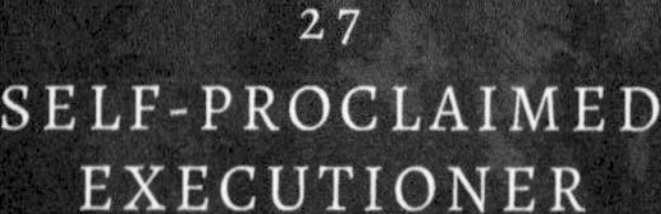

27
SELF-PROCLAIMED EXECUTIONER

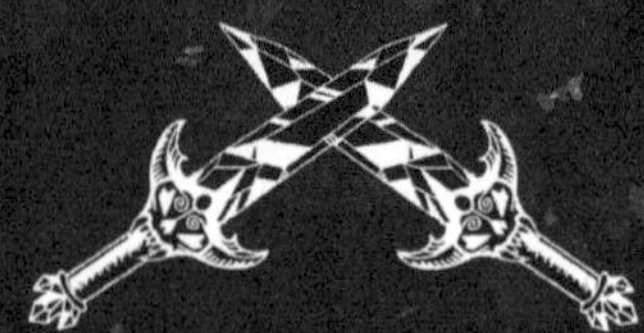

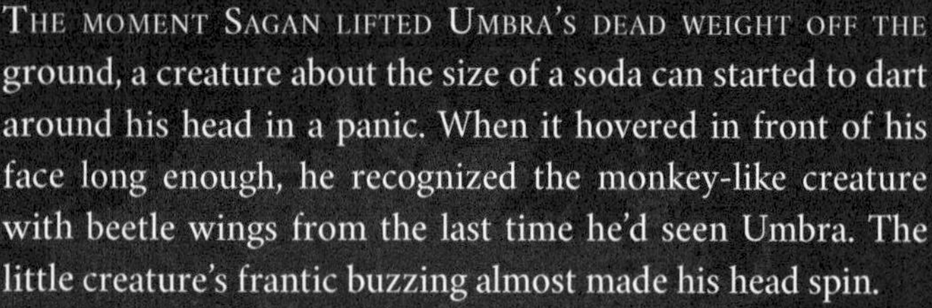

The moment Sagan lifted Umbra's dead weight off the ground, a creature about the size of a soda can started to dart around his head in a panic. When it hovered in front of his face long enough, he recognized the monkey-like creature with beetle wings from the last time he'd seen Umbra. The little creature's frantic buzzing almost made his head spin.

"Either shut up or help me," he growled, almost wishing he had a free hand to swat the creature away.

The little monkey hovered in the air for a few moments, and then, gesturing for Sagan to follow, it zipped toward the door at the end of the hall.

Sagan hustled to catch up, trying hard not to jostle the unconscious woman in his arms. The lush, otherworldly greenery engulfed him once again, but he didn't stop. Instead, he allowed himself to be led into the kitchen and gently laid Umbra on one of the marble countertops.

Cursing himself for leaving his own first aid kit back in the car, he looked up at the hovering monkey. "I don't suppose you know where I can find something to stop Umbra's bleeding."

The monkey chittered a response with a firm nod of its head. It darted over to some of the alien-looking plants, tore off a few leaves and flowers, and brought them back to Sagan.

"Uh…" He gawked at the bundle of foliage. "I meant medical supplies. Do you know what a first aid kit is?"

The creature let out a high-pitched screech, then zipped around the kitchen in a flash of iridescent lightning. It opened cupboards and drawers, collecting various items.

Meanwhile, Sagan carefully removed Umbra's leather jacket. With the scissors the monkey had retrieved, he then cut away some of her blood-soaked shirt.

A breath hissed through Sagan's teeth at the sight of the nasty gash along her ribs and lower abdomen. Several other nicks and scrapes gave him the impression Umbra may have been dragged along the concrete at one point.

Thankfully, his hunter upbringing had taught him to deal with a lot of traumatic injuries. With a trained eye, he quickly deduced that if he could stop the bleeding, he should be able to stitch up Umbra's wounds without much trouble.

He eyed a bottle of isopropyl alcohol the beetle-monkey had placed on the counter. As much as the iso would help clean and disinfect her wounds, Umbra needed something more powerful. Again, he wanted to kick himself for leaving his supplies behind.

But… not all his first aid equipment had been left in the car. He always kept a small supply of the most important item with him.

No! Sagan's anxiety flared. *I can't share my Ylixium. What if something happens and* I *need it?*

Immediately, he recoiled at the thought. *Get over yourself! That's just the addiction talking.*

Fighting hard to ignore the intense urge to do otherwise,

he reached into a secret pocket in his jacket and pulled out a small glass vial.

The pearly-white fluid seemed to glow even brighter under the lights in Umbra's kitchen. It always amazed him that the most powerful blood came from the most humble and peaceful of shifter species. The majority of the shapeshifters whose blood was harvested as Ylixium never even picked up a weapon to defend themselves. Shame burned his cheeks and neck. It was just another level of wicked the hunters stooped to. Not even that. Hunting those innocent and defenseless shifters was downright sick. And yet there was no way Sagan would be alive today if not for the diabolical trade of the Ylixium elixir.

His heart rate surged at the sight of the swirling liquid. Even knowing how foul it tasted, his mouth watered all the same, and the need to take a swig became almost unbearable. He screwed up his nose, revolted by how much just a glance at this stuff affected him.

"Screw you," he whispered at the glass vial. Then, before he could stop himself, he twisted off the cap and poured some of the pearl-white liquid over the biggest gash on Umbra's side.

Umbra cried out. Her eyes flew open, and she attempted to sit up.

"Careful." Sagan caught her before her sudden movements sent her sliding off the counter.

"Damn, that's cold," Umbra protested.

Sagan winced, knowing all too well the icy chill she was experiencing, not to mention the surge of adrenaline and acute alertness, followed by the gradual numbing wherever the pearly-white liquid soaked in.

Umbra glanced down at her side, then her accusing smoky-quartz eyes landed on Sagan. "What happened? What did you do?"

"I was just trying to… clean your wound. Here, you should drink some of this."

Umbra frowned and pointed to the pearly liquid on her wound. "You already poured some of that stuff on me, and now you want me to drink it?"

"Uh, yeah. It soothes pain and aids healing. It also kick-starts a more speedy recovery if ingested."

Umbra narrowed her eyes at the glass vial, then shook her head.

"I promise it won't hurt you," Sagan coaxed. "Trust me, if I wanted to kill you, poison isn't what I'd use."

Umbra scoffed, as if she didn't believe he could hurt her if he tried.

He suppressed a smirk at her confidence. "Come on, just take it. It's only a healing elixir."

"I know what *Ylixium* is *and* what it does." Mouth pursed in disgust, Umbra swatted his hand away. "Hard pass. I'm not keen on the idea of chugging shape-shifter blood. Besides, I've heard that stuff tastes like zombies' insides."

Sagan raised a brow. "Zombies? Really?"

"Yeah? As someone whose entire existence revolves around shape-shifters, you're telling me you have a problem with the concept of zombies?" Umbra started to laugh but then coughed a few times, clutching her side. For several seconds, her face screwed up in agony.

She needed more Ylixium to relieve the pain, but Sagan knew he couldn't force it on her. As he pocketed the vial of pearlescent liquid, he tried his best to suppress the utter relief that his stash hadn't been entirely consumed.

Stop being so selfish and focus on the task at hand, he scolded himself.

"Ylixium or not, I still think it's best to stitch that up." He pointed to the gaping wound along her side.

Umbra began to shake her head again, but the little

monkey interrupted by buzzing around her face, chattering at a million miles an hour. Its iridescent wings glimmered in the eerie illumination from the nearby alien plants.

Umbra's face crinkled in annoyance. "Did you have to bring that up? Seriously, Toffee, when will you drop that? It was just that one time."

The little monkey screeched again and pointed at Sagan, then flew over and landed on his shoulder. It continued to chitter, nodding its head and shaking its finger at her.

Umbra glanced between Sagan and the little monkey, amusement briefly outshining the agony in her eyes. "Fine, fine. Only if it will get you off my back." She sighed and slumped back on the countertop with an exhausted *thunk*.

"What was that about?" Sagan gave the beetle-monkey on his shoulder the side-eye.

"Toffee's just reminding me of the last time she dealt with some damage I happened to acquire. She also said I need to quit my whining and let you help me. Consider yourself lucky, hunter. Toffee's not one to trust others easily."

The little monkey—Toffee—tapped Sagan on the side of his face and titched a single syllable at him, as if to say, *"Well, what are you waiting for?"*

Now under the watchful gaze of both Umbra and Toffee, Sagan continued to clean Umbra's wound, working as gently as he could despite a few winces from his patient. He wasn't really one to freak out under pressure, but the constant bleeding soon started to worry him. "Damn. It's still bleeding," he said under his breath.

Umbra pointed to the wall of plants adjoining the kitchen. "Toffee, go get some Tokino lotus leaves."

The little monkey whizzed away and returned with a small handful of what Sagan could only describe as aloe vera leaves edged with petals. Vermilion red speckled the rich green leaves, but the petals were a vibrant, almost toxic blue.

"What is this?" Sagan said.

"It's one of my mother's plants" was all he got in answer.

"What do I do with it?"

"Break one open and pour the sap onto my gash."

"What? You want me to pour *sap* into your wound?"

"Seriously?" Umbra pished. "You think shifter blood is perfectly fine, but plant sap you have a problem with?"

She leveled a look at him that most others wouldn't dare to direct his way. But instead of meeting it with his usual deadly gaze, he gently took the strange aloe-type leaf from Toffee.

When he snapped the leaf open, thick, gooey toxic-blue liquid gushed out. "And you want me to pour this stuff in your wound?"

"No, just stand there and watch me bleed out. Yes! Don't be scared, hunter. Just pour it on."

With a slight shake of his head, Sagan allowed the sap to drip over Umbra's torso. When the liquid mixed with Umbra's blood, it turned a vibrant purple, and the bleeding immediately stopped. A few seconds later, it seeped into her open wound and disappeared.

"Whoa," said Sagan. "I've never seen anything like that before. What is this stuff?"

"My mother named it a Tokino lotus. She was a bit of an herbalist, and this plant is one of her crossbreeding experiments."

When Umbra didn't offer any more information, Sagan snapped open more of the Tokino lotus leaves and dripped the sap into the other gouge marks. While he worked, Toffee mopped up the rest of the blood on Umbra's torso with a small cloth and some saline solution.

As the crimson gore washed away, a collection of older scars became evident on Umbra's body.

"So, just another day at the office, huh?" Sagan said.

Umbra huffed a soft laugh. "Yeah, I suppose you could say that."

She had an impressive number of scars scattered over her abdomen and hints of more along her back—silvery ghosts of cuts, puncture wounds that may have been bite marks, a mottled area with the appearance of an acid burn, and a whole heap of small nicks and scrapes. Her collection wasn't all that different from a hunter's.

"So what was it this time?" Sagan asked. "Not another Godzilla worm, I hope."

Umbra chuckled, then immediately winced. "No giant worms this time. It was a razortusk. Usually, they're not a big deal, but this one was a bit harder to kill compared to the others. Unfortunately the sucker got away before I could finish the job."

"What's a razortusk?"

Umbra waved a dismissive hand. "Just a boar-like creature with literal metallic razors as its tusks. Yet another one of Xabat's experiments gone wrong that I need to keep putting down before they escape. Heaven forbid any of those creatures figure out how to cross the bridge and end up in the city over the river."

"I'm surprised none of them have made it over there by now."

"Hopefully it doesn't come to that. So far, I'm pretty efficient at my job. And if I don't put the creatures down, who will?"

A surge of remorse flooded through Sagan—he recalled all too well the type of creatures involved in Renard and his cronies' experiments. He'd never been able to erase from his mind the surveillance footage of the Godzilla worm's creation. Xabat scientists had strapped a human man to a hospital bed and stuck dozens of tubes into his veins, pumping him full of strange multicolored liquids. Within minutes, the unfortunate soul had begun screaming in utter agony while morphing into his giant, grotesque counterpart.

"'Put down,' huh?" Sagan rubbed his knuckles over a tic in his jaw. "So, you're a self-proclaimed executioner?"

Umbra's brow furrowed. "What I do is a mercy compared to what those people and creatures are enduring in the Xabat facility. I always ensure their release from this world is as swift and painless as possible."

Contemplating that concept, Sagan disinfected a needle and threaded it.

By the time he began suturing Umbra's wound, the beetle-winged monkey had flitted down and perched on top of his patient's chest, keeping a close eye on each stitch. The remaining purple stuff that hadn't yet dissolved into her wound had become quite tacky, making it easier to pinch together the ragged flesh.

While he sewed, he felt Umbra's intense gaze on him.

"What?" he finally said, keeping a steady focus on his work.

Umbra tilted her head to the side. "I've never seen bleached eyes up close before."

A sudden rush of shame heated the sides of Sagan's neck.

"What color were your eyes before the Ylixium bleached them?"

"I can't remember..."

"How long does it take for the Ylixium to begin bleaching?"

"Uh... it's different for everyone."

He finished the last of his sutures, then snipped off the remainder of the thread.

Umbra gingerly sat up, but instead of inspecting her wound, she leaned in closer to him. Sagan froze at her unexpected proximity. Beneath the sharp scent of blood, sweat, and grime, he detected an undertone of sweetness, something fruity. Was it her shampoo? Was she wearing perfume? Or was he just now picking up a fragrance from one of the floral plants nearby?

She regarded him for a long moment, and then her inquisitive expression softened. "Does it hurt?"

After a few heartbeats, Sagan shook his head.

Umbra didn't say anything more about his eyes. For a moment, he wasn't sure if he was relieved or disappointed she didn't ask any further questions.

"You're all done," he said once he'd finished applying the dressings.

Without bothering to scrutinize Sagan's work, Umbra slid off the counter. "You didn't have to help me, you know."

"Oh yeah?" Sagan washed his hands in the kitchen sink, using a hose that ran in from the balcony. "If I hadn't been here, who would have made sure you didn't fall down that hole in the slab and go splat on the concrete below? I doubt your little monkey friend here would've been able to pull you safely away from the edge before you completely passed out."

"Toffee would've figured something out," Umbra insisted, to which Toffee chittered a sharp response. "Oh, shush, Toffee. We've done just fine by ourselves. We haven't needed anyone else before."

"Just a simple 'thank you' would suffice," said Sagan.

Umbra huffed but, with a scolding from Toffee, relinquished a small smile. "I appreciate what you've done. Now, if you're both done lecturing me, I think I'm in need of a decent wash. Feel free to exit the way you entered. I'm sure you can figure out how to reverse the pulley system for the cable."

"Actually… I came here for your help."

Umbra immediately shook her head. "No way."

"I haven't told you what I need help with."

"Doesn't matter. If you've come here looking for *my* help,

then I can only assume you need me to get you back into Xabat, considering last time you and your posse were here you blew up the last unguarded way in. And now you're probably thinking I know of another way."

"Do you know another way?"

Umbra sighed and rubbed her temple. That was answer enough for Sagan.

"Look, all I need is a way in."

"It's not that simple, hunter."

"Just call me Sagan."

"Whatever. What I mean is, getting you in might be a little tricky. Getting out is another thing. Why do you even want to go in there in the first place?"

"Because..." Sagan flicked his gaze over the wall of alien plants while he gathered his thoughts. "My mother was one of their victims. They were experimenting on her. I managed to get her out, but she's... she's not well. I need to know what they did to her so I can figure out how to help her."

Neither of them said anything for several long minutes.

Toffee flew over and perched on Sagan's shoulder again, chittering with enthusiasm. Umbra listened with pursed lips.

"Fine." She threw up an exasperated hand. "I'll help you. But first I need to rest. Tomorrow we'll work out a plan. Toffee can show you where the spare room is."

With that, Umbra gingerly made her way through the kitchen and disappeared down an adjoining hallway.

Toffee spoke a few syllables in her own language, then patted Sagan on the side of his face, as if to say, *"I've done the hard work and vouched for you, buddy. Now don't screw up."*

28
DE-EVOLUTION OF HUMANS

HOW THE HECK DOES ONE FIGURE OUT HOW TO STEAL FROM the king of an underwater shifter race in less than twenty-four hours?

Violet's mind went into overdrive. So far she didn't have a hope in hell of getting that purple spangle—but they couldn't miss this chance of escaping the Nephezai kingdom and making it back to the surface. Exültov and the Ügovs had already made the arrangements. All she had to do was tell Thane to be ready.

But that didn't solve the problem of removing the collar from Solace's neck.

She still needed to get that spangle.

She *had* to get that spangle.

Just get the damn spangle!

What even was that spangle thing, and why was it so important?

Damn Matthias Branstone. Double—*triple!*—damn him for putting that collar on Solace and creating this unbearable situation.

For a moment, she considered coming clean to Exültov

about the whole thing. Considering the fraught relationship with his father, he might not be too offended at the idea of her stealing from Qozzlotl. But Zasf would probably flat-out refuse to take Solace if he knew she'd be bringing an actual bomb into their midst.

No, Violet couldn't risk losing this opportunity to escape.

Once Exültov had guided her and Jhutev back from the Necropolis Ravine, he gave Violet a long, somber look. "I'll be in touch soon."

Before she could reply, he swam away, leaving Jhutev to escort her back to the menagerie.

They glided along the hallways in silence. Violet chewed vigorously on her lip, replaying every word she'd said and analyzing every new thing she'd learned about the Ügovs and the Nephezai.

How stupid was this plan? Only a few days ago she'd been deathly scared of the mutant-like creatures of the deep, and now she was willing to put her life, and the lives of Thane and Solace, in their care.

Oh gosh… Thane was not going to like this idea at all. But surely even he would do anything to free Solace from the bottom of the ocean.

A flicker of movement caught her attention, and she looked up to find King Qozzlotl Nagahld himself near the end of the hallway she and Jhutev had just turned into. With a few snaps of his eel-like tail, he disappeared into a side corridor about fifty feet away.

"What's down this way?" Before Jhutev could stop her, Violet made a break for the corridor, hoping to catch another glimpse of the king before she lost track of him.

"Miss Violet, you've missed the turnoff to the menagerie," Jhutev called after her.

She maintained her course, swimming as fast as she could. Her earlier conversation with Thane echoed through her head: She'd never make any progress with the spangle by playing "little miss obedient hybrid." She needed to shake things up and deviate from what was expected of her.

"Miss Violet, where are you going?"

Violet gritted her teeth. Damn her inability to move fast in this underwater environment, especially while wearing yet another useless gown. Yet even if she were in a swimsuit, Jhutev would undoubtedly have no trouble gliding through the water to catch her.

She turned into the corridor the king had taken moments before, which opened into another opulently decorated room, much like the other ballrooms and dining halls she'd been dragged to many times before. Her eyes swept over the area.

What the heck?

The room was empty.

Where was he? Had she missed a turnoff? Was she even sure it was the king she'd seen come this way? Surely it was. What other Nephezai had the same eel features as King Qozzlotl?

"Miss Violet, you must return to your enclosure," Jhutev warned.

Panic threatened to paralyze her as she glanced around the basketball-court-sized chamber. *Come on brain, think! Which way would the king have gone?*

A spark of hope ignited when she spotted what looked like a door on the other side of the room. Just as Jhutev began to usher her away, she threw her arm out and pointed to a colorful wall in that direction. "What's that? Is that a mural? I love murals."

"Miss Violet, we really should be getting back before someone believes you are missing."

Ignoring the disapproving tone in Jhutev's voice, Violet clasped her hands in front of her. "Please, Jhutev. A quick peek at the mural won't hurt, right? I promise I'll only take a few seconds."

She couldn't quite read what was going on behind those starburst eyes, but with a quick glance over his shoulder, he sighed. "I suppose we can delay your return a few minutes without raising any alarm."

"Thank you!" Violet darted across the room and straight for the far end of the mural, which spanned the entire length of the wall. Only when she'd swum halfway across the chamber did it become clear that what had looked like a door was actually a shallow arched alcove, housing a bronze statue of a majestic hippocampus.

Disappointment almost knocked the wind out of her. She tried her best not to falter, highly aware of Jhutev keeping pace in her periphery.

"I'd forgotten how beautiful this mural is." He looked up at the vast length of multicolored illustrations.

"Uh, yeah," Violet said, a little distracted with glaring at the statue. The large bronze basin beneath it made her imagine that anywhere on land, this display would have been rigged as a water fountain. But unless the king was somehow hiding in the basin, she didn't care to muse over the absurdity of having a water feature at the bottom of the ocean.

Where the heck had that blasted Nephezai king gone? She'd been so sure she'd seen him come this way, and there was definitely no exit… unless there was some kind of secret passage?

Violet ran her hands over the cold bronze face, neck, and ears of the hippocampus. Her eyes roamed around the alcove and surrounding mural until she found Jhutev looking at her expectantly.

She blanched. After a heartbeat, she realized he'd been speaking to her the whole time.

"Sorry, Jhutev. I got caught up in how beautiful this, uh... water feature is."

He gave her a patient smile. "Perhaps I should be the one apologizing. I had been led to believe you were eager to view the *mural*."

Violet arranged her lips into what she hoped was an innocent smile. "Oh yes! Of course I'm interested in seeing the mural. But clearly, there's a lot more going on in this room than I first realized." Her attempt at a giggle was so lame she wanted to kick herself.

Jhutev's eyes narrowed slightly, but his mouth twitched with amusement. Just as she was about to start fidgeting under his scrutiny, he swept an arm out over the expanse of wall. "In that case, to best understand the story the mural tells, we should start at the other end."

"Great. Let's... start at that end."

When Jhutev turned his back to lead the way, Violet dropped her smile and ground her teeth.

She wouldn't be winning any Nancy Drew awards anytime soon. How had she fumbled things so fast? Sure, she'd managed to "break up the routine" a little, but her exploration had been a bust.

Violet suppressed a huff of frustration as Jhutev came to a halt and pointed to the first panel. As he began to explain the mural scene by scene, however, she started to get caught up in the story it told of the Nephezai race's history, particularly the tale of how a few thousand years ago a young Nephezai prince fell in love with an Erathi princess.

The more Jhutev spoke, the closer Violet drew to the mural, which she discovered was actually a mosaic. Her awe soared as she inspected the tiny fragments of colored glass, shattered porcelain, crushed iridescent shells, small marbled pebbles, and countless precious stones, pearls, and jewels. Each tiny piece was expertly inlaid, to the point where the

Nephezai prince and Erathi princess looked as if they could jump off the wall at any moment. Considering the intricate detail, the massive mosaic must have taken a lifetime.

Jhutev described the relationship of the Nephezai prince and the Erathi princess as an innocent romance turned tragic revenge story, which then escalated into a war between the two shifter species. Not until they'd reached the middle panels of the mosaic did a thought strike Violet.

"Hang on a second," she blurted, cutting Jhutev off mid-sentence. "You said the princess is Erathi, right?"

"Yes, quite right, Miss Violet."

"I thought 'Erathi' was another name for humans."

"Again, that's correct."

"But… this princess has wings. In fact, all the Erathi in this mural have wings."

Her fingers brushed over the textured representation of feathers, each one emerald green blending into lapis blue with a sparkling metallic gold tip. Some Erathi had their wings outstretched, a resplendent display of layered feathers; some had them folded behind their backs. But a lot of the wings were unfurled or canopied in mid-flight, especially in the gruesome battle scenes.

Jhutev gave a knowing nod. "Ah yes. I do recall being told that the Erathi have erased the truth of their original forms."

"'Original forms'? What do you mean by that?" Violet frowned. "The Erathi—humans—*don't* have wings."

"No, not anymore."

Violet gaped at Jhutev's patient expression. It took a few moments for the Meruvo's simple statement to sink in.

"You're joking, right? This has got to be some kind of fairy tale."

"Joking? Why would I joke, Miss Violet?"

"So you're serious? It's not just a story, or a fable of some kind, or whatever?"

Jhutev clasped his hands in front of him, his starburst gaze courteous yet confused. "Apologies, Miss Violet, but I'm not sure I understand your question."

"Are you saying that the Erathi, that humans, *used to have wings*?" For emphasis, she jabbed a finger at the mural.

Jhutev gave a slow nod of his celestial head. "Yes. That is correct."

"No, it can't be…"

She stared in stupefied silence until Jhutev went on to explain. "When the Nephezai prince fell in love with the Erathi princess, it became all too apparent that he could never ascend into the sky to live with his lover, nor could she descend into the ocean to live with him, for he could not fly, and she could not breathe underwater."

He moved on to the next panel, which depicted a magnificent imperial city in the clouds and its dazzling counterpart beneath the surface of the ocean. In the middle of the two cities were the prince and princess, wrapped in each other's arms, yet anguish was clear in their features.

"The princess gradually came to understand the harsh reality of their relationship. With a broken heart, she embraced the sacrifices demanded of her to one day be a queen befitting her people. But the Nephezai prince never reached the same level of acceptance. His passion and love for her turned to a raging bitterness, then to pure hate when he learned of her pregnancy with the Erathi prince her parents had chosen for her to wed. And so, the Nephezai prince's heartbreak consumed him. Eventually, the rift between the Erathi and the Nephezai escalated into a war that lasted decades. Water versus sky. The winged versus the thorned."

Jhutev gestured to a panel portraying a vicious battle scene between the Erathi and the Nephezai. The clash consisted of a volley of mother-of-pearl thorns the Nephezai shot at their airborne enemy, but the Erathi weren't defenseless. Several illustrations showed the winged shifters slicing and dicing the thalassic shifters with the razor-sharp edges of their wings. Tiny chips of bright purple stone and fragments of sparkling emeralds represented the vibrant spilled blood of both species.

"Finally the Nephezai overpowered the Erathi," continued Jhutev. "The price of the Erathi's defeat was their freedom, and also their wings."

Violet gasped when she approached the gruesome image of hundreds of chained Erathi having their wings hacked off. Bloodied mounds of emerald, lapis, and gold were destroyed in all-consuming fires.

"Forbidden to fly, never again to see their homes in the clouds above. Wings were amputated from every Erathi born thereafter."

Violet couldn't bear to look at the mosaic of wings being lopped off newborns and children. She quickly moved on to the next panel.

"Over the millennia of the Erathi enslavement, the Nephezai's unrelenting oppression began to take its toll. For hundreds of years, wing after wing was amputated until, finally, Erathi babies were born with no wings at all."

Violet stared in horror at a series of Erathi figures. The first had the largest set of wings, proud and impressive, while the following figure's wings were smaller and a bit crumpled. The next Erathi in the lineup had wings that looked deformed, probably incapable of flight. On and on it went, until the last figure represented the wingless human form Violet knew.

Jhutev pointed to a section of the "de-evolution" panel. "Another sign of the Erathi's oppression was a change in the color of their blood—from a luminous emerald green to the red extinguished of its glow that you're now familiar with."

Violet's jaw grew slack as she took in the depictions of Erathi slaves being tortured, the spilled blood transitioning from chips of emerald to tiny fragments of glistening rubies. "This can't be true."

"I can assure you it is, Miss Violet. Even my mother confirmed this history to me when I was a child."

"Yes, but…" Violet shook her head, utterly dumbfounded. "Wings? Emerald blood, now turned red? Before a few weeks ago, I'd never even heard of an underwater shifter race, and now you're telling me my own species used to have wings and could *freaking fly like a bird*. I mean, if that's true, then how is it that there is absolutely no mention of it in our history books? Pyramids, pottery armies, dinosaurs—of all the ancient mysteries and wonders of the world, no one thought to mention that humans used to sprout feathers from their backs?"

"Your point is certainly valid," said Jhutev. "Yet, by the time the Erathi overthrew and banished the Nephezai, they had already long lost their heritage. Since they could no longer reach the heavens, the Erathi decided to move ahead from their dark past and start their new regime fresh, wiping their own history clean. And what better way to punish their oppressors than to scrub them from all memory, including what the Nephezai had done to cause the loss of their wings. But as for the Erathi's *true* ancient history, perhaps not all is lost."

Jhutev glided through the water, skipping past several of the mural's panels until he reached the ones at the very end. He raised a hand to indicate a faint impression within the mosaic clouds at the top of the last scene.

When Violet peeked closer, she could make out some subtle geometric shapes within the organic swirls. "Is that supposed to be a city in the clouds?"

Jhutev nodded. "My mother believed so. Some whispered

stories speak of the possibility of a small number of winged Erathi remaining in their cities in the clouds during the war, taking extreme caution to remain out of reach of their oceanic enemies."

"Okay..." Violet squinted at the geometric shapes, willing her eyes to make the subtleties clearer. "If there are still winged Erathi somewhere in the clouds, why haven't they come down out of hiding? And with all our modern-day technology, how is it there's been no talk of a satellite capturing images of flying humans, or an airplane bumping into a floating building?"

Jhutev inclined his head in acknowledgment. "My mother had heard speculation that the winged Erathi were remaining vigilant, anticipating the day the Nephezai would rise up from their banishment and seek revenge. But as for all the 'modern technology' you speak of, I know no theories on how the winged shifters have remained hidden from their land dwelling descendants."

The two fell into a contemplative silence, both staring transfixed at the mosaic mural.

Violet wound a strand of beads around and around one finger, the freshwater pearls and crystals biting into her flesh. Although the ancient story of the winged Erathi seemed very far removed, she couldn't deny a rising sense that these brutal bygones would somehow affect her and her loved ones in ways she could never imagine.

Her mind flooded with a thousand more questions, but before she could utter a single one, a small projectile whizzed past Violet's head and embedded in the mural in front of her. A single mother-of-pearl thorn had shattered the emerald gemstone it pierced.

She and Jhutev spun.

Panic surged through Violet as she came face-to-face with Yigtheez and his viperfish shifter friend.

"Well, well, well. This is a stroke of luck for us to find the hybrid *and* the Meruvo, wouldn't you say, Frizgitl?" Yigtheez said to his slimy friend.

The viperfish's ominous cackle sent chills down Violet's spine. "I'd say it's a lucky bit of luck, Yigz." His grin widened, displaying more of his transparent needle-sharp teeth.

Violet couldn't help but float back a few feet.

"Oh, forgive me, Miss Violet," Jhutev blurted. "The time has slipped away from us. Let's not leave His Reverence waiting too long for our arrival." He gave the two Nephezai a respectful nod. "Yigtheez. Frizgitl. A pleasure as always."

He clasped Violet's wrist, but as he made to swim to the exit, Yigtheez let out one of his signature booming laughs.

"I do believe this Meruvo takes us for a couple of fools, Frizgitl."

The viperfish shifter cackled. "Fools? Not us, Yigz. We were there when the prince was coasting the halls to convince his little ones to get back into bed."

"Quite right, Friz. I'd even wager the prince is tucked in for the night himself by now, and I doubt he'll be expecting any visitors until well into the morning." The parrotfish shifter gracefully glided closer to Jhutev. "But I will say that only a fool would pass up an extraordinary opportunity such as this."

Quick as a flash, both the Nephezai lunged, pinning Jhutev and Violet to the wall behind them.

The hard, textured surface of the mural felt cool on the exposed skin of Violet's shoulders and back. Her frantic breath was cut off as the viperfish's hand pressed against her throat, his transparent fangs and mother-of-pearl thorns edging closer to the air bubble around her head.

But the viperfish shifter didn't even look at her. Instead, his greedy attention remained locked on Yigtheez, who had his own hands wrapped around Jhutev's neck.

"Now, my little Meruvo, how about we play a game? It's called 'Grant Your Wish or Die.' These are the rules: you grant me your Meruvo wish, or you die."

The viperfish shifter cackled with laughter. "That's a good one, Yigz. The funny thing about that is either way he's gonna die."

"No, don't," cried Violet, her shock paralysis finally wearing off. "Leave him alone."

The viperfish shifter struck her hard in the stomach, knocking the wind from her lungs. "Shut it, hybrid, or I'll—"

A fiery teal washed over Violet's vision, and the viperfish shifter's wicked grin faltered. "Uh… Yigz…?"

"Just deal with her," Yigtheez said through clenched teeth, darting wary glances at the teal flames flickering from Violet's eyes. "We may never get a chance like this again. I'm not leaving until I get my wish to be the new king of Scylorethyz. Now, Meruvo, give me my wish."

Jhutev gasped, trying to breathe past the Nephezai's grip on his throat.

"Give it to me!" Yigtheez slammed Jhutev against the mosaic.

"Stop it!" Violet shouted, though with a bit more wheeze than she'd like since still recovering from Frizgitl punching her in the diaphragm.

The viperfish shook her roughly, trying to silence her, as Yigtheez hammered Jhutev against the wall again and again.

"I would rather die," Jhutev said between ragged gasps.

"If that is your wish, then there is no use wasting *my* wish," growled Yigtheez. "One way or another, Meruvo, no one will be leaving this room until I become king. *Now grant my wish.*"

A flash of reflected light caught Violet's eye, and her fear heightened when she spotted the sharp silver dagger in Yigtheez's hand. He brought the tip to Jhutev's throat, barking more threats, but Violet heard none of them—not after she saw the trail of glowing black blood seeping from the Meruvo's flesh.

Her fear turned to rage. "Stop it!"

Remembering her training from Nathan, she brought her arms up outside the viperfish shifter's, clamped her hands together, and slammed her forearms down, breaking Frizgitl's hold. Then she brought her knee up between them and thrust him back.

The viperfish shifter charged her with a cry, but his shout was cut off when Violet kicked him in the chest. He sailed back, though not as far as Violet would have liked. The momentum also caused her to smack back into the mosaic wall, but thankfully, the water helped soften the blow.

Frizgitl snarled at her. Transfixed by his needle-sharp teeth, Violet didn't see the end of his tail until it whipped out and slashed her across the shoulder.

She hissed from the immediate sting of the gaping wound, the salt water causing the cut to burn more fiercely. A small cloud of marbled teal and magenta blossomed in the water by her head.

Again, Frizgitl lunged. Violet dodged left, and the Nephezai's claws sliced through the water inches from her face. Relief surged through her when her air bubble remained intact.

Grinding her teeth with determination, Violet clenched her fists, and teal flames ignited over her hands. She drew her arm back and served a right hook to the viperfish's eye socket.

Despite the infuriatingly slow speed of her punch through the water, Frizgitl still cried out in pain from the teal flames. The Nephezai's shrill scream tore through Violet's eardrums as severe blisters fizzled over his face.

She went to strike him again, but when she drew her hand back, a tentacle whipped out and restrained her wrist.

Looking up, she found Belitozzl and Pwevül, the blue-ringed octopus shifter and the stingray shifter, hovering over them.

Violet could hardly believe her relief.

The viperfish shifter's screeching cries died down as he floated a foot or two away from Violet. Even Yigtheez halted his abuse of Jhutev.

"What in all the seven seas is going on?" hissed Pwevül.

"I'm so glad you're here," said Violet. "Jhutev was leading me back to the menagerie when we were attacked by—"

A mother-of-pearl dart flashed past her face. Violet would have screamed at the sudden stinging in the soft flesh above her collarbone, but the paralytic toxins in the thorn of Neptune worked instantly. Her scream died on paralyzed lips. Every muscle in her body froze. Apart from the ability to breathe and blink her eyes, she had become as still as the legion of purple effigies in the Necropolis Ravine. She would have floated away in the water if not for the tentacle still anchored on her wrist.

Belitozzl directed a glare at Yigtheez. "When you said you were going to take over the kingdom, you didn't mention anything about stealing the Meruvo's wish."

For a moment, confusion engulfed the still-paralyzed Violet.

The parrotfish shifter shrugged. "How else did you expect me to do it? Becoming the king isn't just stealing a crown. I need his power and authority. I need to ensure that all will swear their fealty to me. Qozzlotl still has far too many supporters in the kingdom, and I will no longer wait for frivolous and entitled Nephezai to make up their minds to overthrow him. I want the kingdom now. I need this Meruvo's wish *now*."

Violet's confusion gave way to ice-cold fear. She needed to help Jhutev. She needed to get him away from these imbeciles.

"But you assured us your takeover would be effective and immediate," said Pwevül.

"Stealing the Meruvo's wish *will* make it effective and immediate."

"And yet everyone knows that stealing a Meruvo's wish is next to impossible," countered the blue-ringed octopus shifter. "Why do you think the prince hasn't been able to convince this Meruvo to use his wish? Even the Meruvo's mother died in her old age, stoic and stubborn since the day she was brought down here. Absolutely nothing the king did to her convinced her to relinquish her wish to him."

"That's because he and his son are cowards." Yigtheez practically spat the words. "Neither of them has the courage to do what is necessary for this kingdom." He tightened his grip on his dagger and returned his attention to Jhutev. "But I will cut this Meruvo apart piece by piece until he gives me what I want."

Jhutev bared his teeth in defiance. "Traitors. If you're foolish enough to think you can overthrow the king and His Reverence, I will have no part in it. Not even with my dying breath."

Yigtheez's sinister laugh sent dread prickling down Violet's spine. "Frizgitl is right, Meruvo. You are going to die, either by my will or by your own."

"What about this one though?" Pwevül pointed to Violet. "If this doesn't work out the way you think it will, Yigtheez, none of us can afford to have any witnesses." His tone implied he didn't believe Yigtheez would be successful at all.

"We should just kill her now," said the viperfish shifter with a strained growl. He tenderly patted his face where she'd burned him.

"Poor little hybrid," crooned Belitozzl. His slimy tentacle drew her closer until she was looking straight into his cephalopod eyes. "The king will surely be sad when he hears about the unfortunate accident of his little pet's air bubble failing."

Violet's feral gaze darted to the razor-sharp thorns adorning Belitozzl's arms and shoulders. They were all far too close to the air bubble over her head.

"The king won't have the chance to hear about any of this. Not when I get my wish." Yigtheez raised his dagger above his head. "Meruvo, I wish for you to make me the new king of Scylorethyz and the Midnight Seas. I will be the new heart of the bleeding ocean. I wish to be king of all the Nephezai for now and forever."

Jhutev snarled a phrase Violet didn't understand. Whether in the Nephezai or Meruvo tongue, it caused Yigtheez to roar in outrage. He pinned Jhutev's hand to the wall and skewered the dagger into the middle of his palm.

Instead of crying out in pain, Jhutev hung his head, closed his eyes, and pulled in deep, labored breaths.

Violet wanted to scream, to kick, punch, and fight. Jhutev needed her help. He wasn't a fighter. He'd been born in captivity and never taught to defend himself.

But the thorn's paralytic still gripped her. Hopeless tears streamed down her face as Yigtheez continued to threaten and maim Jhutev. The parrotfish hacked off one finger, then a second, then a third. Jhutev tried his best to fight his tormentor off, but Belitozzl and Pwevül quickly moved in to restrain him.

The Meruvo's determined silence soon turned to anguished groans.

Violet's mind grew frenzied, even as her body remained frozen. Fear and heartbreak turned toxic within her rage.

Her rapid heartbeats pounded in her ears, growing louder each time Jhutev cried out.

The teal flames that had ignited with her first punch still remained over her hands, and the heat inside her and all around her intensified. Soon she would become molten. Soon she would become her fury's inferno incarnate.

The screaming in her mind reached a crescendo.

She needed to help Jhutev. He needed a shield to protect him from any more danger.

Violet began to shake.

No, it wasn't *her* shaking… The ground beneath her had started to tremble.

All the Nephezai froze.

"What's happening?" shouted Yigtheez.

Violet almost didn't hear his words over the rising roar all around her. Her entire world—inside and out—was engulfed by teal flames. They scalded her core and flooded her veins, searing her entire existence until something within her snapped.

The toxins in her blood fizzled. In an instant, she regained control of her body.

Relief surged through her—until she saw Jhutev crumpled on the ground at the base of the mosaic wall. Except for the small, unsteady rise and fall of his chest, he looked as if he could be dead.

The light in his eyes flickered as his lids fluttered open. He looked directly at her, and Violet couldn't stand how faint the starlight in his eyes was. Even the swirling galaxies in the inky midnight of his flesh dimmed with each ragged breath he took.

Working on instinct, Violet channeled her combined Veniri and Magneii abilities into her light-forging skill. She pressed her hands together, then pulled them apart, creating an ever-growing globule of teal-and-magenta light between her palms. In her mind's eye, she called up the structure she wanted, then threw the ball of light toward Jhutev.

Right before the globule hit the Meruvo, it stretched into a membrane about half an inch thick, billowing out like an umbrella before the edges connected with the mosaic wall and the seabed. The final structure enshrouded him in a cocoon of safety, much like the one Qozzlotl had made for her, Thane, and Solace to protect them from the Nephezai mobbing them the day they arrived in Scylorethyz.

Even with Jhutev now safe from his tormentors, Violet felt no relief. Things were far from over. Her flames flared brighter as the last few minutes of Jhutev's suffering played over and over in her mind.

Her attention turned to the Nephezai shifters. All four of them now faced her—the viperfish shifter, the blue-ringed octopus shifter, the stingray shifter, and the parrotfish shifter. The bloodlust in their eyes had long since vanished.

Violet reveled in the terror with which they now regarded her.

Her seething anger burned white hot, soul deep. The heat tingled right down to her toes, then rose in a chaotic inferno, along with the trembling of the ground.

Frizgitl darted away. Before he could make his escape, Violet screamed.

She threw both hands out, the heat beneath her surging. The trembling ground directly under the viperfish shifter split open, and a jet of molten lava spewed from the earth. The water around him bubbled and boiled right up until magma swallowed his last scream of agony. Every inch of flesh, every mother-of-pearl thorn, and every glowing purple marking turned to a sizzling charcoal black.

The entire gruesome scene lasted mere seconds.

When Violet lowered her hands, the lava jet dropped back into the earth, and the ocean bed sealed shut.

Silence followed.

Violet gaped at the floating, sizzling corpse. A few glowing embers scattered over the charred shifter gradually fizzled out.

Her gaze then drifted to the ground, though her awareness drifted even further. She swore she had connected with a slow, swirling, tremendous power source a few miles below her: magma, the lifeblood of the earth itself. She wasn't stupid enough to believe she could control it—not the planet's entire inner inferno. But it was as if the magma recognized her fire abilities and allowed her to tap into a minuscule portion of its force. Like called to like.

Perhaps that explained why she'd been feeling so overheated down here while others were always chilled to the bone. Despite being farther from the warmth of the sun, the deeper she went into the ocean's abyss, the closer she got to the earth's magma.

In the seconds it took her to comprehend all this, Yigtheez, Belitozzl, and Pwevül made a panicked dash for the exit, just like the viperfish had.

But Violet's own fear, misery, and rage still churned within her at hellfire proportions.

The second they moved, she again raised her hands and screamed. As before, the ground trembled. Fissures cracked open beneath the three Nephezai, and three jets of pure molten earth streamed upward.

By the time her own fury burned out and her hands fell back to her sides, three more charred corpses had joined the floating viperfish shifter.

Breath heaving in and out of her lungs, she gaped at what she'd just done. She should feel appalled at herself for causing so much destruction. She should be afraid of her own newfound abilities. She should—

A small, agonized groan stole her attention.

She'd process the last two minutes later. Right now, Jhutev needed her.

Violet rushed to the light-forged shield around the Meruvo, then punctured a hole with her fingers and stretched the membrane back, as if it were made of gum. "Jhutev, are you all right?"

A low groan replied.

"Thank the heavens," Violet said through a sigh.

Just as she was about to help him up, Votloxo appeared in the doorway, a half dozen guards behind her. The fighter fish shifter wavered, aghast at the sight of the two guards—her friends—now just charred tentacles and fire-blackened stingray wings.

Her deadly glare turned to Violet. "What the hell have you done?"

29
"MODIFIED" HUMANS

When he awoke, it took Sagan a few minutes to recall his whereabouts. The couch in the spare room where Toffee had led him hadn't been too terrible to sleep on, and the crocheted and patchwork cushions were a comfy and homey touch.

He shrugged on his black jacket, which he'd used as a makeshift blanket, before softly making his way into the hallway. His body clock told him it was about half an hour before dawn. Umbra might not even be up yet, especially considering her injuries from the night before.

He should probably stay put, but he figured it wouldn't hurt to do a quick check to see if Umbra was much of a morning person or not. Besides, his nerves would never allow him to get back to sleep at this point.

Ensuring each step he took was silent, Sagan trod into the kitchen. No sign of Umbra, and no sign of her little beetle-winged monkey.

He slowly scanned his surroundings. The whole place would have been awash with the gray of predawn if not for the ethereal ambiance the alien forest emitted. Neon blues, yellows, pinks, reds, and of course green made the space look like a nightclub.

Part of him wanted to take a closer look; the fact that a leaf with bright blue sap had healing properties almost as powerful as Ylixium fascinated him. Yet the more wary part of him felt it best to steer clear without knowing which plants could be harmful. Deciding to err on the side of caution, he chose to go back to the spare room.

Just as he pivoted to return the way he'd come, something caught his eye. Within a little nook at the edge of the kitchen was an L-shaped desk completely covered with scattered papers and piles of notebooks, some of them laid open on top of one another. A variety of pots with succulent-type plants had been spasmodically placed wherever they happened to fit. On the walls above the desk, hand-drawn sketches, pages upon pages of handwritten notes, photographs ranging from black and white to full color, dried leaf samples, dried flower samples, and other unfamiliar specimens were all tacked to the wall with push pins.

An illustration in an open notebook on the desk jarred him into stillness. The way it combined human anatomy with animal traits was all too familiar.

Sagan picked up the book and began flipping through the pages. With each page flick, another ominous chill slithered down his spine. All these images and notes theorized the possibility of traits and abilities in one species, or even several species, being infused into the DNA of another creature—particularly a human.

"Good book?"

Sagan almost dropped the notebook when he spun around to face Umbra, who regarded him with a raised eyebrow.

The urge to blurt out apologies hit him instantly, but all he managed to say was "What is all this?"

Instead of anger at his snooping, amusement tucked in a corner of Umbra's mouth. "It's just some of my parents' old research notebooks," she said with a shrug, then went over to one of the plants and tore off a few purple flowers, so dark they almost looked black. "You hungry?"

"Hang on a second. What kind of research?" Sagan was almost certain he knew the answer. After all, he'd spent half his childhood listening to his grandfather and father belabor the possibility of humans being genetically enhanced—enhanced to be like their shape-shifter counterparts.

Umbra shrugged again before filling her mouth with a few of the purple-black flowers. He noted the cautious way she moved, likely still tender from her injuries. The Ylixium vial weighed a little heavy in the secret pocket of his jacket. Another dose would take the edge off her suffering.

Not acknowledging her pain, Umbra gestured to the office nook. "My parents were trying to develop some kind of serum or something that could benefit the human race." She turned her attention back to the plants, picking up a spray bottle to spritz them.

"'Benefit the human race'?" Sagan's mind flooded with all the horrific memories of the caged animals, and even humans, located beneath the building he currently stood in. "You know what all this is, right?"

He didn't like his accusing tone, but he could hardly contain his rising fury. The sudden urge to tear the notebook into pieces and burn it nearly overwhelmed him. Over every single hand-drawn depiction of a "modified" human inside, he kept seeing his mother's face.

Umbra leveled a cool gaze at him. "Of course I know what it is. It's not like I'm out there every day and every night, trying to clean up the mess my parents unintentionally made as a result of their research. If they'd had their way, there wouldn't be any of these mutated animals running around. There certainly wouldn't be any people being tortured and brutally disposed of—all in the name of science and 'biological enhancement.' My parents committed their lives to helping people with their work, only to have their legacy ruined by greedy, power-hungry lunatics."

Sagan took half a step back. During Umbra's rant, she'd taken several formidable strides in his direction and stopped mere inches from his face. Her features twisted into a steely glare, the rage in them rivaling his own.

"I'm… sorry," he said after a few heartbeats. "I didn't mean to accuse you of anything."

Umbra's shoulders sagged, and the tension in her face softened. In that moment, Toffee buzzed over and landed on her shoulder. The little monkey softly chattered and patted Umbra on the cheek.

Guilt rising, Sagan closed the notebook and placed it back on top of the pile.

"My mother had cancer."

After a long pause, Sagan could only think to respond with "Oh."

Toffee took a lock of Umbra's purple-tipped hair and began stroking it over her own furry face as Umbra pointed to a photograph pinned above the desk. "This photo was taken not long after my father moved halfway across the world to study at a specialized university in Japan. He met my mother, who was in a few of his classes."

Sagan noted the university logo on the wall behind the couple but couldn't make out what the kanji symbols in the insignia meant. "Your parents look… happy."

Umbra nodded. "They were."

As he continued to study the photo, Sagan found himself trying to think of any "happy family" photographs of his own parents together, but all he could remember of their relationship was discord. He couldn't mentally dig up any evidence his parents had ever liked—let alone loved—each other. The pain, anguish, and violence of his childhood drowned out almost all the good memories he still held on to.

"When they first met, my mother said my father's Japanese was atrocious," continued Umbra. "She took pity on him and offered to tutor him in the language. She said he was so bad that after a few months, she was beginning to think there was no hope for him. Then she found out he was being terrible on purpose to ensure their tutoring sessions together wouldn't stop."

A sad smile tugged at Umbra's mouth. "When I was a kid, I used to think they had come out of their own fairy-tale love story that Disney hadn't made into a movie yet."

Despite the sadness, it was the first time Sagan had seen a genuine smile grace Umbra's usually guarded face. Granted, he didn't know her at all, but he couldn't help wondering what caused her to smile on a general basis.

"Where are your parents now? Are they still back in Japan?"

"No, they left Japan not long after I was born. Both my parents were biologists, my mother in botany and my father in zoology. They merged their passions together, becoming a dynamic duo, and really pushed the boundaries in their fields. They were driven to be bold, especially in the hopes of benefiting others. Their work was garnering interest far and wide when a company offered them an opportunity they couldn't refuse. It only meant they'd have to leave Japan and move halfway across the world."

"This company, it wasn't Xabat Biogenetics, was it?" Sagan asked.

Umbra nodded with a heavy sigh. "Xabat Biogenetics did everything to entice my parents to join them. They looked after them really well. At the time I didn't understand what their work was all about, but I remember thinking it must have been really important, as lots of people fawned over them.

"But after a few years, my mother discovered she had cancer. Within two years of being diagnosed, she passed away."

Umbra shook her head. "When my mother got sick, my father spiraled into desperation to find a cure. Both of them were so certain their work held the answers."

"What happened?" Sagan asked when she didn't say anything further.

"In the end, my mother didn't make it. But even with her gone, my father still couldn't accept the fact that he wasn't able to help her. He threw himself further into his work, determined to complete what he'd started with her. He was constantly slaving away in the Xabat facility."

Sagan glanced back up at the happy couple on the wall. "What exactly were your parents working on?"

Based on what he'd already experienced at Xabat, and what he'd seen scattered all over Umbra's desk, he had a good idea what the answer was, but he wanted to hear her perspective.

"In a nutshell, they were working on the concept of cross-species breeding, like how plants can be grafted and cross-pollinated to produce a brand-new plant." Umbra winced. "I've oversimplified it. Their research goes much deeper than that." She reached for one of the notebooks and began flipping through it. "Here, it's probably easier to show you."

She held up the book to show a detailed drawing of a rat with wings. It almost could have been a bat if it weren't for the bright red and green feathers.

At the sight of the image, a familiar sinking feeling began to tug at Sagan's gut. The feeling grew deeper with every cross-species animal concept Umbra flipped through: cats with fins, sharks with leopard-print fur, pigeons with echidna spines. Each page brought more and more complex combinations.

Umbra also became more and more animated in her explanations. "My mother spent years crossbreeding her plants to create all these new specimens here in my apartment. Both her and my father were determined to make that a possibility for humans. Just imagine having gills. Or the regeneration ability of an axolotl or a starfish. Or what about being able to adjust our skeletal structure at will? And just think of—uh… Sagan?"

"Huh?" He tore his eyes away from the book in Umbra's hands.

A crease formed between her eyebrows. "You don't look all that well."

He started to nod but stopped when his eyes fell back on the image he'd seen earlier: a human with various animal traits, outlandish abilities written in notes alongside it.

"Sagan, are you all right?"

"Yeah… just feels like I'm in a state of… déjà vu or something." Sagan could have sworn he'd heard this entire explanation before—almost word for word—except in his grandfather's voice. Every one of his childhood memories of Renard included him drilling into Sagan the possibility of humans one day being genetically enhanced.

"Sagan, are you sure you're—"

"I'm fine."

Umbra pressed her lips together. "I'm sorry, I don't usually babble on like this, especially to someone I hardly know."

"I don't mind. Tell me about your father. Did he ever end up completing his work?"

Umbra hesitated for a few moments.

Before she could speak further, Toffee interjected with some of her screechy chatter and then buzzed off. A second later, the little beetle-winged monkey returned with a comb and a handful of hair ties.

Umbra settled down on one of the kitchen barstools while Toffee got to work. Her raven hair gleamed in the growing sunlight, the purple ends flicking around from Toffee's combing and braiding efforts.

"I'm not certain if he completed his work or not," she finally answered, "but what I do know is one day he came home and he was much more excited than I'd seen him since Mom was diagnosed. He claimed he was on the verge of something big—a massive breakthrough.

"A lot of what he and Mom worked on was beyond my understanding. But he said he'd developed a serum that had the potential to combine the biogenetic traits and abilities of different species. Then two days later... he never came home."

She gestured to a photograph of her parents looking a little older, a younger version of Umbra between them. "We were living in the city across the river while my parents commuted to Xabat Biogenetics. When my father went missing, I came looking for him. I was confused to find this shell of a city but scoured it anyway. It took me ages to actually find the facility, and I was beyond shocked to discover that all this time he'd been working in a highly secure and highly secret underground lab.

"When I finally found a way in, no one would help me. No one even admitted they knew my father, nor would they confirm he'd worked there. I began to think I was crazy—or that he was crazy and had become delusional after my mother died. I got kicked out by some security guards, and after a while, I began to believe that maybe I had it all wrong, that maybe my parents hadn't been working for this place after all.

"Just as I was about to give up, I snuck in one more time.

Just to prove to myself that my father had nothing to do with their lab."

"Did you find him?" Sagan thought he could probably guess the answer, but he couldn't help but hope Umbra was about to deliver a happy ending to her story.

She shook her head. "There was no sign of my father. But what I did find was Toffee."

The little monkey perked up at her name. She chittered in response as Umbra smiled down at her.

"In that moment, I remembered some of my mother's research and notes outlining the concept of a pygmy marmoset—the smallest monkey in the world—having wings like the jewel beetle she always admired as a child growing up in Japan."

She picked up the notebook Sagan had been flipping through earlier and showed him a page. "I remember loving this drawing as a kid. It was something my mother always dreamed about making a reality. She used to tell me all about her idea, marveling at the possibility of combining two of her favorite creatures.

"When I saw Toffee locked up in a cage in Xabat, that's when I knew my father had been right. He *had* made a breakthrough. He'd made my mother's drawing come to life. Xabat had lied to me. I soon found signs of my parents' lifelong work *all over* the lab."

Her lips pursed in disgust. "I saw what those people—what those sick scientists were doing. All those poor animals, and all those poor humans. I even discovered the existence of shape-shifters." She gave Sagan a bemused look. "I never even knew how lucrative hunting shape-shifters could be."

Sagan fought to keep his face impassive. He leaned against the wall and crossed his arms.

Umbra returned her attention to her parents' notebooks. "I was devastated to find out the truth of what Xabat was doing with my parents' work. I didn't have to think about what I did next. I rescued Toffee, and I've stayed close by ever since—hoping and praying I'll find any kind of clue that will lead me to my father."

A small, glistening tear rolled down Umbra's cheek. Toffee fluttered up and caught the jewel drop before it rolled off her face.

Sagan couldn't stand to watch the anguish in her eyes. Instead, he glanced around the home Umbra had made for herself. "How long have you been here?"

"I'm not entirely sure. Probably close to three years."

He humphed in admiration. "Any progress in finding out about your father?"

"Nothing. Whatever happened, Xabat has buried it deep —whether figuratively or literally, I'm not quite sure yet."

Sagan reached for the chain around his neck, rolling it between his fingers as he considered Umbra's predicament. "How about I make you a deal? You help me find out what happened to my mother, and I'll help you find out what happened to your father."

Umbra looked up from stroking Toffee's head. "What do you already know about what happened to your mother?"

30
HIDE AWAY LIKE VERMIN

"I'll make sure His Reverence has your head for this," Votloxo spat. She pointed a slender claw-tipped finger at Violet. "Seize her."

Without hesitation, the six guards lunged.

But before they could reach her, an almighty *boom!* almost tore Violet's eardrums to shreds.

Everyone halted. All eyes snapped up to the rocky ceiling as it began to spiderweb with cracks.

"The hunters found us," came Votloxo's hushed words over the ringing in Violet's ears.

All rage on the guards' faces turned to pallid terror.

"Quick!" shouted Votloxo. "Seize the hybrid and the Meruvo. We must find the royal family and lock them in the secret chamber, *now*!"

"No!" screamed Violet as cold, thalassic hands grabbed her. "We need to get to Thane and my baby!"

"Move it!" ordered one of the guards when she kicked and thrashed against their grip.

"Someone needs to get Thane and Solace!"

Another earth-shattering *boom!* resounded all around

them, drowning out Violet's desperate cry.

"Violet!"

She turned at the sound of her name.

Exültov rushed into the mosaic chamber. "I've been looking all over for you. Quick! We must leave, now!" He motioned for her to follow, then noticed Votloxo and the guards holding her captive. "Votloxo, bring her."

"But, Your Reverence, the hunters—the king and your children—we must lock you in the secret—"

The prince rounded on her. "There's no time to argue. Bring Violet and follow me!"

Before anyone could react, Zasf and half a dozen Ügovs surrounded Exültov. All the Nephezai guards froze in shock. Violet had never seen Votloxo look so dumbfounded.

"Exültov, we must leave." Zasf grasped the prince's arm. "No time to spare. We must get you to safety."

"Wait, we can't leave without Violet and her family—"

A teeth-rattling *BOOM!* shook the entire room.

The cracks in the ceiling gave way. Big chunks of rock and debris fell all around them. A few of the guards were struck by boulders, while others tumbled in different directions as the water surged with erratic currents from the explosions. Nephezai hands released their grip on Violet as she, too, was hurled to the side.

"No! Violet!" Exültov's cry broke off as Zasf and the Ügovs hauled him back, away from the deadly cave-in.

Violet crashed into the mosaic wall, crying out at the jarring impact. After a few terrifying moments, the hammering of rocks ceased, and the churning water settled.

The mosaic room had been obliterated.

Exültov and the Ügovs were gone, as were Votloxo and the Nephezai guards—either dead or on the other side of a wall of debris. She hoped and prayed she wasn't trapped.

Relief surged through her when she spotted a small opening she could wriggle through.

But wait! Jhutev!

The Meruvo was still cocooned in the light-forged shield. The hole she had punctured before had resealed. Thankfully, the shield appeared to have protected him from the worst of the blasting water and rocks.

"Jhutev?" The membrane gave way to her touch, much like bubble gum popping at her fingertips. He was still breathing, the air bubble over his head soundly intact. "Come on. We've gotta get out of here."

As swiftly and as gently as possible, she picked up the limp Meruvo—which, with his buoyancy in the salt water, turned out to be easier than expected. While boulders completely blocked the exit to the mosaic room, one of the side walls had crumbled, leaving a big enough gap for Violet and Jhutev to squeeze through.

For a moment, she didn't recognize the hallway they'd entered, but soon some familiar markings helped her get oriented. "Don't worry, Jhutev. I know where we are. We've just got to get to Thane and Solace."

Another *boom!* went off, this time a bit farther behind them. Startled, Violet jerked, and the sudden movement made Jhutev groan with pain.

"I'm sorry. I'll get us to safety as soon as I can."

A water surge from the explosion caught up to Violet, sending her and Jhutev in a swelling whirl down the passageway. Small bits of coral and other debris whipped around her. She hissed when a few sharp edges sliced at her arms and back.

The hallway they'd just passed through had collapsed to rubble. What was once an ornately arched ceiling adorned with abalone inlays now lay cracked open to the ocean above.

Violet's stomach dropped at the sight of two submarines, at least 150 feet away. Their blinding spotlights panned over her.

She turned and fled.

Jhutev groaned again.

"It's okay, Jhutev. I'll get us out of here."

He slowly shook his head. "No, leave me."

"No way."

"I'm just holding you back."

"I'm not leaving you behind!"

"Miss Violet, please. I've endured many beatings and much worse torture my entire life, even under His Reverence's protection." His breath hitched as he took a moment to wince.

"Shh, Jhutev. It's okay. I've got you. I'll get you out of here."

"Violet, listen to me, I can no longer endure."

"Don't say that!"

Jhutev weakly latched on to the front of her dress. "There is nothing left for me. Leave me. Find your family, and escape from here."

Violet shook her head violently. She swam with all her might, darting through the twists and turns as quickly as she could, hoping against hope she'd be able to lose the hunters before they blasted another hole in the passageways to find her, or worse, blasted a hole through her—

No! Don't think like that. She gritted her teeth. *Swim faster, Violet!*

She almost cried with relief when she saw the tunnel entrance to the menagerie ahead.

"Thane!" she shouted when she was halfway through. "Thane! Solace!"

Her heart plummeted. The entire menagerie had been decimated. The towering walls had crumbled, enclosure bubbles had burst, and drowned animals and other land dwellers floated aimlessly through the water. Violet couldn't even think about the number of casualties, not when Thane and Solace were nowhere to be seen.

She cried out in horror at the sight of her own crushed enclosure. Massive boulders had smashed through the bed, crib, and other furniture.

"Thane! Solace!" The names shredded her vocal cords. She looked around, frantic, searching for any sign of them.

Where were they? Where could they possibly be?

"Thane! Solace!"

"Over here."

Violet whirled around. She almost let loose a hysterical laugh as Thane swam toward her from beyond a pile of rubble, with Solace strapped to his chest in a thick width of fabric he'd fashioned into a sling.

"We're here," said Thane, arms stretched out toward Violet. "We're fine. I was just about to come find you. Are you okay?"

Violet nodded. She pointed to the air bubbles over his and Solace's heads. "Your bubble, who—"

"One of the guards removed us and gave us air moments before the ceiling caved in. A chunk of rock hit him. He, uh… didn't make it." Thane looked down at Jhutev still in Violet's arms. "What happened?"

Just as she opened her mouth to explain, a new voice called out from behind her.

"There you are!"

She turned to find Votloxo and six guards. Before Violet could react, the fighter fish shifter sent a fist right into her jaw. The force of the blow snapped her head to the side and sent stars bursting across her vision.

Votloxo barked an order, and the guards rushed her and

Thane. Despite Violet's protests, two guards took Jhutev from her, while another latched on to her arms and yanked them behind her back. In a whirlwind of rushing water, Votloxo and the guards dashed them all out of the menagerie.

"Why the king thinks you're worth keeping alive, I'll never understand," the Nephezai growled.

More booming rang out as they swam down passageway after passageway, dodging falling debris and fighting chaotic swells of seawater.

Disbelief struck Violet when she found herself being dragged back into the destroyed mosaic room through the very same crack in the wall. The guards hauled them up to the now dented bronze hippocampus statue. Votloxo shouted a phrase in the Nephezai tongue, and the statue's alcove swiveled around to reveal a dark opening beyond.

This must have been how the king disappeared when she'd followed him here earlier. She had been so close to finding him—and yet so far. Even if she'd figured out about the passageway, she'd never have been able to guess the password.

When the hippocampus statue had spun completely out of view, the guards shoved Violet through the opening.

"Where are you taking us?" Thane asked.

"Silence, air breather," Votloxo barked.

The guards tugged them forward. Just when she'd thought they couldn't travel any deeper into the ocean, they swam down, down, down a dark tunnel periodically lit by purple-tinged orbs attached to the ragged rock walls. The booming still continued above, but it grew more faint the farther down they went.

Soon hushed voices could be heard. The tunnel opened into a chamber where various Nephezai huddled in groups, their fearful expressions glued to the ceiling above. Everyone grew tense and clutched each other when another faint *boom* went off.

But Votloxo didn't stop; she led them through a side passage where a cluster of guards were stationed outside another entryway. The guards nodded at the fighter fish shifter and moved aside to let her and her entourage pass.

"Your Highness, the hybrid, the Veniri, and the halfling, as requested," said Votloxo, giving a low bow. She motioned for her guards to shove Violet and Thane forward.

The moment Violet was released, Thane drew her into his side, and Solace reached for her and fussed. If the baby weren't securely strapped in Thane's sling, Violet would have pulled her out and cuddled her close, but with a bit of shushing, Solace settled within the confines of her parents' embrace. For a moment, Violet relaxed. Despite the arms around her being Thane's, she hadn't felt this safe in a very long time.

That was, until she remembered they had been brought to the king.

She looked up to find King Qozzlotl lounging on a chaise on the other side of the immaculately decorated suite. His elbow rested on the armrest, and he had his head propped up on one hand. He glared through his splayed fingers, as if suffering from an excruciating migraine. "Ah, such a heartwarming moment for this little family. You'd hardly think my entire kingdom is about to be decimated. Is this all that remains of my collection of pets?"

Votloxo glided forward. "Many apologies, my king, but the menagerie was destroyed. These were the only ones we found alive."

Rage flashed in Qozzlotl's eyes. "Hmm, now that is a pity. A lifetime of work… *destroyed in seconds*." He tilted his head to the side and looked past Violet. "What else do you have there?"

"Just the Meruvo." Votloxo's voice remained as emotionless as if she were stating the time of day.

Violet's hands clenched at her sides. The guards drew closer, no doubt perceiving her wish to punch the fighter fish shifter. Even Thane's arm around her grew tighter.

"He's been attacked," she said.

Votloxo shushed her, but Violet continued to speak.

"Yigtheez and his minions ambushed us. Jhutev needs medical attention, desperately." She hated the pleading in her voice, especially toward the Nephezai king, but she couldn't minimize her worry.

Qozzlotl responded only with a lazy gesture of his hand, and the guards brought the Meruvo shifter forward. Violet's stomach churned at the faint trail of black blood in their wake as they laid him down by the end of the king's eel tail.

"The creature looks half dead. When will my son learn to look after his toys?" Qozzlotl glanced up at Votloxo again. "Speaking of my son, where is he?"

"I, uh…" A plague of emotions crossed Votloxo's face. "We were separated in a cave-in. I sent a troop of guards to find him and take him and his children to one of the other emergency lockdown chambers. They'll be safe there for as long as the hunters are overhead."

Violet's brow furrowed at Votloxo's blatant lie. She had seen the look of pure shock on the fighter fish's face when the Ügovs dragged Exültov out of harm's way.

A faint *boom* went off overhead.

The king's flinty glare turned to the rocky ceiling. He clicked his tongue with disapproval. "It galls me to hide away like vermin. My father and his father never would have hidden when the hunters tracked them down."

"It's for the best, Your Highness," said Votloxo. "Our people have faced hard times in recent years. We've lost too many to the Ügov skirmishes and the plague of air breathers as it is. We must do all we can to ensure you and your kin survive. Wait until the Erathi hunters grow tired and leave. Live to fight another day."

Qozzlotl shot forward, halting several inches from Votloxo's face, his teeth bared in a growl. "And when do you suspect 'another day' will be?"

Violet had to give the fighter fish some credit when she didn't flinch.

In a sudden fit, the king pivoted and swiped at a crustacean-like guard at Votloxo's side. The crustacean shifter didn't buckle under the blow, but he did start to tremble, especially when the king released a tumultuous roar. Mother-of-pearl thorns darted from Qozzlotl's body, at least five of them hitting the crustacean in the chest with a sickening crunch of shell.

Thane yanked Violet back when a few rogue thorns zipped past, slicing through the water with a *thwip-thwip-thwip* right where she'd been. Two other guards weren't lucky enough to dodge, and both collapsed within an instant of being struck.

"The Erathi hunters never grow tired!" the king bellowed. "For millennia we dominated the land dwellers, and now we cower from them whenever they discover any safe haven we endeavor to establish."

Another faint *boom* sounded overhead.

With a menacing scowl, Qozzlotl tilted his head back, extended his hands in front of him, and clenched the seawater as though strangling someone's throat. "I swear I will tear every last Erathi apart. I'll shred them to pieces with my teeth and my bare hands. I will bring every land dweller to their knees. They will pay for all that they've stolen from us. I will take back what is rightfully mine—"

A small cough came from Jhutev, claiming the king's hateful attention.

"—and I am done waiting."

He darted over to where Jhutev lay on the ground.

"No!" Violet cried when Qozzlotl hauled the Meruvo up by the throat. She tried to rush to Jhutev's aid, but Thane held her back, and the guards crowded in closer.

The king brought a limp Jhutev up to his eye level and shook him. "Wake up, Meruvo."

Jhutev's eyes flew open, and he gave a low groan of pain.

"Leave him alone!" Violet called out.

A cold, clawed hand slapped over her mouth, pressing the bubble against her face and nearly suffocating her. "Speak again, hybrid, and I will cut out your tongue," Votloxo whispered in her ear.

"Hey, get away from her!" came Thane's strangled voice as he tried to wrestle free from his own guards.

Votloxo whipped around and backhanded Thane across the face with a stinging *crack*.

A small cry came from Solace.

"Shut that infant up," growled Votloxo.

Violet's inner battle was wreaking havoc, close to tearing through any tether she still maintained on her sanity. Every instinct screamed at her to reconnect with the molten power beneath her feet and blast the entire safe room with magma.

But her daughter…

She glanced down at Solace, then at the dreaded collar around the child's neck. A light-forged shield had protected Jhutev from her magma blasts. Would one also protect Solace? Could the blazing heat of the magma set off the collar bomb?

The king's seething voice cut through her thoughts: "You are so close to death, Meruvo. I can sense your failing heart with every breath you take."

Jhutev gave a slight wheeze, as if to emphasize the king's observation.

"Give me your wish!" the king demanded, enunciating each word with painstaking authority.

When Jhutev's eyes only fluttered shut, the king pointed to the guards and barked an order in the Nephezai tongue. A stonefish shifter, a lionfish shifter, and an Irukandji jellyfish shifter surrounded the helpless Meruvo.

Violet thrashed and fought against Votloxo's grasp as Qozzlotl ordered the three guards to sting and stab Jhutev with their venomous claws and barbs. Tears burned her eyes when his agonizing wails began again, more drained and exhausted than before.

When the king gave a signal, the three guards ceased their attack and moved back.

"Give me your wish, Meruvo." He clasped Jhutev's injured hand and squeezed.

Jhutev released a low groan, and a stream of luminescent blood seeped from his mouth and nose. Even more spilled from his hand and body, dispersing through the water in a billowing cloud of black.

"You have mere minutes, or even seconds, left of your miserable life," said Qozzlotl. "Grant my wish. Set the Nephezai free. Obliterate our banishment." He fumbled with the many necklaces around his neck.

Violet's attention zoned in on the purple spangle, but of all the glimmering and sparkling jewels he wore, the king selected one small vial on a chain. Her eyes widened when she recognized the white pearlescent liquid inside. It looked just like the elixir she'd seen Sagan consume when he'd been on the brink of death.

"I needn't tell you how excruciating the neurotoxins of a stonefish are," the king said, "or of the severe muscle cramps and nausea Irukandji venom induces. There is no need to live out the rest of your life in crippling agony, and it would be pointless to waste your wish by allowing the hope of all

Nephezai to die with you. Your entire existence—even your mother's existence—would be for naught. Give me your wish, and all your pain goes away."

Jhutev gave the king a slow blink, his face contorted in agony. The temptation was clear in his eyes each time his gaze swerved to the vial in the king's hand.

Violet shook her head, on the verge of screaming with frustration. Her fists ignited with teal fire, and she latched on to Votloxo's hand over her mouth. The fighter fish shifter roared when the Magneii flames scorched her flesh.

"Don't do it, Jhutev!" Violet rushed to say while her mouth was free. "Think of your mother. Remember how strong she was. Think of how proud she'd be of you for staying strong too."

With a hiss, Votloxo shoved her to the ground, and at least two more guards helped pin her down. Thane raged, but he immediately hit the ground alongside her. Hundreds of mother-of-pearl thorns surrounded them on all sides. If they came any closer, she and Thane would be impaled.

But her fear of the thorns diminished when Jhutev tilted his head to look at her.

Violet fought against the flood of tears and choking sobs. Whatever Jhutev chose to do would still result in his death, but a spark of determination had returned to his starlit eyes.

The king roared and crushed the vial in his hand. Wisps of pearlescent white trickled from between his fingers and dissipated in the water. Small tendrils even drifted over to Jhutev, almost as if they possessed a sentient desire to help the Meruvo.

But Violet knew the elixir was better ingested. None of it would benefit Jhutev due to the air bubble over his head.

"If you choose to die in vain," Qozzlotl roared, "then so be it. Know this, Jhutev, you have doomed us all!"

The king raised a fist high above Jhutev's head. But the

moment he was about to strike the death blow, Violet screamed.

"Wait!"

To her relief, the king paused.

"Let me speak to him," she pleaded. "I'll convince him to relinquish his wish."

31
MY TURN TO BEAT PUNY PLIOKAI

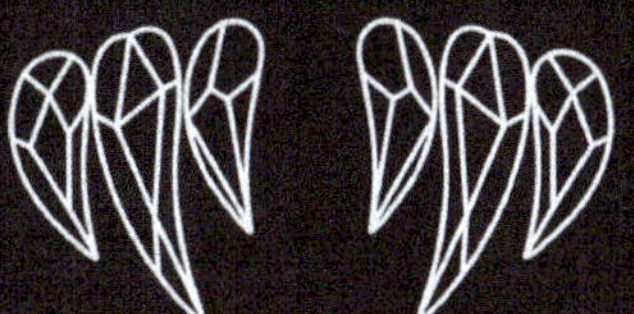

"That's it, Gus. Strong form. Keep him in your sights," Nathan called out. "Don't turn your back on him. Just because your mother knew how to do all those fancy spins doesn't mean it's ideal in combat."

"Aw, come on, the spins are fun," Gus said, not even losing his stride.

His staff clashed against Tio's with an echoing *clack-clack-clack* that rang out in the evening air. After Lazareth had challenged him that first night and then proceeded to wipe the floor with him, Gus was figuring out the hard way that, Glixus skills or not, he still had a lot to learn about bōjutsu. Thankfully, Lazareth had upgraded his son's staff from the crude stick he'd found in the forest that first night, digging out Dawn's old collection from one of the recreational sheds.

Almost immediately, Gus had zoned in on one made of carved red oak, bypassing all the colorful aluminum staffs. Lazareth had claimed it was Dawn's favorite. Brushing his fingers over the decorative carvings etched into the wood, he'd reminisced about having the staff commissioned as a gift when they were dating.

The rediscovery of the staffs sparked an ongoing challenge for Tio and the Jiovis shifters to best Gus at bōjutsu, especially since Gus didn't have the guts to be humiliated by his father again. Lazareth still offered a few tips and tricks; however, Nathan oversaw most of the training, as Lazareth was often occupied with either meal prep or supervising sleeping patients at the medical tent during the night.

"Watch your footwork, Tio," Nathan called as Gus started to drive Tio back.

"I'm trying," Tio growled.

What had begun as shifter training for Gus had become bōjutsu training for everyone. It had taken only two nights for Gus's body to really claim the skill as his own—in human form and Pliokai form. It seemed to come more naturally in Pliokai form, his body ducking, diving, and swishing the bō through the air with splendor and speed. Tio, En'gorr, and the Jiovis guards had also picked up the new skill rather well, probably due to having trained in combat all their lives.

They'd all taken careful note of Gus's explanation of striking, blocking, and sweeping maneuvers. Nathan hadn't been familiar with the art of bōjutsu before, but he'd paid close attention to what Gus had to say about the sport.

"Come on, Tio, stand your ground," Nathan prompted. Gus had been dominating for most of the spar, but he'd started to show signs of fatigue. "And hold on to your Pliokai form, Gus. I can see the hazing ripple from here."

Both Gus and Tio were in their shifter forms. Pliokai versus Jiovis. Pluto versus Jupiter. The gold-blooded versus the orange-blooded.

Gus's bō sliced through the air with a *swish,* his long strands of green and gray cable hair flicking about in a frenzy.

Tio managed to advance on him.

Bō staffs connected. *Clack-clack-clack.*

Now on the back foot, Gus's strikes and counterstrikes became a little labored. Elven ears would morph into rounded human ears before snapping back into points. The brilliant gemstone green of his eyes would dim into his human color, then return to glowing in a flash. His soft short brown hair would elongate and thicken into cablelike strands of gold, gray, and deep peridot green.

"Push through, Gus. Remember to breathe," said Nathan. "Try to hold on to your Pliokai form as long as possible."

Just when Tio was about to claim the match with an overhead strike, Gus ducked low and, within the same move, swiped at Tio's ankles, sending the young Jiovis crashing to the ground.

"Aw, man!" Tio groaned, rolling onto his back. "I thought I had you this time."

Gus wheezed out a chuckle. "For a minute there, I thought the same thing." He doubled over, corded hair falling over his eyes as he rested a hand on his knees. A split second later, all aspects of his Pliokai form hazed back into human form. He continued to heave in big gulps of air. "With my mother's knowledge and skill, I may still have the upper hand, but sheesh! My body isn't built for athletics."

Tio sniggered as he pulled himself up. "Sounds like we need to increase your cardio. How about we go for a three-mile run in the morning before breakfast?"

"What did I just say about not being built for athletics?"

"Come on." Tio clapped him on the back. "Don't you want to maintain your perfect bōjutsu record?"

Gus groaned. "I hate running."

"What about you, Nathan?" Tio asked. "Are you going to join us for a run in the morning?"

"I would, but I need to check in with Autumn's online surveillance. Afterward, I was going to trek around the ocean cliffs with En'gorr and his guards."

"Again?" Tio asked. "Nika already took you to the cliffs."

"I know. I just want to make sure we didn't miss anything. If I'm going to reconnect with my coast guard buddies, I want to make sure I've got all the information before I start fabricating a missing persons story that doesn't include shape-shifter details."

"Okay, I supposed that's an adequate enough excuse to get out of a morning run," said Tio with a nod.

Still in Jiovis form, he was a "living metal" statue of deep metallic gold from head to toe. The metal—or rather, Metallikite—formed a tough exterior for the Jiovis but could also be molded like putty, allowing the Jupiter shifters to adorn their flesh with sculpted accents. Tio's own face and head were decorated with an exaggerated skull and organic whirls and swirls. Two golden tusks, about three inches long, also protruded from the corners of his mouth.

Tio twirled his bō in a few practice moves Gus had previously shown him. The holographic royal-blue vinyl wrap over the aluminum staff shimmered under the LED tripod light Lazareth had set up for the nightly matches. As the young shifter twisted and spun, Nathan caught an embellished metallic mark on his bicep: the Jiovis symbol for Jupiter.

After tossing and catching the bō a final time, Tio dug one end into the ground and leaned against it, his expression serious. "Did Autumn say if she's found any security evidence on how Sagan may be faring?"

Nathan shook his head. "Not since the last time I checked with her, about two hours ago. She assumes he hasn't broken in yet. Nika's sent him a text or two, but his replies have been limited."

"Well, we'd better make sure we're ready, in case Autumn thinks he needs our help."

"Of course," agreed Nathan. "And after we help him, then I'll be whooping his ass."

"But Nika said the reason he took Violet and Thane to the hunters was to try and save his mother."

"Yes, and now Violet, Thane, and their baby are prisoners of the Nephezai." Nathan huffed out a frustrated sigh. "Whatever Sagan's reasoning, I need to hear it from him. Either way, he's still getting a butt-whooping."

"I'm not saying he did the right thing. But if it was someone you loved dearly… Hypothetically, who would you be willing to sacrifice to set Violet free from a decade of being experimented on?"

Nathan dug his hands in his pockets. He knew in his soul what the answer to Tio's question was, but he didn't have the guts to say it aloud.

"Okay," said Gus, standing upright. "I think I've recovered enough." He raised his bō and spun it a few times. "I'm ready to go again."

Someone called out from behind Nathan. He, Gus, and Tio turned to find one of the Jiovis guards strolling over to them, pounding his chest to indicate he'd be next to spar.

Tio handed him the royal-blue aluminum bō. "Here you go, Va'atuu. He's all yours."

With a pat on the guard's back, he hazed back into his human form and went to stand beside Nathan.

"What do you think?" Tio said in a low voice only Nathan could hear. "Can Va'atuu beat Gus this time?"

"We're about to find out," said Nathan.

Once again, Gus hazed into his Pliokai form and turned to face Va'atuu. In his Jiovis form, Va'atuu looked like a metal statue, same as Tio, but instead of rich gold, his Metallikite tones were copper. While more subtle than Tio's, Va'atuu's molded armorlike designs covered him from head to toe and would daunt any opponent on a battlefield.

The sparring match commenced, and again, while Gus dominated in skill, he clearly struggled to hold on to his shifted form.

Nathan started his coaching callouts. "Push through, Gus. Don't let metal-man get the best of you."

Gus's face grew tense with stress and determination.

Clack-clack-clack. Timber clashed with aluminum. The weapons swiped and slashed with ferocious speed.

Gus's puffing was becoming more pronounced.

"Come on, Gus. Hold that form. Fight through," Nathan barked.

An aggressive yell escaped Gus as he threw his might into a forward strike toward Va'atuu's head. The Jiovis stepped back, narrowly avoiding the blow, but Gus quickly followed up with a side to side. Then he finished with—what Nathan liked to think of as—a round-house strike.

Unfortunately for Va'atuu, Gus had lined up a perfect shot, and he knocked the Jiovis's head to the side.

Va'atuu stumbled back a few steps, surprise evident in his wide eyes—especially when he wiped his forearm across his mouth and found a smear of bright orange blood. He looked up at Gus, who had hazed back into his human form.

"Uh oh," said Tio in a low voice when Va'atuu regarded Gus for several long seconds.

Finally, the copper Jiovis began to shake. It took a moment for Nathan to understand Va'atuu was laughing, not quaking with rage.

Hazing back into his human form, Va'atuu lowered his bō and strode over to clap Gus on the shoulder. "Mother of August was ferocious warrior. I must train more for if ever I succeed to victory over August and his stick." He bowed his head and smiled.

"Aw, no need for all that stuff," said Gus, a cheesy grin

plastered on his face. "It's impressive how much you've improved in a few days with no prior bōjutsu training."

A hint of a smile crossed the stoic Jiovis's face. "Forever thanks, August."

"Well, there you have it," said Nathan, turning to Tio. "Gus still reigns supreme."

Tio snorted a laugh. "For now."

Just as Gus started explaining some further techniques to Va'atuu, the other Jiovis shifters sauntered onto the field, the pewter twins flanking Prince En'gorr.

"Nice of you to join us," said Tio.

En'gorr nodded in greeting. "Autumn is now sleep."

"Seriously?" Tio raised an eyebrow. "How did you manage that?"

"Not me. In day time, she at infirmary. At night, she searches for Sagan. Watching Xabat. Hunting for information of spangles—how to defeat Matthias. Autumn works hardly."

Nathan and Tio shared a glance of confusion.

"Uh… do you mean 'Autumn works hard'?" Tio asked.

En'gorr nodded. "Working, working. Finally… Autumn sleeps."

"Sounds like she needs it," said Nathan.

En'gorr then pointed to Gus and Va'atuu and spoke a phrase in Jiovis.

"It was a close match," said Tio. "For a second there, it looked like Va'atuu almost had him, but as always, Gus kicked ass." He shook his head. "It's hard to believe that only a few days ago Gus hadn't picked up a combat weapon of any kind in his life. And yet here we are, a bunch of Jiovis princes and royal guards, getting our butts handed to us night after night."

Nathan gave a dry chuckle. "It's probably a good thing academia and knowledge is preferred by the Pliokai. Can you just imagine an army of Pliokai whose ancestors had mastered the art of war and passed on their cumulative skills?"

A low whistle trilled through Tio's lips. "They'd only need maybe two or three generations' worth of combat and strategy training, and they'd be unstoppable."

Silence fell as En'gorr, the pewter twins, Tio, and Nathan all exchanged glances.

"So… like I said," Nathan reiterated, "perhaps it's a good thing the Pliokai value academia and knowledge instead."

The group responded with nods and grunts of agreement.

En'gorr then called out to Va'atuu. When the copper Jiovis turned to acknowledge him, the prince said, "My turn."

Before anyone could say another word, he strolled onto the sparring field and retrieved the blue aluminum staff.

Facing Gus, En'gorr gave an unsettling smile. "My turn to beat puny Pliokai."

* * *

"Nathan?"

A hand gripped his shoulder, rocking his body from side to side.

"Nathan, you awake?"

Groaning into his pillow, Nathan swiveled his head and cracked one eye open. Autumn's and Tio's faces hovered above him.

"What's-a-matter?" he slurred.

"You'd better get up," said Autumn. "We need you to come check something out."

Tio nodded. "Yeah, but first you'd better get your bandages on."

Before Nathan could protest, Tio yanked on his arm and pulled him into a sitting position.

"What's wrong? Why the urgency?" Grogginess faded as Autumn and Tio started wrapping bandages around his arms.

"Someone arrived not long ago, and they've been causing a bit of a ruckus," said Tio.

"Not really a 'ruckus,' more like throwing demands around," amended Autumn.

Nathan's brow creased. "Demands? Who's making demands?"

"That's the thing. No one knows who this person is," said Tio.

"Maple Shire hasn't really been the kind of place to get suspicious of newcomers—not until recently," said Autumn. "Nika was lucky she arrived by a back road. Raiden Tanner would have flexed his 'I'm the leader' skills and thrown a tantrum if he found out she hadn't been here the whole time. The shire leaders are usually chill, but when they get on edge, the whole shire gets on edge. And with the reasons for the explosions still a mystery to most, wild rumors and mistrust have been going around.

"So, this morning, a woman rocked up out of the blue. She had a run-in with a few of the other community members who were on roadblock duties, and Raiden Tanner demanded she leave. When she refused, En'gorr and his guards got involved. They've now reached an impasse. They refuse to let her out of their sight, and she refuses to leave."

"I think you might need to intervene." Tio looked pointedly at Nathan. "Her scent tells me she's not a shifter, but she smells a little too strange to be just a human. Best to help out before the leaders of the shire learn more than just humans reside in this little community."

In record time, Autumn and Tio had Nathan bandaged up, complete with work gloves and sunglasses. They led him toward the outskirts of the living areas and farther along a dirt road that wove through the forest and eventually onto the nearest highway. Somewhere up ahead, he could make out several people having an argument.

"I'm telling you, I've been here before," stated a woman in an assertive tone.

"And I've lived in this shire most of my life. I've never seen you before."

That was Raiden Tanner's voice. Nathan generally stayed out of shire politics and out of the way of shire leaders, but everyone at Maple Shire knew Raiden—and most loved him. The guy was laid-back, like most of the residents, but still enjoyed a good spotlight and never discouraged any of the fawning and doting from other members. Nathan sometimes wondered how this guy would react if someone else was ever voted in to be top dog in the community.

"Maybe you didn't see me because I was only here for a short time," snapped the woman. "Now get out of my way."

"Out of the question." Raiden's voice rose a few decibels.

Nathan sought out the four Jiovis shifters, who, even in their human forms, still made a formidable roadblock when standing side by side. As Nathan got closer, he recognized the other two elders with Raiden—all now arguing with a female driver of a maroon sedan.

Voices began to overlap. With wild hand and arm gestures, the three human men huddled closer to the open driver's-side window, clearly not about to back down. And the woman was just as persistent that they needed to let her pass.

"All right, I'm here," Nathan called out.

The argument ceased, and all heads turned in his direction.

Nathan gave a nod to the Jiovis shifters, who moved aside to let him, Autumn, and Tio pass. "What seems to be the trouble?"

Raiden stabbed a finger at the driver. "This woman keeps demanding to enter without giving us a reason why. With no valid reason, I must insist she leave *immediately*."

"Understood," said Nathan. Rounding the car, he prepared to add his own voice to the chorus telling the woman to get lost. This community had already suffered enough.

But when he came in full view of the driver, he stopped dead in his tracks. His mouth went dry; his mind went blank.

She stared directly back at him.

A half second later, Nathan's tongue began working again. "Gloria?"

"You know her?" Raiden asked, his tone a little incredulous.

"Uh… yeah. From a long, long time ago." He tried to rake his fingers through his hair, only to remember his head was wrapped in a thick layer of bandages.

"Who is she?" Tio asked.

Nathan took a moment to clear his throat. "This is Gloria Chambers… Violet's mother."

32

IT IS WHAT I, JHUTEV, WISHES…

Qozzlotl regarded Violet with a steely, contemplative expression, his mighty fist still poised above Jhutev's head.

"Please," Violet said, loathing the begging tone of her words. "Please let me speak with Jhutev. I know I can convince him."

Encouraging Jhutev to stay strong and withhold his wish was one thing, but when he was faced with being slaughtered by the king, Violet couldn't handle it.

The Nephezai king raised a single eyebrow, the fury in his eyes momentarily replaced by suspicion. But Violet could sense his temptation. After all, he hadn't yet struck Jhutev, and while the Meruvo was still alive—though barely—the king obviously had hope he could get what he wanted.

Even without flicking her Veniri tongue, she could practically taste Qozzlotl's desperation.

"Are you not aware of how notoriously stubborn the Meruvo are when it comes to guarding their wish, even unto death?" Qozzlotl asked, his expression now an emotionless mask. "What makes you so sure you can convince him to relinquish his wish?"

Violet hesitated, her mind furiously searching for something believable. In her own desperation to save her friend, she'd blurted out the first thing that came into her head, without any thought to how she'd convince the king of her claim.

"I can understand him," she finally answered, steeling her expression into what she hoped appeared to be unwavering confidence. "When someone has lost everything—their family, their hope, their freedom—they believe there is nothing left to lose and no need to preserve their life. But I know what Jhutev wants."

A hint of surprise, along with a spark of greed, crossed Qozzlotl's features.

Violet's heart stung when Jhutev's eyes widened, whether with horror, curiosity, or a spasm of pain, she couldn't quite tell. Either way, she hoped he could trust her.

"Care to enlighten me?" The king's fist slowly lowered to his side, and the end of his eel-like tail twitched back and forth, reminding Violet of a cat contemplating its prey. "What is it you think the Meruvo wants in exchange for his wish?"

"Well, to ensure I've got him figured out correctly, I'd need to speak with Jhutev," said Violet. "Would you mind telling your brutes to let us go?"

A small hiss came from Votloxo.

Qozzlotl's eyes narrowed. Taking up precious seconds of what remained of Jhutev's life, he released the Meruvo, crossed his arms, and contemplated, his fingers mindlessly tapping the sides of a few mother-of-pearl thorns on his biceps. Jhutev fell through the water to land in the silt beneath the king.

Finally, Qozzlotl gave a small nod to his guards, and the fighter fish shifter reluctantly let Violet go. She floated up from the ground, overcome by a small wave of relief—until she saw Thane still pinned to the ground with Solace cocooned in his strong arms.

She opened her mouth to protest, but the king spoke before she had a chance.

"Make the Meruvo give me what I want, and I'll allow your loved ones to be released."

Violet's breath hitched as one of the guards snatched Solace out of Thane's protective embrace. As if pulled by gravity, she surged toward her child, arms outstretched, but Votloxo and her guards barred her from going any farther.

A deep, dark chuckle came from behind Violet.

"The Meruvo may be difficult to persuade," said Qozzlotl, "but there's no question as to what will motivate you to do my bidding, hybrid."

Votloxo glided over to Thane and Solace, her voluminous fins rippling while the king spoke. The vicious expression on her face contrasted sharply with her elegant fins as she grabbed a handful of Thane's hair and yanked his head back. She cupped her hand over his exposed neck and dug her sharp claws into his flesh. Violet's heart leaped to her throat when teal blood seeped into the seawater.

The hammering in her chest pounded like it would crack her ribs. Beneath her feet, an inferno roiled as if on the verge of erupting—the fine crust of seabed an all too thin barrier between the currents of cold ocean and the currents of liquid fire.

The king had made his intention crystal clear.

Whoever she tried to save, someone would still die.

Her impending defeat roiled within her, much like the magma below. Panic and terror bombarded her restraint, but she couldn't risk hurting her family and Meruvo friend with her newfound link to the planet's raging lifeblood.

Sweat trickled down her temples—the manifestation of her frustrations, overwhelming fears, and effort to calm the small portion of the earth's molten power willing to answer her call.

Just as the anguish over her dilemma threatened to consume her, a faint *boom* drew her attention to the ceiling.

"Hybrid!" the king barked, his patience clearly disintegrated.

A guard shoved Violet in the back. She surged through the water, closer to the king, closer to Jhutev. Silt flurried up around her, and her knees scraped on something sharp hidden in the sediment. A rock? Coral? Did it matter?

Her throat constricted in agony to suppress her sobs. How she hated the sight of Jhutev crumpled at the base of Qozzlotl's eel-like tail. Her hands clenched and unclenched at her sides, still burning with her teal Magneii fire.

A guard shoved her again.

She didn't fight back. Instead, Violet drew closer to Jhutev. She extinguished her flames and gently took hold of his wrists, hoping she wasn't causing further pain.

Jhutev's eyes grew fearful as Violet leaned over him, the faint starbursts within even more heartbreaking to behold.

"It's okay," said Violet, regardless of the fact that everything was far from okay. A sharp pain stung her elbows, and adrenaline surged through her body.

Jhutev looked down. His eyes flashed when he caught sight of the crystal blade protruding from her elbow, a blade only he could see. His expression turned hopeful.

It would be a mercy, just one quick slice. A crystal shard cutting through a swirl of galaxies. The end would be swift, and Jhutev's suffering would be no more.

Violet bit her lip, fighting back uncontrolled sobs.

Her Diamantium blade retracted back into her arm.

"Quickly, hybrid," the king yelled as another *boom* came from above. "The Meruvo is fading from us. If you don't get his wish before he dies, you forfeit your little air-breathing family."

"I'm sorry," Violet whispered when Jhutev looked back up at her.

He patted her hand in wordless understanding.

She was too much of a coward to end his life. She thought she could do it, to put him out of his misery, to free him from his underwater prison and allow him to be with his mother.

"I'm sorry. If only I knew how to get you out of here." Violet shook her head. "I don't even know how to get myself out of here."

"It's okay, Miss Violet," Jhutev wheezed. "You have everything you need right here." His head rolled to the side, to look over at Thane and Solace.

Thane's fierce expression softened when his eyes met Violet's. There was a peace in his gaze, one Violet couldn't quite comprehend, not in this time of utter defeat.

Then a sudden thought ignited a spark of hope.

What was it Jhutev had said? *You have everything you need right here?*

Jhutev groaned in agony and tilted his head back. His eyes fluttered shut.

"Jhutev! No!" Violet couldn't hold back a sob as she leaned over him, resting a hand on his chest. The pounding of his heart was faint but thankfully still present.

When King Qozzlotl loomed closer, Violet shook her head. "It's okay, he's not gone yet. He's just resting." She leaned over Jhutev again, as if listening to a whisper, before raising her tear-stricken eyes to meet the king's. "He says he's ready."

Eagerly, and without prompting, Qozzlotl drew right up next to them.

"There's just one thing," said Violet.

Impatience flared in the king's eyes. "What is it?"

"Please tell Exültov I'm sorry I couldn't fulfill my promise to him," said Violet.

Qozzlotl's eyes bulged with shock right before Violet slammed her fist into the side of his neck. Clenched in her hand was her own thorn of Neptune.

The king's body froze in place.

With one fluid motion, Violet snatched the purple spangle from around his neck, raised her knee, and kicked the king in the belly. As he sailed back through the water, she turned and threw her remaining two thorns—one at the guard who held Solace and one at Votloxo.

As if Thane had read her mind, he dove the second Votloxo released him, catching Solace as she fell from her guard's arms.

Violet screamed, no longer able to contain her anguish and fury as she hurled her teal flames. Like torpedoes, they soared effortlessly through the water, directly at the remaining guards.

The lionfish shifter ducked and swooped, avoiding her flames, but he couldn't avoid Thane's crystal blades. With a swift slice of his elbow, Thane impaled the guard on a deadly Diamantium shard. Clouds of vibrant purple blood swirled in the ocean water, joining the teal and black.

In a matter of seconds, the king and his guards had all collapsed to the seabed or were drifting with paralysis.

There was no time to celebrate their victory, as an earsplitting *BOOM!* shattered the ceiling above.

"Go! Go! Go!" Thane roared. With one arm wrapped securely around Solace, he helped Violet pick up Jhutev with his free hand.

The ceiling shattered.

Dodging falling rocks, Violet and Thane swam with frenzied determination back through the passageway they'd been dragged down previously. Violet cried out when a barnacle-encrusted chunk of stone sliced through the flesh of her arm, but her injury didn't cause as much alarm as the wall of collapsed rocks blocking their path.

"There's no way out!" she yelled over the blood pounding in her ears and the roar of swirling water. All hope dissolved when she saw the despair in Thane's eyes.

Another deafening *boom!* shook the world around them.

Thane hugged everyone close, and in one last act of desperation, Violet raised her arms high. Waving her hands through the water, she gathered every fleck of light she could forge and hastily created a shield. In moments, a hollow glowing orb tinged with marbled teal and magenta enclosed all four of them. With another explosive blast from the hunters' submarines, rocky fragments of ceiling slid through the shield's fissures right before Violet sealed them up tight.

Her arms collapsed. She released a gasp when the impact of the rippling blast and several enormous chunks of ceiling crashed onto the orb shield only a split second later.

"It's okay," said Thane when the shield held fast. "You did it, Vi. We're safe for now."

He sounded far from relieved, but his tone held enough confidence for Violet to believe him. Adrenaline ebbing and energy spent, her body went slack. She would have collapsed if not for the salt water's buoyancy and Thane's steadfast presence for her to lean against.

Another blast went off, this time slightly muted by the shield. As more chunks of debris pounded against the teal-and-magenta orb, a new fear threatened to throttle the air from Violet's lungs.

Oh no... What have I done? I've trapped us in a bubble to be buried alive.

"You haven't trapped us," said Thane. "You've saved us from certain death."

Violet's chest heaved with quick, shallow breaths. Before

she could wonder if she'd spoken aloud or not, Jhutev let out a low groan.

"Jhutev, are you all right?" She laid a hand on his shoulder.

Thane still held him up with an arm crooked around his back. Gently, Violet took hold of her friend and helped him sink to the curved floor.

"Jhutev?"

The Meruvo coughed, and immediately his face screwed up in a wince. Black blood still seeped from his wounds. Violet could see some fresh cuts, most likely caused by the rocks, coral, and shrapnel raining down on them before she'd created the shield.

A painful knot formed in her throat. Out of all the abilities she'd gained since becoming a shape-shifter hybrid, none involved healing. Hot, frustrated tears flooded her eyes. "I'm so sorry, Jhutev. I wish I knew what to do. I wish I knew how to help you and get you out of here."

His eyes fluttered open, their light much too dull. "Miss Violet, are you crying?"

Violet bit her trembling lip. "Is there anything I can do for you? What do you need?"

Jhutev gave her a weak smile. With much effort, he raised a hand and patted her on the shoulder. "Do not worry yourself about me, Miss Violet. I am on the brink of death."

Violet shook her head. "No. I won't let that happen. Tell me what I need to do. I don't understand what a Meruvo needs to heal. You need to tell me what I have to do."

"Peace, Violet."

She clamped her mouth shut but still shook her head.

"I will soon be reunited with my mother," Jhutev said. "I have accepted my fate."

As she squeezed her eyes shut, hot tears scorched down Violet's cheeks. "I'm sorry" was all she could think to say.

"There is no need," said Jhutev.

"But I couldn't—didn't stop them in time. Yigtheez and his friends. I should have acted sooner, made them stop sooner. And the king—Votloxo and her guards. I should have—"

"Enough." Jhutev shushed her, but it came out as more of a wheeze. "You have done enough. You have done all you could do. You were kind to me and tried to help me, despite the consequences to yourself. You did not leave me behind, even when I told you to. It is I who should have done more. I should have done more to help you and your family get out of here long before now."

Violet frowned. "No, Jhutev—"

He coughed again with a bit more force than his fragile body could handle. The jolting stirred up the black blood still clouding the water around his wounds.

Jhutev looked up at Thane, who was crouching down beside Violet and helping prop up his head. Even Solace appeared to be gazing at the Meruvo with sorrow. He reached out and clasped the baby's little hand. "I, too, was blessed with the fervent love of a parent. And I can see, little Solace, that you are blessed with not one but two parents with devout love for you."

He touched a finger to the collar around the infant's neck. Violet glared at the hateful object.

When Jhutev looked back at Violet, his fading eyes were brimming with sadness. He coughed again, and this time, viscous black blood coated his lips and splattered onto his Nephezai air bubble.

Violet bit her cheeks hard to stop herself from violently sobbing.

Another *boom* went off overhead, and more debris plummeted down onto their sphere. Solace began to cry out, squirming in Thane's arms as he tried to soothe her.

With all the noise, the chaos, the dire situations all around, Violet wanted to clamp her hands over her ears and scream.

"Peace, Violet," Jhutev wheezed.

"Tell me how to help you." Her voice cracked with desperation as more tears dripped off her chin. "Please."

Jhutev smiled, the agony on his face fleeing for a split second before returning with a vengeance. "Save your tears, Miss Violet. There is no longer any hope for me."

"No, don't say that. We can help you. We will take you with us. You'll finally be free from this underwater prison."

The starlight within Jhutev's night-sky flesh flickered.

"No! Stay with me, Jhutev."

Eyes closed, he patted her arm. "I'm still here, for the moment."

His lids drifted open again when Solace let out another whimper. He laid a hand on her, and the small girl held still for several seconds as she stared directly into Jhutev's starburst eyes.

The silent interaction astounded Violet. She shared a curious glance with Thane.

"Look after your father and mother, little Solace," Jhutev said in an unsteady voice.

The baby clung tight to his thumb as her face screwed up in distress. Despite Solace's young age, Violet had to wonder how well her daughter understood the gravity of Jhutev's condition.

Jhutev gently squeezed Solace's hand. The celestial light speckling his skin flared bright for a split second before fading into the galaxies across his body.

"Don't cry for me," he said, stroking Solace's hand with his thumb. "It is time for me to finally be free of this place. It's time for me to reunite with my family. It's been so long since I've seen my mother."

Solace's whimpers intensified.

Another *boom* sounded, and Thane growled at the shockwave that pounded through the boulders around them. For a heart-racing moment, Violet studied the shield, searching for any cracks or fissures, any sign it might be failing. How much weight and explosive force could a light-forged shield withstand?

Jhutev took hold of her hand. "I do not possess a great power, like that which stole the wings of an entire shifter species. And you also don't have that power, Miss Violet. But I can see your spirit. You have the power to change the world around you, for the good of all shifters. One thing I do know: I have the power to elevate you to your full potential. Someone needs to help awaken that which lies dormant within you."

He gave her a faint smile. "From the moment I was born into my underwater captivity, I've been kept alive for one purpose only. While I'm still able, it is time I fulfill my purpose."

Violet's eyes grew wide with horror.

"No, you can't!" Thane exclaimed.

"Don't do it," said Violet. "Don't give the king what he wants. Don't let him win!"

"No. That is not what I meant." He sucked in a breath, his eyes losing focus as he stared off into the distance. "Oh, how I wish I'd had the chance to see the sun, to feel its warmth, even for just a second. Or see the silvery light of the moon with my own eyes."

He closed his eyes. His breathing grew more ragged, but his face became relaxed, serene.

"I'm sure you'll see a world even more beautiful when you're reunited with your mother." It was the best thing Violet could think to say without blurting out a whole bunch of empty promises.

"Mother. Yes…" A small smile graced Jhutev's lips. Then his brow creased, and the smile fell away. "Mother?"

His eyes flew open, as if he'd just remembered something important.

"Quick," he said, in almost a whisper. "We don't have much time. Violet, give me your hand."

She clasped his hand, his bony fingers icy to touch.

Jhutev turned his attention to Thane. "I know we didn't have much opportunity to become well acquainted, but I have observed your unwavering dedication to your family. So whatever happens, promise me you'll protect them. Protect Miss Violet and your daughter."

"With my life." Thane placed his hand on Violet's shoulder.

Jhutev nodded once, a severe determination in his gaze when it once again found Violet's. "It's been an honor and a privilege." He squeezed her hand with his uninjured one, the effort weak but the sentiment undeniable. "May you and your family find the joy and peace my mother and I were never able to achieve. May you find the freedom we always dreamed of. What was taken from you, may it be restored. What was killed in you, may it be revived. What was destroyed in you, may it be re-created. It is what I, Jhutev Iha of the Arundhati lineage, wishes…"

His eyes lost focus, though his lips continued to move, mumbling what Violet assumed was a phrase—or perhaps a prayer—in the Meruvo language.

"Goodbye, my dear friend." He squeezed her hand one last time.

The instant Jhutev ceased speaking, Violet gasped.

The galaxies within Jhutev's skin blazed until every inch of him glowed with the Meruvo's paradoxical black light. He became the vision of a star, burning so bright Violet had to turn her eyes away.

One moment Jhutev was humanoid; the next, he burst like a solar flare, sending forth an explosion of glittering dark-light embers and stardust. An astronomical, vibrant power filled the spherical shield, churning the water within. With a cyclonic wave, the water whipped around Violet, Thane, and Solace. All three whirled round and round within the whirlpool.

Violet screamed until her voice was left in shreds, but no sound could rival the roar of Jhutev's exploding power. Each particle, speck, and mote of his life force rippled through every cell of her being, until something quaked deep within her. Something sleeping burst to life like a new star.

Ears ringing, heart pounding, breath heaving, she collapsed against Thane, and they tumbled to the floor of the light-forged orb.

All the water within their shield had vanished, whether dispersed or absorbed by Jhutev's supernova, Violet didn't know. She also couldn't tell if they'd been plunged into darkness or not, as the afterglow of Jhutev's intense flare speckled Violet's vision with each blink.

"Violet? Are you okay?"

"Yes, I'm fine… I think." Her body felt… different actually, but she couldn't comprehend how. She felt around until she found her daughter still in Thane's embrace. "What about Solace?"

A small cry came from the baby; distress, anguish, confusion, or pain—it could have been anything. Patting over her child, Violet searched for any kind of external injury or problem. Her hands bumped against Thane's, who she realized was doing the same.

"I think she's okay," he finally said. "Definitely shook up, but I don't think she's been harmed after Jhutev did… actually, what did he do?"

Violet blinked, relieved when the spots in her vision began to clear. "I think… he made a wish."

"What was it?"

Violet slowly shook her head, trying to assess the "new life" she now felt, trying to decipher any clue as to what Jhutev had wished for. "I don't know. I think—it's going to sound stupid, but… I feel very different somehow. What about you?"

"Um… other than feeling like I went through the explosion of a sun, I don't notice anything different. But what about Jhutev? Is he…?"

"Jhutev—" His name burned Violet's soul like acid. He had been in her life for such a short time, yet he had made such an impact on her. She couldn't bring herself to accept that she had, again, lost someone near and dear.

Her eyes scrunched closed as the heat around her intensified.

"Violet?" Thane's concerned tone rolled off her.

"He's gone." Her chest rocked with several shallow breaths.

Jhutev was gone.

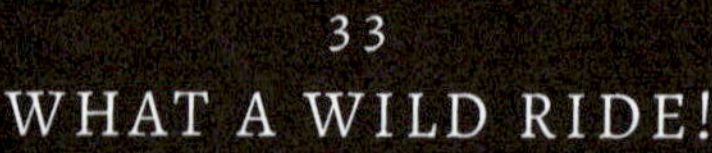

33
WHAT A WILD RIDE!

THEY WERE STILL TRAPPED AT THE BOTTOM OF THE OCEAN.

Explosions still sounded all around them.

Rocks and coral still pounded against their shield.

And there was still the nauseating problem of the bomb strapped around Solace's neck.

Violet hadn't been able to save Jhutev. She couldn't even save herself. *Oh, Solace, how am I supposed to save you?*

The inferno deep inside Violet's core churned. She'd remained at the brink of boiling for weeks, and now she was on the verge of exploding. Each rapid inhalation of breath fanned the flames like a bellows.

She pressed her palms flat against the bottom of the shield. The searing heat just beyond her fingertips matched the searing heat of her pent-up terror and rage. For a split second she wanted to shy away, for fear of also being incinerated by the ferocious power only a few miles beneath her. But just as it had before, like called to like. The flames of Earth called to her flames of Mars.

Her choice was clear: either she allowed herself to be consumed by her intense fear and helplessness, or she allowed herself to be consumed by her burning rage. Her instincts took over.

Violet embraced the inferno.

As her own power connected with that of the molten earth beneath her, the rising heat of her Magneii abilities singed away her uncertainties. Her teal flames erupted to life, burning away the last of the white spots in her vision, bringing her world into teal clarity.

Thane's eyes grew wide as he looked down at her, as if seeing her for the first time. "Violet, you're… you look so—"

An avalanche of rocks pounded against their shield, urging Violet into action. She expanded her flames to engulf Thane and Solace, until the menthol barrier of teal fire encased all three of them. "Hold on to me, and don't let go," she ordered. "I know what to do."

Thane circled his strong arms around her, sandwiching Solace between them.

Violet wrapped her legs around his waist to free up her hands. "Ready?"

He gave a sharp nod. An edge of worry hid behind the determination in his eyes, but his trust in Violet remained evident. Even Solace looked up at her with confidence. Her little hand reached out and touched Violet on the cheek.

Violet gave her a tense smile and kissed her on the head. "Hold on, little one."

The purple spangle she'd swiped from the king was still in her hand. After tying the broken cord around her neck, she set her awareness on the ocean floor and focused on the heat below—the magma below. Determined to avoid the frenzied bursts she'd used on Yigtheez and his friends, Violet strove for calm and control as her Magneii power latched on to the liquid fire, drawing it up through the shallow crust of the earth.

"I can feel it now, the heat. It's definitely getting warmer."

Thane wriggled a bit, but his grip on his family never faltered. "It feels hot, like... really hot. But with the menthol sensation of your Magneii flames, it's not uncomfortable."

Violet didn't respond. Instead, she kept her attention on the small portion of magma under her control. If she lost focus now, there was no telling how badly she would hurt Thane and her daughter.

Before her hybrid shifter days, she would never have been able to bear the heat she was putting Thane and Solace through. But no pain showed in either of their expressions when the temperature rose high enough to start melting their light-forged shield away.

A deafening rumble ensued as the rocks above them began to shift. Gaps in the shield let sprays of seawater in, which instantly sizzled to steam when they hit the now exposed magma. Rocks, coral, water, and who knows what else began to rain down as the integrity of the shield failed further, but the flames and magma disintegrated anything that threatened to come near. Even so, the incoming seawater and steam threatened to overwhelm and drown them, especially since the air bubbles over their heads had burst after Jhutev's supernova.

Violet reinforced her teal flames, expanding the cocoon of fire until an air gap of a few inches surrounded all three of them. She had only a moment to marvel over this new method of shielding with an air supply included before a crash came from behind her.

A gap in the rocks had opened up to her left, leaving a sizable hole for several angry Nephezai faces to peer through. But their anger morphed to sheer shock when they observed Violet and her family in the flame shield.

Among the faces, dead center, was King Qozzlotl.

Violet had no idea how much time had passed since she'd stabbed him in the neck with the paralytic thorn. Minutes?

Hours? It had only been seconds since Jhutev passed away, and yet it already felt like an eternity.

In any case, the neurotoxins in the Nephezai thorns should have lasted much longer. Perhaps the Nephezai had some level of immunity, and the paralysis wore off much quicker than for other shifter species. Or maybe the king had access to some kind of antidote.

Either way, their sudden appearance caught Violet by surprise.

"Hybrid!" Qozzlotl's steely gaze promised soul-killing torture if he ever laid hands on her.

Despite the chill the king's roar sent down her spine, Violet gave him a victorious grin. She patted the purple spangle hanging by her sternum, more for her own reassurance she still had it than as a taunt, but the action still caused the king's face to darken with rage.

He pointed at her and barked an order, and in a flurry, the guards surrounded him. With deadly speed, a torrent of mother-of-pearl thorns darted through the gap in the rock, straight for her, Thane, and Solace.

Qozzlotl shot one of his own mother-of-pearl thorns, his aim second to none. Knowing the thorn would hit her directly between the eyes, Violet raised her arm to protect her face—but no sting from the thorn came.

"Heavens above."

Thane's whispered exclamation felt wholly inadequate for the wall of lava raised in front of them, its vibrant white orange concealing their view of Qozzlotl and his guards. When the liquid earth dropped, it took Violet a second to understand the molten wall lowered at the same time her arm did.

"What the hell just happened?" Thane asked.

Violet shook her head, unable to form words.

She, Thane, and Solace stared down at the ground just

outside their flame shield. A thin crack in the earth, about two feet long, glowed faintly from the magma now several feet below. At the edge of the fissure, the charred remains of the Nephezai king's deadly thorn floated harmlessly in the bubbling water.

Violet released a breath. "That was close."

"Yeah," agreed Thane. "But whatever it is you have planned, perhaps do it now."

She dropped her arm lower, and the fissure in the ocean floor resealed.

As soon as the Nephezai guards saw the lava wall had disappeared, they erupted into action. Violet couldn't understand what they were shouting, but judging by the way they tried to drag the king away to safety, the surrounding water must be reaching temperatures high enough to fry fish.

The shock of what Violet had done was still evident on the king's face when her eyes found his. His sinister glare had been replaced with widened eyes and a hint of uncertainty. Or was that fear? Or regret?

Violet couldn't help but whip out her forked tongue. A plethora of flavors smashed through her senses. Most, she deduced, belonged to Thane and Solace, while the flavors of sour apple and peppermint confirmed everyone's fear and terror.

But the bouquet of flavors she sensed from the king gave her pause.

Neither the presence of seaweed for severe determination nor blood orange for his obvious disdain came as a surprise. But other complex flavors she wouldn't have guessed the king capable of possessing: persimmon to hint he was ashamed of something, along with the cold tang of stainless steel, revealing Qozzlotl believed himself to be worthless.

In the microseconds it took for Violet to assess the king's emotional cocktail, his scowl had returned.

For a moment, she wondered if it would be worth trying to work out some kind of agreement with Qozzlotl. After all, she wasn't the only one who wished to be released from the bottom of the ocean. All the Nephezai wanted to be free from their banishment and return to the surface, and Exültov was a testament to the fact that not all Nephezai were bitter and bloodthirsty.

She was on the verge of reassessing her choices when a whimper from Solace and a high-pitched beeping caught her attention.

"Violet! The timer!" Thane's voice rang through Violet's ears, and her eyes landed on the collar around her daughter's neck.

Glowing red numbers had appeared on one side of the collar—numbers that hadn't been there when Matthias locked it around her neck.

The bright red numbers glared up at Violet.

A gut-splitting nausea punched her in the pit of her stomach. Solace's death sentence had just been announced; they had seventy-two hours left before the collar detonated, and the numbers were now ticking down.

"We need to get out of here." She could feel the blood drain from her face. "I think I can get us out of here, but it's obviously a huge risk."

The flame shield, which had intensified in her panic, abruptly faltered at the staggering thought of what she was about to attempt.

When Thane's gaze met hers, though, it held only confidence. "It's okay, Vi. Whatever happens, we do this together."

Violet didn't trust herself to respond, understanding the meaning of his words—he believed in her to pull off the impossible. Even with the high chance she'd fail, he wouldn't let her go through it alone.

Another crash came from behind them, and the unmistakable pinging sound of a submarine grew closer.

"Get ready to take a big breath at any moment," Violet said, hoping Solace also understood. "I'm not sure our Magneii flame shield will survive this."

Thane nodded. His arms cinched tighter around her and Solace.

Closing her eyes, Violet held her hands parallel to the ocean's floor and pummeled her power into the liquid inferno below.

"Hybrid!"

The king's roar was cut off by the almighty blast of lava beneath her and Thane's feet. Violet's stomach shot through her pelvis as they rocketed up with the eruption, crashed through the collapsed underwater cavern, and darted up toward the ocean's surface.

She and Thane craned their necks to look up. Lava surrounded them on all sides except for above, giving them a tunnel view of the dark ocean and the direction they were heading. The menthol coolness of Violet's teal flames felt odd mixed with the infernal heat.

Up, up, up they traveled, faster than any roller coaster Violet had ever been on.

Excitement hitched in her chest as the water gradually became brighter. It was working. Her insane idea was working! Surely any second now, they would break through the surface.

The sizzle and hiss of lava as it met the cool water was almost deafening. Sweat had long ago broken out over Violet's face, neck, and back and started to trail down her body.

She gritted her teeth, fighting to maintain her control, fighting to keep the lava hot and malleable enough to continue their upward trajectory through the water. Yet the closer they came to the surface, the farther away they got from the lava's heat source. The higher they went, the more the magma started to cool and grow brittle. There was only so much her Magneii heat could do to help maintain their momentum.

Thane's grip had become like an iron vise. Solace's high-pitched screech joined Thane's and Violet's own cries of desperation and anguish.

"I don't know how much longer I can keep this up!" Violet wasn't sure Thane had heard her over the roar until he responded.

"Keep going!"

"Are we close to the surface?"

"Closer than we were before."

"What if I don't get us close enough?" Violet glanced at the surrounding lava. Curiously, the vibrant red-orange liquid had started to turn slightly teal, but it was the blackening spots that gave her greater concern.

"Just keep going!" Thane shouted again. "You can do this!"

But despite his encouragement, fatigue was rolling in.

She was losing her claim over the lava. The ocean's formidable cooling power was becoming too much. Not only had their upward momentum begun to slow down, but their teal fire shield was starting to flicker.

How much farther did they have to go?

When would they no longer be going upward?

Thane's roar of pain intensified. He bowed his head closer to Violet, enclosing Solace even tighter in their embrace. Only when Violet heard a slight sizzle did she realize the flame shield was no longer keeping the extreme heat at bay.

Thane's flesh was beginning to burn. He was shielding Solace with his own body.

Solace's safety, as well as Thane's, kicked Violet's desperation up a notch. She couldn't keep them surrounded by her blue fire and the lava much longer. Digging deeper than she'd ever done in her life, she forced a final wave of her shifter energy into the magma. A blast of teal, magenta, and emerald light shot out from her body, giving them a jolt of speed.

"We're almost there!" she screamed. "I can see the surface."

Thane didn't look up, didn't move an inch from Solace.

Violet couldn't guess how far away the surface was. Maybe twenty feet? Thirty? Glorious sunshine waited almost within reach. But just as Violet's hope began to bloom, it immediately shriveled.

The rampaging force of the lava had come to a halt. Her Magneii energy stores were drained.

Solace screamed.

Urgency flared to life in Violet's mind, but her body had gone limp, unable to react to Solace's severe discomfort from the still unbearable heat.

Thane's strong arms adjusted around Violet and Solace as he took over pushing the trio toward the surface. His strong kicks propelled them through the hole in the top of their lava cocoon, gradually getting them farther away from the horrendously hot chunks of char. Smaller lava stones floated around them, making their way to the surface as well.

Mercifully, their flame shield—and, by extension, air bubble barrier—was still intact, but just barely. Perhaps her Veniri shifter energies still fueled the teal flames, but even those stores were nearly used up.

With mere feet left to go, the flame shield fizzled out, and a second later, water gushed in to fill the void. The three of them were engulfed for a single heartbeat before their heads burst through the ocean's surface.

Air whipped over Violet's face, and she drew in a deep breath of the briny sea breeze. For a few moments, the only sound she heard was the sweet music of Solace's and Thane's ragged gasps of fresh air mingled with her own.

Since her own strength was depleted, Thane held both her and Solace above the water. "Is everyone okay?"

Violet nodded and gazed down at Solace. Her little girl still looked a little shaken from their unorthodox journey from the deep. "Yeah, I think we're fine. You?"

Thane nodded, albeit the movement seemed a little strained. Violet couldn't see the state of his back, but she was sure he was putting on a brave face despite the lava burns. He gave a halfhearted chuckle. "That was crazy. What a wild ride!"

Violet let out her own exhausted laugh. She leaned her head back and squinted into the bright blue sky, her body almost weightless, her hair swishing with the gentle lapping of the water.

Thane swiveled his head back and forth, then ducked his face under the surface. The second time he did this, Violet asked, "What are you looking for?"

"I'm checking if anyone has followed us."

With a start, Violet shoved her own face beneath the waves. She squinted through the blurry water, searching for any obscure shadow that might have the features of a Nephczai.

"We came straight up," said Thane, "and we left a clear trail behind us." He reached out for a small chunk of cooled lava, one of many floating to the surface. A few larger ones gently drifted along in the current. "If someone followed us, I would expect them to show up soon. I'd suggest we start swimming away from here, but…" He made a point of looking in every direction. "I'm not sure which way land is likely to be."

With an anxious glance at the countdown clock on Solace's collar, Violet deduced it had taken them about fifteen minutes to reach the surface. Her jaw dropped. How fast had they been going?

Thane frowned, also looking at the glowing numbers on Solace's collar. "What are the chances this thing has already sent a signal to Matthias and his thugs now that we've resurfaced?"

Violet blanched. As much as Matthias showing up would hopefully guarantee Solace's safety, she hated the idea of him homing in on their exact location and showing up out of the blue.

"Oh no. We've got company," said Thane.

Violet followed his gesture to the dark oblong shadows far, far below. At first they appeared to be part of the collection of floating lava debris, but the faint purple glow was unmistakable. While the Nephezai couldn't move as fast as the lava explosion, they were much more adept at water travel than either Thane or Violet. If she had to guess, it wouldn't take them more than five minutes to reach the surface.

She whipped her head around, her drenched hair slapping her in the face. "We have to go. But... which way?"

Thane was right; all she could see was ocean and sky. Nothing suggested land in any direction she looked.

"We have to..." Her mind went blank. What could they possibly do?

She raised her gaze to the heavens, then gasped when she felt the presence of her connection with Venus and Mars. A melodic hum, one only she could hear, rang through her body as her depleted shifter energies began to rekindle. Unfortunately, there wasn't enough time to refuel before the Nephezai reached them.

"What do we do?" Thane said, more to himself than anyone, repeating the phrase over and over. "We have no choice. We just have to swim."

Violet's body immediately felt heavy at the thought of trying to swim away. She dipped her face in the water again. The shadows were getting bigger, their tentacles and fins starting to take shape. The Nephezai were still too far away to identify, but at least twenty were heading straight for them.

This couldn't be happening, not after everything she, Thane, and Solace had suffered through to escape. She couldn't—wouldn't—allow them to be dragged back down below.

The numbers counting down on Solace's collar sent a surge of hysteria through her, a desperation that kindled something in her core. But this time, it wasn't the familiar ignition of her Magneii abilities or the slicing force of her Veniri abilities. It was something very different. Something more intrinsic, more fundamental to her very being.

It was the same sensation she'd felt after Jhutev made his life-giving wish.

"What?" said Thane when he saw her expression change. "What is it? What's wrong?"

She looked him dead in the eye. "I now understand the wish Jhutev made."

Thane's confused look deepened, but his perplexity turned to shock when Violet wrapped her arms around both him and Solace. "Hold on tight, like you did before, and again, don't let go."

Without hesitation, Thane sandwiched Solace between them.

Violet's adrenaline spiked as the Nephezai drew ever closer, their vicious scowls now clear and unmistakable. King Qozzlotl led the charge.

Violet threw her head back, face turned to the heavens. "Please, please work," she said under her breath.

Refusing to allow fear to consume her, she focused her

attention on her shifter melody. Not her Veniri or Magneii melody—a *new* melody. It was so strong, much stronger than the other two, and as much as she knew she'd never heard this melody before, she could swear it had always been a part of her.

Releasing her fear, she hazed.

Her body shifted, morphing into a form she'd never experienced but could picture clearly in her mind. A humanoid form much like the ones Jhutev had shown her in the mosaic mural back at Scylorethyz.

A new, revitalizing energy surged through her, sending a pulse of power through her extremities until it ruptured through her shoulder blades.

Wings!

Strong, massive wings spread out from her back.

The instinct was instant, primal. Violet gave a mighty flap of her wings, and the three of them darted upward.

Thane's and Solace's shouts of shock and exhilaration reached her ears as she soared into the sky. Again, up and up they rose. The wind gusted around them, reminiscent of the ocean's currents.

A crash of water blasted below as the small army of Nephezai broke the ocean's surface. Seawater sprayed into the air, along with a flurry of mother-of-pearl darts.

Violet caught a thermal that pitched them even higher into the heavens.

"Hybrid! I will find you! You will never escape me!" Qozzlotl roared, but the rushing breeze snatched his voice away, and the words of the raging king grew fainter and fainter the farther away they flew.

Shifter Species

MERUVO - (mer—roo—voh)

Celestial Body Allied To ~ Mercury

Blood Color ~ Glowing Black

Hunted For ~ Meruvo Wish

Appearance ~ Humanoid embodiments of the night sky with nebulous colors and speckled starlight morphed and whirled over midnight flesh like a hundred tiny galaxies.

Facial features like the mouth, nose, and ears appear blurred.

Eyes are strikingly bright with irises like two radiant starbursts, or like the birth of a sun. A vibrant white light halos each eye, and when the being's eyes roam to a particular angle, a small beam of white light flashes out beyond the Meruvo's face.

Abilities ~ Can grant a single wish. Is "invisible" when in shifter form unless a beam of black Mercurial light is shone on them.

Weaknesses ~ Meruvo shifters are not a race to encourage war or fighting, instead prefer to deal with problems diplomatically or remain hiding in shifter form if diplo-

☆ ☆ ☆

macy isn't successful. When faced with hunters, most Meruvo find begging and persuasion is not a method that stops hunters from killing or enslaving them.

Other Facts ~ Almost every shifter race has in various stages of history hunted and enslaved Meruvo in hopes of tempting the Mercury shifters to relinquish their wish.

<u>VENIRI</u> - (ven—ee—ree)

Celestial Body Allied To ~ Venus

Blood Color ~ Teal

Hunted For ~ Diamantium Skeleton

Appearance ~ Reptilian humanoids with iridescent scales of mostly teal dispersed with organic patterns of black and white. Veniri stand on giant raptor feet.

Crystal spikes and shards protrude over their body.

Triple set of Diamantium fangs protrude from top lip.

Long forked tongue that whips out periodically.

Second set of inner eyelids.

Abilities ~ Uses foot long shards that protrude from elbows and run parallel to forearms in fighting and combat. Also uses knees with clusters of Diamantium shards while fighting. Veniri fighting style is very similar to Muay Thai.

Can sense others' emotions and intentions with a whip of their forked Veniri tongue.

Can sense others' "soul-trails" while using a combination of their Veniri forked tongue and their second pair of inner eyelids. Veniri can be proficient at tracking and getting a "snapshot" of an event in time where emotions can be at their strongest.

Weaknesses ~ Veniri hide is tough and generally can't be cut by anything other than a shard of Diamantium. Hunters have forged their weapons out of the crystal spikes and skeletons of Veniri shifters. However repeated gouging of silver

Lycan claws will eventually cut through. Nephezai thorns are sharp enough to pierce and release the paralytic toxins, but not integral enough to slice through. Erathi feather blades are the only other weapon known to easily slice through Veniri hide.

Other Facts ~ A cluster of poison glands surround the heart of each Veniri. The poison eats through flesh and bone at a rapid pace. A stab to the heart with punctured poison glands is a quick, yet agonising death to a Veniri.

Veniri babies are born with inch-long teal fur that covers most of their body except for the face, neck, hands, and feet. Veniri fur is shed during early adolescence. When the last of the baby fur is shed, Veniri are considered full grown and begin initiation into combat training and learning royal protocols in protecting the Veniri royals.

Baby Veniri skin not covered in fur show faint impressions of the scales to come in a pastel shade of aquamarine, with a distinct pattern of white and darker blues around cheeks and forehead. Small bumps risen along eyebrows and across cheek bones will one day have protruding shards of Diamantium at a centimeter long at most. Two rounded nubs of glittery teeth peek out from top lip to one day become part of a triple set of fangs.

<u>LYCAN</u> - (lie—can)

Celestial Body Allied To ~ Moon

Blood Color ~ Silver

Hunted For ~ Lycan Leather

Appearance ~ Humanoid wolves of various shades of thick fur, from midnight black, russet red, topaz gold, platinum grey, lupine white, and the most rare being the arctic blue with transparent green eyes.

Lycan claws on hands and feet are made from sharpened solid silver.

☆ ☆ ☆

Abilities ~ Heightened sense of smell and hearing. Vicious speed and berserker mode when fighting.

Weaknesses ~ Fire. Beheading.

Other Facts ~ Lycan leather is cured and dyed black which human hunters use as armor when hunting shifters. Veniri hide is much tougher than Lycan leather, but cannot be fashioned into armor like Lycan leather due to its rapid decay after death.

Lycan shifters are much easier to find and much more predictable for human hunters to track down. A portion of Lycans not skinned for their leather are sent to Tempecrest Island, a prison where shifters are forced to fight in a gladiator arena.

<u>ERATHI</u> - (eh—ra—thee)

Celestial Body Allied To ~ Earth

Blood Color ~ Emerald Green

Hunted For ~ Wings

Appearance ~ Typical human appearance. In shifter form feathered wings from between shoulder blades. The colors of each feather are emerald green blended into lapis lazuli blue and tipped with metallic gold. Erathi wingspan reaches about fifteen to twenty feet wide.

Erathi shifter flesh holds an incandescent decorative design with an inner radiance like a shimmer of light or a lustrous pigment under the skin similar to UV tattoos that can only really be seen under a special light.

Abilities ~ Flight. Harnessing the wind and clouds to create "skyhooks" or "sky anchors" which is fundamental in engineering castles and buildings among the clouds.

Winged Erathi use their wings as weapons, slicing through flesh and bone with the razor sharp edges of the metallic gold tips of each feather.

Weaknesses ~ Wings can be used as a weapon and shield.

Slice off the wings and Erathi are as susceptible to damage and death like any other "earth bound"human.

Other Facts ~ Humans today are "wingless" or "earth bound" descendants from the ancient winged Erathi. The winged Erathi are widely thought to be either extinct or creatures of mythology.

The Nephezai enslaved the Erathi by cutting the wings off every Erathi born in enslavement. After hundreds of years of severe oppression, the Erathi underwent a "de-evolution" where they eventually were born without wings, and their glowing emerald green blood turned to the blood red know of humans today.

There are rumours of castles and buildings sometimes seen among the clouds where it's possible a number of winged Erathi have been in hiding since losing the war against the Nephezai.

<u>MAGNEII</u> - (mag—nee—eye)

Celestial Body Allied To ~ Mars

Blood Color ~ Magenta

Hunted For ~ Luxium Power Cores

Appearance ~ Charred flesh like cooling magma with crackled fissures revealing the magenta fire within. Eyes ignite with magenta flames. Hands ignite with magenta flames, but entire body can be engulfed with magenta fire when desired.

Abilities ~ Flaming fireballs can be flame-thrown from palms.

Magneii can connect with the power of the magma beneath Earth's surface and manipulate a small portion of the Earth's lifeblood.

Weaknesses ~ Beheading, or smashing the Luxium power core.

Other Facts ~ A Magneii's Luxium power core is about

☆ ☆ ☆

the size of a baseball and is located in the skull between their eyes. The Luxium power core is the source of the Magneii's flame and heat abilities.

Human hunters aim to behead Magneii shifters to avoid destroying the Luxium cores. Luxium cores are used as a power source in the hunter world, powering anything that uses a battery or motor. Luxium orbs can be found in a large variety of things such as torches, computers, even vehicles and explosive weapons.

JIOVIS - (jee—ov—is)

Celestial Body Allied To ~ Jupiter

Blood Color ~ Orange

Hunted For ~ Metallikite

Appearance ~ Life-sized statues of the living metal Metallikite. Jiovis shifters can range in various precious metals, such as gold, silver, bronze, copper, pewter, brass, rose gold, cobalt blue, purple gold, and the rarest being bismuth.

Abilities ~ Adept at warmongering and battle strategy. Living metal statues in shifter form. Metallikite flesh can be moulded into decorative details to enhance appearance.

Ability to regrow limbs. If damaged in war, Jiovis shifters have the option to amputate to regrow healthy and functional Metallikite limbs. Regrown limbs are obvious by the highly polished, "chrome-like" appearance.

Jiovis shifters have a heightened sense of smell which is useful in tracking and sensing other shifters.

Weaknesses ~ Rust Rot

Other Facts ~ With their heightened sense of smell, Jiovis shifters can scent out their Seh'Vuthi, or soulmate. Jiovis didn't scent emotional flavors like the Veniri do, but they can pick up one's chemical signals—adrenaline surges, subtle sweat secretions, pheromones, and so on.

☆ ☆ ☆

When Metallikite is removed from a Jiovis shifter for long enough, the Metallikite will harden, or "cure" into a greyish-green. The cured Metallikite is practically unbreakable, and human hunters use cured Metallikite for most of their prisons and crates for capturing and transporting live shifters.

The Jiovis heart is located in their throat, and is very vulnerable. A plate of cured Metallikite is fused into the shifted form of a Jiovis to permanently protect the Jiovis heart.

When displaying love and affection to a Seh'Vuthi soulmate, Jiovis shifters lay hands on each other's throats to show trust and vulnerability. To lay hands on a Jiovis throat who is not a soulmate is a severe offence and punishable by death.

<u>SATHOI</u> - (sah—thoi)

Celestial Body Allied To ~ Saturn

Blood Color ~ Absinthe Green

Hunted For ~ Viscid

Appearance ~ There are two main versions of Sathoi shifters, insectile humanoids and fungi humanoids.

Abilities ~ Camouflage. Spitting Viscid.

Weaknesses ~ Poison

Other Facts ~ Each Sathoi shifter spits a particular type of Viscid, but it is possible for a Sathoi to be able to spit up to three different types of Viscid. The main types of Viscid range from acidic, sticky glue, or a hallucinogenic or mind altering substance. Human hunters use a particular type of Viscid to create their Myst atomisers to paralyse their prey.

<u>YRANUM</u> - (ee—ran—um)

Celestial Body Allied To ~ Uranus

Blood Color ~ Pearlescent White

☆ ☆ ☆

Hunted For ~ Ylixium

Appearance ~ More alien in appearance compared to the other shifters, with elongated necks, tall thin bodies, usually bald heads, big feline like ears, and large eyes. Eyes have black pupils, but colored irises fill the rest of their eyes.

Iridescent skin is pale, whether frost white, ghost white, eggshell white, or moonstone white.

Skin is adorned with embedded pearls and chips of crystals and diamonds. Sometimes embedded skin modifications can be purely aesthetic, or added to create a protective layer.

Abilities ~ Control over ice and water. Sensing and healing various sicknesses and diseases. Adaptability to harsh environments such as the desert and arctic locations.

Weaknesses ~ Slow. Always chooses peace over violence, and tend to be easy prey to human hunters due to their refusal to fight back.

Other Facts ~ Ylixium is the pearlescent white blood of Yranum shifters and has concentrated healing elements which human hunters use as an elixir for rapid healing. However, overuse of Yranum blood can lead to addiction, less effectiveness of the healing elements over time, and "bleaching" of color from eyes.

Yranum live in small villages, and are masters at hiding from human hunters. But human hunters always easily decimate any Yranum village they're ever able to find.

<u>NEPHEZAI</u> - (nef—eh—zai)

Celestial Body Allied To ~ Neptune

Blood Color ~ Royal Purple

Hunted For ~ Mother of Pearl Thorns

Appearance ~ Thalassic humanoids in all types of aquatic and amphibious species. Mother of peal thorns about two to three inches long cover most of their upper arms and shoulders. Neon purple markings speckle over their bodies like birthmarks, and glow in the darkest of oceans.

Abilities ~ Mother of pearl thorns are filled with paralytic toxins that can be shot at enemies.

Nephezai can create bubbles of air to go over land-dwellers' heads for breathing underwater.

Some Nephezai have the ability to cause a sonic boom to blast enemies to disorient and/or enable a fast getaway.

Weaknesses ~ Human hunters with submarines. Pride and stubbornness.

Other Facts ~ Nephezai shifters have been banished to the bottom of the ocean since their Erathi slaves overpowered them. The Nephezai have been banished long enough that most Erathi, now mostly known as humans, have forgotten that Nephezai even exist.

In fact the humans have practically re-written their history to erase most evidence of Nephezai shifters, and most of the other shifters, as a testament to their growing domination throughout the Earth. What worse punishment to one's oppressors than to erase any part of their existence.

<u>PLIOKAI</u> - (plee—oh—kai)

Celestial Body Allied To ~ Pluto

Blood Color ~ Metallic Gold

Hunted For ~ Glixus

Appearance ~ Flesh of a very pale grayish green, or pale blue, or pale gold, or pale purple. Deep seam lines along brow, down one cheek, across jaw, and back up the other cheek, giving the impression of a mask made up of panels. A few other smaller "panels" materialized over neck and the rest of exposed skin.

Elongated ears split into panel-like structures.

A golden glow shines out from each of the seams, as well

☆ ☆ ☆

as from distinct markings over face like a cross between Viking warpaint and cybernetic face tattoos.

Eyes hold an almost mechanical glow, but instead of golden, they are a deep peridot green, sapphire blue, alexandrite gold, or tanzanite purple to match pale color of skin.

Hair is made up of thin strands of transparent cords like wire cables, where dots of light pulsed from skull to the tips of the twenty-or-so-inch lengths. The "cable hair" is a mixture of glowing gold like their blood, the pastel color like their skin, and bright color of their eyes.

Overall, Pliokai are best described as "cyborg elf" in appearance.

Abilities ~ Each Pliokai contain a Glixus (plural - Glixees) which contain the memories and abilities each Pliokai obtains throughout their lives. When a Pliokai reaches the end of their life, they can give their Glixus to another Pliokai who can "download" and instantly learn the memories and skills given to them.

Weaknesses ~ An overload of information from too many Glixees from other Pliokai can lead to madness, haemorrhaging of the brain, and ultimately a premature death where all the accumulated skills and abilities die with the Pliokai before being passed on.

Other Facts ~ All Pliokai have a tri-tone inflection to their voices, almost as if there is a half-second delay to one of the bass tones in their register.

☆ ☆ ☆

CHARACTER LIST

Autumn Novak - (aw—tm, no—vak)

~HUMAN~

Daughter to Skye and Cruz Novak. Cousin to Gus (August) Farrow. Resident of Maple Shire. Was roommates with Violet Chambers at collage. Adept with computer technology and hacking.

IDENTIFIERS - Petite. Chestnut dreadlocks hang down to mid-waist. Sun-tanned golden skin.

Axel - (ak—sel)

~HUMAN~

Hunter of shapeshifters. Right hand man to Matthias Branstone. Resident of the Branstone hunter barracks.

IDENTIFIERS - Gray biker beard. Wields a trident made from Diamantium.

Belitozzl - (belly—toz—zl)

~NEPHEZAI~

One of the Nepehzai guards. Resident of the hidden city of Scylorethyz at the bottom of the ocean.

IDENTIFIERS - Blue-ringed octopus humanoid.

Brutus - (broo—tuhs)

~HUMAN~

Hunter of shapeshifters. Resident of the Branstone hunter barracks. Killed by Matthias.

IDENTIFIERS - Bulky man with a shaved head.

Cruz Novak - (krooz, no—vak)

~HUMAN~

Husband to Skye Novak. Father to Autumn Novak.

Killed by Magneii mercenaries who were hired to kidnap Solace.

Dawn Farrow - (dorn, fa—row)

~PLIOKAI~

Wife to Lazareth Farrow. Mother to Gus (August) Farrow. Adopted sister to Skye Novak. Doctor and resident of Maple Shire. Killed by hunters in the Maple Shire bombings.

IDENTIFIERS - Dead-straight fair hair, short hairstyle.

Ebele - (ee—bel—eh)

~MEGALODON SHARK~

Currently at 55.7 feet (17m) in length.

Was a pup when Prince Exültov Nagahld found her and raised her for a time until she became too big to keep hidden from the other residents of Scylorethyz. She now lives with the Ügovs and is a constant companion to the Ügov clan leader Zasf. She always comes and visits Exültov when he's in the Necropolis Ravine.

Elias Ragefire - (ee—lie—us, rayj—fai—uh)

~HUMAN~

Son to Stellan Ragefire. Older brother to Peony Ragefire. Resident of the Ragefire hunter barracks.

IDENTIFIERS - Tall, dark brown wavy hair, honey-brown eyes.

En'gorr Droth - (en—gor, droth)

~JIOVIS~

Older brother to Tio (It-thio) Droth. Royal prince to the Jiovis shifters. Zhivotza soulmate to Autumn Novak.

Carries the Jiovis royal spear but is yet to undergo the coronation ceremony to become king of the Jiovis shifters. Postponed the coronation ceremony to find Tio after he went missing.

IDENTIFIERS - In human form: large, dark skin.

In Jiovis form: Golden Metallikite living metal. Has sculpted a fierce golden mask of sharpened teeth around his mouth and a highly detailed pair of skeletal hands with the bony thumbs and forefingers framing his eyes.

Exültov Nagahld - (ek—zool—tov, na—gaah—ld)

~NEPHEZAI~

Son to Qozzlotl Nagahld. Husband to Nepthyz Nagahld. Father to Therizüs Nagahld and Zümgroz Nagahld.

Reverant prince to the Nephezai shifters. Resident of the hidden city of Scylorethyz at the bottom of the ocean.

IDENTIFIERS - Sea nettle jellyfish humanoid.

Falco - (fal—koh)

~VENIRI~

One of the Veniri babies Nika rescues when Matthias Branstone and his army of hunters attack the Veniri hive hidden beneath the Stony Hearted Highlands in the middle of the Boiling Void desert.

IDENTIFIERS - An eagle image on his shirt.

Frizgitl - (friz—git—tl)

~NEPHEZAI~

One of Yigtheez's cronies. Was once a resident of a small underwater village on the outskirts of Scylorethyz until human hunters destroyed the village. Yigtheez took in the survivors to his own home in another village on the outskirts of Scylorethyz.

IDENTIFIERS - Viperfish humanoid.

Giztherrel - (giz—theh—rel)

~NEPHEZAI~

One of Yigtheez's cronies. Resident of the hidden city of Scylorethyz at the bottom of the ocean.

IDENTIFIERS - Mantis shrimp humanoid.

Gloria Chambers - (glaw—ree—ah, chaym—berz)

~HUMAN~

Mother to Violet Chambers.

IDENTIFIERS - Cranky.

Gus (August) Farrow - (gus (aw—guhst), fa—row)

~PLIOKAI~

Son to Dawn Farrow and Lazareth Farrow. Cousin to Autumn Farrow.

Full name is August, but prefers Gus.

Striving to be the next Maple Shire doctor since his mother had been killed. Also in training to learn his shape-shifter skills after finding out he's Pliokai.

IDENTIFIERS - In human form: Tall, dark brown hair in a messy quiff. Half-dozen necklaces made from black thread, gemstone beads, copper, and silver. A faded turquoise wrist cuff adorned with a few bracelets that match necklaces.

In Pliokai form: Flesh very pale grayish green. Deep seam lines along brow, down one cheek, across jaw, and back up other cheek, giving the impression of a mask made up of panels. A few other smaller "panels" over neck and the rest of skin. A golden glow shines out from each seam, as well as from distinct markings over his face that look like a cross between Viking warpaint and cybernetic face tattoos.

Elongated "elven" ears split into panel-like structures.

Eyes hold a mechanical glow of a deep peridot green.

Hair made up of transparent cords where dots of light pulse from skull to the tips of the twenty-or-so-inch lengths. His "cable hair" is a mixture of glowing gold, peridot gray like his skin, and bright peridot green like his eyes.

Hestus Branstone - (hes—tus, bran—stohn)

~HUMAN~

Younger brother to Quill Branstone. Older brother to Nika Branstone. Cousin to Sagan Branstone, and Lyla-Rose Branstone. Nephew to Matthias Branstone. Grandson to Renard Bransone.

Hunter of shapeshifters. Resident of the Branstone hunter barracks.

IDENTIFIERS - Lean, brown hair.

Hunter amulet is of the Branstone family crest, and holds three blood samples: silver Lycan blood, teal Veniri blood, and magenta Magneii blood.

Hildez - (hil—dez)

~NEPHEZAI~

Nanny to Exültov Nagahld's children, Therizüs Nagahld and Zümgroz Nagahld. Resident of the hidden city of Scylorethyz at the bottom of the ocean.

IDENTIFIERS - Leafy seadragon humanoid.

Idalia - (ee—da—lee—ah)

~VENIRI~

Daughter to Imoranda.

Queen of the Veniri hive hidden beneath the Stony Hearted Highlands in the middle of the Boiling Void desert.

IDENTIFIERS - In human form: Unknown.

In Veniri form: Beautiful, goddess-like.

Imoranda - (ee—mor—ran—dah)

~VENIRI~

Mother to Idalia.

Previous queen of the Veniri hive hidden beneath the Stony Hearted Highlands in the middle of the Boiling Void desert. Cause of death unknown.

Jhutev Iha - (zhoo—tev, ee—hah)

~MERUVO~

Slave of the Nagahlds, specifically to Exültov Nagahld. Resident of the hidden city of Scylorethyz at the bottom of the ocean. Of the Arundhati lineage.

IDENTIFIERS - In human form: Unknown.

In Meruvo form: Midnight/navy blue flesh with nebulous colors and speckled starlight whirled like a hundred tiny galaxies. Facial features like the mouth, nose, and ears also appeared blurred within his "midnight sky" flesh.

Eyes with irises that look like two radiant starbursts, or like the birth of a sun. A vibrant white light halos each eye, and small beams of white light flashed out beyond his face when he blinks.

Kronan - (kroh—nan)

~VENIRI~

Cousin to Idalia. Enslaved to Matthias Branstone.

IDENTIFIERS - Wimp.

Lazareth Farrow: - (laz—ah—reth, fa—row)

~HUMAN~

Husband to Dawn Farrow. Adoptive father to Gus (August) Farrow. Resident of Maple Shire.

A jack of all trades. Mainly organises meals for the community. Award winner for his goats milk cheese. Makes the best fig and lychee cheesecake. Adept at bōjutsu.

IDENTIFIERS - Blonde, shoulder-length "surfer dude" hair.

Levana - (lev—van—ah)

Mysterious…

Lyla-Rose (Lyla) Branstone - (lie—luh—rohz, bran—stohn)

~HUMAN~

Daughter to Matthias Branstone. Half sister to Sagan Branstone. Cousin to Nika, Hestus, and Quill Branstone. Granddaughter to Renard Branstone.

Best friend to Violet Chambers, met Violet at school when Violet was fostered by Nathan and moved to Brookhaven. Killed by Soren Alvarez, Thane Alvarez's brother.

Matthias Branstone - (ma—tie—us, bran—stohn)

~HUMAN~

Son to Renard Branstone. Ex-husband to Odette Branstone. Father to Sagan Branstone and Lyla-Rose Branstone. Uncle to Nika, Hestus, and Quill Branstone and sometimes gets called Uncle Ty.

Hunter of shapeshifters. Resident of the Branstone hunter barracks.

IDENTIFIERS - Six foot two. Dark brown hair with graying sideburns, a trimmed moustache, and a goatee. Broad shoulders. Muscular. Brown eyes. Has a "shark-like" grin.

Nathan Delano - (nay—thun, del—ah—noh)

~VENIRI~

Foster father to Violet Chambers.

Was once a detective at the Brookhaven police precinct. Used to reside in Brookhaven until captured by Matthias Branstone and forced into the Tempecrest Island shifter gladiator arena. Survived Tempecrest with Thane Alvarez and Tio (It'thio) Droth. Now a resident of Maple Shire.

IDENTIFIERS - In human form: Tawny eyes. Early forties. Silver streaks in dark hair. Stubble. Now faceted all over with the appearance of a "live-sized Swarovski statue"

In Veniri form: The usual appearance of a Veniri with reptilian teal, white, black scales from head to large raptor feet. But is now faceted all over with the appearance of a "live-sized Swarovski statue"

Nepthyz Nagahld - (nep—thiz, na—gaah—ld)

~NEPHEZAI~

Wife to Exültov Nagahld. Mother to Therizüs Nagahld and Zümgroz Nagahld. Reverant princess to the Nephezai shifters.

Killed by hunters while giving aid to a small underwater village on the outskirts of the city of Scylorethyz.

IDENTIFIERS - Blue dragon nudibranch humanoid.

Nika Branstone - (nee—kuh, bran—stohn)

~HUMAN~

Youngest sister to Hestus and Quill Branstone. Cousin to Sagan and Lyla-Rose Branstone. Niece to Matthias Branstone. Granddaughter to Renard Branstone.

Hunter of shapeshifters. Resident of the Branstone hunter barracks. Known as Nika "Iron Maiden" Branstone in the hunter community.

Carer to three young Veniri boys, Orson, Falco, and Raoul, after rescuing them from the hunters destroying their Veniri hive.

IDENTIFIERS - Petite 22 year old. Light brown "Shirley Temple" curls. Periwinkle blue eyes.

Hunter amulet is of the Branstone family crest, and holds three blood samples: silver Lycan blood, teal Veniri blood, and magenta Magneii blood, and orange Jiovis blood. Hunter amulet was destroyed by Sagan.

Orson - (aw—sun)

~VENIRI~

One of the Veniri babies Nika rescues when Matthias Branstone and his army of hunters attack the Veniri hive hidden beneath the Stony Hearted Highlands in the middle of the Boiling Void desert.

IDENTIFIERS - Has a plush green bear.

Peony Ragefire - (pee—uh—nee, rayj—fai—uh)

~HUMAN~

Daughter to Stellan Ragefire. Younger sister to Elias Ragefire. Resident of the Ragefire hunter barracks.

IDENTIFIERS - Six years old.

Pwevül - (pweh—vool)

~NEPHEZAI~

One of the Nepehzai guards. Resident of the hidden city of Scylorethyz at the bottom of the ocean.

IDENTIFIERS - Stingray humanoid.

Qozzlotl Nagahld - (koz—lot—tl, na—gaah—ld)

~NEPHEZAI~

Husband to Sozzüxl Nagahld. Father to Exültov Nagahld.

King to the Nephezai shifters. Resident of the hidden city of Scylorethyz at the bottom of the ocean.

IDENTIFIERS - Eel tail, gray complexion. Wears a big collection of necklaces of precious metals and jewels, including a vial of white pearlescent Yranum blood, and the purple disc-like spangle Matthias Branstone is hunting.

Quill Branstone - (kwil, bran—stohn)

~HUMAN~

Oldest brother to Hestus and Nika Branstone. Cousin to Sagan and Lyla-Rose Branstone. Nephew to Matthias Branstone. Grandson to Renard Bransone.

Hunter of shapeshifters. Resident of the Branstone hunter barracks.

IDENTIFIERS - Brunet, bulky.

Hunter amulet is of the Branstone family crest and holds three blood samples: silver Lycan blood, teal Veniri blood, and orange Jiovis blood.

Raiden Tanner - (ray—dun, tan—nuh)

~HUMAN~

Leader of Maple Shire.

Raoul - (rah—ool)

~VENIRI~

One of the Veniri babies Nika rescues when Matthias Branstone and his army of hunters attack the Veniri hive hidden beneath the Stony Hearted Highlands in the middle of the Boiling Void desert.

IDENTIFIERS - A wolf image on his shirt.

Renard Branstone - (reh—naad, bran—stohn)

~HUMAN~

Father to Matthias Branstone. Grandfather to Sagan, Lyla-Rose, Nika, Hestus, and Quill Branstone.

Leader of Xabat Biogenetics, the bio-hacking and experimental laboratory hidden underground beneath the ghost city of Rivermyre.

IDENTIFIERS - Ultimate douchebag.

Sagan Branstone - (say—gn, bran—stohn)

~HUMAN~

Son to Odette and Matthias Branstone. Half brother to Lyla-Rose Branstone. Grandson to Renard Branstone. Cousin to Nika, Hestus, and Quill Branstone. Often gets called Saggy-Aggy by cousins.

Was raised in the Branstone hunter barracks.

IDENTIFIERS - 24 years old. White-blond hair. Eyes were once navy blue, now "bleached" to pastel blue from overuse of Ylixium healing elixir.

Hunter amulet is of the Branstone family crest and holds unknown number of blood samples.

Skye Novak - (sky, no—vak)

~HUMAN~

Mother to Autumn and wive to Cruz Novak. Adoptive sister to Dawn Farrow. Aunty to Gus (August) Farrow.

Killed by Magneii mercenaries who were hired to kidnap Solace.

IDENTIFIERS - Petite. Chestnut dreadlocks hang down to mid-waist. Sun-tanned golden skin.

Solace - (soh—luhs)

~VENIRI~

Daughter to Violet Chambers and Thane Alvarez. Was born in Maple Shire. Was kidnapped by Magneii mercenaries when a few weeks old and taken to Xabat Biogenetics Laboratory. Was about ten weeks old when captured by Nephezai shifters with her parents and trapped in the hidden city of Scylorethyz at the bottom of the ocean.

IDENTIFIERS - In Veniri form: Face, throat, hands, and feet a pale shade of teal with faint impressions of scales to come. A distinct pattern of white and darker blues around her cheeks and forehead.

Rest of her body is covered in velvet soft fur an inch or so long. Fur is mostly teal with various markings in white and dark blue.

Small bumps along her eyebrows and across her cheek bones, marking areas where shards of Diamantium will one day protrude.

Peeking out from her top lip are two rounded glittery teeth, which will one day become part of a triple set of Veniri fangs.

Soren Alvarez - (soh—ren, all—vah—rez)

~VENIRI~

Older brother to Thane Alvarez. Veniri trapper for human females to be enslaved as breeders for his hive. Was one of the Veniri who captured both Violet Chambers and Lyla-Rose Branstone. Killed by Nathan Delano.

IDENTIFIERS - Black hoodie.

Sozzüxl Nagahld - (soh—zook—sl, na—gaah—ld)

~NEPHEZAI~

Wife to Qozzlotl Nagahld. Mother to Exültov Nagahld. Grandmother to Therizüs Nagahld and Zümgroz Nagahld.

Queen to the Nephezai shifters. Killed by hunters while on the outskirts of the city of Scylorethyz.

IDENTIFIERS - Sea nettle jellyfish humanoid.

Stellan Ragefire - (stel—uhn, rayj—fai—uh)

~HUMAN~

Father to Elias and Peony Ragefire. Human hunter. Leader of the Ragefire barracks.

Thane Alvarez - (thayn, all—vah—rez)

~VENIRI~

Father to Solace. Seh'Vuthi soulmate to Violet Chambers. Youngest brother to Soren Alvarez. Was once a Veniri trapper for human females to be enslaved as breeders for their hive. Was one of the Veniri who captured both Violet Chambers and Lyla-Rose Branstone. Was helped to escape his hive by Nathan Delano. Was captured by Matthias Branstone and forced into the Tempecrest Island shifter gladiator arena. Survived Tempecrest with Thane Alvarez and Tio (It'thio) Droth.

IDENTIFIERS - In human form: Deep chocolate eyes with flecks of gold. Trimmed goatee. Sandy-blond hair, streaked with vintage gold and sun-kissed white. Irregular star-shaped and bluish-black scar over heart where Violet Chambers stabbed him with her switchblade.

In Veniri form: Unknown. Refuses to shift into Veniri form since escaping his hive and living in the "human" world. But will use his Veniri elbow shards while fighting.

Therizüs Nagahld - (theh—ree—zoos, na—gaah—ld)

~NEPHEZAI~

Daughter to Exültov and Nepthyz Nagahld. Older sister to Zümgroz Nagahld. Granddaughter to Qozzlotl and Sozzüxl Nagahld. Princess to the Nephezai shifters. Resident of the hidden city of Scylorethyz at the bottom of the ocean.

IDENTIFIERS - Sea nettle jellyfish humanoid. 8 or 9 years old

Tio (It'thio) Droth - (tee—oh (it—theo), droth)

~JIOVIS~

Younger brother to En'gorr Droth. Royal prince to the Jiovis shifters. Was captured by hunters in his early teens and forced into the Tempecrest Island shifter gladiator arena. Survived Tempecrest with Nathan Delano and Thane

Alvarez. Has since been a resident of Maple Shire after escaping Tempecrest Island.

Adept with computer technology and hacking. Met Autumn Novak online in a chat forum.

IDENTIFIERS - In human form: Large and tall for a 16 year old. Dark skin.

In Jiovis form: Golden Metallikite living metal. Covered with elaborately designed flesh manipulations typical of the Jiovis race. His face had been sculpted into an overemphasized skull, with an organic design of whirls and curls accenting his brow and cheekbones. Two tusks protrude from the edges of his mouth. Jiovis symbol for Jupiter is embellished on his bicep.

Tior'vul - (tee—or—vool)

~JIOVIS~

Twin brother to Urg'vhul. Royal guard to Prince En'gorr Droth.

IDENTIFIERS - In human form: Bulky and tall. Dark skin.

In Jiovis form: Pewter Metallikite living metal. Jiovis symbol for Jupiter is embellished on his bicep.

Toffee - (toh—fee)

~BEETLE-MONKEY~

Animal companion to Umbra. Was bio-engineered in Xabat Biogenetics Laboratory. Was rescued by Umbra. Toffee was designed from a drawing done by Umbra's mother.

IDENTIFIERS - A a pygmy marmoset—the smallest monkey in the world—with jewel beetle wings. About the size of a soda can.

Umbra - (um—brah)

~HUMAN~

Self proclaimed "executioner" to the mutant animals that escape the underground Xabat Biogenetics Laboratory. Has established a home in an abandoned skyscraper in the ghost city of Rivermyre. Adept with herbology, and dabbles in alchemy which she learned from her mother.

IDENTIFIERS - Japanese descent. Black hair with ombre purple tips. Arm rocket that launches silver ninja stars.

Urg'vhul - (erg—vool)

~JIOVIS~

Twin brother to Tior'vul. Royal guard to Prince En'gorr Droth.

IDENTIFIERS - In human form: Bulky and tall. Dark skin.

In Jiovis form: Pewter Metallikite living metal. Jiovis symbol for Jupiter is embellished on his bicep.

Va'atuu - (vah—ah—too)

~JIOVIS~

Royal guard to Prince En'gorr Droth.

IDENTIFIERS - In human form: Bulky and tall. Dark skin.

In Jiovis form: Copper Metallikite living metal. Jiovis symbol for Jupiter is embellished on his bicep.

Violet Chambers - (vai—oh—let, chaym—berz)

~VENIRI & MAGNEII HYBRID~

Foster daughter to Nathan Delano. Mother to Solace. Seh'Vuthi soulmate to Thane Alvarez. Daughter to Gloria Chambers, but abandoned as a baby at the hospital.

Met Autumn Novak and Gus (August) Farrow at college. Resident of Maple Shire.

IDENTIFIERS - In human form: Gray-blue eyes. Dark

brown, shoulder-length hair. Defined, angular cheekbones. Acid like scars in the two divots of her lower back.

In Veniri/Magneii form: Can alternate between Veniri scaled form with Magneii flames of teal, or Magneii flesh of charred and crackled fissures of teal with protruding Diamantium crystal shards. Even in human form, can ignite teal flames from her eyes and over her hands.

Votloxo - (vot—tl—ox—oh)

~NEPHEZAI~

One of the Nepehzai guards. Resident of the hidden city of Scylorethyz at the bottom of the ocean.

IDENTIFIERS - Siamese fighter fish shifter.

Yigtheez - (yig—theez)

~NEPHEZAI~

Son to King Quozzlotl's best friend who was killed by human hunters. Born of a noble family. Usually seen with his obnoxious friends including Frizgitl the viperfish Nephezai and Giztherrel the mantis shrimp Nephezai. Yigtheez is a resident in a village on the outskirts of Scylorethyz but is a regular long-stay visitor to Scylorethyz.

IDENTIFIERS - Parrotfish humanoid.

Zasf - (zah—sff)

~ÜGOV~

An Ügov clan leader. Survives and protects his clan from the harsh environment outside the protection of the city of Scylorethyz. An acquaintance of Exültov Nagahld.

IDENTIFIERS - Bulbous eyes of a pale and sickly green glow. Humanoid but disfigured—mashed-up mutations of fins, gills, claws, thorns, shells, and tentacles. A mouthful of jagged teeth plus hundreds more in rows upon rows over his face and head.

Attire consisting of scraps of metal scavenged from shipwrecks, decorated with bleached bones from a myriad of underwater creatures.

Zümgroz Nagahld - (zoom—groz, na—gaah—ld)

~NEPHEZAI~

Son to Exültov and Nepthyz Nagahld. Younger brother to Therizüs Nagahld. Granddaughter to Qozzlotl and Sozzüxl Nagahld. Prince to the Nephezai shifters. Resident of the hidden city of Scylorethyz at the bottom of the ocean.

IDENTIFIERS - Blue dragon nudibranch humanoid. 3 years old.

☆ ☆ ☆

Glossary of Terms

Arundhati Lineage - (aah—roon—da—tee)

A family clan of the Meruvo shifter species. Meruvo shifters announce their lineage in formal settings such as meeting others, or in declaration of making their Meruvo wish.

Eg. "I, Jhutev, of the Arundhati Lineage, am pleased to meet you..."

Diamantium - (die—ah—man—tee—um)

The bio-crystal that makes up the skeleton and spikes of the Veniri shifter's anatomy. Diamantium is iridescent and clear in appearance like aurora borealis crystal. Diamantium has a distinct whirled pattern within the facets where each Diamantium shard is unique like a fingerprint.

Scaled Veniri hide is almost impossible to cut without the use of a Diamantium shard. Human hunters forge their hunting weapons from Diamantium.

The razor sharp feathers of an Erathi shifter wing is the only other known item that can cut through Veniri hide.

Ethoseez - (ee—thoss—eez)

Hidden at the center of each Glixus are several glowing tangles of a dense, writhing spiderweb-like substance. Though pea sized at first, once out of the confines of the

Glixus, the tangles expand to the size of small pumpkins, each a different color. These are *ethoseez.*

Each ethoseez tangle is a strand of information and emits a soft hum and crackle when the Glixus is opened.

Each is a different component of a Pliokai's mind, things like memories, knowledge banks, interests, passions, and other mental traits. The number of ethoseez is dependent on how much a Pliokai learns and experiences over a lifetime. That number can also be increased by fusing other Pliokai's Glixees ethoseez.

Grayed-out strands of ethoseez within a Glixus are deactivated. They can never be erased entirely, but leave a permanent scar. Yet a Pliokai is able to function much better regardless of the scarred ethoseez if they are in danger of madness and brain haemorrhaging from too much acquired information and skills from other Pliokai.

However, Pliokai rarely deactivate the information they're given, to avoid demotion in the Pliokai social hierarchy and fear of losing valuable information and skills acquired over several generations. Instead, most Pliokai choose to endure to best overcome any madness and certain fast-coming death.

Every Pliokai aims to be the most learned and most skilled among their peers and shifter species, believing it's possible to reach pure intelligence with persistence in acquiring information and skills to hopefully achieve an ultimate cure.

Glixus - (glik—sus)

A cylinder about an inch and a half in diameter and about the length of a soda can. Gold in color but not in material. A decorative, organic circuit-board-like pattern flickers and dances over the surface, illuminating more brightly when comes in contact with a loved one.

A Glixus (plural: Glixees) house the ethoseez, which are the stands of information containing all the memories, knowledge, skills, and thoughts of the Pliokai shifter it belonged to. Where beings of other species can spend a lifetime perfecting their chosen skills only to lose it all at the expiration of their life, the Pliokai can store their wisdom, expertise, and inner thoughts and pass them on to other Pliokai.

Glixees can be removed from a Pliokai via a hidden panel at the shifter's temple. When removed, the Pliokai can still function as normal, yet no new information is recorded without the Glixus present.

Hunter Medallions:

When human hunters come of age, they are all given a hunter medallion of their family crest made of black metal which hangs on a black chain. Each hunter medallion contain ten tiny glass vials. When a hunter achieves the first kill of each shifter species, they fill a glass vial with a sample of shifter blood from their kill, until all ten vials are filled with all the different shifter blood colors.

Hunters are ranked in the hunter community by the number of "colors" in their medallions.

One color shows a hunter has completed initiation.

Two colors is not too bad.

Three colors and you're becoming a pretty decent hunter.

Four colors and you're starting to make a name for yourself and may start to be recognised more within your own hunter barracks.

Five colors and more is rare and you're basically becoming a hunter celebrity and known throughout all the hunter barracks in the country.

It is unheard of in modern hunter history for a hunter to fill all ten vials in their medallion.

Jiovis Royal Spear:

Rather than a typical blade, the spear-like shaft is a decorative metal head with a glowing orange orb floating at its centre.

Surrounding the orb are several metal semicircles and rings, like a kinetic solar system sculpture.

The Jiovis symbol for Jupiter etched into the metal above the kinetic sculpture. The symbol glows with a fierce orange even richer than the orb itself.

The glowing orb contains the blood of the first Jiovis king. A drop of blood from each royal successor is added during every coronation ceremony.

Light Forging:

The ability to condense beams of light into a tangible putty that can be molded to create various items that can be as little or as big as the creator desires.

Light forged elements can range from but are not limited to trinkets, jewellery, tools, weapons, shields, construction of buildings and much more.

Highly adept light forgers can construct more specialised creations of mechanised light-locks and keys, such as gateway vortexes to create a shortcut from one place on Earth to another.

Light forging is also used in creating portals to other worlds, but the practice is considered extinct or that of mythology.

Luxium Power Orb:

A Magneii's Luxium power core is about the size of a baseball and is located in the skull between their eyes. The Luxium power core is the source of the Magneii's flame and heat abilities.

Human hunters aim to behead Magneii shifters to avoid destroying the Luxium cores.

Luxium cores are used as a power source in the hunter world, powering anything that uses a battery or motor. Luxium orbs can be found in a large variety of things in the human hunter world such as torches, computers, even vehicles and explosive weapons.

Lycan Leather:

Human hunters hunt Lycan shifters for Lycan hide which is fashioned into leather. Lycan leather is cured and dyed black which human hunters use as armor when hunting shifters.

Veniri hide is much tougher than Lycan leather, but cannot be fashioned into armor like Lycan leather due to its rapid decay after death.

Meruvo Wish:

Meruvo shifters are hunted and enslaved for their Meruvo wish. Each Meruvo shifter has the ability to grant a single wish. However, the wish is powered by the sacrifice of the Meruvo's own life. The wish can only be granted if the Meruvo is deeply sincere in wanting to grant to wish. No amount of gentle persuasion, manipulation, or torture can force a Meruvo to relinquish their wish. The Meruvo wish is the one thing every Meruvo shifter has the ultimate authority to grant.

Meruvo shifters are notorious for not being persuaded in granting their wishes, believing it is the ultimate revenge to their captors in taking their wishes to their own grave.

Metallikite:

Jiovis shifters are hunted for their "living metal" or Metallikite. When in shifter form, Jiovis shifters a walking and breathing embodiments of metal statues. Jiovis shifters can hold and manipulate their own Metallikite like putty, creating intricate and fierce designs all over their metallic bodies.

Colors of Metallikite can range in various precious metals, such as gold, silver, bronze, copper, pewter, brass, rose gold, cobalt blue, purple gold, and the rarest being bismuth. But when Metallikite is removed from a Jiovis shifter long enough, it begins to "cure" and turn solid and practically unbreakable.

No mater what color Metallikite was originally, all cured Metallikite turns a light greyish-green color.

Human hunters "drain" or "flay" Jiovis shifters of their living metals, to create prisons, bunkers, crates to transport live shifters, and much more out of the cured Metallikite.

Myst - (mist)

Myst is a paralytic spray created from Viscid harvested from Sathoi shifters. Human hunters use Myst when hunting and carry it in small atomisers. Myst is used in close proximity.

Nephezai paralytic thorns are a preferred method for hunters to use, as thorns can be used in ranged weapons. However, acquiring Nephezai thorns is an arduous and inconsistent resource, due to Nephezai needing to be hunted at the bottom of the vast depths of the ocean.

Atomised Myst is an alternative to the Nephezai thorns. Myst is mainly used by more experienced human hunters, due to the nature of needing to be in close proximity to their prey to spray them with Myst.

Nephezai Thorns:

Every Nephezai shifter have a few hundred mother of pearl thorns that adorn their upper arms and shoulders. The

Nephezai thorns are roughly two to three inches in length and a couple millimeters in diameter.

Each Nephezai thorn contains a paralytic toxin that can be shot at enemies or prey like darts. The paralytic toxin reacts instantly.

Pre-Eminent:

In Pliokai politics, the Pre-Eminent is the top most leadership role, like that of a prime minister or president of all Pliokai

The Pliokai value knowledge and skill over all else. The more knowledge and skill one attains, the more likely it is for a Pliokai to be elevated to the role of Pre-Eminent. And one way a Pliokai can fast-track their education is to inherit a Glixus from various other Pliokai.

The Pre-Eminent role can be held by a single Pliokai, but it is preferred for a married couple to take the role as equal and impartial partners.

Rust Rot:

Jiovis shifters are sensitive to iron and rust.

Although human hunters prefer to use their Diamantium weapons, they do also carry iron weapons in their arsenal. Their most effective weapon against Jiovis shifters is to use molten iron. Jiovis shifters are adept in combat and are highly trained to deflect iron weapons, but only if iron is not in molten form.

Molten iron is much harder to deflect and quickly adheres and melts into the Jiovis shifter's Metallikite flesh. Iron rusts and rots away at Jiovis shifter's bio-metal flesh, much like sepsis and gangrene. The only treatment to avoid rust rot is to cut away the affected Metallikite and regrow the metal flesh.

Regrown Metallikite flesh and limbs are obvious by the highly polished, "chrome-like" appearance.

Seh'Vuthi - (seh—voo—thee)

A love bond, commitment, or "soulmate" connection. The Seh'Vuthi bond is not widely common, and not always recognised until the Seh'Vuthi bond is completed.

The preliminary signs of Seh'Vuthi include small speckles of floating lights emitted from either/or both members of the Seh'Vuthi pairing. The speckles of floating lights range in various colors, and it's not known how the different colors are selected to represent each person.

The speckled lights can also glow within each person's eyes when an intimate connection is experienced.

Other preliminary signs of Seh'Vuthi include the ability to "feel" when the other person is being looked upon by the other. This tends to heighten trust and familiarity within the bond.

Seh'Vuthi is a consensual bond, and will only be completed when both parties reach willingness and acceptance of the pairing.

Tempecrest Island - (tem—peh—crest)

A shape shifter prison where human hunters force shifters to fight in a gladiator arena.

Tempecrest is an island that contains only the prison, and is in a location in the middle of the ocean known only by human hunters.

Hunters come from far and wide to bet big on their favourite shifter gladiators.

Many hunters fall into the trap of gambling addiction at Tempecrest Island.

Ügov - (ooh—gov)

Disfigured aquatic humanoids—mashed-up mutations of fins, gills, claws, thorns, shells, and tentacles.

Ügovs have round, bulbous eyes made of a pale and sickly green glow.

Their attire consists of scraps of metal scavenged from shipwrecks decorated with bleached bones from a myriad of underwater creatures.

They fashion weapons out of larger bones sharpened into long spears, spiked mallets, sawfish swords, and various others.

Ügovs are creatures of the deep with mouths overfilled with transparent needle like teeth, and jagged shark-like fangs.

Ügovs flick lanky, slimy-looking tendrils about in the water, like feelers on insects tasting and testing the environment around them.

Some believe the Ügovs are a mutated portion of Nephezai shifters that got lost in the harsh environment of the ocean's cruel depths. Over time these Nephezai may have adapted and mutated over a number of generations to survive.

Umibudo - (ooh—mee—boo—doh)

A type of green algae that looks like tiny sea grapes and green caviar. It mostly comes from Japan and the Philippines. Has a subtle "taste of the sea" saltiness. The flavor bursts in your mouth like caviar, releasing a fresh briny taste where some may notice an acidity with a hint of sweetness.

Viscid - (vis—kid)

Each Sathoi shifter spits a particular type of Viscid, but it is possible for a Sathoi to be able to spit up to three different types of Viscid. The main types of Viscid range from acidic, sticky glue, or a hallucinogenic or mind altering substance.

Human hunters use a particular type of Viscid to create their Myst atomisers to paralyse their prey.

Ylixium - (ee—lik—see—um)

Ylixium is the pearlescent white blood of Yranum shifters and has concentrated healing elements which human hunters use as an elixir for rapid healing. However, overuse of Yranum blood can lead to addiction, less effectiveness of the healing elements over time, and "bleaching" of color from eyes.

Zhivotza - (zhee—vot—zah)

The Jiovis term for "Seh'Vuthi". In the Jiovis tongue Zhivotza means "drug" or "medicine." But in the context of a soulmate it means "life source."

Zhivotza is used as a term of endearment for a Jiovis's soulmate.

☆ ☆ ☆

Veniri Soul Scents

- Amazed – Cherry Popping Candy
- Anxious – Molasses
- Ashamed – Persimmon
- Bitter – Black Cherry
- Comfortable – Lavender
- Confused – Nutmeg
- Curious – Ginger
- Deepest Sorrow - Black Liquorice
- Depressed – White Vinegar
- Determined – Seaweed
- Deceit – Almonds/Arsenic
- Delighted - Watermelon
- Disdain – Blood Orange
- Disgusted – Pipe Tobacco
- Distrust - Bicarb Soda
- Dread – Apricot
- Envious – Saffron
- Fear - Sour Apple
- Grieving – Cider Vinegar
- Hatred – Rhubarb
- Heartbreak – Nougat
- Hopeful – Macadamia
- Inadequate – Champagne
- Insecure – Burnt Sugar
- Inspired – Vanilla

- Jealous – Marshmallows
- Jubilant - Pomegranate
- Lonely – Peanut butter
- Love / Loving – Pine Needles
- Motivated – Chillies
- Murderous – Cinnamon
- Nervous – Aloe Vera
- Overjoyed - Lotus
- Overwhelmed – Rosewater
- Peaceful – Truffles
- Proud - Wasabi
- Relieved – Jasmine
- Resentful – Chalk
- Restraint – Salt
- Revenge/Vengeful – Vodka
- Sad – Balsamic Vinegar
- Scared/Fear – Sour Apple
- Self-Conscious – Egg Yolk
- Shocked – Rhubarb
- Suspicious – Elderflower
- Tense – Lilly Pilly Berry
- Terrified – Peppermint
- Truth – Bleach
- Worthless – Stainless Steel

ACKNOWLEDGMENTS

Crikey! Can we all shout a big “Hallelujah!” that I’ve finally seceded in getting this next book out into the world! 😂

Gosh! I never intended for this third book in my Celestial Shifters series to take so long since Flames of Mars was published. But now that we’re finally here, it’s definitely a big relief.

Again, I owe a phenomenal thank you to my Lord and Saviour, Jesus Christ. Without His amazing sacrifice, I would have ended it all long ago. I give all credit to You, my Father in Heaven and the Holy Spirit for my life and all that is good in it. I’m still in awe of the fact that I get to live out this dream of being an author. With each new book, I still have no doubts that You to inspire me and give me the words to write. There are a lot of challenges, and much, much more I need to learn about this industry. But thankfully, everything I have achieved so far, You have made possible. Everything for Your glory.

To Kevin, my wonderful husband, again your support and encouragement has been stellar! Getting this book has been a slog, but you’ve always pushed me to keep going and get it finished. Thank you so much for your patience. Words cannot express how grateful I am, nor how much I love you. Thanks for calling this emotional wreck your wife! xxx

Annabelle, my little lady. You keep growing up so fast! Even though you're not a sucker for books like me, I've still loved having you as my little companion to all the bookish and pop culture events that I drag you to. I'm always amazed at your own creativity and the wonderful young lady you're becoming. I love you so much!

A big thank you Janeen Donovan, my Mum. Your support in more than just emotional and financial ways has been truly grateful. It's an honour to be your daughter. Thank you for raising me, for being there whenever I need, for feeding my Enid Blyton addiction and for introducing me to authors such as Frank E. Peretti, C.S. Lewis, and J.R.R. Tolkien. I think I can safely blame you for sparking my wild imagination, haha!

A big thank you to the rest of my family! Oh, Wow! I'm so blessed to be a part of such a wonderful clan. The Hams, Donovans, Colemans, Evans', Drapers, McCuddens, Eveans', Youngs, and all the extended family. Thank you so much for your support in buying my first book and being my behind the scenes cheerleaders.

To my Alphas, the super talented Writer's Unite Group; Carleton Chinner, Julie Dickson, Tim Edwards, Suzie Eisfelder, Tarryn Mallick, and Katarina Smythe (a.k.a. Kaydence Snow). You guys are AWESOME! I'm so glad I found you guys and eventually plucked up the courage to share my budding little story way back since starting Shards of Venus. Thanks for all the feedback, the support, the great laughs and the motivation to keep writing. Gosh, I cringe to think how many tears and whinging you had to put up with from me. But, you guys have been such a solid and steady support in helping me to find the courage to "suck it up" and move on with the next step. You're all such an inspiration and I'm so excited to see what the future brings for you all.

Treece and Dan Stubbs and your adorable little Iggy. You guys are such a blessing! Thanks for being amazing in hearing all my crazy world-building ideas since the very first book. Treece, I'm so amazed with the work you've been achieving since starting your 'Creative Minds Support' business. It's been so cool to watch you flourish in this space. Thanks so much for all the encouragement and support you have given me over the years. I look forward to sharing many more successes and achievements with you!

You guys rock!

A big shout out to all my beta readers who volunteered their precious time to read through my manuscript and to provide me with honest feedback. You all kept me on my toes and picked up several inconsistencies compared with the first book. Taking on a beta reader role is an epic job and I'm truly grateful. Thanks Heaps!

And to my editor, Kirstin Andrews, what words can I possibly use to describe how grateful I am? Once again you've amazed me with the hard work and attention to detail you've put into refining this latest manuscript I sent you. I know I mentioned it to you before, but I feel so "uplifted" when I go through your edits. I can clearly see how you've helped to improve my work. Thank you so much for all the work you put into editing my story. It's been such an honour to have you as my editor. Please don't ever leave me!! 😂

For the amazing cover, thanks so much to the amazing team at Deranged Doctor Design. I was mesmerised by the cover you made for the Shards of Venus book, and it's been so great have you involved in crating covers for the next books in the series. Thank you so much for your fantastic work in bringing my world visually to life!

I hope I haven't forgotten anyone. If I have, I'm so sorry! xoxo

ABOUT THE AUTHOR

Hey Hey!

I'm Tjalara Draper, a small town Aussie who's started turning my whimsical daydreams into the written and bookish format.

My dream of becoming an author has been a fascinating journey of making friends with other authors and meeting readers who enthusiastically enable my book buying addiction.

I'm inspired to craft stories that resonate with readers of all ages. My writing is a testament to the power of imagination and the boundless possibilities of the human spirit. I'm a sucker for complex and wild characters who tend to have a mind of their own and take my stories where I never expect.

I love exploring the ability to forge worlds and magic systems for all my favourite genres—paranormal, fantasy, and sci-fi—all dappled with action, adventure, and amorous entanglements.

Along with side questing as an indie author, I'm also a wife and mother, residing in our quaint little town on the edge of the Australian Outback. When not logged into the left hemisphere of my world building escapades, I'm fearlessly navigating the Aussie landscape, dodging drop bears, and avoiding man eating crocs.

Nah! Just kidding! There are no crocs where I live.

GET IN TOUCH:

Website: www.tjalaradraper.com
Instagram: tjalaradraper_author
Facebook: Tjalara Draper Author
Facebook Group: Tjalara Draper's Reader Lounge
TikTok: tjalaradraper_author

ALSO BY TJALARA DRAPER

Celestial Shifters Series:

Shards of Venus - Book 1

Flames of Mars - Book 2

Thorns of Neptune - Book 3

Wishes of Mercury - Book 4 **(COMING SOON!)**

Celestial Shifters Spinoff:

Nika

HUNT
SHAPESHIFTER
EAT, SLEEP,
REPEAT. . .

WANT MORE CELESTIAL SHIFTERS?

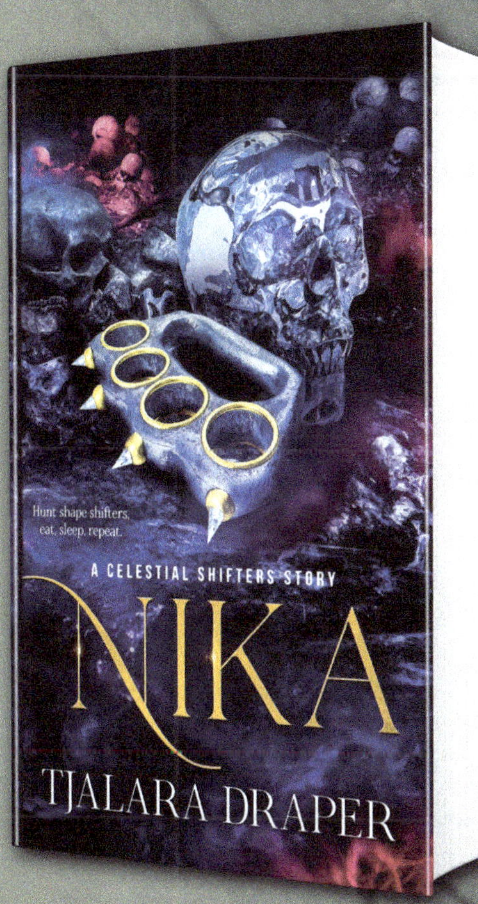

GRAB YOUR COPY OF NIKA TODAY!

www.tjalaradraper.com

www.ingramcontent.com/pod-product-compliance
Lightning Source LLC
Chambersburg PA
CBHW070820020826
48982CB00014B/2

* 9 7 8 0 6 4 5 6 8 8 0 7 8 *